Also by Paul McAuley

The Secret of Life

Whole Wide World

Paul McAuley

TOR

A TOM DOHERTY ASSOCIATES BOOK
NEW YORK

WHOLE WIDE WORLD

Edited by Ellen Datlow

Book design by Jane Adele Regina

A Tor Book
Published by Tom Doherty Associates, LLC
175 Fifth Avenue
New York, NY 10010

www.tor.com

Tor® is a registered trademark of Tom Doherty Associates, LLC.

Library of Congress Cataloging-in-Publication Data

McAuley, Paul J.
    Whole wide world / Paul McAuley.—1st ed.
        p. cm.
    "A Tom Doherty Associates book."
    ISBN 0-765-30392-2 (alk. paper)
        1. Police—England—London—Fiction. 2. Artificial intelligence—
    Fiction. 3. London (England)—Fiction. 4. Internet—Fiction.
    5. Murder—Fiction. I. Title.
    PR6063.C29 W47 2002
    823'.914—dc21

                                                                2001059653

First Edition: May 2002

Printed in the United States of America

0   9   8   7   6   5   4   3   2   1

For Georgina, encore

I am nothing but must be everything.
—*Karl Marx*

Whole
Wide
World

PART ONE

The Silver Chair

1

I was running laps in the local park when my mobile rang. I managed to drop my headphones around my neck and hook the headset over my ear without breaking stride. I was hoping it would be Julie, but it was Detective Inspector Pete Reid, T12's duty officer. He said, "I need you to make a pick-up."

"I'm not on call," I told him, and rang off.

I could just about stand up to Pete Reid, a dedicated alcoholic at the end of an undistinguished career. At least, I could do it over the mobile, which rang again almost at once, with the insistent warbling of a small and very hungry bird. I let it ring and put on my headphones (the extended reissue of Elvis Costello's *Armed Forces*) and kept running.

Sunday, early June. The sky hazy with heat as if bandaged in gauze, the sun burning through it like the business end of a welder's torch. According to the watch Julie had given me the previous Christmas, it was eighty-eight degrees. It felt hotter. People in various states of undress sprawled on browning grass like a horde of refugees from one of the European microwars. I was aware of the brief snags and thorns of their drowsy inattention as I ran past.

I'm not a natural runner. I run as self-consciously as an actor in some low-grade drama. I run to stay in touch with my body; at a certain age, especially after you've been badly hurt, you become horribly aware of its tendency to sag and sprawl and seize up, of its obdurate otherness. I run because there's virtue to be wrung from moderate exertion. In the good old days of cohabitation, I'd come back boiled red and trembling, and after some heroic hawking in the sink my announcement to Julie that I'd managed six kilometres (a judicious doubling of the actual distance) would earn me a cold beer or a glass of nicely chilled Colombian Chardonnay.

I ran past a man rubbing sunscreen into the trembling flanks of his boxer dog. I ran past a family eating from styrene clamshells. Sweat soaked my T-shirt, gathered at the waistband of my shorts. My left leg hardly hurt at all. I ran past a kid resting his head between the speakers of a sound box broadcasting heavy pulses of raga metal to the indifferent world. I ran past a temporary security checkpoint on the other side of the park railings, where coils of smartwire and high kerbs of hollow, water-filled plastic blocks choked the road down to a single lane. Three peace wardens in red tunics, black trousers, and mirrorshades— pit bulls in *Star Trek* leisure gear, their paws resting on belts laden with shock sticks, plasticuffs, extensible batons, and canisters of riot glue and pepper spray—scanned the sparse traffic for bandits who just might be heading into the City Economic Zone to liberate building materials.

The mobile was still ringing. I pressed the *yes* button.

Pete Reid said, "Where are you?" PoliceNet's quantum encryption made him sound as if he was shouting through a metal pipe crammed with angry bees.

"Shoreditch Park. Doing laps."

I ran past a couple of men drinking beer and watching a

portable TV shaded by a cardboard box, like a shrine. The TV
said, "Bandwidth totally secure and safe for all the family."

Pete Reid said in my ear, "I see you."

"Fuck off."

"I'm in the system, Minimum. White T-shirt, red shorts."

"Lucky guess." I shouldn't have resented Pete Reid's use of
my nickname, but sue me, I did.

"Watch the birdie," Pete Reid said.

Tall steel poles wore planted at intervals along the park's perimeter, coated in gluey grey antivandal paint and topped with
the metal shoe boxes of CCTV cameras and their underslung
spotlights, the cameras linked via RedLine chips to ADESS, the
Autonomous Distributed Expert Surveillance System, which
watched all London with omniscient patience.

One night in March, I'd seen these same cameras track a fox.
The hapless animal had become increasingly frantic as it dashed
to and fro, trying to outrun spotlights that fingered the darkness
with unforgiving precision, until at last it could run no more and
stood still, scrawny flanks heaving, eyes blankly reflecting the
glare of overlapping circles of light that briefly twirled around it
before snapping off. That's when I'd become aware of something
new and nonhuman at play in the world; an intelligence vast and
cold and unsympathetic testing the limits of its ability.

Now, one camera and then another and another turned to follow me as I ran past. Watching the detective. I gave them the
finger.

"A 92 per cent recognition factor," Pete Reid said. "Even
without the caring gesture."

"For someone who wears elasticated boots because he can't
tie a proper knot, you're a very technical boy all of a sudden."

"We have search filters and microwave links. We have polygonal forcing routines. We have eight crucial physiognomy
points, too, whatever the fuck they are. There's some kind of
slogan on your T-shirt but I can't quite read it. No doubt some-

thing sarcastic. You're a sarcastic little fucker, Minimum, but I'll let it slide because I need you to do something."

"Who's running the rig? Someone has to be helping an old-fashioned one-finger typist like you."

"I'm with Ross Whitaker," Pete Reid confessed, "hacked into the system through his phone. We're in a squad car in Waltham-stow, waiting for the word to go in and seriously hassle this pinko journalist."

"Was sitting in the office waiting for the phone to ring too boring for you?"

"I have a weakness for journalists. And I didn't know I was going to get two fucking call-outs on a Sunday."

"I hope T12 isn't paying for your time on ADESS."

"Don't you worry. Ross has a mate in the Bunker."

"Because Rachel Sweeney will carpet you when she finds out."

"It's off the books, Minimum. Stop trying to give me a hard time, you aren't built for it. Now listen, you got your warrant card?"

"This is a favour you're about to ask me, isn't it?"

"Do a lap around the corner," Pete Reid said, and gave me an address. "It's a pick-up, that's all. See the exhibits officer, grab the gear, in and out, bing bang boom, no problem. I'll send a uniform with a car and an evidence kit."

"Make that a pretty massive favour," I said.

"In and out, what's the problem? Get the job done, and I'll have Ross here suck your dick by remote control."

That's how it began. I didn't know that it was about a suspicious death. I didn't know it was about the dead girl in the silver chair. The information was only partial.

The poor young trees the council had put in along the road two years ago, those which hadn't been snapped off by kids or poisoned by dog piss, were hanging their heads like ballerinas about to faint. Cars smacked over speed bumps like boats on a choppy sea, trailing music in their wakes. People sat on the balconies of council flats like spectators at the Apocalypse. A very fat black woman enthroned on a red velour armchair held a little electric fan under her chin. The noise of televisions and stereos pounded out of open windows. I ran past a church, a discount off-licence with the no-nonsense offer of *CHEAP BOOZE* painted across its steel-shuttered windows and a burly guard just inside its door, burnt-out live/work flats carved from an old cinema that had started life as a music hall, a row of almshouses. There had been hamlets in marshy fields here, once upon a time. A priory. Country lanes in the drowsy shade of elms and oaks. Then a clutch of theatres, houses creeping north, paved streets, factories and warehouses thrown up on either side of the new canal. Fifteen years ago, artists and pop stars had made the area fashionable. Developers had moved in, turning sweatshop garment factories into loft-style flats for City workers flush with easy money. The InfoWar had wiped them out; now there was talk that the artists might be moving back.

I ran over shattered paving stones, heat-softened tarmac. I ran past an old woman wrapped in a heavy woollen coat despite the heat, a scarf tied tightly over a wig the approximate shape and texture of a Brillo pad. She was pulling a wheeled shopping basket as slowly and steadily as if ascending the north face of Everest. I ran past a couple of gangbangers on the corner, as nervously alert as gazelles, eyes bloodshot from too much crumble. Advance troops of the yardie gangs that were once again trying to push across the river onto Turkish turf. They were serviced by kids on scooters and mountain bikes, kept their stashes hidden, did their deals in burnt-out buildings, hidden from ADESS's sleepless scrutiny. At night, their whistled alerts and signals permeated the neighbourhood like the cries of curlews in some mournful marsh; every few weeks, one was found dead on some patch of waste ground, stabbed in the heart or shot in the head.

I ran easily and sweetly, my T-shirt sticking and unsticking to my sweaty back, my feet cased in Nike Victory 9s that, sprung with argon pockets and flexing sheaths of smart elastomers, could probably have run better by themselves.

I had no trouble finding the address Pete Reid had given me. It was halfway down a narrow street jammed up with police vehicles—three patrol cars, a Ford Transit van, a couple of unmarked Scorpios, a sleek silver Saab. Two men in black trousers and buttoned-up white shirts leaned against a black van, quietly smoking. The van's motor ticked over; the metal box of a refrigeration unit outlet clung to its roof.

I didn't have to be a detective to know that this was not a routine shout.

A woman Police Constable was squatting down to talk to an old woman in widow's weeds who sat in the back seat of a squad car. A young constable in a short-sleeved shirt was stretching blue-and-white tape from a drainpipe to the lamppost in front of a three-storey house which was squeezed between a wreck of a building with an abandoned office-supply shop at street level and boarded windows above, and the blackened shell of a late 1990s flat conversion I'd seen burning on the first night of the InfoWar. The house had two narrow doors on either side of a plate-glass window protected by security bars; clearly it had been subdivided beyond its means. The orange sticker of a security firm glowed in one corner of the window, and a sign in retrostyle computer type, *Mobo Technology*, hung above a row of dead ferns in plastic pots. The metal box of a CCTV camera was perched on a bracket above the right-hand door.

A squad car pulled up behind me. I showed the driver my warrant card.

"I was told just to drop this," he said, meaning the evidence kit on the backseat of his car. He had put on his cap when he had climbed out of the car; now he took it off and blotted sweat from his forehead with the back of his hand.

"You'll have to wait," I said. "There'll be something to take back to T12."

A hard-faced WPC came out of the left-hand door and had a word with the two men by the van: the coroner's appointed undertakers. They dropped their cigarettes and ground them under their polished black brogues, opened the back door of the black van and pulled out a stretcher with an unfolding wheeled frame and went inside. I leaned against the squad car, sweat drying in my hair, my skin giving up volumes of heat to the hot air. I badly needed a cigarette, but as part of my new discipline I had left my tabs in the flat, and the driver didn't smoke.

"What's this all about?" he said.

"We don't need to know."

"A suspicious death, it looks like."

He was very young, eager to impress.

"We're cogs in the machine," I told him. "We don't need to know anything. Kick back and enjoy the sunshine."

At last, the undertakers manoeuvred the loaded stretcher out of the left-hand door. The young constable lifted the crime-scene tape for them with a ceremonial flourish. I grabbed the kit, showed my warrant card to the constable, went inside. Someone in plain clothes was talking with a uniform on the stairs at the end of the narrow corridor. He broke off his conversation to challenge me. A tall man at least ten years younger than me, unforgiving blue eyes behind steel-rimmed glasses, thinning blond hair brushed straight back. He was sweating through the pink shirt under his charcoal suit (there was a small silver cross centred on the fashionably wide lapel), and he wore disposable plastic overshoes.

"You're late," he said, after I told him who I was. He had taken a good look at the slogan on my T-shirt, and it clearly made him unhappy.

"And you're in charge?"

"DI David Varnom. I'm the crime-scene coordinator, Mc-Ardle's in charge. What did you do, run here?"

"I know Tony McArdle. Are you going to show me what needs to be done, or is he?"

I didn't like Varnom. I didn't like his bully-boy attitude, the curl of his lip, his automatic assumption of superiority. I didn't like the way he stood two steps above me.

He said, "I suppose you might have worked a suspicious death before."

"I have an idea of what goes on. What happened?"

"A girl died." Something must have showed in my face. Varnom allowed himself a smile and said, "You were waiting for the body to be taken away."

I didn't deny it.

"I can have the stuff brought down," he said, "if you can't face what's up there."

"I have to document it in place."

"All right, but I'm not having you go up like that," he said, and told the uniform to find me a set of coveralls.

I said, "Are the techs still working the scene?"

"It's a question of decorum."

As I pulled on white coveralls, and fitted overshoes over my Nikes, Varnom said, "If you're going to throw up, do it outside. No smoking—whoever did this sprayed solvent around to mess up DNA typing. And watch where you put your feet. Tony will go ballistic if you knock something over or contaminate the DNA profiling. It was a very nasty death, and Tony wants the evidence processed as quickly as possible."

"I'm sure Tony can tell me that himself," I said.

"Just do your job and don't give me any grief," Varnom said, and turned his back on me and went up the stairs.

I wonder now if any of this would have happened if Varnom hadn't pissed me off quite so badly.

Above the ground-floor offices, the property had been split up into what estate agents used to call studio flats. It was late Victorian and no doubt had been cared for by the *petit-bourgeois* family who had first lived in it—I'd noticed the bit of stained glass over the lintel of the front door and the iron bootscraper on the step when I came in, and there was intricate plaster moulding along the slope of the stairwell's ceiling—but the place had fallen on bad times since, and had clearly missed out on Hoxton's microboomlet. Landlord's miser switches of the kind that gave you thirty seconds of forty-watt light, not quite enough to get you from one landing to the next; cheap builder's carpet on the stairs; woodchip paper on the stairwell walls, that had been badly painted with one coat of obliterating emulsion some time in the last century and were marked now with sweeps of silver-black fingerprint powder at waist height, where a suspect might brush his fingers on the way up or down.

A pair of narrow doors stood side by side on the first-floor landing, where a couple of plainclothes were consulting a palmtop and a photographer was packing equipment into an aluminium case. The right-hand door stood open and a rack of floodlights had been set up inside, illuminating the room like a stage set.

"Mind where you tread," Varnom told me. "There's a broken mug just inside the door. We want it to stay there."

Anticipation was worse than actuality.

The high-ceilinged room looked smaller than it was because of all the people crowded into it. Two crime-scene technicians in white coveralls identical to mine, hoods pulled tightly around their heads, were working the kitchen area at the far end, brushing aluminium powder and spraying for fingerprints with the autistic concentration of trainspotters; a third was bagging papers spilled across a trestle table under a sash window with black blinds. The police surgeon was talking to a middle-aged man in suit trousers and shirtsleeves: Detective Chief Inspector Tony McArdle.

It was very hot in the room, and the air was full with the smell of blood, a heavy black stink that went right to the base of my brain. I had to stamp down on the sudden urge to turn around and walk right out of there.

The floor was uncarpeted, its wide oak planks spattered with flecks and spots of paint. The smooth plaster walls, once light blue, had been spray painted with dense patterns of multicoloured squiggles. There was a mattress covered with a white rug and a heap of cushions. There was a cheap, aluminium tubing rack crammed with dresses and jeans and shirts, and two plain cardboard boxes with reinforced corners and rope handles. Big church candles stood either side of a Victorian cast-iron grate piled high with dusty fake fruit. A stacking stereo, no TV. Fairylights were strung across the ceiling and tiny webcams clung to two corners, like eyeballs stuck on inverted pyramids.

The candles and the fairylights and the painted walls might have made the room look eerie and festive, but in the harsh glare of the floodlights it looked as flat and unreal as a child's picture of a witch's cave, a backdrop for the thing in the centre of the room.

A chair. An ordinary stacking chair with a moulded plastic seat set on four splayed metal legs, the kind of chair found in row upon row in municipal halls, in leisure centres, in hospital waiting rooms. It had been painted silver, and the blood looked black against the silver paint. Two long pools of blood in the saddle of the seat, and jellied blood in a kind of pile beneath.

Varnom said, "The computers are over there," and Tony McArdle noticed me for the first time.

"Not an ideal way to spend a Sunday," he said. He'd grown up in Bow: a hard man from a hard part of town, with a reputation as a fair, intelligent and highly motivated boss. Bull-necked, a five o'clock shadow like a tattoo, dark eyes that gave nothing away, black hair greased down, an old-fashioned short-back-and-sides. His shirtsleeves were rolled up high on his meaty arms; a Glock 17 was slung in a shoulder holster under his left arm. He wore white overshoes and white vinyl gloves, the gloves tight on his big hands, islands of sweat trapped between vinyl and skin, and he had flipped his tie over his shoulder—to keep it out of the blood. After the victim had been photographed and pronounced, before she had been taken down, he had leaned in and taken a close look at her. His gaze passed over me. If he saw my T-shirt's slogan beneath the semitranslucent plastic-treated paper of my coveralls he gave no sign. He stripped off the gloves and balled them up and said, "I suppose you've come for the computers. Is that where you're at now, John? ITU?"

"T12," I said. "It changed its name six months ago."

"T12 then. A bit quiet after H and E, isn't it?"

We knew each other from a siege I'd worked when I had been with the Hostage and Extortion Unit; an armed robbery suspect strung out on crack cocaine and Valium had kept us at bay all day and most of the night by holding a replica pistol to his girlfriend's head.

"I go where I'm told," I said.

"It's good to see you back on active duty. We need more men like you."

"I'm no hero, sir."

"You wouldn't happen to know anything about computers, I suppose."

"I've picked up a little knowledge."

"This one's a bit of a puzzle," McArdle said. "Someone sent a fax to the Yard this morning. It said that a girl by the name of Sophie Booth had been killed. No address was given, and it took a while to check up on all the Sophie Booths in the country. It wasn't signed, and it came from somewhere in Cuba."

"Probably routed through an anonymous remailer," I said. "They're very keen on anonymous remailers in Cuba."

"The computers, sir," Varnom said.

McArdle noticed him for a moment. He said, "This man was hurt in the line of duty, David."

"I know," Varnom said, giving me a hard look.

"Then don't treat him like a flunky," McArdle told him, and said to me, "What's this about remailers?"

"Every email message comes with a header that shows where it originated. If you send a message through an anonymous remailer, the header is stripped off and a new one is put on, with only a random number as identifier. And some remailers will forward faxes."

"So it can't be traced," McArdle said.

"Not exactly," I said. "Remailers keep the details of every message they forward. If the one that sent you the fax was sited in this country, you could get an Information Disclosure Order."

"But it's in Cuba. And we're at war with Cuba."

"Not exactly war, sir, but I take your point."

"It's still a long way from anything useful, except to confirm my idea that whoever did this is playing games with us. You saw the cameras. I have a nasty suspicion about them," he said, and went over to the silver-painted chair and stood behind it. He looked up at the webcams, looked at the chair, looked at me.

I said, "I noticed it too."

"And they're linked to the computers, so their output could have been sent anywhere over the Web."

"Absolutely."

Andy Higgins had set up a camera to monitor the coffee machine outside our offices, so that his gang of tech-heads could check on the level in the pot and save themselves the walk downstairs if it was empty.

McArdle said, "It was a nasty death. One of the worst. A young girl, twenty-one, and the bastard took his time with her and he knew what he was doing. I think he's done this kind of thing before. He washed her down afterwards, spritzed the area

with solvent, left her to be found. Very neat, very tidy. People
who want to get rid of DNA traces usually torch the scene, but
not our boy. And then there are the cameras, and the computers."

"You think he did it for an audience, sir."

"It wouldn't be a first, would it? Yes, I think it was for an
audience, or for a souvenir. In any case, he smashed the computers and took their hard drives. I'd like to know what your
people can tell me about them, as soon as possible."

Varnom said, trying to find a way into the conversation, "There
are the wraps of blow, sir. She might have been dealing, and
made someone unhappy enough to have her killed."

"Two wraps, probably stepped on so hard they wouldn't give
a buzz to a goldfish. Forget about the blow," McArdle told Varnom, and said to me, "I want your technicians to find out everything they can. Chase them hard, John. I want this one badly."

"I'll do my best, sir," I said, and gave Varnom a nice shit-
eating grin.

There were two computers, one a beige box without a monitor,
the other a new and expensive model, a Macintosh G10, the kind
of machine popular with graphic designers. Its translucent blue
casing had been cracked open and its motherboard dangled by
a couple of wires. The beige box had been opened up and
stripped too. I got out the evidence kit and used the digital
camera to photograph the cables and plugs at the back of the
computers, so that they could be reconfigured exactly by one of
our techs. Keyboard, mouse, the much-scuffed mouse pad a lam-
inated photograph of fireworks bursting above Tower Bridge, a
Millennium souvenir. I bagged and tagged everything and wrote
up the inventory on an evidence form while the techs worked
quietly with brush and powder, tweezers and magnifying loupe,
swabs, sticky tape. Looking for prints, for fibres and hairs, for
flakes of skin and fingernail shards, flecks of blood. We were
engaged in a ritual so familiar that we did not need to acknowledge each other's presence as we moved about our painstaking

tasks. The ingathering of information. The flare of the camera flash. Silvery powder scattered like smoke from a thurible.

When I had finished, I gave a copy of my notes to the exhibits officer, a young woman detective sergeant with a neat blonde bob, and asked her about the data spikes.

"There aren't any data spikes," she said.

"Did you look carefully? There are always data spikes."

"Not this time, sir."

"Zip discs, then. Or DVDs. Maybe a tape-streamer. A few diehards still use tape-streamers. You might have thought it was an answering machine, and bagged it separately."

The DS shook her head. "Sorry, sir. Everything is as found."

A constable helped me carry out the computers. Varnom followed me down the stairs, watched as I stripped off the white coveralls. "Don't worry," I said. "I'll take care of everything."

"What does it mean?"

"What does what mean?"

He jabbed my chest with a hard finger. " 'Information wants to be free.' "

"It keeps me in work."

"I don't like it."

"You don't have to like it."

"Next time come properly dressed."

"I'll make a note."

I wrote out a memo to Andy Higgins, taped it to the smashed G10, bullied the driver Pete Reid had sent to take everything to T12. And walked home through the hot streets, feeling my skin grow colder and smaller, as if it was being drawn up towards the back of my head. Halfway there, I threw up in a litter bin.

2

I was working on my third beer and my fourth tab when Julie, my not-quite-ex-girlfriend, phoned. I was sitting on the tiny, triangular balcony of the flat I'd been renting ever since my own place in Stoke Newington had been torched eighteen months ago, while I was still in hospital (no one had ever been caught for that: it could have been terrorists or it could have been police, which back then was my life in a nutshell). The flat was up on the third floor of a converted carpet warehouse beside the Regent's Canal, and I was idly watching the cyclists and sparse foot traffic pass to and fro on the towpath. A fisherman sat on a folding stool directly opposite my observation post, holding a tiny radio to his ear and sipping from a can of lager. A pair of swans patrolled the water beyond the bowed span of his carbon-fibre rod. The sun hung above the city's roofscape, swollen and reddened by smog; the air under the balcony's tent of mosquito netting was hot and still and prickled with static electricity. It had not rained for more than two weeks. If I had been feeling morbid, my watch, continuously updated by a weather station on top of Centre Point, could have told me the precise levels of ozone, nitrogen dioxide and carbon monoxide parching my lungs. It could have told me the percentage chance of rain (zero), my altitude above sea level, my position to within ten metres, my pulse rate and blood-sugar level. It could even have told me the time. There is too much information in the world. In a hundred years, every dust particle will be tagged and coded.

I had showered, put on a fresh T-shirt and a pair of khaki pants. My hair had dried in stiff, short spikes. Steely Dan was playing softly inside the flat. The bug-killer hummed its one-note mantra inside its eerie blue aura. Archimedes the Wonder Owl sat on his perch just inside the sliding door. I was thinking of cameras and computers, the silver chair and the dead girl, when Archimedes turned to look at me and my mobile rang.

"There you are," Julie said, after my mobile, resetting from PoliceNet encryption to the civilian band, had run through its repertoire of clucks and chirps. "There you are," my not-quite-ex-girlfriend said. "Drinking beer and smoking, like the king of the world."

I raised the bottle of Tiger beer in salute to Archimedes' unblinking camera eyes. "I salute your omniscience. You are as God."

"I'm just a very wired-up girl, Dixon."

That was her nickname for me. A comfortable father figure, anchor of Saturday evening TV in the 1960s. Blue lamps. Whistles in the fog. Villains who called you "Governor." Young tykes set on the straight and narrow by no more than a clip to the ear. Julie believed that at heart I was an old-fashioned copper. Well, I was old-fashioned all right, that much was true. I was so old-fashioned I didn't even carry a gun.

Julie said, "I hope Archimedes has been behaving himself. Is he still bumping into things?"

Archimedes the Wonder Owl was her pet. A simulacrum gizmoed up from nylon feathers, plastic skin stretched over a lightweight carbon-fibre frame, and more than two hundred microelectric motors and a dozen parallel microprocessors, but Julie treated him as if he were real. I was looking after him while Julie was in Brussels because he was too sophisticated to be switched off or left alone. Sometimes the knowledge that at any time she could be watching me through his lucent eyes gave me the creeps, but mostly I found it reassuring. A sign of interest, of the potential for jealousy, of continuing emotional connection. We had split up a month ago on a provisional basis, and Julie was still trying to work out if we should get back together or become no more than Just Good Friends. I played along with this because I had no choice—I'd even shamelessly parlayed it into a couple of mercy fucks that had been almost worth the postcoital guilt and tears.

I said, "Did you call to talk to me, or to talk about him?"

"I'm worried about the bumping thing."

"He's trying to get it under control. He just isn't used to this flat."

"Perhaps you should take him to Gabe Day."

"He's fine. He just needs a couple of days to settle down here. How's Brussels?"

Julie was a partner in a firm of architectural consultants; she was in Brussels to lay the groundwork for a radical redesign of the offices of the European Parliament building. We'd met last year, just after I'd returned to the job. I had been investigating the theft of chips and hard drives from a company her firm had been working for, a no-brainer inside job as it happened, and she'd asked me out for a drink. She was flamboyant and fizzing with energy; I was quiet and undemonstrative. For a little while it seemed that we were the perfect odd couple, two wary survivors of serial bad relationships who wouldn't admit that we were in love until it was too late.

She said, "Brussels is splendid. I don't know why there are so many jokes about it. I had lunch in the Grand Place, with all the other tourists in the city. The food wasn't bad, apart from the famous mayonnaise on the chips, but you don't have to have mayonnaise on your chips. It comes in a little paper tub. You can choose to go native or not. I chose not. Then I went for a long walk through a big park, past the palace, and now I'm in my room, waiting for room service."

"How was the King?"

"I didn't see the King, but I did find a Communist shop."

"Isn't that a contradiction?"

"It was selling busts and tracts and spikes for the good of the cause."

"Lenin's complete speeches? Mao reading his own poems? Soundtracks to Stalin's favourite Westerns?"

"Music spikes, unfortunately."

"What kind of music do Communists listen to?"

"Not The Clash, I can tell you, but stuff that's just as retro. Twelve-tone serial stuff. *Musique concrète*. Very twencen," she said, knowing how much I hated that neologism. "I also found a British bookshop, in this long, sad street near the hotel that's crammed with bad restaurants and seedy clubs."

"I suppose British politicians don't read French or German."

"Or Walloon or Flemish. They buy remaindered Jeffrey Archer novels at a terrible markup and sit reading at lonely tables in bad pizza parlours. Oh, and I saw a fabulous wedding procession. Twenty people crammed into two white convertibles, setting off firecrackers and blowing whistles."

"It doesn't sound very Belgian. What happened to the famous grim grey dourness?"

"I think the secret of Belgium is that no one has told the Belgians about their awful reputation for being boring. The bride was in a cute white minidress and holding up her veil while swigging from a champagne bottle."

A pause. I said, "How's work?"

"Still at the pre-fucked-up stage. What have you been doing, Dixon?"

"Nothing much. I visited Grandma C.'s grave. I read the papers. I had a minimal lunch of salad and hummus. I went for a run."

"Your leg was fine?"

"The leg is good. I think the leg will outlast me," I said, trying to be casual about it, "I was called out to a job."

"That's unfair. It's your day off."

"No one else available. Pete Reid sent me."

"Pete Reid of the caveman ethics and the long lunchtime absences?"

"The very same."

"And it shook you up, this job."

I shifted the mobile from my right ear to my left ear. Archimedes watched me, and Julie watched me through Archimedes' camera eyes. I said carefully, "It wasn't fun."

I told Julie about the dead girl, the gutted computers, the webcams. "I packed everything up and sent it all down to T12. The techs will look at it first thing tomorrow."

"And you're brooding on it and drinking beer."

"The beer is necessary. It's very hot here."

"Come off it, Dixon."

"My head is in a funny place," I admitted.

"Because of this murder? Was it very bad?"

"I didn't even see the body. It was horrible, but exciting too. For a moment, I felt I was doing real police work again."

We talked for half an hour. Julie was often away on assignments—a day, a couple of days, a week—but we kept in touch. Phones. Email. She emailed me pictures taken with a digital camera no bigger than my thumb and more intelligent than a dog. We talked for the sake of talking, Just Good Friends, until the mobile told me I had another call. It was Nick Francis. Julie and I said our goodnights, and Nick said, "I want to buy you a drink, man."

"What's up?"

"Let me buy you that drink first."

"The usual place?"

"I'll be there in half an hour."

It was eight o'clock. The air was hot and oppressive. The fisherman was packing up his gear. The swans had gone to wherever it was swans go for the night. I finished my beer in two swallows and locked up the flat and got out my Mini and buzzed up to Islington, found a spot at the Head's bar and bought a pint of Kronenbourg. The Head is popular in summer because it has a terrace where you can sit under big canvas umbrellas and watch people go by in the lanes of the antiques market. I like it because it has a big, old-fashioned square central bar; you can lean at it while you sip your pint and see what's going on in the rest of the place, which is just how it should be in public houses. That night it was business as usual: regulars from nearby council flats on one side of the bar; a healthy mix of media brats, antique traders and chancers on the other. Joey Jones, one of the oldest regulars, was collecting glasses from the tables, his way of earning a couple of free drinks. Ernie Mitchell, a former bank robber now well past pensionable age, who served coffee and croissants to commuters from a little cart outside the Angel Tube station, was at his usual spot just inside the door, and touched two fingers to his brow when I caught his eye.

Nick Francis slouched in and slapped my shoulder and ordered a Kronenbourg to replace the pint I'd nearly finished, and a bottle of Sol. A scary-looking fellow if you didn't know him, what with his biker's stubble (a big improvement on the gypsy-pimp greased-back quiff with dangling pigtails he'd worn for most of the 1990s, or the white soul-boy Afro he'd had before that, which had made his head look like a mushroom sliced in half), rings in ears and nose and eyebrows, a vertical stripe of beard under his lower lip, a bare chest under a grungy black leather vest, black tattoos on his bare arms. In fact, he's a pussy-cat, gentle, genial and urbane, an uxorious husband and proud father of two lovely daughters, and so soft-spoken that as usual I had to lean close to him to hear him over the roar of the pub.

"The usual shit," he said, when I asked him how it was going. We touched glass to bottle, drank. He added, "I might be on the way to working out how to finish the book."

Nick had been working on an exhaustive biography of the legendary blues singer Robert Johnson for half his life. I'd known him a lot longer than that. We'd grown up together on Wormholt Estate, close by Shepherd's Bush, had both been at Christopher Wren School, the same school that Paul Cook and Steve Jones of the Sex Pistols had gone to, although they'd left a year before Nick and I had started. We'd been a band of two, Nick and I, sharp-tongued oddballs deeply into punk rock, even though its glory year had been and gone, and wearing rows of safety pins in the lapels of our school blazers and cutting off the ends of our ties was about as punk as we got. We both agreed that The Clash at the Hammersmith Palais, 17 June 1980, was the best gig ever, argued passionately about the merits of PIL, Kraftwerk, The Style Council and Dexy's Midnight Runners, compiled lists ranking obscure soul singers, lied about our ages to get into the Beat Route, the Dirtbox, the Gold Coast, clubs whose playlists were eclectic enough to match Robert Wyatt with Gil Scott Heron, John Lee Hooker with King Sunny Ade. We grooved on afrobeat, jazz soul, and funk, nerved each other to chat up impossibly glamorous girls. I left school at sixteen; Nick, brighter and possessed of an almost perfect memory, went to sixth-form college, Oxford University, and then near starvation while he earned his chops as a freelance rock journalist. Even though we might not see each other for a year, we never quite lost touch, and neither of us had quite grown up, either. We'd stayed best mates through thick and thin. He was the only person who knew the real story about what had happened to me at Spitalfields, in the InfoWar.

I let Nick explain his new idea about framing the biography

as a fantastic ghost story. He said, "Of course, I need to make another trip to Mississippi first. I've found a couple more people to interview."

"And then you'll finish the book."

He smiled, showing teeth pitted by years of taking speed. "You should come along. It's a genuine murder mystery."

Robert Johnson died in Greenwood, Mississippi, 16 August 1938, after drinking from a bottle of poisoned whiskey that had been given to him by a jealous husband. Nick wasn't interested in the murder, though, but in the mystery of Johnson himself. The mystery of how someone from the same impoverished background as tens of thousands of others, an uneducated loner who had been a cipher even to his contemporaries, could have created a body of work of such scope and universal power.

We shot the shit for a while. I bought another round, and Nick asked me if I knew anything about the journalist who'd been raided in Walthamstow that afternoon.

I thought of Pete Reid. I said, "Not really."

Nick drew on his skinny, hand-rolled tab, pinching it between nicotine-stained finger and thumb. He had a big silver skull ring on his thumb, with rubies in the eye sockets. He said, "The guy, a friend of mine, is a film critic. An American, name of Jeff Hersch."

"I don't know half your friends, Nick."

Nick screwed the wet stub of his tab into the battered ashtray. "He's more of a friend of a friend. Anyway, they busted him for possession of unlicensed videos, took every DVD and spike he owns. Took his fucking laptop, man, and took his passport too."

"That's in case he tries to flee the country."

"Yeah, but he has his family here. A wife and a kid, his wife lectures in media studies at Westminster University. He hasn't been charged with anything, and I was wondering if you could find out whether it's just the usual bullshit harassment, or if it's something more serious. I mean, it's serious enough, he was working on a book and they took all his files and research material."

"These were American DVDs and spikes?"

"Of course they were. Jeff's book is about slasher movies. Some of that shit is banned, the rest is cut to ribbons. These days a two-hour mainstream film routinely loses thirty minutes to the BBFC. Even Disney cartoons are cut these days, man, and these were the kind of big bad horror flicks," Nick said, rolling his eyes and holding clawed fingers either side of his face, "that were banned when there was all that hysteria about video nasties in the 1980s."

"I'll see what I can find out. But he won't be getting his stuff back."

"Maybe not the DVDs and the spikes, but won't the laptop be going through T12?"

"I can't make a copy of the hard drive, Nick."

"I guess not, but it was worth asking."

"But I can ask about the case."

"If you find something I'll definitely buy you another Kronenbourg or two. But right now I've got to run for a late-night screening of the latest Clint Eastwood. More proof of life after death, but at least it's the American print."

"Well, I hope you don't get busted by Vice."

"This is a private show in Sony's very own screening room. The only way journos can see the real thing any more."

Nick gave me a spike, a copy of the first album of a new, shit-hot blues guitarist from Alabama by the name of Carpenter Hill, drained his Sol, and split. I sank my Kronenbourg and moved on as well. Too restless to go home, I walked over to Upper Street and rambled through the crowds promenading under the gaze of dozens of security cameras, past lighted shops and crowded bars and islands of tables that spread across the pavement outside restaurants. Half the pubs in Islington are dressed up like farm-house kitchens or Mongolian yurts or mini–rain forests full of ferns and palmettos and ambient birdsong (in one, there's a rain shower every hour on the hour; they hand out slickers at the door); the rest are buzz bars, full of baby tech-heads wearing interactive lovehi badges, people who never get any nearer to poetry than a Hallmark Moment, who make shopping lists and stick to them, who network at parties and think they're having serious fun. I stopped off at the Post House, the last proper, smoke-filled pub on Upper Street, packed out every lunchtime with postal workers fresh off their shift, packed out now with men watching the Brazilian women's water ski championships, sank a couple of pints and smoked half a packet of tabs and wandered down Cross Street towards Essex Road. I bought a six-pack of lager from the Drinks Cabin and a fried supper from the Greek place by the old Egyptian cinema, and drove the old routes with the parcel of fish and chips open on the passenger seat, a cold can between my knees, a tab between my lips.

The old restlessness. The old habits. Drinking and driving. Driving and smoking. Driving and drinking and smoking.

Back when I was a uniform on patrol, one of my favourite things had been driving at night, especially on bandit pursuits. A pursuit enlivened a dull shift and always made for a good anecdote, even if nothing came from it. For two years I had in Trevor Bailey a tolerant partner who was as fearless and terrific a driver as he was a policeman. He never once mentioned my height. He hardly ever used any of my nicknames. He said that I was as good as any WPC at delivering bad news to anxious disbelieving relatives. He was killed the February before last, when he tried to take a knife off a maniac who had walked into a supermarket and started slashing at the customers and staff—it was just after the InfoWar, food rationing was still in force, and Trevor's killer was a bankrupted day trader. I like to remember him late at night, intent at the wheel as he drove very fast and with absolute precision, lights and siren going, other vehicles pulling over to let us past, half the time weaving on the wrong side of the road and shooting through red lights, the overrevved motor screaming and the car filling with that lovely smell of hot oil.

Now I drove our old routes in my Mini, a classic Cooper SE, British Racing Green with two white stripes on the bonnet and an English White roof, an S Works engine, chrome wheels and half-leather seats. I had let it get in a dreadful state. Occasionally I remembered to top up the radiator or change the oil and put in a new filter, but it was rusting out at the sills, I'd patched the smashed quarterlight on the offside with plastic tape, and I knew the brake lights didn't work because a patrol car had pulled me over for it a couple of months ago. The stuffing was coming out of the split seams of the seats, and the back was piled up with plastic carrier bags full of spent newspapers I vaguely intended to dump at the recycling bank but never did, half-empty canisters of antifreeze and oil, a scurf of fast-food containers, and half a dozen parking tickets.

I drove north and west, a compilation tape playing at maximum volume on the Blaupunkt deck I'd wired up myself. The deck had been worth more than the car once upon a time, but it was dead tech now, superseded by CDs, DVDs, spikes. The Specials: "Ghosttown." The Jam: "Beat Surrender." The Clash: "London Calling," "Armagideon Time." Iggy Pop: "The Passenger." Singles Nick and I had searched out in Woolworth's bargain bins, the soundtrack of my past. All I had left of my past, after my flat was burnt down.

Holloway Road:

A man at a bus stop raging at the traffic, a Turk or Kurd waving a can of lager like a hand grenade. "Fucking English! Fucking stupid English wankers!"

Students milling outside the Garage. A boy on his knees, being sick into the gutter.

An entire Muslim family, the women veiled from head to foot and chivvying a flock of children behind a vanguard of men in leather jackets and loose white trousers, moving north past shuttered secondhand-furniture stores.

It was ten past ten. The air temperature a sultry seventy-seven degrees; humidity 88 per cent.

Cameras everywhere, clinging to the sides of buildings, watching doorways, watching the pavement, watching the traffic. Turning, tracking.

And I drive and I drive.

I was on the beat for five years, and then was transferred to the Yard, where I became one of the drones who invisibly manage file systems and information flow. I was good at it. Sometimes I even liked it. It was steady work, thirteen years' worth. I ended up in charge of a team of forty civilian clerks, part of a big initiative to completely reorganize the Yard's data-retrieval service. If my staff had a nickname for me they kept it to themselves. But it wasn't exactly police work.

On the side, I took an Open University degree in applied psychology, and wrote speeches and tidied up drafts of position papers for an Assistant Commissioner. Just before he retired I asked him for a favour he couldn't refuse. On his word, I was transferred to the Met's Hostage and Extortion Unit.

I talked down jumpers who didn't have the nerve. I talked out armed villains trapped at the scene of crime by one or another of the Flying Squad's rapid-response teams. I talked out men raving on their own, men holding knives to the throats of their wives, men threatening to kill themselves and their children. I talked out domestic sieges. I talked crazy men into submission. I kept frightened men calm. I listened to men raving about real or imagined grievances. I listened to men threatening to kill themselves, or to kill others. I made assurances. I kept the stress level down. I told men that they had all the time in the world to sort out their problems. I told them there was no hurry. I told them that they would be treated fairly. I told them that nothing dramatic would happen to them. I allowed them small victories after long delays. Simple demands were subjected to exhaustive debate. A cup of tea? No problem at all, but what kind of tea? English Breakfast, Orange Pekoe, Earl Grey, Assam, Darjeeling? Something special, perhaps, Jasmine or Oolong. Or something flavoured, raspberry or lemon or peppermint. Just ordinary tea? Well, but what brand? Milk? Ordinary milk or semi-skimmed or skimmed? In the tea or not? And if in the tea, just how much milk? Sugar? Lumps or straws or loose? Brown or white? You could talk an hour about a cup of tea, and don't get me started on pizzas, or how chicken should be cooked. I turned demands into favours, yielded to small requests to give the illusion that progress was being made, stalled endlessly on larger demands.

Only at the death, when I thoroughly knew the man, could anticipate what he was going to say next, had talked him up and talked him down, did I address the key issue. Only then did I say, "Why don't we start talking about you coming out of there?"

Six years of talking and listening. And then there was the InfoWar. And then there was Spitalfields.

The official story, the one everyone knows, is simple, like all the best lies. And like all the best lies, it doesn't embroider or distort the truth. It's a lie not because it tells an untruth, but because of what it leaves out.

The official story is this: on the third night of the InfoWar, after an anti-capitalist march turned into a riot, after unidentified terrorists (the Iraqi government, two Kurdish Communist groups and three gangs of Irish Nationalists all claimed responsibility) used the riot as cover to mount their attack, with the City of London cordoned off and under curfew, half a dozen major buildings bombed out and dozens more set ablaze by computer chips that overheated after viruses switched off their cooling fans, in the middle of all that chaos, a police patrol group spotted two bandits and gave hot pursuit. While one police officer radioed for help, three others were killed outright and a fourth was fatally injured when the cornered suspects set off a satchel bomb.

I'm the survivor. I know what was left out of that nice, neat story. I know, for instance, that the girl was caught at once, but her comrade escaped. I know what the other police did to the girl, and what happened when her comrade came back to save her. I know that one policeman, blinded, both legs gone, lived long enough to give a deathbed statement in the ambulance, claiming that I had run from the scene.

There were no other witnesses. No one else saw what happened. The authorities decided to let the two versions cancel each other out, cooked up a nice, neat version for public consumption, bought my silence with threats, and buried me in T12.

I turned off Holloway Road and cut along York Way, through the tangle of narrow streets behind St Pancras, lairy second-hand office-furniture shops and respray places shuttered and dark under railway arches, toms (this year they were mostly Slovaks and Scots, with a sprinkling of ultraglamorous Somalian transvestites) standing two by two at street corners. Then back into Islington, past the narrow wedge of a park full of trees and black rocks, rows of Georgian houses, the street where in a fit of pathological jealousy Kenneth Halliwell murdered Joe Orton just a few weeks after Paul McCartney came to visit their shabby bedsit, the tree-lined cut of the Regent's Canal and a tangle of old factories and Victorian terraces.

At one point, somewhere in the ruins of Old Street, a squad car came up behind. I drove very carefully as it followed me, my heart quickening when it switched on its blue lights and siren—but it pulled out onto the wrong side of the road and flashed past, screaming away on a call. I wobbled to the kerb and cut the motor just as Television segued into Jonathan Richman and the Modern Lovers, and cracked the last can of lager.

I knew that this drinking and driving had to stop, but I needed the driving when I got restless, and I couldn't face the driving without the drinking, the buzz that lifted me out of myself, that made me a passenger in my own head, along for the ride but not part of it.

I thought of Chris Fraser while I finished off the lager. Another colleague at Islington, he'd been off-duty the night he got hurt, walking down Green Lanes towards his flat when he saw a commotion in an off-licence. A man with a baseball bat was smashing the bottles of wine in the display shelves and screaming at the owner, telling him he'd be next if he didn't open the fucking till. Chris walked in and told the man to put the bat down. There was a struggle; Chris slipped in spilled claret; the man beat him badly and snatched up a couple of packets of chewing gum and ran off. Chris was a month in hospital, fractured skull, broken ribs, most of the bones in his right hand smashed where he'd tried to fend off the blows. He came back on the job but suffered from blinding headaches and had completely lost his nerve. He started drinking badly. He was disciplined twice, then stood down; six months later, blind drunk, he walked in front of a lorry on the A10.

I didn't know if I'd lost my nerve or not, after what happened to me in the InfoWar. After Spitalfields, the dead girl and the dead boy and the dead police, the in-camera board of inquiry and the political compromise. I hadn't put it to the test. I didn't have the nerve to quit, that was certain, although I knew that my bosses would be very happy if I did quit because they had already offered me early retirement. When I had turned it down they gave me the safe, quiet job at T12, fetching and carrying, filing and collating. It was my natural habitat, but it was no longer enough and I tried to fill the hole with the drinking and driving, and sooner or later I was going to get caught at it by some peace warden or police without any sympathy.

My mind kept going back to that silver chair, the way your

tongue will go back to a cracked tooth. A child's play-throne standing in a pool of blood, triangulated by the webcams, vibrant with the imprint of what had been done to the girl who had died in it. I had talked up the computers and the webcams to McArdle because I had wanted to annoy Varnom, but I knew that they were important. Because, like their owner, the computers had been violated. Someone, almost certainly the monster who had taken the girl's life, had stolen the computers' memories, had taken the information they had contained. There were angles to be worked. A chance for redemption, a change of luck.

The dead girl. The silver chair. I threw the empty can out of the window and drove home.

3

I know that I'm an unlikely policeman.

The ideal detective has no history, no family. He's a solitary knight who has dedicated his life to the search for absolute justice, or a stubborn eccentric possessed of arcane knowledge and corkscrew intuition. The reality is that although most police will tell you they're on the job because it's a vocation, and can look you straight in the eye and dare you to say anything different, everyone has a different reason for signing on. One may be looking for excitement; another wants a secure job to raise her kids and pay off the mortgage. I joined because I couldn't get into the army, and I'm pretty sure now that I wanted to join the army because I was looking for a family.

I was brought up by my grandmother, Grandma C. (for Cecily). My father left my mother when I was six and my mother had some kind of breakdown and had to go away for a while, so Grandma C. took charge of me. Later on, my mother, discharged from the sanatorium but doped up with Librium, went to live with her unmarried aunt in Chiswick. I used to go down there every Sunday, and sometimes when the weather was fine my mother would take me to play in the park beside the Tube line, or we would walk along the path by the Thames to Kew. She was a vague, fine-boned woman, my mother, her nerves worn on the outside of her skin. Dulled by Librium, she seemed to live two or three seconds behind the rest of the world. Small things— a cloud blotting out the sun, an unreasonable demand for ice cream—would spin her into a flurry of panicky indecision and then bitter tears at her impotence. To my shame, I was relieved when she died after six years of slow decline; I was a selfish, unsentimental twelve-year-old who at her funeral fled from the clumsy sympathy of adults and walked aimlessly until, long past nightfall, I was picked up by the police in Dulwich and brought home.

I never found out why my father abandoned us. I remember bitter whispered arguments behind closed doors, shouts, sobs, stifling silences, but I was too young to understand exactly what was going on. Now, I'm pretty sure that there had been another woman. My father was twenty years older than my mother, a sergeant in the army and then an insurance salesman after his discharge, going on the knock from door to door, selling to the poorest of the poor policies costing a few pennies a week to cover the cost of a Co-op funeral with the trimmings. I put him out of my mind until my fortieth birthday, the exact age he had been when he left, when I discovered that he had moved to Southampton and remarried and died, and that I had a half brother. I also found out that he had been dishonourably discharged from the army after serving two years for stealing and selling supplies, and that he had been twice arrested for burglary. Although neither arrest had led to a conviction, I'm convinced that thieving, rather than selling insurance, had been his real trade.

Grandma C. had been widowed in the Second World War; my grandfather's smooth young face gazed out of half a dozen fading photographs in cheap frames on the mantelpiece over the gas fire. He had been a merchant seaman, drowned when his ship was torpedoed in the North Atlantic in 1943. Grandma C. had never remarried. She eked out a living on her war pension and by doing alterations and mending for a posh dry-cleaning establishment in the West End. She kept her tiny two-bedroom council flat spotlessly clean. Every Monday she boiled up all the laundry in an aluminium cauldron, stirring it with a great wooden ladle and running everything through the mangle. She scrubbed her front step every Monday, too, made jam from blackberries picked on waste ground, and liked to sit in her armchair in the evenings, working on the intricate stitching of a ballgown or letting out the sleeves of a jacket while listening to Radio Two on a valve radio whose dial, as round and glowing as the full moon, was marked with dozens of exotic names: Luxembourg, Hilversum, Helvetia, Athlone.

My grandfather had left behind little more than a clutch of yellowing paperback detective novels he had bought on shore leave in Baltimore, Boston, and New York. When I was thirteen I came down with mononucleosis, and for two months, listless and febrile, my throat reamed with barbed wire, I lived on a diet of chicken soup, hot Bovril, and pulp fiction. Raymond Chandler, Dashiell Hammett, W. R. Burnett, William P. McGivern. Cornell Woolrich, Frederick Nebel, Erle Stanley Gardner. Stories set at the margins of city life, brimming with rough individualism and rude wit, bad men, *femmes fatales* and patsies. Stories in which crimes never went unpunished even if motives were never clear, where detectives were uncommon common men, tough but sentimental loners, helplessly possessed by an absolute sense of moral duty, who never ran out of cigarettes, bullets or quips.

I do not think that it was then that I decided that I wanted to be a detective. I read my grandfather's books and everything in the genre that my grandmother could find in the local library, and then I went back to school and it seemed that my passion for *noir* pulps was extinguished, like a brush fire running out of fuel. I was two months behind my classmates, and two months is a long time when you are thirteen. Except for my enduring friendship with Nick Francis I had fallen out of the intricate tangle of alliances and hierarchies, but I did not mind. It confirmed my romantic notion that I was a quixotic loner, just like the heroes of the novels I had devoured.

Grandma C. was felled by a stroke one hot August night. She lay in hospital for a week, and then a second stroke carried her away. I was sixteen. I lived with my aunt for a little while, and then through Nick's father got a job making up orders at a wholesale greengrocer's, and stayed on rather than going back to school. The job was mindless, but I had enough money for records and clothes and roaming the clubs with Nick. I tried and failed to get into the army, and then I saw an advertisement in the *Evening Standard* and on a whim decided to try for the Metropolitan Police.

Nick's father knew a local constable, Jeff Rimmer, who took me for a ride in his patrol car to see what he got up to in the normal way of things, and later helped me get into the Met, coaching me on the interview ("Whatever you do, son, don't say you want to help the public. They'll think you're a fucking social worker."). Jeff retired five years ago. He lives out in Essex now, in a bungalow with an orchard where he's built a tree house for his grandchildren. I hadn't seen him since I got into trouble, although we'd spoken on the phone a couple of times about my coming to visit, and now I doubt that I'll ever see him again.

He did ask me, just once, why I stayed in the police after Spitalfields. I couldn't give him a sensible answer. All I could say was that I wasn't ready to quit.

Or there's this:

After being moved around various manors as a rookie uniform, I finally ended up in Islington. I was there for five years, longer than my marriage lasted.

(I'm not going to talk about my marriage. There were only the two of us involved. We were very young, and we had the arrogance of the young. We thought we could make a go of it. We thought that the simple force of our love would overcome the problems that all police marriages face. The shift work that leaves you feeling permanently jet-lagged; the irregular hours; time off cancelled at the last moment because of court appearances; and of course the usual shit that goes with the job, the stuff you make jokes about with your mates on the scene or in the canteen, a burden you bring home but never unwrap. No, the fear and the horror come out in other ways, and unless you and your partner are prepared to work at it, work hard and persistently, it will wear down your love until there's nothing left. That's how my marriage went. She's somewhere in Leeds now, married to a media-studies lecturer. They have two kids. Like I say, I'm not going to talk about it.)

Like anyone in the police who's a little bit different from the common run, I came in for some ragging, but I learned to bear it. Laughed when a joker stuck a height chart to the door of my locker. Bore my nicknames (Soapbox, Hutch, Minimum, Bonsai, Bridget) with good grace. Oh, we had some fun at the station all right.

Most police work is mundane; long stretches of routine and boredom unpredictably punctuated by moments of intense stress and fear, but there are also moments that are windows into the strangeness of the human soul. I once tried to explain this to my mate Trevor Bailey, and he laughed and said I sounded like some sad hippie.

"This isn't about any hippie nonsense," I told him. "It's about reality. It's about opening your eyes to what's around you."

"I'd as soon enough not know," he said. "I get enough reality as it is. That one who topped herself last week, as an instance."

We'd broken into her flat because the neighbours had complained about the smell. She'd managed to hang herself in her bedroom, using a short length of electrical flex and the doorknob. Judging from the mail piled behind her front door, she'd been there at least a month before we found her. The place had been crawling with maggots, flies, and yellow ants, and she'd left a grease stain six feet across on her bedroom carpet.

"That's not what I mean," I said. "That's just death, and it's all the same in the end. I mean the glimpses into people's lives, the way they think, the way they see the world."

"Dealing with what they do is bad enough," Trevor said, "without knowing what they're thinking."

I never could find the words to explain it to him, even though we went through a lot together. Trevor was a good copper, but he saw it, or pretended to see it, as no more than a job.

Anyway, in this story, I was still a uniformed constable on patrol. We were called, Trevor Bailey and I, to a supermarket on the Holloway Road, where an old man had collapsed. A doctor shopping with his wife had pronounced him at the scene. I later learned that he'd had a massive cerebral haemorrhage. A little bit of tubing, a pipe of elastic and gristle not much thicker than a thread, which unthought of had carried millions of gallons of blood over more than ninety years, had ruptured, and he had dropped as dead as a stone between shelves of canned soup and dried pasta.

We got his address from an electricity bill he was carrying and went round to break the bad news to anyone who might be there. As it turned out, he lived alone. I found out later that his wife had been killed in the Blitz, they had had no children, and (like Grandma C.) he hadn't remarried. But what wonders were revealed by that mean, squalidly public death!

The place was a bedsit on the first floor of a converted Victorian villa in Tufnell Park. A single bed neatly made up with army corners, a worn leather armchair, a radio-cassette on a dark wooden chest of drawers, a Baby Belling cooker on an old-fashioned washstand: the furniture of ten thousand solitary London rooms. But the walls were covered with paintings and watercolours—and not the kind of stuff you find on display on the railings of Hyde Park of a Sunday afternoon. There was a tiny early Francis Bacon watercolour, half a dozen Eric Gill lithographs, a Paul Nash cornfield, a Graham Sutherland watercolour portrait, a red-and-black Howard Hodgkin, a small, exquisite Barbara Hepworth bronze bull's head on top of a bookcase stuffed with first editions. The lot went up to auction and fetched half a million pounds, which went to some distant cousin in Aberdeen.

I did some background work in my spare time. The old man had been a senior clerk in a law firm, but had spent most of his money and his life on art. Every day he would leave his work and make his way to Soho, where he would drink in the Colony Room or the Coach and Horses or the French pub; he'd been a friend of many of the artists, helping them out when they were getting started and taking his reward in kind. I discovered that he'd been a fireman in the war, and had been one of those who had saved St Paul's from incendiaries—he had a signed letter from the Dean, and a George Medal. Who would have thought of that, to look at the poor dead old man lying curled up on his side on the supermarket floor, with his neat old-fashioned suit, his wispy crown of grey hair, his false teeth askew in his mouth?

I'm trying to tell you that we all contain mysteries. I'm trying to tell you why the girl murdered in the silver chair meant so much to me.

4

At the turn of the century, the government established an elite squad within the National Criminal Intelligence Service, NCIS, to counter the growth in computer-related crimes—fraud, money laundering, identity theft, distribution of pornography, and information about paedophilia and terrorism. It grew massively after the InfoWar, and now absorbs half the Home Office's crime budget and most of NCIS's manpower. It chases hackers and crackers, spammers and culture-jammers, phone phreaks and cypherpunks. It draws on experts in the private sector, the Inland Revenue, and Customs. It has links with MI5, MI6, and GCHQ. It liaises with Interpol and the FBI.

In short, it's the big time, and it should have made places like T12 redundant years ago. But like most of the regional forces, the Met has stubbornly retained its own computer-related crime unit, and despite name changes, budget cuts and structural overviews, T12 has survived more or less intact. Its civilian technicians are kept busy processing evidence and maintaining the security of the Met's intranet, but the police officers attached to T12 are either on their first posting and are too green or too stupid to realize where they've been sent, or have reached bottom through exhaustion or some fuck-up not quite major enough to warrant dismissal. They liaise with crime-scene coordinators and exhibits officers, and oversee transportation of evidence. They write up report forms, archive forms, evidence forms. They're supposed to keep up with the endless flood of action papers, memos, circulars, procedural updates and the rest, but unless Rachel Sweeney decides to try and stir things up they mostly sit around drinking bad coffee and working at their artless little scams and dodges. T12: formerly the Information Technology Unit, and before that Electronic Crimes, generally known as the Donkey Sanctuary. That's where I had been sent after I had refused early retirement and had been declared fit for active duty.

It occupies a gimcrack early 1970s steel-framed office building that's inadequately dressed in spackled panels painted a shade of green not found in nature, backed into a corner of a cramped car park with blank brick walls towering over it on three sides and a razor-wire fence at the front. The barber-pole gate and security cameras are operated by a private security firm, FourSquare, which because it employs old villains supplied with fabricated IDs and pays less than the minimum wage, is able to underbid its competitors and make itself highly attractive to the Met's accountants. The building has a flat roof with a mobile leak, there's enough asbestos dust floating in the air to make the Devil a nice set of pyjamas, and because it has to be patched and tended like a patient dying from a variety of unspecific symptoms, there's always construction work nagging away somewhere. Cables are fixed to the walls with silvery duct tape. The green nylon carpet tiles on the ground floor are lifting from damp that's working its way through cracks in the foundations. Buzzing fluorescents, permanently lit, give the place the blankly exhausted look of someone kept awake under heavy interrogation.

As I expected, Rachel Sweeney, the detective-superintendent

in charge of T12, was at the opening of the Martin trial and
wasn't due back until after lunch, so I had a few hours' grace.
I fired up my computer, checked my emails, and found that Julie
had sent me a photo of herself. A slim, thirtysomething redhead
with a mannish brush cut, her long handsome face shaded by a
panama hat with a band of fake leopardskin, she was sitting in
a crowded outdoor café, holding up a tall glass of dark beer and
giving the camera a big cheesy grin. She collected amber and
garish Dr Martens boots, went to the opera for the spectacle
and the buzz—she cheerfully admitted that she had no idea
about music. She spent an hour every day at the carbon-fibre
exercise machines of the Muscle Factory, things that looked like
they were stamping dies and lathes for parts of some kind of
exotic sports car. She drank milk from the carton, wiping away
with the back of her hand droplets that clung to the fine hairs
above her lip. She didn't shave her armpits or her legs, couldn't
cook, preferred beer to wine, left the bathroom a wreck in the
morning, had a habit of wrapping the entire duvet around herself
in the middle of the night. She did not believe in mysteries, was
candid and garrulous and restless. I missed her more than I
could tell her, and seeing the picture made me want to talk to
her more than anything else in the world. But I had work to do,
and I didn't want to risk doing anything that might tip the bal-
ance towards our becoming no more than Just Good Friends.

I called up the browser, started to work through the search
engines. T12 has an open server, and although every click trail
is logged, it's wide open to the Web's spew of data, unchecked
by nanny programs, black-box filters and RIP search engines. It
didn't take me long to find a link to the dead girl, Sophie Booth.
I clicked through the pages, excited and scared. I told myself
that anyone on McArdle's team with a bit of computer experience
could have found this too. I saved everything to disk and went
upstairs.

The top floor had been knocked through into one long workroom, full of benches cluttered with electronic equipment and trays of parts, battered desks on which computers permanently hummed, cubicles partitioned by shoulder-high screens scaled with postcards and colour photocopies and printouts. Raw sunlight burned through a row of dusty windows and the air smelled of electricity and warm plastic. It was always hot on the top floor; the windows were welded shut for security, with heavy steel grilles inside and out, and the air-conditioning couldn't cope with the heat sink of the flat roof and the heat generated by a hundred computers. It was not yet nine o'clock, and only one technician was at work, T12's resident übergeek, Charlie Wills. He was hunched in front of a terminal, greying hair tied back in a long, loose ponytail that swayed across the back of his white lab coat as he clicked his mouse with the cool precision of a gunfighter. The lab coat, like the ponytail, was an affectation; so was the soldering iron clipped to its top pocket.

"I've got a good one today," he told me, without looking up from the screen. "Some maniac has broken into the sarcophagus at Chernobyl—he must have used a robot—and wired it up with webcams. Impressively spooky. Or how about a smoker cam? A mile below the Pacific, watching albino crabs crawl around this chimney belching superheated black water."

"All that screen radiation is softening your brain. Not to mention the porn I know you look at after hours. Doesn't anyone do any work around here?"

"Apparently, some people like to clock in and out on a regular basis," Charlie said. "You should appreciate this stuff, John. Private obsessions made public: that's what the Web is all about."

Andy Higgins, the chief technician, was in his little corner office, tamping tobacco in his pipe. He didn't seem surprised to see me. He said mildly, "You misspelled *urgency*."

"I was in a hurry. Did you take a look at the gear, or just the evidence form?"

Andy tapped his Out tray with the stem of his pipe. A heavyset, affable, ruddy-faced man in his late fifties, he looked more like a retired farmer than an electronics expert, but he could take apart anything you gave him, squeeze every recoverable byte out of damaged disks. He had started working with computers as an RAF technician, back when mainframes with less processing power than a pocket calculator filled an entire room, had spent thirty years in GCHQ before moving to T12. He still kept on his shelves packets of green or orange or pink programming cards held together with thick rubber bands, and would sometimes take a packet down and slowly thumb through it, the way you might thumb through a favourite book you know that you will never read again.

He told me, "It was a nice bit of kit, the G10, almost brand-new as you might expect—that model has only been out for a few weeks. Pity someone took such a dislike to it. The other one, the beige box, was a standard multimedia model about three years old."

"Is that it?"

Andy lit a match, held it to the bowl of his pipe and drew wetly on the stem until it got going. He put the spent match in a tin ashtray someone had pinched from one of the local pubs. "The hard drives had been removed, so yes, that's about it. Still, webcams and two computers, this is pure speculation, but it's possible she could have been running an illegal website. The beige box could have been the server. It was cabled to the G10, and it was connected to a fat line, too."

"She was dirty all right. I did a search on the Web, and turned up something."

Andy squinted at me through the sunlit haze of tobacco smoke. "What's your role in the investigation, exactly?"

I lied like a hero. "At the moment I'm a sort of unofficial advisor."

"I've written it all up," Andy said, and pulled a form from a stack and gave it to me. "You'll need to give me a signed copy."

"I know."

"You had better tell Rachel Sweeney, too."

As I went out, Charlie Wills said, without looking around from the glowing screen of the computer monitor, "If you're going downstairs, put on some more coffee, will you? The pot's empty."

5

The murder room was in an anonymous annexe of Scotland Yard. The usual scene: two civilian aides entering data into ancient computers, half a dozen plain clothes, haggard from fifteen-hour shifts, working telephones, writing up reports and action dockets. A WPC was pinning blue duty sheets to a notice board. The blonde DS I remembered from the scene, the exhibits officer, carried a stack of orange dockets into one of the offices off the main room.

A 360-degree photomosaic of the bedsit was pinned to a big display board. The dead girl was centred in it, tied naked to the silver chair, her head hanging down over an apron of blood. There were dozens of close-ups—all glare and shadow in the brutal light of the camera's flash, a lunar skinscape sliced by knife cuts, each wound circled in red and neatly numbered, as if quantifying the murderer's handiwork could begin to explain it. A whiteboard was covered in names circled and linked in red and green and blue ink, and in the middle of this multicoloured web was a grainy, blown-up snapshot of Sophie Booth. Taken from life. She had her arm around someone who had been cropped out of the picture, and was grinning straight at the camera, bold and defiant and vital. Her hair so black it must have been dyed, cut in an asymmetrical pageboy bob that suited her neat, oval face. She wore very dark lipstick and silver eye shadow. The camera's flash had caught the blood at the back of her eyes, so that they were capped with red.

While I was studying this picture, DI David Varnom unfolded himself from behind a desk and came over like a shark angling towards a likely morsel. His white Pierre Cardin shirt was neatly ironed, the top button fastened under his yellow silk tie, the sleeves rolled back to his elbows, exposing pale, hairless forearms. He lamped me with the full force of his Jesuitical gaze, all flint and frosty rectitude, and said, "Like what you see?"

"I have something for your boss," I told him.

"You can leave it with me."

Yes, I thought, and then you can bury my name at the bottom of a ton of paperwork. "Tony McArdle has to see this himself," I said, and wafted the data spike under his nose.

Varnom adjusted his steel-framed glasses with finger and thumb. "I understood the computers were trashed."

"They were. This is something else. Something your boss has to see right away."

"What part of 'you can leave it with me' don't you understand?"

He didn't bother to disguise his contempt, which made it so much easier for me to hate him back. I put the spike in the top pocket of my jacket. "My boss asked me to give an important piece of evidence to Tony McArdle. If that's not possible now, I'll take it away and come back another time."

A simple bluff which worked far better than I expected. Varnom flushed and said, "For your sake, this had better be worth it."

Tony McArdle, rumpled and red-eyed, had obviously pulled an all-nighter. He ran an electric razor over his chin and cheeks while I explained that I had done a simple search of the Web using Sophie Booth's name as the keyword, and had found plenty of leads to her website. That was down, naturally enough—every link yielding the same 404 error—because the computer she had used to run it had been trashed.

"But I did find something else. It seems that she had an admirer. He downloaded pictures from her site and put them on his own website. Illegal, of course, but intellectual property is a rather vague notion out on the Web."

McArdle laid the razor on the stack of papers in his Out tray, fingered the folds of his face. "This admirer wouldn't happen to live in London, would he?"

"In the States. Champaign, Illinois. You can find out all about him from his website. There's even a picture of him. He looks very young."

"If this is about the cameras," Varnom said, "we already know what she was doing with them."

"You do?"

"Sophie Booth was an art student, at Central St Martin's," Varnom said. "We talked with her tutor last night, and she told us that Sophie was using the cameras to put her work on to the Web. Through what was most definitely an unlicensed server."

I said, "What I found is not what I'd call performance art."

"He's making it out to be more than it is, sir," Varnom told McArdle. "That's why I let him see you, against my better judgement."

"And now he's here, so I might as well take a look. Go on, John," McArdle told me. "Do your worst."

I fired up McArdle's computer, found the Web browser and pointed it at the files on the spike. The first page was the index to the fan's website, his name, Iggy Stix, rendered in red spray-paint lettering above a thumbnail photograph of a sallow-faced kid with a goatee beard and long hair brushed back from a high forehead. He stirred and grinned and said, "What's up?" if you held the pointer over him. The text underneath told the world that he was twenty-five years old, that he had a degree in computer science from MIT, that he worked as a programmer for a defence firm in Champaign, Illinois (*can't tell you what I do, but it keeps me very busy and it's fun!!!*), that he had a cat called Starbucks. There was a picture of the cat.

Click **here** *if you want to hear what I'm listening to. Click* **here** *if you want to know what books I've recently read. Click* **here** *if you want to go to some of my favorite sites on the Web. Click* **here** *if you want to visit Starbucks' home page. It's worth the visit! I know the site's pretty sparse but I'll put up some more stuff when I have the time. Take a look here to see my favorite* **web girl***. She's an English chick who IMHO is cuter than the original Jenni (remember Jenni?!?!). Check out her site, where she gets up to strange* **arty things** *with her pals. Or you might prefer these* **intimate moments** *she's shared with us. Very retro but very hot!!!!*

"Lead on," McArdle told me, and I clicked the mouse, aware of Varnom at my back.

First a geeky little boast, the kind of territorial assertion these people like to make about stuff they've taken from elsewhere.

These thumbnails are all 256-color JPEGs which share the same palette. Consequently the index should render well even in 16-bit color-mapped displays.

This slowly faded into two grainy, low-definition pictures of Sophie Booth sleeping on the mattress under the white rug, amidst a scattering of cushions. Long shadows striped the floor. In the first you could just see her head and the curve of one shoulder; in the second, she had partly kicked off the rug, exposing a long pale leg.

We've caught her napping was Iggy Stix's comment under the first. *A tantalizing glimpse . . .* under the second.

And then the rest. McArdle leaned back in his chair and clucked his tongue and said, "Sophie. Sophie, girl, did you know what you were doing?"

Here was Sophie Booth in a burlesque of a schoolgirl outfit—
blazer and white blouse, and a very short skirt that showed the
tops of her stockings. She was sticking out her bum and looking
at the camera with a finger to her lipsticked lips and a knowing
gaze.

Wouldn't you like to go to school with her?

And here she was with the blouse open, leaning forward and
offering her breasts in the cradle of her bra, eyes closed, lips
slightly parted to show a glint of teeth.

I wonder what's behind that adorable, sly smirk . . .

Now she was down to knickers and stockings and suspenders,
cupping her breasts and looking down at them.

I'm going to censor what this picture makes me think!

Here she was naked, bent over sideways to the camera, hand
curled around to press something, an orange cylinder, between
the cheeks of her bum. Here she was sitting on that kitchen
chair facing the camera, legs apart, the orange cylinder, probably
a vibrator, between her legs; you couldn't see much because her
hands splayed above and below. Her head was back, offering the
white length of her throat, hair falling around her bare shoulders.

Mr Iggy Stix had no comments for these two pictures. As
McArdle studied them, I wondered again why she had done this.
What had she been thinking, there in the room? It was less
explicit than hard-core porn, but more shocking because Sophie
seemed to be acting out her own fantasy, and making whoever
viewed it an accomplice.

But she hadn't just displayed herself to the camera. She had
opened herself to the world. And the world had answered back.

"Very nice," Varnom said, in a tone that suggested the opposite.

"Have some respect for the dead, Dave," McArdle told him.
"What's your opinion, John?"

"There are plenty of dirty pictures on the Web, sir. And plenty
of sites like Sophie Booth's. In America or Japan, Holland or

Russia, anywhere where cyberprostitution isn't illegal. Some of them are amateur, but most of them are run by professionals. They recruit good-looking kids, set them up in an apartment wired up with webcams, and pay them a wage to wander around naked and give regular sex shows. They have full-motion video and sound. This, though, is very amateur."

"And completely illegal," Varnom said.

"In this country," I said. "Not in most of the rest of the world."

"But she wasn't in America or Cuba," Varnom said. "She was playing her dirty little games here, and she was breaking the law."

"She made herself visible," McArdle said. "That's all we should care about. Is that all there is?"

There were a few more pictures. One a grainy blur, catching Sophie in the act of rising naked from the mattress.

We nearly missed her.

Another of her bending over the sink, the cylinder of the electric water heater above her head, again naked, brushing her teeth. No comment from Mr Iggy Stix; he was silent before the power of her casual nakedness.

And then the last, a close-cropped headshot in three-quarter profile. Perhaps she was sitting at her computer, looking at its screen; perhaps she was looking at a mirror; whatever held her intent gaze was out of shot.

I wonder what that adorable smile is hiding . . .

"I wonder too," McArdle said. "I think we should have a word with Mr Stix."

I said, "He hasn't updated his site for more than two months."

"That doesn't mean that he might not have seen the murder if it was transmitted over the Web," McArdle said. "And while our Mr Stix is most likely a silly lad with a bit of a personality deficiency, there is just a chance he's a little bit more sinister than that. There was a case a few years ago where an American exchange student became infatuated with a girl, continued to bombard her with letters and flowers after he went back to the States. Then she was found dead. Turned out he bought a cheap flight on his father's credit card, flew over and killed her, flew straight back. Have a word with the local police, Dave, and find out what you can about this Iggy Stix. Let's make sure he doesn't have anything more to tell us."

I said, "It might be an idea to close down his website. Anyone can access those pictures."

"Including the eager ladies and gentlemen of the press, I suppose." McArdle massaged the bridge of his nose with both forefingers. "Is it possible to get it closed down? I have to confess that I don't have much time for the Whole Wide World."

"The Whole Wide World, sir?" I didn't have McArdle down as a Wreckless Eric fan.

"It's what my youngest daughter calls the Web," McArdle said, looking me straight in the eye and daring me to smile. "WWW. World Wide Web, Whole Wide World. She's six, knows more about computers than I ever will."

I said, "The local police probably have a computer-crime section. You could ask them to lean on Mr Stix's ISP."

"Organize that, Dave," McArdle told Varnom. "Get it done before these pictures turn up in the tabloids."

Varnom said, "Shouldn't we alert NCIS, sir?"

"I think NCIS has better things to do than bother with our one little murder," McArdle said.

"I wasn't thinking of murder per se, sir," Varnom said. "Just the computer aspect, such as it is."

"T12 has liaised with murder investigations before," I said.

Varnom ignored me. "These pictures are clearly illegal content, sir, put up on an unlicensed server. We should let NCIS investigate that side of things."

"Let's leave them out of it for now," McArdle said. "I want you to chase up this Iggy Stix, Dave. Oh, and find someone who can get these pictures printed out, too. I'm going for a breath of air with our computer expert. I want them on my desk when I get back."

We walked down Queen Anne's Gate towards St James's Park. McArdle asked questions about Sophie Booth's computers, and I did my best to answer them. He said, "You like the work over at ITU?"

"T12."

"Whatever. How is it for you?"

"There are good days and slow days."

"I remember the siege we worked on together. You did good work, you got the girlfriend out, it wasn't your fault the SO19 boys had to go in at the end."

"I must admit that at the end I deliberately went downstairs for a cup of tea and left them to it, sir."

"I rather thought so. It must have been hard, Danny Hamilton off his head on drugs, ranting and making demands and sticking his gun through his letter box, while you tried to talk him down and the SO19 team sat in the flat opposite, aching to get on with the game."

"That's the way most of the jobs went."

"You were in the information service before you became a negotiator."

"Thirteen years, sir. Then they discovered that I could talk as well as file."

"You handled the paperwork on quite a few suspicious deaths, I suppose."

"A bit of everything, sir."

"But no actual experience in the field."

"I was on the beat in Islington. I saw my share."

"I don't think you were to blame for the Spitalfields fuck-up, by the way."

"Thank you, sir."

"There's a few that do, of course. Friends of the dead. But it was a crazy time, and Spitalfields was the least of it. Still, it must have been hard, coming back on the job. Toby Patterson for one was well liked."

"I got some stick, and I took it. Since then, I've mostly been blessed with some nice quiet desk work."

"I think I'd find it hard to give up the job too," McArdle said.

We crossed Birdcage Walk and entered the park's calm green eye. It was very hot and close. Cameras perched on top of steel poles along the paths. People lay everywhere on the grass in various states of undress. A couple of suncare patrols were about, wholesome-looking teenagers in decal-spattered tracksuits and sunhats offering free applications of brightly coloured sunblock to the insufficiently protected. People pushed pushchairs beside the lake, their babies and toddlers hidden behind layers of fine black antimosquito netting. Three skinny, tanned American boys in psychedelically patterned surfer jams were throwing a Frisbee back and forth; it made a UFO warble as it sliced through the sunlit air. It was all horribly normal.

McArdle stopped to buy two ice-cream cones from one of the park's gypsy vendors. We stood and ate our ice cream and watched the Frisbee players. Two middle-aged men in suits, taking the air, idly chatting about murder.

"We interviewed Sophie Booth's college tutor and some of her classmates last night," McArdle said, "the ones who helped her out with her performance art. We might reinterview in light of what you found, see if they know anything about this unlicensed server of hers. Tell me what you think."

"There are thousands of unlicensed servers in the country, sir. They have spoof addresses and use freeware firewall programs to hide from RIP search engines. If this was a professional site— one where you have to pay a subscription to gain full access— she'll have a bank account which should show plenty of small credit-card payments."

"We'll check it out, of course," McArdle said. "So she could have been earning money flaunting herself. Poor silly girl."

"It isn't exactly prostitution."

"That's what the girls in the Soho peepshows used to say." McArdle licked a trail of melting ice cream from his wrist with a deft gesture. "It keeps coming back to computers. There's the fax, sent through this anonymous remailer in Cuba. Sophie Booth was running an illegal server, those pictures she posted are very definitely against the Protection of Children Act, her computer hard drives were taken after she was murdered. And it turns out that her uncle, the man who gave her those computers and holds leases on the flat and the office below, runs a very successful software company. Something to do with CCTV, the chip that links everything together."

"RedLine," I said, and thought of the fox caught in the implacable lights.

"That's the one. The smart chip they've been putting in all the CCTV cameras."

I said, "I suppose he has government connections."

"I've been made aware of them," McArdle said dryly. "He's in Scotland on business, but he's flying back tonight."

"There was a camera above the office door."

"Linked to ADESS. We pulled its picture file. No sign of anyone but the residents going in or out of the flats, but that doesn't mean anything. There are a couple of back doors, too. Nothing to indicate that they were forced, or that their locks were picked, but our chum might have had a key. He brought rope and solvent with him, after all, so this wasn't a simple b and e turned nasty."

"It was planned."

"It was definitely planned. Our chum knows Sophie Booth is in, gets inside the building, knocks on the door to her flat. Maybe she knew him. Maybe she was expecting him. Anyway, she opens the door and he saps her, one blow to the forehead. A sock filled with sand, the surgeon thinks. He ties her to the chair and spends some time working on her before he finally cuts her throat, one deep cut that severed the jugular veins and the carotid arteries. She would have passed out in a few seconds from blood loss; she would have been dead in only a few more." McArdle crunched up his cone and added, "It was the only mercy the fucker showed her. The coroner found high levels of serotonin and free histamines in her blood. She suffered horribly before he killed her, and I think that he wanted people to admire his handiwork. The setting and methodology didn't ring any bells with the behaviourial people, but we're waiting for HOLMES to come up with a list of similar crimes. The worst possibility is that it was a professional carrying out a one-off commission."

I finished my ice cream and lit a cigarette.

"I'll have one," McArdle said, twiddling his fingers. "I gave up for New Year and I haven't bought one since, but I'm a shameless cadger."

I handed him a tab and lit it for him.

McArdle took a deep drag, slowly exhaled, then took the tab from his mouth and examined it critically. "Christ, what's a policeman doing smoking Tropica Ultras? They could hand these out in hospital."

"I'm on my way to giving up, sir."

"You've given up on cigarettes," McArdle said. "Now all you have to do is give up these." He took another drag. "This isn't an easy shout. It has a red flag flying over it, but my budget hasn't been increased. I need to get to work on all the likely leads as soon as possible, and my squad has two other suspicious deaths and a kidnapping to deal with. Dave Varnom's right. I should ask NCIS to look into the computer side of things. But I've tangled with NCIS before. They have a habit of taking the case away from you, they like to grab headlines because it helps justify their enormous budget. This poor girl doesn't need to become anyone's trophy. All she needs is that her killer is found."

"I'd like to help, sir."

"I wouldn't be wasting my time with you if I didn't think that."

McArdle dropped his cigarette stub and ground it under his heel. "Let's be getting back."

As we walked through the park, he said, "I love this place. I come here at least once a day. Fresh air, a gentle stroll in no particular direction, there's nothing better." He glanced sideways at me and said, "Where would you go with what you found?"

"I would make a full-scale search on the Web. And I would try to track down everyone who took a look at her website or otherwise had access to her server."

"A lot of work for one man. Let's try you out on something easier. Sophie Booth had an Internet account with her college, like every student, but she never made use of it."

"Because she had her own server."

"Maybe so, but we discovered from her mobile phone records that she also had an account with an outfit called Wizard Internet. I want copies of her recent emails. Think you could handle that?"

"It's a routine Information Disclosure Order, sir."

"Then you shouldn't have any problem with it. You'll have to work on T12's books, mind, not mine. I can't afford to pay overtime to my own people, let alone subsidize other departments."

"If I'm going to work for you, sir, I'll need to clear it with Detective-Superintendent Rachel Sweeney."

"The word is, Rachel Sweeney is going to lose T12 under the new decentralization scheme, that she needs all the points she can get. But you already know that. You want to be back in the action, and you've been working out the angles."

"Something like that, sir."

"I'm short-handed, and I'm under a lot of pressure to put this away as quickly as possible. I need someone who can shovel shit, not a showboat looking for a large piece of the glory. All I ask is that you do some good work for me, and try not to piss off Dave Varnom. In return, I'll make sure you're mentioned in dispatches."

"I have the impression that Varnom knew Toby Patterson," I said.

"They were at Hendon together. Dave's an ambitious lad, and very upfront about his likes and dislikes, but he knows I won't stand for them getting in the way of his work. Say hello to Rachel from me," he added, and we parted in the shadow of the rotating signage of Scotland Yard.

6

I didn't wait for Rachel Sweeney to get back from court. I wrote up an Information Disclosure Order, made an appointment with the Technical Director of Wizard Internet, and drove around to the site of the murder. I wanted to see it again because there was so much Tony McArdle hadn't told me. I wanted to put myself where Sophie Booth had been when she had died because I wanted to be at the heart of the mystery. I had a strange airy sense of dislocation, *déjà vu* all over again. Six months ago I'd been watching a completely illegal spike of *A Clockwork Orange* that Julie had brought back from the States, and had started weeping during the first rape scene, the one in the disused theatre that ends as a rumble between the two gangs. And hadn't been able to stop. So I didn't know if I could handle this, and I didn't know what I would do if I went to pieces. But I knew that I had to know.

I parked outside the building and took a medicinal nip from a quarter bottle of Jack Daniel's I happened to have brought with me, got out, and made a circuit around the block. Three burnt-out cars squatted like toads, all brown-and-orange rust and black char, in an abandoned building site; I clambered on to the bonnet of one so I could look over the brick wall into the tiny, rubbish-filled yard of the building where Sophie Booth had died.

A steel fire door at ground level presumably belonged to the office; a spiral stair led up to another door on the first floor. There were shards of glass stuck in the rough concrete that capped the wall. I supposed that the Forensic Science Service people had checked them for fibres and blood. I walked all the way around to the front, where festive pennants of blue-and-white crime-scene tape fluttered in the hot, dirty breeze. I squinted through dusty glass into the empty office, then rang the bell for Sophie's flat.

The uniform on watch noted my name and number and led the way upstairs and unlocked the door to the flat. He was young and blond and unreasonably gangling, with traces of acne scars along the line of his jaw and Chinese hairs at the corners of his mouth. An affable boy who'd be better suited to directing cows in some deep green Somerset lane than confronting the spooks and monsters of the inner city. He was sweating through the back of his white, short-sleeved shirt. A Walther P990 pistol rode in a black button-down holster at his hip.

"Someone was here first thing, sir," he said.

"DCI McArdle?"

"No, sir, an inspector, same as you."

"I think I know who that would be."

"He wanted to talk with the victim's neighbour," the boy said.

"Did he?"

"That's what he told me, sir."

"I mean did he talk? With the neighbour."

"No, sir, the guy hasn't been back. He lives somewhere in Oxford, stays in town during the week. You know, while he's working."

"And this is a Monday, and he isn't here."

"Well, I suppose so. Maybe he's off on his summer holidays."

"I expect DI Varnom told you to keep an eye out for him."

The baby constable nodded. "Is he a suspect, do you think?"

"I wouldn't know. Who else lives here?"

"A nice old lady, Greek, nearly a hundred. Dressed all in black and as deaf as a post. She gave me tea," he said. "In a glass. It had a mint leaf in it."

He said it with a kind of wonder. No, the inner city wasn't for him at all.

I told him, "You go and have another cup of nice minty tea."

"I have to stay here, sir."

"I know you went upstairs to get the tea. After all, you wouldn't have wanted the old dear to be climbing up and down those stairs just to bring you a refreshing beverage, not at her age."

"It was only for a minute," he said. "I've been here on my own since six."

"Count yourself lucky it isn't in a tower block on the Mile End Road."

"I know," he said. "I was on watch at a block of flats in Dalston last month. Kids kept trying to drop dogshit on me from one of the balconies."

"You were lucky it wasn't a TV. Go and get some more tea or go and stand outside in the sunshine for a bit. I need to think, and I can't do it while you're looming over me or flexing your size twelves outside the door. Oh, one more thing. Is there any way into the yard at the back?"

"I don't know, sir. Through the office, I suppose."

"You don't have a key for the office?"

"Just the front door and the flat, sir."

He went off, his boots making a lot of noise on the stairs. My stomach was clenched tight and I was sweating hard. Not for the first time, I wished that I could have a quiet moment with Friedrich Nietzsche, so I could tell him exactly what I thought about his *that which does not kill us makes us stronger* bullshit. I took a breath. I opened the door.

It was quiet and dim in there, and very warm and close. A few flies buzzed about. I could hear the rumble of the upstairs neighbour's television. Knives of sunlight prised at the closed black blinds. I shut the door and stood with my back to it, my hands in my trouser pockets.

The mattress had been stripped. There were smudges of silvery dust all over the trestle table by the window, on the black telephone that sat on a stack of directories on the floor, around the frame of the door. The blood was still under the silver-sprayed plastic chair, black and dull now. I told myself that I couldn't smell it, and I was pretty sure that I couldn't, but I was breathing through my mouth as I looked at it and saw what I hadn't seen before, blood speckles in a wide irregular fan in front of the chair. Sophie had moved after he'd cut her throat, managed to lift her head so that blood had sprayed out. Perhaps she had been trying to get some on him, but probably it was no more than a reflex, straining against her killer's grip for a last glimpse of light.

A small spark of anger tripped my heart. I thought that it was a good sign.

A fan came on when I pulled the light cord in the tiny bathroom. A washbasin jammed beside the toilet, a shower in the corner, its white tiles gridded by black mildew. A shelf crammed with little bottles of soaps and lotions over the sink, and a big, gilt-framed mirror with postcards untidily wedged into it, cheap glossy pictures of New York. I turned one back with my ballpoint; there was no writing on it. No shaving kit or men's aftershave or deodorant. The fridge held a banana going black, half a dozen yoghurts, a slice of pizza curling on a plate, a carton of skimmed milk. Lentils and three kinds of rice in the cabinet above the sink, a clutter of spices, ordinary tea, rose-hip tea, camomile tea, lemon tea, a sprouting onion.

I went back to the door and looked at the room again. I wanted to think it through for myself, like a proper detective.

He had come up the stairs. There was only a cheap Yale lock on the outer door. Any kid could have opened it with a bit of plastic, but the CCTV camera which overlooked the door had recorded nothing unusual, so perhaps he had come in through one of the doors at the back. In which case, since neither of them had been forced, he must have had a key. Anyway, he had got inside, and Sophie Booth had opened her door to his knock, thinking it was her neighbour or the old dear. Or perhaps she had been expecting him. In any case, she had been drinking from a mug and she had carried it with her when she answered the door, casual and unworried. She had opened the door to him and he had hit her, hit her once and with precision. She had fallen and the mug had shattered (a day later, Dave Varnom had warned me not to disturb its fragments) and he was inside with her. Had he stripped her there and then? Or had he waited until she came around, and then made her strip? Had he made a show of it, or had he got down to business straight away?

No, I thought, he had made her strip. Because it had been staged, played out under the gaze of the webcams. From the moment he had made her strip to the moment he cut her throat. She had bled out, and then he had washed her body to remove any trace of himself. He'd known what he was doing, which suggested that he had done it before. I wondered if he had taken a souvenir. They did that sometimes, as an *aide-mémoire* of the good time they had had, the way a bride might keep a single rose pressed between the order of service of her wedding. They would take it out, sniff it, fondle it, masturbate over it.

Maybe the webcam pictures were his trophy.

McArdle's people would have fed every detail into HOLMES,

the Home Office Large Major Enquiry System, and Flints, the Forensic Led Intelligence System. The things done while Sophie Booth had been alive. The particular way she had been tied up. The way her throat had been cut. The washing of the body. McArdle had told me that they had failed to get a match with previous murders, but perhaps that didn't matter.

Because the murder was only half of it.

Because the last thing the murderer had done was to open the computers and take their hard drives.

I thought then that Sophie's killer might have taken them because he knew they held information which might lead to him. And he had known to take them, not just smash them. He had known that information could be retrieved from reformatted or broken hard drives. He had taken them, and he had taken all of Sophie Booth's data spikes and Zip disks too.

He knew about computers. I was sure that he had found Sophie Booth because she had put her little fantasies, her teases, her dares or challenges, on the Web. He had traced her, watched her in real life, made his plans, pounced. And he had killed her, and washed her body, and broken into her computers and stolen her information.

At least one person had seen him do it. Probably more, perhaps many more, although only one had taken the trouble to find the fax number of Scotland Yard and call it in.

The webcams were still up in the corners of the ceiling, on either side of the door. There was a chair by the little table in the kitchen nook, and I stood on that to look at them. Connectix IntelliCam 5s, small cheap things which sold by the tens of thousands.

I looked back over my shoulder, at the silver-sprayed plastic chair in the middle of the room. I climbed down and went over and stood behind it and looked up at the webcams. There was blood on the seat of the chair, two shallow, cracked ovals. I poked them with the tip of my ballpoint. They were quite dry.

I sat in the chair and looked up.

The round black eyes of the webcams stared back at me.

I drove down Commercial Road to the Isle of Dogs. In the good old days before the InfoWar, I would have submitted the Information Disclosure Order to the National Communication Data Storage Service, whose supercomputer had held cross-referenced records of every telephone call, email, and Web connection made in Britain. But the NCDSS supercomputer had been wiped out by a microwave bomb, and its replacement was still unfinished because of budget overruns, construction delays and interdepartmental wranglings; to dig out copies of Sophie Booth's emails, I had to take the IDO directly to her Internet Service Provider.

Stuck in stop-ago traffic, I rustled through the litter of cassettes in the Mini's broken glove box and came up with Wreckless Eric: "Whole Wide World." His plaintive *faux-naïf* voice anchored by a beat as steady as an engine bearing a ship away from shore, the voice of a helpless romantic, tough yet vulnerable, wearily cynical yet eternally hopeful, boasting that he would travel the whole wide world to be with his girl, yet uncertain whether this will win her affections. Like the guileless defiance of a playground dare: I'll die if you don't! I remembered Tony McArdle quoting his daughter's malapropism, and knew that in Sophie I'd found my own obsession. Like Wreckless Eric, I was a wannabe tough guy fatally weakened by romance, a helpless dancer. I had to redeem Sophie's death or destroy myself trying.

It was very bright and very hot, ninety-two degrees by my watch. The dry wind blowing off the river was full of the sulphurous stink of sloughs of algae which had recently bloomed and died in the Thames's warm stew. The tarmacadam of the roads shimmered, cupping little rippling mirages. Sunlight burned on glass-walled buildings, flashed from the pyramid that capped the central tower at Canary Wharf. Docklands, with its glass-skinned office blocks and windy squares, the inhuman scale of its abstract sculptures, its toy railway slung across reaches of water and between buildings, seemed like an illustration from an old sci-fi magazine, an ideal, bloodless futurescape with all human mess and confusion erased, the last refuge of capitalism in post-InfoWar Britain, another country.

I queued in the razor wire tunnel of the checkpoint under the gaze of a hundred CCTVs. The security guards in Imperial Stormtrooper body armour, better armed than any police, were not much impressed by my warrant card, but one of them stuck a six-hour pass on the windscreen of my Mini and waved me through. I swung around the big underground roundabout and promptly got lost, drove halfway down the length of the Isle of Dogs before realizing it, reversed in front of a busy building site, and turned back.

Wizard Internet's offices were in a two-storey glass-and-steel building on Heron Quays. An arc of yellow bricks led up to the automatic glass doors of the reception area. *We're off to see the Wizard* . . . was inlaid in silver calligraphic script above them.

I gave the name of the man I was to meet to the receptionist, and she told me that another police officer would be attending the meeting, a police officer from (she pronounced each letter of the acronym with endearing care) NCIS.

I had plenty of time to think about that while I waited on a fat black leather couch. Sunlight streamed through the bronzed-glass curtain wall, throwing across the white carpet the shadows of palms and tree ferns that stood in big stainless-steel planters. The receptionist typed at her computer behind a sweep of blond wood, under the company's cartoon logo of a cheeky young chap who, in a dishevelled robe and a crooked pointy hat, was brandishing a wand from which a stylized lightning bolt crackled. She was pretty in a corn-fed, bottle blonde Essex girl kind of way, wore a microphone headset, and didn't stop typing as she answered calls. When I went over to remind her of my appointment, she said, without looking up, "I'm sorry, sir, but Mr Mc-Lean told me that the meeting can't start without the other police officer."

"Did the other police officer tell Mr McLean to say that?"

"I wouldn't know, would I?"

"Perhaps I should go and find out."

I would have done, too, if the way hadn't been barred by the kind of armoured-glass gates that need either a swipe card or a chip embedded under your skin to open them.

"I could page Mr McLean again," she said, "but he was quite insistent as to that point."

"My appointment was for half past twelve. It's almost one o'clock now. Let me through and I'll go and find him myself."

"I'm sorry, sir, but I really can't do that."

The receptionist was about the same age as Sophie Booth, her face carefully made up, neat and trim in a grey jacket of thin ribbed rubber over a black T-shirt. Her fingers, long nails painted with silver, rested on the keyboard; her gaze was half-directed at the memo she had been typing up. I tried another tack. My famous charm. "What's it like working out here? Where do you go for a drink?"

"You wouldn't be trying to chat me up, would you?" She looked at me now. Her accent had slipped slightly. "An old man like you, I should hope not."

"Let's pretend that I was just asking about pubs."

"We usually go down the Anchor," she said. "It's back past the station, in the old bit opposite the hotel. What they call the Heritage Village. There's shops there too, although they mostly sell business stuff. If you don't like that, some of the cafés across the water in Canary Wharf are all right, if you don't mind paying five quid for a cup of milky coffee."

"Maybe I'll stop by the pub when I'm done here. I could do

with a spot of lunch. If you happen to be there, I'll stand you a drink."

"I still can't let you in," the receptionist said, but at least she gave me a smile.

I went back to the couch and waited. At last, a young woman in a severe charcoal jacket and skirt came in. She introduced herself as DI Anne-Marie Davies from NCIS, and told me, "Your IDO rang alarm bells."

"Then it wasn't DI Varnom who let you know about it."

"We have an expert system that monitors all IDOs," DI Davies said.

She wore her shiny black hair in a kind of cap, and her thin, not unpretty face was white and clean, as if made from some synthetic superior to ordinary human skin. A slim leather document case was tucked under her arm; a discreet bulge in her jacket suggested a shoulder holster. If she hadn't been wearing heels, she would have been exactly my height. Like David Varnom, she was the new type of police, one of the horde of ambitious graduates armed with spreadsheets and statistics and corporate policies, brimming with enthusiasm for zero tolerance and profiling and all the other policies of the moment imported directly from the United States without any regard for whether or not they would work on the streets of London. They had no time or sympathy for traditional police work, were more interested in enforcing laws cooked up by politicians eager to pander to mass prejudice because that was where promotional points were earned. They worked in teams, and regarded insight, instinct and individualism with suspicion. They liked to keep their hands clean, referred to victims as clients and crimes as incidents, loved statistics more than anything else in the world. There was no place for the ambiguous messiness of real life in their world-view: if a crime didn't correspond to any of their computer profiles, it didn't exist.

I said, "Why would NCIS be interested in a routine murder?"

When it was clear that DI Davies wasn't about to break the silence, I said, "I'm here because I believe that your company might be able to supply some information which could be of use in a murder investigation."

"Of course," McLean said, with reflexive sympathy. "Dreadful business. Do sit down. I suppose this is going to take some time."

We all sat down. I said, "I expected to see more kit here, Mr McLean."

"Oh, this is merely the head office," McLean said. He had the faintest trace of a Scottish burr. "All our servers are in the Telehouse at East India Dock, like most of the UK's ISPs. It's effectively the centre of the UK's Internet, rebuilt from the ground up after the InfoWar, 154 gigabytes of bandwidth and fantastic security. We have a thirteen-thousand-square-foot suite housing our equipment, with twenty-four-hour access for our staff. We also have our old node in Clapham, which is where our offices were when we started up, and the customer-service offices in Southend. Fantastic telecommunications at Southend. Fantastic security too, on lease from the army."

"But if I had a question about one of your clients, no matter where they were, you could find the answer here."

McLean's smile showed perfect white teeth. "Well, that's the point of the Web, isn't it? By the way, I'm intrigued by your department, Inspector. Perhaps you could have a word with our magazine editor. We print a quarterly magazine for our customers, and an article about a police unit that tackles information crime would be just the ticket." He glanced at his watch and said in a slightly different tone, one that meant business, "Now, how exactly can I help you?"

I handed him a copy of the IDO. I started to explain it to him, but he cut me short. "Don't worry, we see plenty of these, and we're always happy to cooperate. Can I ask how you found out that Ms Booth had an account with us?"

"She was connecting with your server every day, presumably to download her email."

"We supply a free email service, yes, together with a home-page facility that gives each of our customers fifty megabytes of server space. Enough for a small and fairly basic site. We have more than thirty-eight thousand customers who make use of the service, and beyond that, we offer commercial Web services on a sliding scale of fees, depending on how much server space is required. We have more than four thousand commercial clients. We have our own team of white-hat hackers working around the clock to counter attempts at infiltration and sabotage, and of course we are fully compliant with the requirements of both the Child Protection and the Regulation of Investigatory Powers Acts. Our clients' websites are scrupulously monitored, and we take down all inappropriate material at once."

This last addressed to DI Davies.

I said, "I want to know if I can find anything about this particular client's emails."

"Of course." McLean pulled his keyboard onto his lap and typed rapidly. Pages flashed past on the flatscreen. "There's not much to give you, I'm afraid. Ms Booth only signed up with us two weeks ago."

"She also had her own server," I said. "The man who killed her took the hard drive of the computer that was hosting it, but I was wondering if she had anything stored with you, or if perhaps she had set up a mirror site."

McLean hit the space bar of his keyboard; a new page came up on the flatscreen. "No," he said, "she didn't make use of her homepages. And I'm afraid there aren't many emails, either."

I said, "But Sophie Booth did receive email through you."

"Oh yes, of course," McLean said. "That's a basic service."

"And copies of those messages will be stored somewhere on your system."

"We have by law to maintain records for seven years. Unfortunately, Ms Booth's account has been stripped out, almost certainly by a mail spider."

DI Davies said sharply, "What about backups?"

"We make a backup every day, of course. But unfortunately for your enquiry, the new backup overwrites the previous one."

"Then you can't take your duties very seriously," DI Davies said. She sat primly upright in her chair, her small pale hands resting side by side on the leather document case in her lap.

"If you mean the emergency data storage legislation," McLean said blandly, "then as a matter of fact we're fully compliant. However, mail spiders are a very recent development, and the law has yet to catch up. And because mail spiders are not yet illegal, like every other ISP we do not go to the unnecessary difficulty of removing any which may be lodged in our clients' accounts."

"I'm sure like every other ISP your company spends as little money as possible on compliance," DI Davies said tartly. "As a result, you're unable to provide proper information when presented with an IDO."

I told McLean, "If you gave me the appropriate tape, or whatever it is you use, T12's technicians could probably recover something."

"Perhaps. Unfortunately, your IDO does not extend to hardware. You would need a court order for that."

DI Davies said, "We may well get one."

I said, "Perhaps you can tell me when this mail spider activated."

McLean typed some more. "Judging by the emails queued in the system, some time on or around the fifth. I wish I could tell you more."

"This kind of slipshod security is one of the reasons that more than 10 per cent of Web traffic in this country is illegal," DI Davies said.

"With respect, Ms Davies, we spend more than 10 per cent of our gross income on compliance," McLean said. "While other ISPs have made only half-hearted attempts to resist data-control legislation, or have even moved overseas to escape it altogether, our policy is to cooperate fully and to provide safe and secure service bandwidth for all the family."

I said, "I don't want to make your job any more difficult, Mr McLean. All I want to do is see the emails that were sent to a young woman who was murdered only two days ago. Can you get them right away?"

"It's not a problem," McLean said. "We'll even decrypt them for you, no extra charge."

"We will want her encryption keys anyway," DI Davies said.

"Of course. They're in escrow with us. Would you like the emails on a spike, or as hard copy?"

"I don't know about DI Davies," I said, "but I'd like to be able to read them."

I found the pub which the receptionist had recommended, at the corner of two short streets of terraced houses turned into chichi retail units selling tailored shirts, hand-tooled leather goods, palmtop accessories and all the other kit office drones can't live without. It was only just gone two, but the pub had stopped serving food, and the lunchtime crowd, mostly men in suits, were finishing up their drinks, taking last drags at their cigarettes, and looking at their watches. I bought a pint of Kronenbourg and a packet of cheese-and-onion crisps, and sat outside in the heat and leafed through the thin sheaf of paper I had been given.

DI Davies had taken away on a data spike her own copy of what remained of Sophie Booth's email account. She hadn't told me whether NCIS would take it any further when we had parted on the yellow brick road outside Wizard Internet's offices, but I had a bad feeling that I hadn't seen the last of her.

Like all emails, the headers showing the route of the messages were far longer than the actual messages themselves, but this was an advantage as far as I was concerned, because it meant that each email could be traced back to the unique address of the computer from which it had been sent. Unless, of course, the sender knew a thing or two about disguising their electronic mail.

Most of those left in Sophie Booth's account had been sent from the USA. There was a lot of traffic between 3 and 4 P.M. Eastern Standard Time on the fifth, 8 and 9 P.M. here. The earliest posted at 8:09, the last, with one exception, posted at 8:52. I wondered how that fitted in with the activation of the mail spider and the timing of Sophie's murder. They fell into three groups: questions about why Sophie Booth's server was down; concerned enquiries about Sophie herself; demands for more of the same kind of show. The first group would have missed what happened because they hadn't been logged on at the time, and then of course the server had been smashed up. The second group weren't quite sure if what they had seen was real or not. The third group either didn't care that someone had been killed, or had got off on it.

Every email in the second and third groups was a confirmation of Tony McArdle's guess. The killer had made a performance of it, all right, in front of those two webcams. The images of Sophie's murder had gone out live, over the Web. And more than that, I recognized the name of the person who had posted a message to her Wizard Internet account long after it was over, long after the hard drives had been stripped from her computers.

7

I went back to T12 and had a quick word with Andy Higgins.
I hung around the schedule board and when no one was
looking moved an evidence-processing docket from one slot
to another, then went downstairs. Rachel Sweeney was in her
office, watering the plants that grew lushly in pots on the sill of
her window, a microjungle of fronds and glossy leaves obscuring
the unedifying view of a slice of car park and soot-stained brick
wall outside. When I knocked on the frame of the open door,
she set down the toy-sized watering can and said, "I hope you're
ready for a bollocking."

"I take it Tony McArdle has been in touch."

"He's been in touch all right," my boss said. She was a
chunky, thirtysomething blonde who kept her hair in a tight
French braid and wore sober jackets with calf-length skirts. She
knew that T12 was a poisoned chalice, but still took her job
seriously. She fought her corner. She would survive, and one day
she would move on, and T12 would be someone else's problem.

"Then you know what I want to talk about. I've been some
help to his suspicious-death investigation—"

Rachel Sweeney silenced me with a raised hand. "The building is falling down," she said. "I can't make the budget stretch beyond September. Fraud are setting up their own computer-crime section as part of the new decentralization initiative, Vice want to liaise directly with NCIS, and now one of my officers is so fired up over a simple evidence pick-up that he has to go and volunteer his services with a squad at Serious Crimes. And the first I hear about it is not from my officer, no, but the SIO, who phones me up to ask how it's going."

"I did the pick-up on Sunday, Boss, and then I found some pertinent information on the Web this morning. You were in a meeting, and because it's a suspicious-death investigation, I took it over to Tony McArdle straight away. Did he tell you about the computers and the webcams?"

"There are computers everywhere you look," Rachel Sweeney said. "The presence of computers at a crime scene doesn't mean they have anything to do with it, nor do the webcams."

"I think this is different, Boss. So does Tony McArdle. So does NCIS."

Rachel Sweeney sat on a corner of her desk. "NCIS is involved?"

I told her about DI Davies.

"Well, what do we know about the computers at this particular crime scene, aside from the fact that someone complained that the chain of evidence wasn't properly handled?"

"A complaint made by a DI David Varnom, by any chance?"

"Apparently the evidence from the murder scene went off unescorted."

"He's complaining because I didn't ride in with it? I wasn't even on duty, Boss, but I took the call and went to the scene anyway, and I bagged and tagged the evidence and saw off the dispatch."

"In future do a proper job whether you're on duty or off."

"I'm trying to keep T12 in the frame."

A half-truth at best, but it seemed to satisfy her. Perhaps she wanted to believe it. She said, "What do we have?"

I told her about the computers and the webcams, the missing hard drives, Mr Iggy Stix's website and the emails retrieved from Sophie Booth's account with Wizard Internet, but I didn't tell her about the name I had recognized. That was my gift to Tony McArdle, a way of staying in the game.

Rachel Sweeney thought about it. She said, "You think the people who sent these emails witnessed the murder?"

"It was broadcast over the Web. Judging by the emails, most of the people who saw it thought it was just another of the arty performances Sophie Booth had been putting on with her student friends. The rest either didn't want to believe what they'd seen, or they didn't care."

"And not one of them thought to call the police."

"Well, one of them did, in a way. There was a fax."

"A fax. Dear Christ. What does Tony McArdle think of this?"

"He guessed that the murder went out live over the Web. I haven't yet told him that he was right."

Rachel Sweeney thought about this. She said, "I suppose you had better get on with it."

"I'm definitely on secondment?"

"I thought I'd already told you. I'll be tied up with the Martin trial for the next few days, but make sure that you keep me informed."

T12 had worked the Martin case with Vice and then with NCIS, but it had been T12's collar, and Rachel Sweeney wanted to make sure that her people got the credit. The three men up for trial had been queer for each other. Since they were all over sixteen that was no crime, of course, or not yet it wasn't, but they were also paedophiles. They'd been caught because one of them, Michael Martin, had been posting pictures of his special favourites on a clandestine bulletin board. That's what he called them—special favourites. Naked eleven- and twelve-year-old boys cowering in the glare of his digital camera's flash. Martin was a social worker, and part of his job had involved patrolling the area around King's Cross, spotting runaways and getting them into sheltered accommodation before the pimps and nonces could find them. But because he himself was a nonce, when he found an especially good-looking boy, well, what could you expect? They got special treatment. Special treatment for special favourites. A rented room of their own, a little pocket money, introductions to his friends, a photoshoot for his bulletin board. Oh, he looked after them, all right.

Martin gave everything up in the interview room, blubbering like a shoplifting granny caught with her cardigan full of tinned salmon, but his remorse was not for his victims, but for himself. He wasn't full of guilt, but self-pity.

Martin's friends, it turned out, were bad men, much worse than him. (What could be worse than him? Well, we found out: there's always something worse, worse is an infinitely elastic concept in police work.) Martin claimed that they had made him do it. They were casual labourers, working on demolition crews in the City. He liked a bit of rough with the smooth, did our social worker, with his mediocre degree in social history, his Marks and Sparks cardie and neatly ironed jeans, his nice one-bedroom flat in a mansion block in St Pancras, his computer with its hard drive full of pictures of his special favourites.

His two friends were picked up and interviewed separately. The younger one, Oisin Kernan, with a soft Irish accent, a quivering lip and wet spaniel's gaze, gave it up as quickly as Martin. The other, Keith Locksley, was a harder man. Locksley was married, two kiddies and another on the way, and he denied everything, even after a forensic team dug out the body of the poor kid he and Kernan had buried under one corner of the ruins of a burnt-out office block in the City. Kernan said that there were others, but the west side of a thirty-million-pound mall development would have had to be demolished to get at them, so of course they stayed where they were. I said at the time that it wasn't right, and got into an argument with Pete Reid about it.

"No one missed them," he said, "and holding up a shopping mall is probably more than the poor fuckers would have achieved in life."

"We're the only ones who can speak for them," I said, "and if we let them lie there unnamed we're as bad as the men who put them where they are. Worse, because we're supposed to have consciences, it's what we're paid for."

"All I'm saying is that if we started digging up London for missing bodies, we'd never stop," Pete Reid said.

He had a point, and I told him so. "But in this case, we know they're there, and we'll always know. That's the problem with our system. It makes too many compromises to get convictions."

"Come off it, Soapbox," Pete Reid said. He'd found out about my nicknames, of course. It was the kind of thing he made a point of finding out. "If you'd earned your pips in the front line, you wouldn't have such silly notions. Those fuckers will get life without remission in the labour camps for what they did to that one kid. Digging up the other two won't make any difference."

Anyway, the three of them, Martin, Locksley, and Kernan, were on trial for murder. Martin and Kernan were pleading guilty with diminished responsibility, hoping for manslaughter. Locksley was still denying everything, despite the advice of his counsel.

"It might seem like an easy win," Rachel Sweeney told me, "but I never count on anything until I see the villains go down. I was in court this morning. Alison was as pale as death."

After NCIS had taken over, Rachel Sweeney had fought hard to make sure that Alison Somers stayed on the case. She was the young DC, just twenty-six, who had stumbled upon Martin's clandestine bulletin board; no matter what happened at the trial, she had her ticket out of T12. I had my own chance now, of course, the name of a likely suspect who just might crack the

Sophie Booth murder wide open, and although I was too experienced not to doubt my luck, I was still riding on the moment when I had discovered that name in one of the emails in Sophie Booth's account.

I said, "There's no way the jury won't convict."

"Yes, but NCIS will take the credit because we had to pass it up to them after we'd uncovered it."

"Well, perhaps we'll have better luck with this suspicious death," I said.

Rachel Sweeney gave me one of her hard stares. "Don't try and pretend you're doing me or T12 a favour, John. I know this place is a backwater. I know why people are sent here. I know what it's called behind my back. And I know you've twice asked for transfer since you came here."

"I've always been straight about that."

"A case like this—I'll be frank, it could do us a lot of good. It could raise our profile. But don't pretend you're doing me a favour, okay?"

"Yes, Boss."

"And don't think that this relieves you of your other duties. There's been a break on the porn spike case. A school liaison officer spotted someone selling them outside the gate of a private school while she was on her way in to give a drug-awareness class."

I groaned. "How old is the perp?"

"Twelve or thirteen. I want you to set up an interview."

"This mastermind is probably a twelve-year-old with access to a computer, a stick-burner and his parents' credit-card numbers."

"Get on with it, John. And keep me informed."

I went downstairs and made photocopies of the emails from Sophie Booth's account with Wizard Internet. Pete Reid was hanging around the vending machines in the corridor, talking with one of the computer operators. As I was leaving, he called out to me, and said, "Looks like it's you who owes me for that shout."

"You're chancing it," I said, "considering you went for a joyride when you were supposed to be minding the store."

"Whenever you need someone to ride along with you," he said, "I'll be there."

Pete Reid was a big man in his early fifties. His suits always seemed to be slightly too small, and his ties were spotted with greace stains. He was a professional rugby linesman on the side, and had the thickened ears and confrontational manner of an ex–prop forward. He also had the watery eyes, dry hair and burst veins of a serious drinker, and it was common knowledge that he'd been busted from Street Crimes to T12 for inefficiency. Rachel Sweeney might not think T12 was a rest home, but she was the only officer in the Met who didn't. Every time I saw Pete Reid I thought, That could be me. If I'd quit the force after Spitalfields. If I hadn't met Julie. If I could hold my booze better, if I didn't get drunk when I drank but could become a proper drunk who drinks because he needs it to function. Pete Reid was the ghost of one of my unrealized futures.

I told him, "The trouble is you're there for anybody."

He took a sip from a plastic cup of the vile tomato soup the vending machine dispensed; he was the only person who worked at T12 who liked it, and even he had to stir three sugars into it to make it palatable. He said, "I don't deny I like a bit of excitement."

"What's happening about that journalist?"

"You should have heard him go on about his rights while we were tossing his place," Pete Reid said. "Fucking American, wasn't he? Very big on their rights, Americans."

"Will he be charged?"

"Caught red-handed with a pile of nasties, and him with a little kiddie? I should hope so. What about this thing I gave you yesterday? I'm hearing that it could be something big."

I could smell his lunchtime whisky on his breath, and wondered if his bravado on Sunday had been fuelled by a few illicit nips. I said, "It's early days."

"Well, don't forget I did you the favour in the first place."

"Not likely."

I drove through blocked, balked, baffled traffic to Scotland Yard. It took only an hour, something of a record. Talking Heads: *Remain in Light*. David Bowie: *"Heroes."* Happier than I'd been in a long time, feeling that the whole world lay open to me, an intricate machine transparent to thought. A hero, just for one day.

Tony McArdle wasn't in his office. A moon-faced, prematurely balding DC by the name of Keen put his hand over his phone, told me that McArdle was at a press conference, and added, "We found the neighbour. He was in Brighton, used his credit card to book a hotel room."

"It doesn't sound like he was trying to hide." I wasn't interested in the neighbour. I had my red-hot lead.

Keen shrugged. "The local plods are driving him up," he said, and went back to his phone conversation.

The pressroom was in the main building, a new auditorium on the ground floor, hard by the museum and the shop where you can buy Metropolitan Police T-shirts, plastic helmets, inflatable truncheons, replicas of Jack the Ripper's taunting letters, picture postcards of murder scenes, word-processor typefaces based on the handwriting of famous murderers. When I arrived at the back of the room, clutching the folder full of paper to my chest like a shield, the conference was beginning to wind down. McArdle and Varnom were up on the podium, sitting behind a long table covered in blue cloth, a bouquet of microphones planted square in the middle, darker blue curtains as a backdrop. The middle-aged man and woman beside them had to be

Sophie Booth's parents, Simon and Angela. A picture of Sophie glowed on a TV monitor, a studio portrait that must have been taken a few years ago. Sophie's hair was long and straight, rich chestnut with glossy highlights, brushed back from her slightly chubby face. There was a cute spray of freckles over the bridge of her snub nose. She stared boldly through the camera, through time, through death, straight through the people in the half-full room, the cameras from the BBC, Carlton, Sky. It wasn't a big turn out: murder isn't news these days. I recognized a junior reporter from the *Guardian*, a woman from the *Mirror* who had done a lengthy and not too unfriendly piece on me after Spitalfields, when I had been briefly notorious.

McArdle parried a few half-hearted questions, then announced that Sophie Booth's mother would like to make a brief statement. A slight stir at this, attention refocusing on the handsome, strong-boned woman in a neat lilac suit. She leaned towards the microphone and tried to speak, and her fragile composure collapsed. She sobbed and gulped air and averted her face; her husband covered her hands with his. He was tall and craggy, with gold-rimmed bifocals and grey hair that brushed his collar. The black jacket over his unironed white shirt didn't quite fit. He whispered something to his wife and she shook her head and he turned to the microphones and said, "My wife and I would just like to say that someone must know who did this terrible thing to our daughter. A neighbour or a friend or a family member may have seen something suspicious. Bloody clothes being washed, an unexplained absence, a sudden change in mood. To those who are protecting this person, to those who are unsure of their suspicions, let me say that we have come here to talk about our daughter's murder because we do not want anyone else to suffer the way that she did, or to suffer as my wife and I are suffering now. By coming forward, you can help prevent that."

It was a good speech, unflinchingly delivered with a strong

and vibrant actorly voice straight to the cameras clustered at the front of the podium. Simon Booth held his wife's hands while half a dozen cameras flashed, and McArdle thanked the ladies and gentlemen of the press.

The reporter from the *Mirror* cornered me, wanting to know why I was involved. I made a comment about running an errand, which she clearly didn't believe, lied about an appointment to get away, and went back to the Murder Room, where a friendly young DC, Sandra Sands, told me that I had been assigned a desk. It was small and battle-scarred, stuck away from the others in a corner to one side of the whiteboard, and littered with fast-food clamshells and plastic cups. I looked at the chair and said, "Is this a joke?"

"There's a shortage of proper office chairs," Sandra Sands said. "I think someone must have raided the canteen. Are you all right, sir?"

I kicked one of the legs of the plastic chair with the toe of my shoe. It jumped back like a live thing. I said, "I was wondering about something. Has the time of death been established yet?"

"The coroner puts it between six and ten Saturday evening." Sandra Sands was young and pretty and had a bold, searching gaze. The scent of a fresh, lemony perfume lifted from her. Her long brown hair was pulled back in a ponytail. She added, "There's a coffee and tea pool, sir. Two quid a day, three if you want biscuits."

"Ground coffee?"

"Freeze-dried, but it's better than the canteen."

I paid my sub, booted up a computer on an unattended desk and pulled a file from HOLMES and started to read. After a few minutes, I became aware of the scent of piny cologne and turned and looked up at DI Dave Varnom. "Take a seat," I said. Not even Varnom could puncture my generous good humour. "I'll tell you what I found."

"Would this be something to do with your unauthorized intrusion at the crime scene?"

Most of the people in the room, obviously used to the sound of Varnom's voice raised in anger, didn't bother to look up, but a young man with a sharp suit and a ferrety face ornamented with a thin moustache was openly enjoying the scene.

Varnom said, "I'd like an explanation, Inspector."

"I wanted to look at it," I said. It sounded inadequate. I added, "I wanted to confirm a suspicion I had."

"Any suspicions you have, run them past me first. I don't like loose cannons or fast operators."

"But you don't mind mixed metaphors, clearly."

"Don't be so fucking cheeky," Varnom said, just as McArdle ambled into the room.

He had loosened his tie, and he was smoking a cigarette he must have borrowed from one of the reporters. Barely glancing at us as he went past, he said, "You two. In my office. Right away."

I brought the folder full of photocopies.

"Shut the door," McArdle told me. He draped his jacket over his chair and sat and swivelled to and fro, staring at Varnom, at me. When neither of us spoke up, he said, "Let's hear it."

Varnom started in at once with a long complaint about my intrusion on the murder scene, his voice pitched high with indignation. I let him have his say. When he was finished, and McArdle looked at me, an eyebrow raised, I said, "I'm taking an interest, sir."

Varnom said, "It's abundantly clear that he's not a team player, Tony."

I said, "You wouldn't be friendly with a DI Davies, would you? She works for NCIS, and she just happened to turn up at Sophie Booth's ISP when I did."

"You see what I mean," Varnom told McArdle.

"Shake hands," McArdle said, "and stop acting like a couple of drama queens."

We shook. Varnom wouldn't meet my eyes.

"Good," McArdle said. He asked me, "What's this about NCIS?"

"This DI Davies claimed to have spotted the IDO I filed, and took it upon herself to come along to the meeting at Wizard Internet. She took away copies of emails sent to Sophie Booth." I opened the folder and took out the photocopies and laid them on McArdle's desk. "These emails. All but one sent on the day Sophie was murdered."

McArdle lifted up the first page. "And do they tell us anything?"

"You were right, sir. The emails prove that the killing was staged for the benefit of the webcams Sophie Booth had set up. It was staged from beginning to end, and transmitted over the Web."

"Christ," McArdle said. He put his hands together and touched the tips of his fingers to his lips. "How many people saw it?"

"Thirty-eight people sent emails between eight and nine o'clock on Saturday, which fits in with the coroner's ETD."

"Christ," McArdle said again.

"Some thought it was a show, one of the pieces of performance art Sophie Booth liked to put on. Some were sick enough to like it. One or two even offered criticisms and advice. But others expressed concern, and I think that at least one was motivated to do something about it, and sent that fax through the anonymous remailer in Cuba."

"Unless that was the murderer," Varnom said.

"That's true," I admitted. "He wanted people to see what he'd done, after all."

"Ironic really," Varnom said.

"I won't have that kind of talk," McArdle said sharply.

"I only meant that those who live by the sword, and so on," Varnom said blandly.

"I won't have anybody making judgements," McArdle said. "If we can't find out who sent the fax, can we find out who sent these emails?"

"You can trace them back from the headers," I said, "but most of them came from outside the country, and almost all of them were sent from freemail servers. Anyone can set up a freemail account over the Web, using any name they like."

"But they can be traced."

"In this country, yes, but not in the US or in any country where they have privacy-protection laws."

"How many from the UK?"

"Just four."

"Put a couple of people on this," McArdle told Varnom. "I want the names of everyone who can be traced, and then we'll get them interviewed. Either by us, or by the local police."

Varnom said, "I don't know, sir, if the statement of anyone residing overseas will be admissible in court."

"They're still witnesses," McArdle said, "and they might make the case even if we can't use them in court. We've checked her bank statements. No sign that she was receiving payments. And we traced the bloke with the website you found."

"Mr Iggy Stix."

"He claims not to have seen the murder, according to the local police. And they claim they can't take a look in his computer because it would be a violation of his rights."

"He probably isn't lying," I said. "His site hadn't been updated for the past two months."

"Am I right in thinking that anyone anywhere in the world could have logged on to her site?"

"If they knew about it."

"So we only have the whole world to consider," McArdle said.

"Two more points," I said. "Someone, perhaps Sophie Booth,

perhaps not, sent a mail spider to her email account, and it was activated just before she was killed. That's why there are so few emails. The rest were erased."

"A mail spider," McArdle said.

"A bit of freeware, sir. It sits in an account as an email attachment until it is activated, and then overwrites everything including itself with random ones and zeros. A common tool for those who like their privacy, and as yet not illegal."

"All right. What was the other thing?"

I'd spotted this myself, and although I'd had Andy Higgins confirm it, I laid it out with pride. "I'm certain that all but one of these emails were bounced from Sophie Booth's illegal server. They come from different places, but all share the same bit of routing code. Here, and here, and here," I said, pointing to the same string of numbers in the headers of successive emails. "I think she was using the account with Wizard Internet as a backup or archive. But there's one more email, sent directly to her account the day after she was killed and her server was ripped apart. From someone by the name of Barry Deane."

"I don't know him," McArdle said, after a moment's consideration.

"He was interviewed by Vice a couple of weeks ago about porn-filled data spikes that are being hawked around schools. T12 is involved in the case, and I happened to be present at the interview."

"Then I suppose we should talk to him."

"Sooner rather than later, sir. He's only visiting this country. These days, he lives in Cuba."

8

arry Deane designed pornographic websites for a Maltese
family, the Vitellis, who in the good old days at the beginning of the century, before the InfoWar and the Child
Protection Act and the Decency League, had owned half the peep
shows, skin clubs and sex shops in Soho, not to mention four
restaurants and a pâtisserie. They still owned the pâtisserie, but
had moved most of their sex business offshore: to Cuba. Which
didn't necessarily mean anything, because anyone in the world
could have rerouted that fax through the Cuban remailer, but
Barry Deane's name was on an email that had been sent directly
to Sophie Booth's account at Wizard Internet, and the HOLMES
files showed that he had a long record.

There were petty offences stretching back to age eleven—
shoplifting, damage to property, suspected arson. He'd been
banned from keeping pets for ten years after he had doused a
cat in petrol and set it alight—to see if it had the sense to run
to the river, he'd said. He had been fifteen at the time. Three
years later, while he was studying for a degree in computer science at the University of York, he was interviewed about an

incident in which the room of a female student he had been pestering was set on fire. Nothing was proved, and Deane had been let off with a warning and allowed to graduate. Then he was arrested for flashing in Green Park, and soon after that he had been sacked from his computer programming job because he had been harassing women working in the company by sending emails—

I followed you into work today and could see your knickers through your skirt. Are you wearing a thong?

I want to buy some knickers for my girlfriend. Do women like crotchless panties?

—with attachments in the form of video clips of women eating shit or being beaten or having sex with animals, all of them fixed so that the embarrassed recipients couldn't turn them off.

Six months later Deane was pulled for a serious offence involving a single mother who was on the game in a casual way to top up her social security. She was found wandering down the street, high on Ecstasy and with superficial knife cuts to her face and thighs. She couldn't remember how she'd been cut, but a bottle of spiked Coca-Cola was found in her flat, and when a formal statement was taken, she mentioned Barry Deane's name. He had been a customer just the once, but kept hanging around her flat, banging on her door early in the morning and late at night, dropping notes and bunches of flowers through the letter box, following her in the street. Deane wouldn't give anything up when he was interviewed, there was no hard evidence that he had spiked the Coke, and the woman's claim about harassment wasn't followed through because any half-decent defence brief would have used her part-time tomming to destroy her credibility. But Deane's card was marked, and when he tried it again a couple of years later, he fell hard.

This time it was a woman who ran a drinking club round the back of Oxford Street. The same routine, hanging about her workplace and her home address, following her, notes, flowers, threats. She called in the police through a DS she was friendly with, and after a bit of surveillance Deane was pulled for harassment. He was carrying a pocketknife when he was arrested, stood trial, and went down for nine months. He kept to himself in prison, got out on parole in the minimum time, started working for the Vitellis, moved to Cuba a year ago.

The question was, what was he doing back in Britain? And if he had been involved in Sophie Booth's murder, why was he still here? And why had he sent that email?

I had just begun to plough through Barry Deane's psychiatric reports when the two DCs who had been dispatched to pick him up, Keen and Hampson, came back. They went straight past my desk to McArdle's office. I followed them in and said, "Did he say anything?"

McArdle was putting on his suit jacket. He said mildly, "I like people to knock before they enter my office. Even if the door is open."

"I'm sorry, sir. I forgot my manners in my eagerness to learn if these two had managed to bring our friend in."

Keen shrugged. "He has a rented flat in Soho, and that's where he was. He came along calmly enough. No fuss."

"He's done time for a sex crime," I said. "He should be used to being pulled."

"He's a funny little fellow," Hampson said. He was the young man with the pencil moustache who had been so interested in my recent exchange of views with Varnom. "He does like to bullshit. You'd think he was the king of the world, the way he goes on."

I said, "Did you bring in his computer?"

"We weren't asked to," Hampson said.

"He brought along his mobile," Keen said. "A funny-looking one he said he'd bought in Cuba."

"Told us we could get a discount if we wanted to buy one through him," Hampson said. "Like I said, he does like his bullshit."

I said, "I don't suppose you two thought to take the mobile from him."

"I don't suppose we did," Keen said affably. "I mean, it's not as if he's under arrest."

"Because there might be some interesting stuff in its cache."

Hampson bristled and said, "No one said anything about caches. We were asked to pull a body, and that's what we did."

McArdle dismissed Keen and Hampson, and told me, "I don't care what might be in Deane's mobile, I'm not ready to swear out a warrant just yet. You can sit in on the interview, but Dave Varnom and I will handle the chat. You'll stay in the background. I might ask for your opinion if he starts talking about computers, but that's all. Understood?"

"Absolutely, sir."

McArdle favoured me with the considerable weight of his gaze. "I hope so. And do try not to piss off my men. We're all on the same side."

Edward Wilson, the solicitor for the Vitelli family, was waiting outside the interview room, a tall gent with carefully waved silver hair and a distinguished profile marred by a badly broken nose. He was smoking a black Sobranie, and his calfskin briefcase rested between his polished oxblood loafers.

"There's no smoking here, sir," McArdle said.

Wilson blew a riffle of smoke. "Then I'll step outside, Chief Inspector. Despite my very best advice, my client has waived the right for counsel. Will you be charging him?"

"This is just a routine enquiry, sir."

"My client has been subject to altogether too many routine enquiries in the past, Chief Inspector." Wilson looked at me, and added, "Including one just two weeks ago, at which this man was present."

"That was Vice's call," I said. "I was along for the assist."

"And now you are assisting on yet another investigation that has drawn in my client," Wilson said. "Quite a coincidence."

McArdle said, "Your client is a known sex offender, sir. As he has no need for you, I'm sure you can find your way out if you've no other business here."

Dave Varnom and a uniform were waiting with Barry Deane in the stark little interview-room. Deane was in his late twenties, as small and slight as a jockey; I had a good couple of inches on him. His hair was swept back from the broad shelf of his forehead and straggled in oily rat-tails over the collar of an expensive red leather jacket a couple of sizes too big for him, so that he looked like a child wearing adult's clothes. He had very white skin and bright blue eyes that gazed at us with lively interest.

He smiled at me and said, "I remember you from that silly business about dirty spikes a couple of weeks ago. I'm beginning to think you have it in for me."

"I like to stay in touch, Barry," I said. "I see you haven't gone back to Cuba yet."

"I always thought the Met had a height requirement," Deane said. "It's one reason why I never became a copper. That, and my self-respect."

His voice was high, a boy's barely broken voice. There was something sly in it, and the same slyness was in his bright blue eyes, and the way his tongue kept poking at a corner of his mouth, like an animal peeking out of a cave.

"Shut it," McArdle said absent-mindedly; I wasn't sure if he meant Deane or me. He dismissed the uniform, started the tape and the video, and sat opposite Deane and slapped down the file of emails. I propped up the wall behind Deane, and Varnom stood behind McArdle, watching me as much as Deane.

McArdle leaned in right away. "Have you been told why you're here, Barry?"

Deane gave me a quick glance and shrugged inside his over-sized leather jacket. "When I was living here, I used to be pulled in every time some slag got fucked. I never minded. It brightened up my day."

"You're here to help us with our enquiries concerning the murder of Sophie Booth on the evening of June 5. Have your rights been read to you?"

"Oh yes." Deane's gaze flicked towards Varnom. "By that nice inspector there."

"The suspect indicates Detective Inspector Varnom," McArdle said. "Well, Barry, I'm going to read them to you again." He did, and when he had finished, he said, "Will you now confirm that you have waived the right to be questioned in the presence of a solicitor of your choosing, or failing that one of the duty solici-tors."

"I don't need the old fart who came with me."

"Why would that be?"

"Because I'm innocent, of course."

"I'm not sure about your innocence, Barry. Not a man with your kind of record. Harassing women, it's in your blood, isn't it?"

"I've done my penance as far as society is concerned," Deane said, "but I understand how it is with the police. That you think that everyone has to keep paying." He turned in his chair to look at me and said, "Did you catch whoever's making those dirty spikes? Let me know when you do. My employers would like a word with them, seeing as whoever made them up stole copyrighted material from their sites."

McArdle put an edge to his voice. "I'm asking you about your problems with women, Barry. Be a good boy and don't waste my time, I don't take kindly to that."

"They were just misunderstandings. A couple of silly tarts who tried to pretend they didn't recognize me for what I really am."

His gaze tried to include all three of us. "They both knew, but it scared them. It always does."

McArdle said, "What is it that scares them, Barry?"

Deane folded his arms with a creak of leather, put up his chin and said in his sly, piping voice, "I'm a real man. Not pussy-whipped like most. My own man."

"You fancy yourself as a lover boy, then? One for the ladies?"

"Not at all." Deane stretched. "Look, this is boring me. I have work to do, and I know it's no use trying to explain anything to you. No offence, mind, but I see the ring on your finger, I know you're married. I know you've gone over to the other side."

"Which side is that?"

"Their side, of course."

Varnom said, "You really fancy yourself, son, but I don't know why. Unless it's because no one else ever has, including your mother."

Deane looked at him and said, "Are you married too?"

"That's none of your business."

"I'll take that as a yes," Deane said, "so I don't suppose you would understand, either. Now the wee inspector there, he might know."

"What I don't understand," McArdle said, "is why, if you're such a man, you have to pay for sex."

"If you mean the tart who said I knifed her, then I didn't pay her. That's why she tried to get me in trouble."

"Come off it," McArdle said. "More likely you couldn't perform when it came down to it, she didn't want to waste any more time on you, and you took it badly. Did she laugh at you, Barry? Is that why you came back and cut her?"

"It was never proved."

"That doesn't mean it isn't true. Do you only ever go with tarts, Barry?"

"All women are tarts, don't you think? They prostitute themselves because that's where their power is. Your wife is a tart. So is your mother."

McArdle let that slide. His skin was too thick for Deane's silly little darts. He said, "So you would say that Eva Hallett is a tart?"

"Of course."

"You do know who Eva Hallett is."

"The tart who had me put away."

"The woman who pressed charges when you stalked her with intent to do physical harm."

"Another misunderstanding," Deane said airily.

"Is that how you see it?"

"All of this is old stuff, it's boring me. Tell me what you think I did, I'll tell you I don't know anything about it, we'll go around and around a bit, and then you'll let me go because you don't have anything on me. The same old same old."

McArdle said, heavily and flatly, "You'll talk about anything I want you to talk about."

Deane shrugged inside his red leather jacket. He'd been through this so many times that it no longer bothered him, but he didn't have the sense to keep his mouth shut. Professionals stay quiet in the interview-room. They say nothing. They give nothing away. They know that their silence can be used in court as an indication of guilt, but they'd rather take that chance than open themselves up to psychological manipulation by seasoned interrogators. They listen to the arresting officer tell them what a great, understanding guy he is, how he's put away every guilty man he's come across, how he's going to sit down man to man and talk this thing through, and they say just one sentence: "I want my lawyer."

Deane, though, was stupid enough to think that he could play the game. He was quite happy to talk about the whys and wherefores of his old crimes because he thought he was too clever for us, and he felt no guilt about what he had done. At last, McArdle brought the conversation around to Sophie Booth's murder. He did it in his usual direct fashion, staring straight into Barry Deane's face, watching for the flicker of inattention, the fatal second of weakness, that would give him an opening.

"Tell me about Sophie Booth, Barry. Tell me how you know her."

"I wouldn't say I know her at all," Deane said.

"Bullshit," McArdle said. He slapped the table with the flat of his palm, loud as a gunshot in the little room, and raised his voice a notch, leaning in. "Now we've had a nice little chat so far. I've heard your silly little opinions about women, and frankly, son, I don't think you're quite right in the head. I don't think you quite know what the score is. That's why you get in the trouble you do. That's why you're here now. I happen to know that you know Sophie Booth, and I want you to look me in the eye and tell me how you know her."

"Well, I don't," Deane said.

"I want you to look at this," McArdle said, and took a sheet of paper from the folder and spun it around and tapped it. "Do you recognize this?"

Deane shrugged again. "It's an email."

"That's right. Did you send it? Look closely now. I want to make sure that you know exactly what it is."

Deane bent over it, then pushed away from the table, the legs of his chair scraping on the tiled floor. "What are you playing at?"

"Calm down, Barry. Don't get excited, it won't help you."

"I've never seen that before!"

Varnom stepped around the table, placed his hands on Barry Deane's shoulders and made him sit down. McArdle said, "You agree that that's your name, there in the header."

"So what? Anyone in the world could have sent that email."

McArdle turned the paper around. " 'You're mine for ever.' What does that mean, Barry?"

"I wouldn't know. I didn't send it."

"Then why is your name on it?"

"I think I should have my lawyer in here," Deane said.

"We can bring him in if you want," McArdle said, "but then we'll have to charge you, and take a formal statement, and take your passport away from you. Do you want that? Because this is serious shit, son, and you'd better help me clear it up straight away."

"Charge me with what?"

"Conspiracy to murder would fit you very well," McArdle said. "What do you think, Dave?"

"Oh, I think it would fit him much better than his jacket," Varnom said. He was kneading Deane's shoulders, and Deane wriggled under his grip like an unwilling child.

"You'll feel so very much better if you tell us the truth, Barry," McArdle said. "It'll be like a weight lifting right off."

"Tell this fucker to let go and I'll tell you what I think."

McArdle raised an eyebrow, and Varnom lifted his hands from Deane's shoulders and took a step backwards.

Deane said slowly, "That might be my name on the email, but I didn't send it. It's from a freemail account—anyone could have set it up using my name. It doesn't prove anything, except that someone's trying to drop me in the shit."

McArdle said, "And who might want to do that to a nice boy like you?"

"Him for one," Deane said, turning to look at me.

McArdle said, "Why would he want to fit you up, Barry?"

"He had me in two weeks ago. I was barely off the plane. He couldn't fit me up then, and now he's trying something else."

McArdle silenced me with a look, and said to Deane, "Are you accusing a police officer of setting you up for a murder, Barry? Do try and do better than that. I heard you're an intelligent man, but really, you're grasping at straws. Let's be straight with each other. Start by telling me why you sent this email."

"Look," Deane said, "if you know anything about the Web, you know that anyone could have sent that email."

"You say that you didn't send it."

"Of course I didn't fucking send it."

"But there's your name, Barry, as plain as day."

"I've told you. Anyone can put their name to a freemail account. It doesn't mean anything."

"Your name on an email sent to a dead girl, Barry, it must mean something."

"It means someone is trying to fit me up."

McArdle said, "If you have enemies, Barry, it won't hurt to give up their names. It'll put you in the clear and it may help us catch a murderer. Think how favourably we'll treat you after that."

I said, "We could take a look at your computer, Barry. Just to be sure you're telling the truth."

"Be my guest."

"Your browser's cache file would tell us whether you had been looking at Ms Booth's website."

"I suppose it might, except the computer I'm using is brand-new. I didn't send that email, and you can't pin the murder on me because, you know what, I wasn't even in the country at the time."

McArdle said, "Where were you on June 5, Barry?"

"Well as a matter of fact I was back in Havana."

Varnom said, "You had better be able to prove that. You don't have much of a tan."

"I flew by KLM from Heathrow to Schiphol, and then from Schiphol to Havana, Club Class all the way. I still have the tickets on me," Deane said, and reached into his jacket and set them on the desk. "It should be quite easy to check all this."

"Oh, we'll check," Varnom said, "don't you worry."

"I always keep well out of the sun," Deane said. He was relaxing. The email had been a nasty surprise, but now he was playing the get-out-of-jail-free card he had kept up his sleeve for just this moment. He said, "Sunlight is dangerous, it's well-known."

McArdle said, "What were you doing in Havana?"

"I had to go back to fix a Web server for my employer, Mr Andreas Vitelli."

"Computer porn," Varnom said.

"It isn't illegal in Cuba," Deane said, smiling. "They have freedom of information there, like most of the world."

Varnom said, "It's illegal here."

"It's illegal to post pornography on a British-based ISP, but my ISP isn't based in Britain, and I'm not responsible for who looks at the sites I take care of. Information wants to be free, after all," Deane said, glancing at me.

McArdle said, "I think you're lying, Barry. Even if you happened to be in Havana, and you can be very sure that we are going to check that, you could have logged on to Sophie Booth's website, and you could have sent that email."

"I don't see how you can prove that," Deane said.

I said, "Have you ever used an anonymous remailer?"

"Why would I want to do that? I'm quite open about who I talk to," Deane said. He turned to McArdle and asked, "Do you want me to stay here while you check on me, or am I free to go?"

"You can go for now, Barry," McArdle said, "but we will definitely want to talk to you again, so don't go too far. The two policemen who will take you back will be wanting your passport."

"I'll need it back, in a few days," Deane said. "When I've finished my little bit of work here."

"You'll get a receipt. You'll also report to Vine Street police station at 8 A.M. every day until notified otherwise. Interview terminated at 18:23."

"I'll see you around, Inspector," Barry Deane called after me, as I followed McArdle and Varnom out of the interview-room.

What do you think?" McArdle said, once we were back in his office.

"I don't think he has anything to do with Sophie Booth's murder, and I don't know why we brought him in in the first place," Varnom said, and jutted his chin at me. "Unless it was because you really do have a grudge against him."

"It's true I don't like him," I said, "but any right-thinking human being wouldn't like him. He's done time for harassment, he clearly hates women. But the point is, if he is telling the truth about having nothing to do with that email, then whoever did send it was obviously trying to involve him in Sophie Booth's murder."

"But he happened to be in Cuba when she was killed," Varnom said.

"If he wasn't lying," I said. "At the least we should check his computer."

McArdle said, "I'm not minded to eliminate him from the enquiry, but I'm not going to try and get a warrant sworn just yet. His solicitor would certainly kick up a stink, and I don't think we have enough probable cause at this stage."

"Even if we get a warrant to look at his computer and his mobile," Varnom said, eager to agree with his boss, "he knows enough to have wiped anything incriminating off their caches. Deane is a distraction from James Whitehead. Who lived right next door to Sophie Booth, who has run off, who isn't answering his mobile, who hasn't been in contact with his wife for the past two days. It doesn't have to be related to computers at all."

I said, "Except that we have emails proving that the webcams were live when Sophie Booth was killed, that at least thirty people saw the murder."

"And we'll try and track as many of them down as we can," McArdle said. "You've done some good work today, John, but you have to remember that Whitehead is very much in the frame as of this moment. Where is he, Dave? Shouldn't he be here by now?"

"He was delayed by roadworks on the M23, sir, the last time I checked."

"I'm looking forward to seeing him. Check up his ETA, Dave, and book an interview-room."

When Varnom had gone, McArdle said to me, "I have to ask this, John. Deane said that you were setting him up. There's not a whisper of truth in that, is there?"

"Not at all, sir."

McArdle watched me for a few moments, his slept-in face unreadable. At last, he said, "I hope we don't have to speak about it again."

"You won't, sir."

McArdle nodded. He seemed satisfied, but I knew now that anything I said or did would be tainted by the suspicion that I wasn't playing a straight game.

"Let's clear this up," McArdle said. "Deane claimed that anyone could have set up the account from which that email was sent. Is that true?"

"Well, yes. But if he didn't send it, someone he knows did it. Someone who knew the address of Sophie's account with Wizard Internet. Someone who knew she was dead before we did."

"But not necessarily Barry Deane."

I said, "His name has to be on that email for some reason. When we came into the interview-room, he was relaxed, he wasn't anxious, he knew we were going to ask about Sophie Booth and he had his story straight. That's the way guilty men behave, because they know what they're in for. But the email is another matter. That definitely upset him."

"All the more reason for thinking that he didn't send it," McArdle said.

"But his name is on it all the same. Why would someone want to put him in the frame? Especially as he was behaving as if he expected to be in the frame, but not because of the email. I think he's involved, sir."

"All right," McArdle said. "I'll have someone check up Deane's alibi, I'll have forensics check his DNA against the sperm stain they found on Sophie Booth's sheets. I'll even scrape up something from my dwindling budget to pay to have him tracked by this fancy new surveillance system. But I'm not going to issue a warrant on him until I know more."

"His computer—"

"Enough," McArdle said. "One step at a time. If you want to stay on my team, you'll have to learn to do things my way."

"Sorry, sir."

There was a knock on the door. Varnom came in and said, "Whitehead will be here in an hour, sir."

"Good. I have a job for you two. You're going to see Sophie Booth's uncle. He's back from Scotland and he has kindly consented to an interview. Much as I'd like to go with you, I have a date with our Mr Whitehead, and then I have to deliver a progress report to Assistant Commissioner Frost."

Varnom said, "Boss—"

"You don't speak computer, Dave," McArdle said firmly. "You need someone to go with you, and you might as well take a translator."

"I'll take good care of him," I said.

9

nthony Booth, Sophie Booth's uncle, had clearly done well for himself. His flat was in a new building right on the edge of the river at Bankside, a corner penthouse suitable for a fashion photoshoot or a Bond villain's lair. The wide sweep of its balcony, floored with salvaged wood weathered to a silvery sheen, overlooked the slender arch of the pedestrian bridge that linked the north bank with the little park in front of the Tate Modern. The long living-room had a white lambswool carpet, two couches the size of double beds upholstered in glove-soft brown leather, glass walls on three sides and a huge fireplace set in the rough brick of the fourth. There were framed posters of all six Star Wars movies, a big flatscreen TV, a Bang & Olufsen stereo, a Wurlitzer jukebox, and the biggest lava lamp I had ever seen, shaped like an old-fashioned rocket. In one corner, small black-and-white TV monitors mounted four by four on a recurved piece of steel showed static views of the nearby streets and the river walk, or tracked pedestrians from one camera to the next.

A slender Thai man in black Armani brought in a tray of martinis, handed one to Varnom and one to me, and made himself scarce. Varnom set his on an Allen Jones side table—a life-sized flesh-coloured replica of a naked woman on hands and knees, a whip between her teeth, supporting an oval of glass on her bare back—and looked out at the view while I sipped ice-cold Bombay Sapphire delicately infused with vermouth and examined the stereo and the racks of DVDs and spikes mounted above it.

We had barely spoken on the drive over. Varnom had told me that the interview with Anthony Booth was his, that he would take the lead with minimal interference, and I hadn't thought it worth arguing the point. Varnom was badly fucked off that Tony McArdle had taken the session with Whitehead, but I could see why McArdle had done it. Varnom was a headline chaser, he thought Whitehead a likely suspect, he wanted to be in on what might be the end of the case and would have gone in with all guns blazing; Whitehead would have hidden behind his solicitor and we would have learnt nothing.

I had half finished my martini and moved on to look at the stack of TV monitors when Anthony Booth came in. He was a short, stocky man, at least ten years younger than his half-brother, Simon. He wore glasses with heavy black plastic frames and blue-tinted lenses, a raw linen jacket over a black T-shirt, baggy linen trousers, sandals with thick corrugated treads.

"Everyone but the host seems to have a drink," he said, and went to the tray and picked up a glass of silky martini and dropped in an onion skewered by a cocktail stick. "Your health, gentlemen," he said, sipped approvingly, and collapsed onto one of the couches. He said, "Whom do I have the honour?"

Varnom made the introductions.

"Two detective inspectors," Anthony Booth said, the blue-tinted lenses of his spectacles flashing as he looked from Varnom to me and back again. "Should I be worried, or flattered?"

His manner was lively, almost flirtatious, and there was a

sense of tremendous contained energy and intelligence about him. Although seated, he dominated the room.

"I'm supposed to be the computer expert," I said.

"Well, I promise to try and speak in Basic." Only Anthony Booth smiled at his joke. He said, "How is the enquiry proceeding?"

"It's proceeding as well as can be expected, sir," Varnom said. "This is purely routine—a few background questions. I promise that it won't take long."

"I bet myself you'd say that," Anthony Booth said. He took another sip of his martini, bonelessly relaxed in the couch's embrace. "I was hoping, though, that you would be as candid as possible. Sophie was very dear to me."

"You owned the flat she was living in, didn't you?" Varnom said. He stood with his hands behind his back as if at parade rest, framed by the tremendous view of the river, the glass curtain walls of office blocks on the north bank burning with early evening sunlight, the dome of St Paul's, the ruined towers of the City downriver.

Booth said, "I have long leases on both the office and the flat—they were all I could afford after I gave up my job and sold my house to set up Mobo Technology. Then the government wanted to improve London's security, my RedLine chip won the competition, I floated Mobo Technology on the stock market, and here I am, a filthy-rich technocrat. It happened that quickly. After I moved out, it seemed silly to let the flat go to waste when Sophie needed a place to stay. She was very happy there."

Varnom said, "How did her parents take the arrangement?"

Booth shrugged. Webs of silvery light shivered in his martini. "Sophie was old enough to make her own choices. I was pleased to help her. Simon and Angela are pleasant people, good people, but they are hardly ambitious. They've been stuck in teaching all their lives. They claim to be socialists, but really their politics is that of typical left-wing reactionaries: reflexive complaints and genuflection to the minority view and ethnic correctness. Sophie didn't get on with them very well in the last few years. Typical teenager-parent stuff. I tried to keep out of it, but when I saw the place she was living in when she first came up to London I offered her my old flat. I've been too busy to get around to selling or renting it; it was empty; she needed a quiet place to get on with her work."

"Did you know about her work?"

"I don't know much about art," Booth said. "I'm a computer nerd. A geek."

"But you helped her with it. You bought her a computer, for instance."

"A rich uncle's indulgence."

"Did you know about her website?"

"Of course. I paid for the fat line rental, and I upgraded her computer."

"And did you ever look at her website, sir?"

Anthony Booth smiled. "I'm a typical geek, Inspector. Twenty-hour days at the computer, absolutely no life beyond indulging in the kind of pop culture I loved when I was a kid. Tell me, do you have a suspect yet?"

"We're putting a picture together, sir," Varnom said.

"I saw Simon's appeal on the six o'clock news. Who lent him the jacket, by the way?"

Varnom hesitated, then admitted, "One of our officers."

"Simon did it rather well, but then, he is a drama teacher. However, I do think that he made a mistake when he appealed to people's consciences. I've generally found that greed is usually a better motivating factor. With that in mind, I'm willing to arrange a substantial reward."

"You would have to discuss it with my superior, sir," Varnom said.

"Perhaps I will."

I said, "When did you take Sophie to New York?"

"Ah. I suppose Simon and Angela told you about that. They did complain mightily at the time, but as I pointed out, Sophie was over eighteen and quite capable of deciding for herself."

Varnom was giving me a hard look. I ignored it. I said, "I saw the postcards she bought there. They were tucked around her bathroom mirror. If she was over eighteen, then it would have been some time in the last three years."

"It was for her nineteenth birthday, as a matter of fact." Anthony Booth cocked his head at me. "I'm a little stupid with travel, so perhaps that's why I don't see the relevance of your question to Sophie's death."

Varnom said, "And what were you doing in Scotland, sir?"

"It was a business trip. I was talking with some designers at a chip-manufacturing plant outside Glasgow. We're implementing new upgrades for our RedLine technology."

I patted the stack of TV monitors. "This is receiving feeds from RedLine-enabled cameras, isn't it?"

"As a matter of fact," Anthony Booth said, "it's the prototype of ADESS. Once the network is up and running, it becomes almost a living thing, and because I could hardly kill off my first child, I had it reassembled here. It isn't very bright, but it is still learning. It never stops learning, just like you and me. That's the beauty of it, of course."

"There was a CCTV camera outside your old office," I said.

"Everyone still says CCTV," Booth said, "but it should really be OCTV. Not Closed Circuit TV, but Open Circuit. It's a world of difference. Not uncoordinated feeds to a central control room, but an active, intelligent network, inhabiting and linked by RedLine chips, capable of making decisions and acting upon them."

Varnom gave me another hard look and said, "That camera at your old office, sir, would it have been part of your original network?"

"Of course. We used it as part of a demo system. One camera permanently installed over the door, others set up along the street. We'd send out half a dozen identically dressed people, show potential clients that the system could discriminate between them, could spot and track particular individuals. From little acorns, *et cetera*."

"And would you know, sir, if it was currently active?"

"ADESS covers Shoreditch and Hoxton, and I suppose my little camera might be linked up to it. Did it pick up the person who attacked Sophie?"

"You can be sure that we are investigating every aspect, Mr Booth," Varnom said. "For instance, can you tell me about Sophie's friends?"

"I didn't see much of them. Certainly not after she moved into the flat."

"Boyfriends?"

Booth sipped his martini thoughtfully. "I don't think she had one. Not what you or I would call a boyfriend, anyway."

"I find that a little puzzling, sir, because you said that you were close to her, and that you knew her better than her parents."

"I said that she was very dear to me."

"But that didn't extend to knowing whether or not she had a boyfriend."

"I didn't ask," Booth said, a little too quickly. "Besides, young people today, they don't seem to go in for proper relationships, do they?"

"But you did see her quite frequently."

"Perhaps once a month or so if I was in town."

"Where did you see her?"

"Mostly here."

"Not at the flat in Hoxton?"

"No."

"Did she ever bring anyone here?"

"Such as a boyfriend? No."

"And what did you and Sophie do, sir, when she visited you?"

"Do?"

"What did you talk about?"

"This and that. Am I under suspicion, Inspector? Is that what this is about?"

"You didn't talk about her work."

"Not really."

"Although you were in effect sponsoring it by buying her an expensive computer and renting the fat line."

"I'd hardly call it sponsorship, Inspector. The truth was that she didn't like talking about her work because it wasn't finished." Anthony Booth took off his spectacles and pinched the bridge of his nose between thumb and forefinger, a curiously vulnerable gesture. "She was working towards her graduation show. I would have seen it then."

"You took her out to restaurants," Varnom made a show of flipping open his mobile. "The Oxo Tower. Opera. Luxor. The Ivy. Metropolis. Manga Manga Manga. Trip."

"I don't really remember," Booth said. "Where on earth did you get the list? From Simon and Angela?"

"We found matchbooks in Sophie's flat. All fairly expensive places, if you don't mind me saying, sir."

"I can afford it, Inspector. In case you hadn't noticed, I do have quite a lot of money."

"And did Sophie bring anyone along when you went to these restaurants?"

"No."

"So it was just you and her."

"And sometimes one of my girlfriends."

"You have more than one girlfriend, sir?"

"How does a geek get a girlfriend?" Booth smiled. "He floats his company on the stock market. I've been enjoying the money I've made. Hardly a crime."

"Did you take her anywhere else, sir?"

"A couple of gallery openings, perhaps. Film premieres, that kind of thing. I'm sorry, Inspector, I don't keep track of my social engagements. If you give me some time, I'll try and remember."

Varnom put his mobile away. He said, "Someone will be in touch, to ask for the names and addresses of those girlfriends."

"Does that mean this interview is at an end?"

"Thank you for your cooperation, sir," Varnom said. "There is one other thing. We'll need a blood sample from you."

"Really? What for?"

"We are conducting a DNA analysis of the crime scene, sir. We need to eliminate anyone who might have been there before the murder took place. You did live there, before Sophie moved in, and although you can't remember it, perhaps you visited her once or twice."

"Yes. Yes, of course."

"Someone will phone you and explain the arrangements, sir. You can, if you wish, have a solicitor present when the sample is taken, but I can assure you that it is quite routine."

"I'm sure that won't be necessary, as long as it is quite routine."

"Of course, sir."

"No problem, then," Booth said. He put down his martini glass and clapped his hands. A moment later, the slim black-clad Thai appeared at the doorway. "Bob will see you out. Do keep in touch. And please do keep in mind that I'm serious about that reward."

As we were leaving, I said, "By the way, that's quite a collection of movies."

Booth suddenly looked alert. He said, "I make no secret of my tastes."

"So I see," I said, and followed Varnom and Bob the butler down the long corridor.

Anthony Booth's penthouse flat had its own lift. It was about the size of two coffins and padded with rich red leather. Varnom and I stood shoulder to shoulder as it descended. Varnom's cologne pricked my nostrils.

"So," Varnom said coldly, "what was that last remark about?"

"He had a big collection of porn. American stuff, mostly from the 1970s. You don't like him, do you?"

Varnom studied me from behind his steel-rimmed spectacles. He said, "Let's put it this way: her parents didn't like the set-up, and he has a collection of porn sitting in plain sight."

"And two and two make five, and I suppose you've never had a wank."

Varnom let that one go.

I said, "You're going to type his DNA against the sperm Forensics found on her sheets, aren't you? That's a wild leap, if you don't mind me saying so."

"Not as wild as dragging in Barry Deane."

"*Touché.*"

"You gave your best shot and it blew up in your face. I'd leave suspicious deaths to the experts, if I were you, and go back to escorting evidence."

The lift door slid open on to the brightly lit lobby. I said, "Maybe I'm hacked off about Barry Deane, but you're hacked off too, because you aren't in on the interview with Whitehead. I don't blame you, but that's no reason to go chasing after one of Sophie Booth's relatives."

"Booth could easily have been watching his niece while he was in Scotland. That's the thing about the Web, isn't it? It connects everywhere with everywhere else. And he likes porn, you said so yourself. If we could get access to his computer, we could check what he's been looking at."

"That's not very likely," I said, "given who he is and who he knows, and the flimsiness of your hypothesis." I was beginning to wish I hadn't made that crack about Booth's little collection.

"He might have seen the murder," Varnom said. "And that would make him a material witness."

"If he did see it, he was playing it very coolly."

We were outside now. A hot wind was blowing from the river, lifting litter and swirling it high around the spotlit stands of topiaried evergreens in front of the building. There was a CCTV camera over the revolving door, and another high up on the wall of the building across the street. I wondered if Anthony Booth's system was connected to them.

"He was on his own turf this time," Varnom said. "I'll see how he does in an interview-room, by and by."

"I don't know about you, but I need a drink. A proper one. To get rid of the taste of Mr Anthony Booth."

"I think you know you can count me out," Varnom said.

"I was hoping we might make a go of it," I said. "After all, we're the classic odd couple. You're the establishment man; I'm the maverick, the oddball outsider with something to prove. We could generate a synergy that could crack the case wide open."

Varnom said forcefully, "In my opinion, people like you shouldn't be allowed to stay on the force, let alone get near a suspicious death. You fucked up and four men died because of it, one of them a good friend of mine."

I could have mentioned my exoneration at the Board of Enquiry, or the metal in my leg that set off scanning frames at every airport, or the four teeth that were not strictly speaking my own, grown as they were from implanted buds, but I had long ago stopped making excuses. I was as guilty as the dead. They might have died because of what they did to the girl, but I hadn't stopped it. I had run. My cowardice had saved me.

I tried to cool things down. I said, "I know you were a friend of Toby Patterson. I'm not surprised that you don't like me, but let's try and be civil."

Varnom looked down at me. "I know the true story about what happened at Spitalfields, you sad little man. Not the official whitewash, but the statement Andrew Fuller gave just before he died. If you stay on this case, I'll fuck you up so badly you won't be able to get a job directing traffic. You go and have your drink. I'm going back to write this up."

10

I went for my drink. The river walk was busy with tourists and strolling couples. A gang of kids zoomed by on motorized skateboards, trailing petrol fumes. Water lapped the top of the rubble breakwater piled along the muddy foreshore where an age ago Nick and I had prospected, finding bits of old china and glass, clay pipes, square Georgian ship nails, once even an old penny, worn smooth and black. Now the river always seemed to be at high tide, and there was talk of building another Thames Barrier. A gelid scum of algae lapped the rocks at the brimful river's edge. The air was thick with the stink of decay and the tang of insecticide. Barges anchored in the central current were pumping air deep into the water like paramedics trying to resuscitate a failing patient; effervescent wreaths of foam boiled up around them and trailed downstream.

Despite the smell of decay and the persistent hammering of the barges' pumps, the tables outside the riverside pubs were packed out, so I crossed at Blackfriars Bridge and found a spot at the bar in the back of the Black Friar pub, under the friezes of gold-and-black marble and the black plaster figures of monks.

I bought a microwaved meat pie and a pint of ice-cold Kronen-bourg, sank half the lager in one go, started an absent-minded autopsy of the pie while I leafed through a copy of the *Evening Standard* someone had abandoned. The report on Sophie Booth's murder was on page five, four brief factual paragraphs under a photograph of the distraught parents, nothing about webcams or black servers or home-made pornography.

I tried to get my thoughts straight about the case, but Varnom's hostility had unnerved me, and the details—the missing hard drives, the way the murder had been staged as carefully as a performance, the fax sent through the Cuban remailer, the emails and Barry Deane's claim to have been set up, the shady wariness masked by Anthony Booth's bonhomie—all these things floated free, refusing to click with each other.

I didn't have enough information. Or perhaps I didn't have the right information. Someone should devise a scale of useful-ness or quality that can be applied to information, I thought. It would make our lives so much easier.

I finished the pie and drank the rest of my pint and bought another.

Varnom's barb had struck deep, even though Fuller's deathbed statement was only part of the truth. Despite the Board of En-quiry, the hours of debriefing, post-trauma counselling and psych sessions, I still believed that Toby Patterson and the others would not have died if only I had done things differently. The two terrorists would not have died. I would not have been left alone with my burden of guilt.

Everyone had stories about the InfoWar. About where they had been when the high explosive and microwave bombs had gone off and thousands of fires had been started by overheating computers. About how they'd coped with bank accounts run back to zero, invalidated credit cards, power cuts, food rationing, phone lines dead or randomly cross-connected, the Web inac-cessible, TV channels transmitting porn or insane rants by computer-generated talking heads or nothing but snow, every traffic light in London jammed on red, the Tube shut down, street protests and flash riots, the army on the streets.

My own story had become public property. I'd been made a hero, a survivor of a fanatical terrorist attack. That was the official version, nothing like what had really happened, or the deathbed statement of Andrew Fuller. Which I didn't doubt that Varnom had seen; he wasn't the kind of man to make an empty threat.

I thought about that, and about Barry Deane's malicious pleasure in revealing his alibi. I was sure that it would turn out to be genuine, but the more I thought about it the more I was certain that it was evidence of his guilt, not of his innocence. He was deeply involved in Sophie Booth's murder, all right, despite his angry surprise when he had seen the email.

I finished my second pint and because my Mini was in Scotland Yard's car park walked all the way home through the hot dark streets, restless and unsettled, and limping very slightly. I needed to do some running. I needed to loosen up. I didn't want to think of Spitalfields, the heat and fluttering red light from buildings burning all in a row, black snow falling out of the smoky air, drifts of broken glass over the cobblestones where the girl writhed at the centre of the knot of police. A hand clamped over her mouth, her eyes searching frantically as other hands worked at her clothes. Straight to Hell.

When I got home, the building was in darkness and the streetlights and the blocks of flats on the other side of the canal were dark too. Eighteen months after the InfoWar, viruses that had infected the control systems of the electricity grid were still causing random surges and power cuts. I found my way up the stairs using my pocket flashlight, lit candles in the flat and opened the sliding glass door to let out the heat that had accumulated during the day. The little candle flames danced and flickered in the faint breeze, and points of light reflected in the round glass eyes of Archimedes the Wonder Owl as he swivelled his head back and forth, tracking me as I moved around the flat.

Julie had sent me a postcard of the Manneken Pis dressed in a police uniform. That, the martini and two pints of lager, and Archimedes' unblinking scrutiny, made me feel that I had an excuse to phone her.

"You were watching me," I said.

"Don't be silly."

"Well, your robot sidekick is looking at me in a funny way."

"He does have a mind of his own. Maybe he finds you interesting."

I remembered what Anthony Booth had said about the ADESS prototype. His first child. Not very bright, but still learning.

Julie told me about her work, told me about the restaurant to which she had been taken that evening.

"It's called De Ultieme Hallucinatie," she said, "and that's no lie, Dixon. It's a fabulous art-nouveau place a hundred years old, chock-full of gold statues and stained glass. Absolutely amazing. It made up for the dullness of my dinner companions. I sent you some photos."

"Who took the last one you sent me? The one in the café?"

"Tim."

"Tim?"

"Tim Leyland. My partner in crime on this little jaunt. You've met him. Fortysomething, silly little ponytail, seriously horrible Hawaiian shirts."

"He's been keeping you company?"

"I'm fabulously brilliant at what I do, but this is a big job. Even I need help, sometimes, and Tim speaks far better French than I do." A pause. Dead air crackled in my ear. Julie said, "Something's up. Don't bother to deny it."

"I seem to have become involved in this murder case."

"That poor dead girl?"

"The very one."

I had moved out to the terrace, under the tent of soft, fine mosquito netting. Archimedes watched me from his perch just inside the glass door.

Julie said, "Can you tell me about it?"

"There's not much to tell."

"Is there a computer angle? Come on, Dixon, spill all the delicious details."

She was trying to keep it light. She knew the official version of what had happened in Spitalfields, but she also knew there was more to it than that, and that I could not bring myself to tell her the whole story. It was part of the reason we had split up. That, and my stubbornness, my self-absorption, my black moods and unfocused rages and general wretched fucked-upness.

I told Julie, also trying to keep it light, "If you had a PoliceNet-capable phone I just might."

"Quantum encryption phones are legal here. They're legal everywhere, except in Britain and China and a couple of other repressive regimes. I could go out and buy one right now, over the counter, no questions asked. Think of the kind of photos I could send you then, Dixon."

"How much did you drink at this restaurant?"

"Am I friskier than usual?"

"Just a little."

"I had three glasses of white wine, and now I'm toying with a gin and tonic from the minibar. Come on, Dixon, you can give up a little information. It's good to talk."

"So you keep telling me."

Women are too sensitive to your tone of voice. Even over the phone. Even when they're half-drunk. "Hey," Julie said. "Fuck you too."

"I'm sorry. I had a bad evening. Something didn't work out."

"Just don't take it out on me."

"We'll talk, Julie. Whatever you want."

"If you weren't so preoccupied with yourself, you'd understand that it hurts me to watch you suffer and not be able to get close to you."

"There really isn't anything to tell you about the case. I've only been working on it for a day."

"I have faith in you, Dixon. You know that. If I didn't have faith in you that would be it, you'd never hear from me again. It's good, isn't it, that you're doing some proper police work?"

"I hope so," I said.

We talked a little more, but we both had the feeling we'd gone backwards. The power was still off when at last we said our goodnights. I sat outside in the warm darkness and drank beer and smoked, lighting the next tab off the stub of the one before, their ashy tips crackling brighter each time I inhaled, watched by twin red sparks sunk deep in Archimedes' unfathomable gaze.

11

A ll you have to do," I told the boy, "is tell us where the spikes came from."

Half past nine, the headmaster's office of Bellingham Academy, Highgate, a hitech boot camp subsidized by half a dozen multinationals. A couple of hundred pupils and more networked computers and electronic equipment than the old Stock Exchange crammed into three large detached houses, a mix of reactionary discipline and new technology. Uniforms, mass exercises in the morning, loyalty chants; a ten-metre satellite dish tilted at the sky at the bottom of the playing fields.

Apocalyptic sunlight fell through the big bay window of the office, laid a dazzling sheen on the stainless-steel sweep of the headmaster's desk. Five of us were sitting in leather-and-steel chairs drawn in a half-circle in front of the desk: the headmaster, Dr Christopher Lane; the boy's solicitor, the senior partner of his firm, tall and silver-haired and cadaverous in a chalk-stripe suit; WPC Sheena Gilbert; me, with a couple of aspirins working on my headache and patches of sweat growing in my armpits and down the small of my back; and the boy himself, thirteen-year-old Ben Perry, sitting up straight in his dove grey school uniform, blond hair combed back in a neat wave from his pale, sulky face, refusing point-blank to answer any questions.

WPC Gilbert wiggled the spike she held between thumb and forefinger. Shards of sunlight reflected from its silver casing shot around the room. She told the child, "You're not the only one selling these, Ben. We know someone sold a batch to you, and we know that you went into business selling them to your friends."

"How much of a profit did you make?" I said.

The solicitor cleared his throat and said, "I don't think the idea of profit is germane, Inspector."

"It will be if we have to prosecute, sir. But as I hope I've made clear, just a little cooperation from your client will allow me to overlook the problem."

"I'm sure it doesn't need to go beyond the school gates," the headmaster said. He was much younger than me, bloodlessly prim in a white short-sleeved shirt and tan slacks, with the razored crew cut and rimless round spectacles of a Swiss architect. Watchful pale blue eyes and a thin patrician nose, nostrils flared to sniff out any scent of scandal.

WPC Gilbert said, laying on the sympathy, "Did one of your friends supply you with the spikes, Ben? We understand that you don't want to get anyone into trouble, but by keeping quiet you're only making things worse for yourself."

"Answer the question, Perry," the headmaster said.

"Sir, yes sir! No, ma'am, I don't want to get anyone into trouble."

I said, "Was it someone in the school? Someone older? Someone you're afraid of? I promise you that no one will know that you told me. You can whisper it in my ear, or write it down on a piece of paper. Or everyone else in this room can step outside for a moment, and you can tell me then. It will be between you and me, Ben, and when you've told me, you'll feel ever so much better. It will be a weight lifted from you, believe me. But if you don't tell me now, then you can bet that someone else will tell me all about it, and sooner rather than later. If you're smart, and I think you are, you'll do it first. If you aren't smart, well then, Ben, you will have to take the consequences. Do you understand?"

"Sir, yes sir! I'm sorry, but I don't have anything to tell you, sir."

And so it went, for another twenty minutes.

The solicitor stopped for a word with WPC Gilbert and me as we made for our cars. "I hope you don't take this seriously," he said. "Really, it isn't anything other than boyish foolishness. They're intensely curious about sex at that age, after all."

He was only doing his job, but his chummy attitude touched off WPC Gilbert's priggish self-righteousness. She said, "The spikes were bought from shady merchants with connections to serious criminals, sir, and it's not just about ordinary sex, which would be bad enough. It isn't even anal sex or golden showers, or even rainbow showers, which in case you didn't know, sir, is where the woman throws up over the man during intercourse. There are women in high heels trampling chicks and hamsters and mice. One movie clip is five minutes of a naked woman rolling around in a bath full of crickets. There are very real-looking torture and rape sequences. Wanting to watch that kind of stuff doesn't strike me as the kind of thing that could be categorized as normal healthy boyish curiosity."

The solicitor looked grim. "Nevertheless, Ben Perry is a minor, and I think it would be wise to keep this inside the school gates. Let Dr Lane deal with it."

WPC Gilbert stood up to him. "This is part of a bigger investigation, sir. We can't let it go. We have to protect the children."

I said, "WPC Gilbert means that Ben Perry's file will have to remain open for the time being, but we may not have to act on it if we can find the main distributor."

"As long as the information does not become common knowledge, I suppose there is nothing else I can do for now. However, I think you had better take my card, Inspector," the solicitor said, and gave one to WPC Gilbert too, before folding himself into his sleek silver BMW 18 series and driving off.

I hadn't had time to retrieve my Mini from Scotland Yard, so I rode off with WPC Gilbert in her squad car, which smelled like someone had been very sick in the back. Rainbow showers.

"I'd like to hear what that son of a bitch would have to say for himself after he'd been forced to watch everything on those spikes," Gilbert said. She was in her early thirties, solidly built, her black hair tied in a short, businesslike ponytail. She was also head of her station's Decency League chapter.

"We gave it our best shot," I said, "but I don't think we're going to penetrate that combination of schoolboy *omerta* and heavy-duty legal firepower. Besides, Ben Perry is hardly a dangerous master criminal. He's a silly kid obsessed with trying to impress his friends, just like every other teenager."

"He's been corrupted. That's what pornography does. You seem to be taking this very lightly, sir, if you don't mind me saying so."

"I'll make sure the spikes are looked at as soon as possible, but the most we can expect is to learn that they were burned on the same machine as the others."

WPC Gilbert said, "I know that some police still don't approve of the Child Protection Act, but it does just what it says. It protects children. It represents the views of ordinary decent families."

I could have said that the Child Protection Act was imposed by moralizers who cloaked themselves in a fantasy of traditional family values, who claimed a monopoly on judgement and the power to decide on what is good and right, but had to resort to law to force everyone to conform to their views because they could not win by reasoned debate. I could have said that these self-appointed protectors were really bluestockings who hated whatever was different from themselves, especially if it came close to their own guilty desires; that they were arrogant, insensitive, intolerant, unkind, lacked imagination and sympathy, and were deeply ignorant of the variety of human experience. But I didn't. Sue me. Life's too short to get into arguments with people you cannot argue with, because their beliefs, not being based on reason, are immune to it.

We were coming up on Kentish Town Tube station. I said, "Drop me off here. I have an errand to run."

WPC Gilbert had to have the last word. As she stopped the squad car, blocking a junction, she said, "If we don't get anywhere soon, I think we should have a long and serious talk with the parents. Show them what kind of filth and corruption their darling boy has been peddling. Ten minutes would make even the most spineless Hampstead lefty liberal want to give up their nearest and dearest."

I rode the Tube from Kentish Town to the Angel, Islington, and walked to T12. I left the spikes with Andy Higgins and asked him a couple of questions, chased up the tech who was tracing the names and addresses of the people who had sent emails to Sophie Booth's account at Wizard Internet, and stopped by my office to check my email. Official circulars and news items from computer-crime newslists. The picture files Julie had sent me. And an email sent from an anonymous server in Cuba, with a picture file attached.

Tell anyone else about it and this is all you get. Let me know if you want to see more. Don't use a police computer or any UK ISP.

I felt cold, then hot. Got the shakes as I ran the picture file through my battery of antivirus software. It was clean. I opened it.

A dead woman in a chair.

She was naked, caught in the harsh light and shadow of a desk lamp off to the right. Her arms locked behind her, her skin pale and clean, a column of darkness between her white legs. Her head flopped to one side, so she seemed to be staring off at one corner of the room, craftily oblivious of what had been done to her.

Death porn, starring Sophie Booth.

I pulled up the email, printed it off, header and all, and brainstormed as I rode the Tube to Scotland Yard. Sophie Booth's murder had been transmitted over the Web, and someone had not only seen it, but had kept the pictures. Someone who knew that I was involved in the case. Someone who liked to play games. Someone who liked to flaunt their knowledge. Most likely, it had been sent by Barry Deane, but there was an outside chance it was from Anthony Booth, or even from someone else, someone involved in the murder, perhaps the same person who had sent the spoof email fingering Barry Deane. Mr X. The message was both a challenge and a taunt, but there was no question that I wouldn't take the bait.

I arrived at the tail end of a meeting of McArdle's squad. DC Keen was explaining that the rope used to tie up Sophie Booth was a common nylon twine sold in Wal-Mart superstores, that analysis of its chemical composition might help pinpoint the date it had been manufactured, and that meanwhile he was checking the sales records of all six Wal-Marts in the Home Counties.

Next up was DS Ferguson, chubby and balding, who gave a briefing about the evidence provided by the FSS. The semen on the sheets had been typed for DNA, but Flints had come up with a negative match—it belonged to someone who had never even been caught speeding. Apart from that of Sophie Booth, there was no DNA residue on the rope—it had been soaked in solvent before use, and the killer had worn gloves. And DNA profiling on dust picked up from the scene was inconclusive. Not only had a solvent been used, but the flat had been fluff-bombed with material vacuumed from bus or Tube seats. Preliminary analysis showed that the DNA of several hundred people was present; even if it was all typed and there was a positive result for a known villain or suspect, it would be difficult to prove that he had been in the room at the time of the murder. Conclusion: the killer knew what he was doing, and we might be in for a long haul.

The meeting broke up with little chat. Varnom went past me without a glance or a word. In the Murder Room, I wandered over as casually as possible to the boards and looked at the photographs of the scene, zeroing in on one in particular.

I made myself scope it out slowly. Sophie Booth naked and dead in the silver chair, bled out and washed clean, as in the picture I had been sent. But in this photograph, taken after she had been dead for twelve hours, she seemed to be wearing black, knee-high socks: postmortem lividity, tissue swollen and bruised by all the blood that had drained into it after her heart had stopped fighting gravity. The photograph emailed to me must have been taken just after her death, confirming my suspicion that it had been sent by one of the people who had watched her die.

Barry Deane: flaunting his knowledge.

Anthony Booth: looking for vengeance.

Mr X.

I hassled the exhibits officer, Denise Leary, and got a look at the fax sent through the anonymous remailer in Cuba. And, yes, the fax and the email I'd just received had both been sent through a machine with the same name, aglet.cu, and more importantly (names can be spoofed, names don't really mean any-thing on the Web), the same IP address: [158.152.221.123].

Sandra Sands had found out that Barry Deane had been telling the truth. He'd travelled from Heathrow to Havana on May 28, and returned on June 6. She handed me a folder and said, "Just to be sure, sir, I made a call to Heathrow Immigration, asked if they still had any CCTV footage of passengers from the KLM flight."

I flicked through the stills, and there were two clean shots of Barry Deane, smiling directly at the camera.

"Watch the birdie," I said.

"He does take a nice picture, doesn't he, sir?"

"This is good work, DC Sands. I wonder if you could do me a little favour, and find out the names of all the other passengers on the two flights."

"Any particular reason, sir?" Sandra Sands was wearing a neat black trouser suit and a green blouse. Her blonde hair was scraped back and held by a kind of wooden clip, and she looked appallingly young and eager.

"It's occurred to me that Deane may not have been travelling alone. What happened with Whitehead?"

"He was interviewed and released."

"And?"

Sandra Sands shrugged. "I couldn't say, sir."

"Where were you this morning?" Tony McArdle said, when I knocked on the open door of his office. His abrupt manner wasn't anger, merely exhaustion.

"I'm working another case, sir. Data spikes filled with porn and being sold in schools, nothing important."

"In my day it was *Health and Efficiency* magazine. I didn't even know women had pubic hair until I was sixteen."

I put the photographs on his desk. "Barry Deane came back from Havana on June 6. Here's his photograph at Heathrow. Giving the CCTV camera a shit-eating grin."

"I've seen it," McArdle said. "Log it in with Denise Leary, and forget about Deane for now."

"Not everyone knows they're photographed as they go through Immigration, sir, but Deane does. Look at him. He was working on his alibi well before we pulled him in. He wanted us to know where he was at the time."

"What might be on Whitehead's laptop is more important. I sent it over to T12 this morning, and I'd like you to go there now and chase it up for me."

"Are you telling me, sir, that you like Whitehead for this? I thought he'd been let go."

McArdle said, "I haven't charged him, but that doesn't mean I don't fancy him."

"What was his explanation for running all the way to Brighton?"

"He said that he had work to do, and that he had problems with his marriage, which is why he wasn't talking with his wife. We're doing follow-ups. Dave Varnom is checking traffic camera records to see if Whitehead drove to London on the night instead of going directly to Brighton, as he claims. And he gave up his laptop readily enough, although his solicitor advised him not to. I had to send it over to T12, since you weren't here."

"What did Whitehead say about Sophie Booth?"

"That she seemed a nice enough girl. Kept herself to herself, didn't have many people around. Said she was quieter than Mrs Panopoulos."

"Who would be the upstairs neighbour with the TV."

"Whitehead said that he didn't know anything about Sophie Booth's website, but I think he's not telling the truth. Chase up that laptop, John, I want it ransacked for anything which might be useful as soon as possible. Get it sorted, come straight back with what you find."

"If Whitehead tried to hide something on his computer, sir, it will take the technicians a while to find it. While we're waiting for them, and with your permission, I'd like to reinterview a couple of people."

McArdle rocked back in his chair and looked up at me. "Are you working an angle, John? Are you trying to pull a fast one? If you are, think again. I don't tolerate loners."

"Can I ask, sir, what exactly the terms of my secondment are?"

"As far as I'm concerned, a computer is a cross between an expensive typewriter and a bad TV. You are here, Detective Inspector, to provide expertise in an area where I know fuck-all."

"And to follow up anything I find in that area, sir?"

"What are you about, John? You disappear into a sad little backwater that hasn't been closed down only because everyone has forgotten about it, and now you're coming on like Regan and Carter."

"Sir?"

"*The Sweeney*. Don't tell me it was before your time. Fucking marvellous programme. If only police really were like that, we'd all be having a lot more fun."

"You told me how Sophie Booth died, sir, when I first came here."

"So I did."

"It got my attention, sir, in the worst way. I want the man who did that to her as badly as you. I'll be happy to take someone along with me. After, of course, I've had a word with the chief technician at T12, and explained to him that you urgently need Whitehead's laptop cracked wide open."

McArdle sighed. "You want to reinterview people."

"Yes, sir. From the computer angle."

I told him what Anthony Booth had said last night, and what Andy Higgins had told me this morning. McArdle considered this, then said, "She might have just sold it."

"She might. But almost certainly to someone she knows. That, or given it to her parents. I think it's important to follow this up, sir. The hard drives of the computers in her flat were taken, and so were any spikes or Zip disks that happened to be lying around. Someone didn't want us to have the information they contained. Perhaps there's something on Sophie's old computer that will be useful to us."

"I don't want you going on your own. DC Sands has a sympathetic manner."

"I don't, I take it."

"You don't go pedal to the metal like Dave Varnom, but Sandra is the family liaison officer, so she has to go along in any case. I hope this is going to be worth something."

"So do I, sir."

12

Simon and Angela Booth lived in an anonymous three-bedroom bay-fronted semidetached house deep in the endless repetition of the suburbs that spread around the wannabe skyscrapers of central Croydon. No one answered the doorbell, so DC Sandra Sands and I went through the carport and found Simon Booth kneeling in the middle of the half-mown lawn, fiddling with an upturned lawn mower.

Sandra Sands had phoned before we set off, but Simon Booth seemed surprised by our appearance, and was slow to get to his feet. He looked older than he had under the glare of the TV lights, tentative and uncertain and dazed, like a prizefighter the night after losing the last fight in his career.

"I suppose you'll want tea," he said. "Most of you lot do."

"Not if it's any trouble, sir," Sands said.

I said, "This is a nice patch you have here, Mr Booth."

The garden was long and narrow. A neat lawn bordered by flowers, vegetables and strawberries growing in raised beds, half a dozen gnarled apple trees with rough grass between them. A crude swing, nothing more than a couple of ropes and a bit of wood for a seat, hung from a sturdy branch of the biggest apple tree.

"It's going to be another hot day," Simon Booth said. He was wearing baggy white shorts and a faded T-shirt from the 2002 London Marathon. "I thought I'd get the lawn done. Angela's at work," he added, as he led us through the kitchen into the living-room. "It's her way of coping. You sit down. I'll make tea."

"If it's no trouble," Sands said.

"I'm having some," Simon Booth said, and wandered back into the kitchen.

"He's on tranquillizers, sir," Sands confided.

"I don't blame him."

"I mean that he might not be much help."

"We're just here to take a look, not interrogate him. Don't worry, I'll go easy. I won't even mention the cannabis plants he has growing amongst his sunflowers."

"It's been mentioned before, sir, in a quiet way, but I don't think he's taking much in."

Neither of us felt comfortable enough to sit down. The room was cluttered: a couch and two overstuffed armchairs, a coffee table loaded with books and papers and magazines, more books in cheap white bookcases under the bow window, where spider plants hung in macramé cradles. I fingered through the dusty LPs that leaned against an old stacking stereo. Pink Floyd, Yes, Jethro Tull, Gong, Genesis, the Electric Light Orchestra, Joni Mitchell, Neil Diamond. Apart from a couple of Dire Straits LPs, nothing much later than the midseventies. A few classical records, tapes of Cuban and African music. Photographs in clip-frames covered one wall. Family holidays, Sophie Booth at all stages of childhood, on beaches in swimwear, on moors in walking gear. Photographs of more than a dozen olive-skinned children. Younger versions of Simon and Angela Booth wearing Sandinista T-shirts and straw hats in a sugar cane field, in a field of banana plants, at a long table with a dozen grinning Latin Americans.

"That's where we met," Simon Booth said, as he carried a tray into the room. "El Salvador, 1986. We went to pick coffee to show solidarity for the revolution. We married the next year, and Sophie was born two years later. I hope you don't mind mugs."

I stirred two spoonfuls of sugar into my milky tea. The chipped mug commemorated the miners' strike.

"I haven't seen one of these in a long while," I said.

Simon Booth gave a wan smile. He seemed very tired, and much older than his fifty-five years. His grey hair was uncombed and there was an oil smudge on his cheek. Flecks of grass clung to his T-shirt. He said, "I suppose we might have faced each other across the picket lines, at one time or another, Inspector."

"I doubt it, sir. It was rather before my time."

But only just. As a rookie constable I'd listened to the older men's tales of thrashing the enemy within. They had joined the police for action, and they had got plenty in the miners' strike of 1984: policing picket lines at power stations; escorting convoys of coal trucks; haring around the countryside in Transit vans, chasing secondary pickets. They'd wave a wad of notes in front of the striking miners, working men with absolutely no money except charity because the union's funds had been sequestered, men facing a lifetime on the dole. There had been three million unemployed then.

"In some ways the 1980s were our finest hour," Simon Booth said. "We had real enemies to fight, real causes. The trouble is that our side won by becoming what they were supposed to be fighting against. Still, Angela and I try and do what we can. I saw you looking at our extended family. We've managed to get almost all of them through university." He touched the pictures, one after the other. "Alfonso and Clara are doctors. Mirtha, José Maria, and Alejo are teachers. Jesus here had a hole in his heart when he was born. He's doing research in biology now, at Harvard Medical School."

"We've come to ask you about Sophie's computers, Mr Booth," I said. "We'll try not to take up much of your time."

"Yes, of course. Well, go ahead. Do your worst."

"She had two computers, sir. One was bought by her uncle, I believe."

"We don't see much of him. We're very different, my younger brother and me. He's very much a child of the 1980s—one of Thatcher's children. Ambitious and smart, an opportunist with no charity in him."

"I've met him, sir."

"Angela has no time for him and always made it obvious. A very honest woman, my wife."

I said, "Sophie had two computers, sir. One more or less brand-new, bought by her uncle, the other about three years old."

"They're the ideal consumer product, aren't they? Obsolete before they're out of the box, yet the new models seem to do much the same as the old ones. Anthony gave Sophie a new computer just last month, for her birthday, even though there was nothing wrong with the laptop he gave her the year before." Simon Booth sipped his tea, staring silently into the past for a few moments. "There was a bit of an argument about that, as usual. Angela wanted to send it back. Sophie wouldn't. Anthony is very fond of Sophie, but Angela doesn't like him at all. There were rows, so bad he stopped coming around to see us. We're very different, my younger brother and I. He's done very well for himself, but I don't think he's really happy. He has devoted all his life to his work. He has no hinterland. I suppose Angela was worried that Sophie would take after him."

"The computer your brother bought, that would be the G10."

Simon Booth's hand described a vague circle in the air by his head. "Oh, I wouldn't know about makes and models," he said, meaning that he really didn't care.

"And the other computer Sophie had, the older one she had, did you buy it for her?"

Simon Booth gave a long sigh. "I'm afraid our budget doesn't run to that kind of thing, Inspector. No, She earned the money to buy it herself. She spent the summer after her A-levels doing drawings of tourists in Covent Garden, went on holiday in France with some friends and earned more money picking fruit. She bought the computer with that."

"That would be three years ago."

Another sigh. "I suppose so, yes."

"And your brother bought her a laptop, and then the G10. Do you know what happened to the laptop?"

"If you mean to ask if I have it, no. No, I don't. I don't much like them. We have them at school, of course. Like it or not, every kid needs to know about computers these days, because most of them are going to end up as wage slaves for some multinational. But I have absolutely no use for them."

"You don't know what Sophie did with it?"

"Threw it out, I suppose. There's not much value in old computers, is there? Is this really going to help you? Find who did it, I mean."

"We're following up every lead, Mr Booth," Sandra Sands said. "Would it be possible, do you think, to look in Sophie's room? She may have left some spikes or disks behind that could be useful to us."

"I'm sure that she didn't," Simon Booth said. "She took everything like that with her when she moved to London."

"If it's not too much trouble, we'd like to make sure. It will only take a minute."

Simon Booth shrugged, his silence awful and eloquent.

Sandra Sands leaned forward, trying to catch his gaze. She said, "Would you like to come upstairs with us, Simon?"

Booth heaved himself out of his chair. "I'm sure you know what you're doing," he said. "I'll be in the garden if you need me. I have to fix that fucking lawn mower. The grass needs cutting."

Sophie's room was long and narrow and very hot. There was a single bed with a grey duvet folded on it, a cheap white wardrobe and two bookcases, a battered pine desk. Pictures of pop groups were Sellotaped to the pink-and-yellow-striped wallpaper, and posters from big art exhibitions at the Tate Modern, the Serpentine Gallery, the Royal Academy. The wall over the desk was covered with dozens of drawings in clip-frames—flowers, landscapes, studies of a cat, of the apple trees at the bottom of the garden, all done in bold charcoal.

Sandra Sands drew a breath, let it out slowly.

"Are you all right?"

"She was just an ordinary girl."

"This place is stifling. Let's open a window and get to work."

"The room has already been searched, sir."

"We're looking for data spikes and Zip disks. You take the bed and wardrobe. Check the pockets of everything. I'll take the rest."

The bookcases held old Ladybird books, much scribbled over in thick red and blue crayon, pop annuals, some Point Horror, Tolkien, Terry Pratchett, J. K. Rowling, a row of fat fantasies written by American women with three or four names. All, judging by the pencilled prices on their title pages, bought secondhand. Bleached seashells. A stack of school exercise books. Homemade tapes of the bands whose posters looked down from the walls. The desk drawers were empty; I turned them over in case anything had been taped to the underside. People leave their backup data in all kinds of places, but Sophie had left nothing of her new life here.

"What do you see here?" I said, when we had finished the search.

"Just an ordinary kid's bedroom. Full of childhood things left behind."

"She drew a lot of pictures."

"She was an art student, sir."

"Who was good enough to earn money drawing tourists' portraits in Covent Garden. But there aren't any portraits of her parents."

"Perhaps they're elsewhere."

"Perhaps. The books are all secondhand, and there aren't any CDs or spikes, just home-recorded tapes."

"Perhaps she took the CDs with her."

"Of boy bands she'd grown out of? I'll bet you twenty quid the inventory of her flat will show she didn't. And I'll bet another twenty that a lot of the clothes she left behind are home-made."

"What's your point, sir?"

"Her parents live frugally. They both work, but everything in the house is make-do-and-mend. The lawn mower is on its last legs. They don't have a car—there are no oil stains under the carport."

"They're teachers, sir. And they sponsor children in the Third World."

"I wonder how hard it was for Sophie, growing up without the things all her friends had. Watching her parents settle further and further into the past, knowing they cared as much about strangers as they did for her."

"Well, she had her rich uncle."

"Yes, she did, didn't she?"

I put the drawers back, helped Sandra Sands straighten the bed. As we went downstairs, the lawn mower started up.

13

J ust before one in the afternoon, the air jellied with heat in the choked canyon of Charing Cross Road. Three men in blue coveralls stood around a green junction box, two resting styrofoam coffee cups on its top, another wearing a baseball cap, all of them watching a fourth man, who with a galvanometer probe was testing the sheaves and nests of wires inside the box. A pair of Japanese tourists, a skinny boy and a skinny girl with matching rockabilly quiffs, neatly pressed blue jeans and white nylon jackets printed with pictures of electric guitars, were consulting a map on a mobile's screen, trying to match global positioning with reality. Students were slouching out of the main entrance of Central St Martin's College of Art and Design, drifting away in knots of two or three. After getting directions from the porter, I climbed to the top floor, which a big, polished brass plate informed me was The Magic Doll Laboratory of the Digital Arts, opened on 18 March 2007 by Mr K. R. Choi, President of the Magic Doll Corporation of Korea.

Sophie Booth's tutor, Laura Sills, had an office opposite a big studio room in which two intent young women, video cameras pressed to their faces, were stalking one or another of the dozens of foot-long, turtle-shaped robots crawling this way and that, gears and motors and circuitry visible through their glass shells. I watched for a moment, then knocked on the frosted glass of the office door.

Laura Sills was a slim, fine-boned woman in her late thirties, her hair cropped short and dyed a fluorescent orange. She wore loose black jeans with loops and buckles and pockets, a faded green T-shirt with the sleeves torn off, showing a rose tattoo on her left shoulder. She was hunched at her desk over paperwork. At her elbow, a Macintosh computer, its screen the biggest and flattest I'd ever seen, played a screensaver of silver flying saucers swooping amongst improbably red crags under a starry sky. Although a window was cracked open, the room was hot and full of cigarette smoke. A crumpled cigarette was smouldering in an ashtray, and Laura Sills held another in her left hand while she scribbled on the neatly printed sheets of some student's essay.

I introduced myself and she waved me in without looking up. I sat in one of the two mismatched chairs between the desk and a floor-to-ceiling bookcase crammed with box files and oversized books. A cactus was slowly dying on top of a battered four-drawer filing cabinet beside the door; mobiles of fragile blown-glass globes hung from the institutional fluorescent-light fixture. A collage of drawings and photographs and postcards and posters covered every bit of free wall space.

Laura Sills finally put down the pen and looked at me. Her lipstick was a bright red slash in her scrubbed, elfin face. "End of term," she said, "and I'm behind on the final assessments. I understand you have more questions about Sophie Booth? I thought you guys had wrung me dry."

"I've just joined the team," I said, and asked if I could smoke.

"Of course. It keeps the students away while I'm working— most of the poor things would faint if they inhaled more than a lungful, although Lord knows the air quality is worse down on the street than it is in here."

I refused her offer of a half-empty packet of Gauloise unfiltered, took out my Tropicas. "Wow," she said, as she sparked a fresh cigarette, "you might as well not bother. You know, you're not at all like the other police who've been to see me. You're—"

"More compact?"

"Old-fashioned, I was going to say. Your cuff links, the handkerchief in your jacket pocket, the way you hold your cigarette by the side of your neck. You look more like a TV private eye than a policeman."

"I can show you my warrant card."

"Oh, I'm sure you're genuine. Would you like coffee or tea?"

"No thanks."

"Wise move. I make coffee from instant and water from the hot tap, and I haven't yet got the hang of making tea the English way."

I had been trying to place the twang in her accent. I said, "You're American."

"Canadian. Québécuoise, in fact. Don't be embarrassed; it's a common mistake. Now, how can I help you?"

"I'm looking at the case from the computer angle. I'm especially interested in Sophie's website. Do you know anything about it?"

"It was part of her work. All students have to write a theoretical thesis, and produce pieces of work for our end-of-year show. Sophie was interested in computing from the beginning. I encouraged her in that direction."

"So you knew the contents of her website."

Laura Sills shook her head, blew out a cloud of smoke. "That isn't how it works. The student has to find her own direction. I'm here to encourage and advise, not stand over them. Sophie did show me her completed pieces, of course. Latterly, she was working on videos involving her friends. She was making use of the intervals between an old-fashioned frame-grabbing program, mixing in distortion and morphing effects, multitrack sound. The best were quite haunting. She told me that she was collecting emails from people who had seen her work on the Web, and that she planned to work them into her pieces."

"So you didn't know that she had been broadcasting sex shows over the Web?"

Laura Sills smiled. "No! No, I didn't. Although I know she had been putting up photographs of her daily life on her website. That was something she was particularly interested in, and her written thesis wasn't a bad stab at analysing the impulse behind similar attempts. I didn't know that she'd been putting on, what did you call them?"

"Sex shows."

"Hah. Well, she did have a pretty strong exhibitionist streak. A very fierce girl with an almost neurotic sense of her own self-worth. What kind of sex shows did she do? If it doesn't embarrass you to talk about them."

"I suppose you might say they were copied from pornographic magazines."

Laura Sills laughed. When she reached out to tap a length of ash into a plastic cup, I saw a tuft of black hair under her arm. I was pretty sure that she wasn't wearing a bra under the scoop-necked T-shirt. She smiled when she caught me looking, and said, "Her parents are violently liberal, and Sophie reacted against that by pushing transgression as far as it would go. She went through a period of sleeping around in her first year, and I think that gave her a lot of emotional problems she was trying to work through. Like many kids, she was interested in putting all of her life directly into her art. She didn't see a separation. Really, I didn't think much of her as an artist. She wasn't interested in finding anything original in herself, and she was too full of self-interest to have the natural generosity of the real artist.

She would have probably ended up as a pale copy of Tracy Emin or Sarah Lucas. You look shocked. Don't speak ill of the dead and all that. But I assume you'd rather have the truth."

"I appreciate your frankness."

"Oh, I'm a very frank woman. That's my shtick, it's how I charm the students."

"I might need a list of her boyfriends."

"I don't think she had any boyfriends recently, but let me show you something."

She rummaged around in a drawer, pulled out a spike and slotted it into her computer, briefly attacked the keyboard with nicotine-stained fingers. The alien landscape vanished; a movie player launched itself.

"This was a piece Sophie did at the end of her first year," Laura Sills said, lounging back in her chair, watching me as I watched the screen:

Men's faces, portraits as formally straightforward as mug shots, slowly morphing one into another against a royal-blue background, names and dates flickering underneath. Most of them young, student types. Defiant stares, sheepish looks, dazed smiles.

Laura Sills said, "Those are the men she slept with in her first year at college. She took a photograph of each one after she'd fucked him. It's a derivative piece, but not without its merits."

"I suppose someone has taken down the names."

"I gave them a copy of the spike. Like a lot of pretty girls, Sophie was unsure of her self-image. Sleeping around was a way of validating herself, but she went through that phase and came out the other side with no attachments. She always struck me as a bit of a cold fish, in fact, despite her desperation to be liked."

"You don't seem to have liked her very much."

"Look, as we're being so frank, can I ask if you want a drink? It's lunchtime, the phones and Web access have been fucked by some gremlin left over from the InfoWar, and I've been stuck in this office all morning."

Laura Sills told the two robot-wranglers that she would be back in an hour and if they were going to break for lunch they had better pack everything away and lock it up, and we went down to the street and through one of Soho's security gates, to a basement bar in Frith Street. Orange leather sofas and tall, slim steel tables scattered over a black slate floor inset with panels of glowing blue or green glass. We settled on stools at the steel counter. A bartender delivered a glass of white wine for Laura, a bottle of lager for me. On a nearby sofa, a couple of pert production assistants, blonde bobs, halter tops and tight shorts, their long, gleaming legs unself-consciously stretched out, were discussing someone called Piers who was, apparently, a bit of a cunt.

"Cheers," Laura Sills said, when our drinks came. Her lip-sticked lips left a bold imprint on the wineglass. "We were talking about sex."

"I found some pictures one of her admirers had posted up on his own website. She did a strip show, and then she masturbated."

"Wow." Laura's left foot was idly swinging to and fro. She wore clear plastic sandals. Her toenails were painted bright red. There was a silver ring on her big toe. She said, "Was it the real thing?"

"Nothing was left to the imagination. You don't seem shocked."

"Students naturally gravitate towards the transgressive end of art. It's a phase they go through—it's easier to rebel against received ideas than transform or advance them with ideas of your own. A few years ago, I was teaching in Toronto then, one of my kids put on a *faux* sex-education tape, half an hour of himself masturbating on a bed draped with red velvet and beautifully lit by candles." She smiled at me. She said, "He was very good at it."

"Can we speak confidentially?"

"If you mean, will I speak to the press, no, I won't. They've been at my house, they've been at my place of work. I told them all to fuck off."

"I appreciate the sentiment."

"It's part of my job. They were pushing notes through the letter box. There was an envelope with two fifty-pound notes in it. I went outside and set fire to it. A picture was taken, much to my embarrassment. I suppose that it's all because of her famous uncle."

"If the sex angle leaks out, there'll be a fresh feeding frenzy."

"Is there a sex angle?"

I felt that I could be candid with this bold, frank woman. I said, "I think that Sophie's killer saw her on the Web and found out where she lived. Her murder was transmitted over the Web too. Live."

Laura sipped her wine. Her smile was gone. "I've already had a long session with two of your people about Sophie, but this is a new angle, isn't it?"

"We have some new leads. Did she ever complain to you of someone sending her abusive or disturbing emails? Or of someone stalking her?"

Laura shook her head. "No. No, she didn't. Will you get the creep who did this?"

"I hope so."

"She didn't deserve to die. I tell my students not to ride the Tube after eight o'clock in the evening. I tell them that if they go out on the town they shouldn't try and walk home on their own. But I don't tell them to stay indoors and make sure all the doors and windows are double-locked. We can't live in fear because of a few sickos, can we? I carry a can of Mace, and I'd encourage any of my students to do the same, boys or girls."

"That's sensible, although it is illegal."

"I bought it in Paris, where it is legal. A slim little brushed-aluminium cylinder, *très chic*. I'd use it if I had to."

"I doubt if any good copper would object."

"Is that what you are? A good copper?"

"I want to get Sophie's killer as badly as anyone."

"I'm glad to hear it." Laura Sills finished her wine and glanced at her watch. "I should get back and make sure all the equipment has been put away. We've had a couple of break-ins recently."

We parted outside the security gate. Laura Sills took my card and told me that she'd be in touch if she thought of anything.

"I never thought I'd say this to a policeman, but I do want to help," she said.

I watched her thread her way along the crowded pavement, then turned and went in the other direction.

I visited one of the electronics shops on Tottenham Court Road and drove back to the Yard. Sandra Sands was in the canteen. We found a quiet corner. I offered her a cigarette, but she told me she didn't smoke.

"Good for you. It's a filthy habit."

"There's no smoking in here anyway, sir."

"Shit," I said, but kept the unlit tab between my lips.

"I checked out the flights as you suggested. One man travelled to and from Cuba on the same flights as Barry Deane. By the name of Damien Nazzaro."

"Does DCI McArdle know?"

"He's interviewing Mr Nazzaro now, sir."

"And is Mr Nazzaro dirty?"

"Nothing on record. He came to the country from Malta a

couple of years ago, is the manager of a licensed theatre club in Brewer Street. It's owned by the Vitelli family."

"Who also employ Barry Deane. Well, perhaps he's just a business acquaintance."

"You don't really think that, do you sir?"

"I need to talk with Sophie's friends, and I need someone with me."

"I suppose I should be flattered."

"I need someone else to be there, and you fit the bill. A sympathetic face and a smart manner, it's a lethal combination."

Sandra Sands gave me a candid look. It occurred to me that she wasn't much older than Sophie Booth. She said, "You didn't need anyone when you went off to talk with Dr Sills, sir."

"She's neither a suspect nor a material witness, WPC Sands. But according to the preliminary interviews, these kids were helping Sophie Booth with her video art. I want to know what they got up to, and that is germane to the case."

"Germane, sir?"

"I can't order you directly, but I could ask Tony McArdle for your help. Frankly, I'd rather you wanted to come along."

"As long as it isn't a steady thing, sir. And as long as you don't smoke in the car."

Tim Coveney lived in a bedsit in a late Victorian town house in a grandiose but ruined crescent in Chalk Farm. He didn't answer the doorbell, and his message service clicked in on the second ring when I called his mobile number.

Sandra Sands said, "You're not going to leave a message, sir?"

I took a last drag on my cigarette and flicked it away. "No point in spoiling the surprise."

We had more luck with Lucy Matthews, who had a room in the Ralph West hall of residence, across the river in Battersea.

Sandra Sands and I perched on the single bed like visiting parents; Lucy Matthews sat on a beanbag, hugging a cushion to herself. There were a dozen church candles set on a wonky plastic table, more candles in cheap wrought-iron candelabra, swathes and swags of purple velvet wrapped around the curtain rail. A clutch of rubber bats hung from the ceiling; a bookcase was crammed with paperback novels by Stephen King, Anne Rice, Poppy Z. Brite, Kim Newman. Plastic knives and forks melted and twisted into sculptures. A cork notice board tiled with square Polaroid portraits, the faces distorted into wolfish masks by some kind of manipulation of the photographic gel. Posters for Goth bands and a couple of tattered repro posters (*Dracula A.D. 1972, After Dark*), a dense grid of fairylights linked to motion detectors so that the lights dimmed and brightened when you passed a hand near them.

Lucy Matthews, short, plump with puppy fat, wore a loose, ankle-length black dress and sixteen-hole Dr Martens she tucked beneath her. Long hair dyed dead black, kohl smudged around her eyes, purple lipstick. A young and naive vampire, a child infatuated with the romance of death. I thought, cruelly, that she would be cured of that infatuation for ever if she saw the pictures of Sophie Booth in the silver chair, slumped over the pile of her own blood.

Lucy Matthews admitted straight away that she had helped out a few times with Sophie's video pieces, and I said, "What kind of things did you two get up to?"

"It was silly stuff really. I'm not really into performance art." She had a small, breathy voice, and spent most of her time looking down at her interlaced, heavily ringed fingers.

"Oh? And what are you into?"

Her shoulders rose and fell inside her loose dress. "I don't know. Graphic design, mostly, I guess. I've done some spike cases for the end-of-term show."

I could imagine. I said, "And what did you do with Sophie?"

"All kinds of stuff. Inside and out."

"Inside and out?"

"In her room, which went on her website, and outside, for the security cameras."

"Like the one above the door to the building."

Lucy nodded and squeezed the cushion tight, more like twelve than twenty-two.

I said, "You gave performances to CCTV cameras."

Another nod. In a small voice: "I suppose it was situationist."

She was suddenly crying, the tears streaking black make-up down her cheeks. I looked at Sandra Sands, who leaned forward and said, "I know this is terribly upsetting, Lucy, but what you are telling us is a great help."

A sniff, a gulp.

I shook out a couple of cigarettes, offered one to Lucy. She took it, and I lit it for her.

I said, "If you could tell us how you helped Sophie with her website, it really would help."

"We did what she called a candle rite, only it didn't come out properly because the light level was too low for her webcams. We dressed in these hire-shop monks' robes so only our faces showed, held candles and moved about, made different patterns. Then there were the tableaux in her room. You know, like living statues, changing our poses every thirty seconds. That was the refresh time of the frame-grabbing program, so it was like making disconnected frames of a movie. Anyway, that's what Sophie said."

"This is a difficult question for me to ask," I said, "but it's important. You've been very helpful so far, and I hope you can answer it frankly. Did any of these performances involve sex in any way?"

Sandra Sands gave me a sharp look; Lucy Matthews looked up at me too, black streaks down her cheeks, a bright bubble in one nostril. She sniffed and said, "I know Sophie did that piece in her first year, but after that she was very straight. She liked to flirt, but she didn't follow through."

"So what other stuff did you do with her?"

Another shrug. "Stuff with mirrors. That didn't look too bad, we got some interesting engulfing patterns going. And something with indoor fireworks, using the kind that produce lots of floating flakes of ash? Silly stuff, mostly. And she just liked having us hang out and talk, so that it looked like she had a lot of social life going on for the people who wanted to watch. I didn't like that much, you didn't know who might be watching. Creepy."

I thought of the show Sophie Booth had put on by herself. Obviously she hadn't had Lucy Matthews's problem with cameras. The doors locked, the curtains drawn. Just her and the webcams and the whole wide world. A silly game. A dare.

"It was always you three together," I said. "You and Sophie and Tim Coveney."

"Sometimes Sophie did stuff with just Tim. He used to follow her around, you know, but I don't think it led to anything. Sophie was very self-centred. She knew what she wanted and she manipulated people to get it."

"It sounds to me that you didn't like her that much, even though you hung around with her and helped her out with these performance pieces."

A shrug.

Sandra Sands said gently, "It's all right, Lucy. Anything you can tell us might be a big help."

"I don't know if I liked her," Lucy Matthews said, "but I admired her. She had all this energy, and she knew how to focus it on the one thing she wanted."

"And that was?"

"She always said she wanted to be rich and famous, but that was just a front. I know she really cared about her art, but she didn't want people to know that—she thought it was a weakness."

I said, "Can I ask you about the computers Sophie used, Lucy? We know that her uncle bought her one last month. And he also bought her one the year before—a laptop."

A nod.

"But what we found in Sophie's flat was the brand-new computer, and a much older model she was using to run her website. So we were wondering, what happened to the laptop her uncle bought her last year?"

Sandra Sands asked gently, "Did Sophie give it to someone, Lucy? We need to find out where it went. If it went to someone she knew, they won't get into trouble. We just need to see it, tidy up the loose end. So, did she give it away to someone?"

Lucy Matthews took a deep drag on her cigarette, blew out smoke, and watched it disperse. She said, "Sophie never gave away anything in her life. She was going to sell it. She offered it to me, but I couldn't afford it."

Sandra Sands said, "Do you know who she sold it to? Was it someone you know?"

"Why is this important? The other police didn't ask about Sophie's computers."

"We think that there may be something on Sophie's old computer that could help us."

"We just need to take a look at it, Lucy," I said.

"She was going to sell it," Lucy Matthews said, "but then it was stolen from her car."

We went back to Timothy Coveney's bedsit. He didn't answer his bell, so I rang all the others. At last, a young man stuck his head out of an open window and sleepily asked what we wanted.

"We're looking for a neighbour of yours. Tim Coveney. Know him?"

"He's away," the young man said, and withdrew. I leaned on

his bell until he came back. "Fuck off," he said, "or I'll call the police."

"We are the police. Is Tim about?"

"He went away a couple of days ago."

"Can you tell me where he went?"

"He didn't tell me. I passed him on the stairs. He had a rucksack on his back. He asked me to take in his post, so I guess he's gone away somewhere. Is he in trouble?"

"Not yet."

Sandra Sands scrolled through a transcript of Tim Coveney's interview on her mobile, and told me that he had a placement in a workshop in Hackney. It took me a while to find it, a narrow two-storey brick building tucked into a small triangle of land in the shadow of a railway bridge off the Kingsland Road. The owner, Roger Court, was a skinny fortysomething with tousled hair and glasses with little round lenses. Tim Coveney had been working there that morning, he said, but had taken the afternoon off.

I said, "Perhaps we could have a word with you about Tim, sir."

"Why not? Come in. Would you like some tea? I've just boiled a kettle."

Court appeared to be wearing nothing under his blue denim overalls, and I found out why when we went inside. The place was as hot as one of the inner circles of hell. Worktables piled high with sheets of shaped glass stood on one side, two long furnaces as big as cars on the other, squatting under layers of shimmering air. Grinders and drills hung from a rack, alongside huge ladles and tongs that wouldn't have looked out of place in a dungeon. The floor was crunchy with bits of glass, and there was a powdering of white glass dust everywhere.

"I mostly do large-scale work," Court told us. He turned down a battered radio tuned to *London Live*, emptied a battered kettle into a trio of dirty chipped mugs. "Baths, sinks, shower enclosures and tabletops for architects and private customers; bigger pieces for commercial customers. I just did a glass-brick installation for one of the squares by Canary Wharf."

The tea was lukewarm and too milky, but I was grateful for it; traffic fumes and the workshop's tremendous heat had dried my mouth.

"What does Tim do?" Sandra Sands asked.

"He's into bowls, plates, that kind of thing. He sells quite a bit to one of the shops in Camden Market. He likes the challenge of scaling down industrial processes, and he's especially interested in smart glass." Roger Court picked up a clear glass bowl and shook it. Short spikes erupted over the surface, collapsed when Court shook it again. "Something to do with robots, this one," he said. "Horribly complicated stuff to make, it's built up in layers in special moulds."

Sandra Sands said, "It's generous of you to help him out."

"He's a talented boy. I'm thinking of keeping him on when he graduates. This is about the murder of his friend, isn't it?"

"Just a follow-up, sir."

"I think Tim is still feeling pretty bloody about it. Go easy on him."

I said, "It really is just a few routine questions. Has he said much?"

"Not really. He only came this morning, said he'd like to start work again. He has some pieces waiting to be taken out of the furnace. He took off before they cooled, but he said that he'll be back for them tomorrow."

"How does he seem to you?"

Court shrugged. One of the straps of his overalls fell off his shoulder and he pushed it back absent-mindedly. "He's a quiet lad. A bit intense, a bit interiorized, but clever and capable."

"Did he talk to you about it?"

"No, and I didn't ask."

"I don't suppose you know if he has a girlfriend, sir?"

"A fiancée, actually. In Liverpool. Look, he's just a young lad, and he's had a horrible time."

"We'll be gentle with him," I said.

I gave Roger Court one of my cards. He promised to phone me if Timothy Coveney turned up. Traffic was heavy, and it took me more than half an hour to drive Sandra Sands the quarter mile to the nearest Tube station. One side of a C60 compilation tape of The Only Ones, the first few tracks of a bootleg tape of The Clash, live in the Lyceum, December 1978.

Alan Rudd, the detective sergeant over in Vice who was working with me on the porn spike case, phoned me. He had some news.

"I'll be there," I told him.

"First thing?"

"First thing."

Sandra Sands and I talked about the progress of the case. I said, "How many of the team think that she was asking for it? No names, unless of course you want to name names."

"We're the new improved police, sir. No one thinks like that now."

"No, I forgot, of course they don't. Except for the Decency League people, who think that anyone with a lifestyle gets what they deserve."

A silence stretched through most of "Capital Radio." At last, Sandra Sands said, "He stalked her, didn't he, sir? Through her website."

"Then I wouldn't be on the case, because cyberstalking is the province of NCIS," I said, and remembered DI Davies.

"Dave Varnom says that the neighbour, James Whitehead, is as likely as anyone."

"Running away doesn't mean he was guilty. Everyone feels guilty around us." We were inching forward in stop-go traffic.

The computerized traffic-control system had collapsed during the InfoWar, and three attempts to bring it back online had failed. Gridlock was a way of life now. All around, sunlight flared brutally on glass and candy-coloured metal. I said, "Look, I really need a cigarette. The windows are wound down, and it won't be as bad as the traffic fumes."

"I can see you're suffering, sir."

"Bless you."

"I've never been in a Mini before."

"It's a classic design," I said.

"It's a pity it sits level with most people's exhausts."

"It would probably be quicker for you if you got out and walked, DC Sands."

"I'm quite comfortable, thank you, sir. And I'd like to know why you're so keen on finding Tim Coveney."

"Did you know that he has a criminal record?"

"That doesn't mean he stole Sophie Booth's computer."

"Let's hope that it does, or this line of enquiry will run dry."

"Even if we do find Sophie Booth's old computer, are you sure that anything useful will still be on it?"

I told Sandra Sands what I knew about the persistence of memory. It is very difficult for anyone to remove every trace of past activity on a computer. Operating systems store extra, hidden copies of files; swap files extend a computer's memory by off-loading data into a temporary buffer on the hard drive. Even completely reformatting the hard drive will not touch these files, which are full of earlier copies of documents. Information doesn't vanish into the ether when you press the delete key or move a file to the trash can. All you've done is take away the data about the location of the files on the disk, freeing up that space so it can be overwritten by new data. And files can be retrieved even if they have been partly overwritten—every block of data is allocated thirty-two kilobytes of disk space, enough for twenty-odd pages of single-space typing. Even if the space is reused, there's usually some data left in the odd corner, and superconducting quantum detectors can sometimes pull out ghostly traces of data from the magnetic sectors of overwritten tracks.

"If you want to erase a particular file and know exactly where it is," I said, "you have to overwrite it a hundred times or so. Otherwise, your best bet is to heat your hard drive until it starts to glow—that randomizes the alignment of the magnetic domains."

"Or you could take the hard drive out of the computer," Sandra Sands said, "and drop it into the river, and hope no one finds it."

"Yes, you could."

"Perhaps that's what happened to the hard drives taken from Sophie Booth's computers."

"Perhaps. That's why we need to find this laptop." Sandra Sands had turned down the tape deck so she could hear my little lecture; I turned it back up for "Another Girl, Another Planet." "You don't mind, do you? It helps me think."

"My father liked drum and pipe bands, sir. After that, I can take anything."

"I lost my CDs and records when my flat burned down. These are all I have left."

"Records, sir?"

"I know you've heard of them, DC Sands, although perhaps you've never seen one." The car in front of us edged forward, all of three feet. When I didn't bother to move the Mini, the driver of the car behind tapped his horn impatiently. "Another Girl, Another Planet" segued into "Why Don't You Kill Yourself?". I said, "You did well with Lucy Matthews."

"I'll take that straight, sir, since you were once a negotiator."

"I'm not feeding you a line, DC Sands. You can relax in the knowledge that I really think you did well. You knew when to back me up, when to change tack. That kind of sensitivity is difficult to teach."

"I hope this doesn't mean we're going steady or anything, sir."

"I still want to talk to Timothy Coveney. I could use your fine way with words."

"I was in a big family, sir, the second-youngest. You soon learn about the right way of asking for what you want."

14

It was just gone six o'clock when, after dropping Sandra Sands at the Dalston Tube station, I arrived at T12. The workshop on the top floor was deserted, but Andy Higgins was waiting for me in his office, his feet up on his desk, his keyboard in his lap. He was sucking on his unlit pipe as he typed, and he said around it, "I've been through the hard drive of Mr Whitehead's computer. It was reformatted, but I recovered most of the old files. I looked for picture files, as you asked."

"Any luck?"

Andy took his pipe out of his mouth and said seriously, "I found some bad stuff, John. Some of the worst I've seen."

"I think I can guess."

Andy tossed a data spike to me. "I copied them onto that. What's it like, doing real police work?"

"I'll write you a memo. By the way, what's the word on that journalist's laptop? The one taken in the Walthamstow raid."

"I wouldn't know. I suppose it's waiting its turn."

"It should have been done by now," I said. After all, I'd moved its action docket myself. "Let me know as soon as you can."

"I'll write you a memo."

I signed the forms and took the spike downstairs and stuck it into my computer. Forty-five picture files. Whitehead had been in on it from near the beginning, and had stayed until the end.

Sophie Booth had taken a long time to die.

Click.

She was already naked, tied to the plastic chair, a desperate and fearful look on her face as she stared at something to her right.

Click.

The killer was in the frame, obscuring her as he bent over her. His back was to the camera, but I could tell that he was a big man. He wore a dark tracksuit and had a fall of long blond hair that might have been his, but was probably a wig. Even the pathetic sods who knock over building society branches with spud guns know that pulling the hood of your anorak over your head isn't enough any more, and go in with more prosthetics on their faces than Laurence Olivier in his dotage.

Click.

He was in midswing, slashing at her with a craft knife.

Click, click, click.

He was bent to her, busy. Blood on white skin. Her face mercifully obscured.

Click, click, click.

Needles, the wire from the lamp, and at last the mercy of the knife.

Click, click, click.

She had died between 18:55:32 and 18:56:33. The actual *coup de grâce* had not been captured, but afterwards the killer had posed to show the camera how he held her head down, the long curved knife tucked under the left side of her chin, his face, masked with a caricature of Margaret Thatcher, staring into the camera.

Click.

A picture I'd seen before, her naked body, head down, blood shining black on her white skin.

Click.

Her killer holding her head up by the hair, like a trophy.

My jaw hurt. I'd been grinding my teeth. The worst thing was not the killing, but the clear evidence that the killer had loved his work. I felt a cold pure anger towards him, and for people like Whitehead, who had watched Sophie Booth die and had done nothing about it, who felt guilt only when they thought that they might be caught.

There was a little worm of guilt in me, too. I had not told anyone about the picture I had been sent, and I was relieved that now it did not seem necessary to mention it.

Watching the sequence for the second time, just an hour and a half later, was worse. When it was over, McArdle stubbed out his cigarette and sparked another. He was smoking Bloomsburys, the kind of serious ordnance that could clear a restaurant in California faster than a canister of CS gas. "My wife's giving me grief about starting up again," he said, and offered me one.

"I have my own, sir."

"I forgot you like those non-strength ones."

I lit one of my Tropica Ultras. It tasted as sweetly disgusting as a joss stick, and for a moment I thought I might be sick. McArdle's office, lit only by the computer screen and a desk lamp, was horribly hot and airless. Beyond the open door, the Murder Room was empty and dark. After the first frantic day, the investigation was settling into an 8 A.M. to 6 P.M. routine; red flag or not, the budget didn't stretch to much overtime.

McArdle pushed his chair away from his desk and drew deeply on his tab and said, "I hope I never see anything like that again."

I said, "Well, it wasn't Barry Deane."

McArdle's eyes were bruised, and although he had recently shaved, he'd missed hairs that grew in the deep crevices and pouches of his fleshy face. He said, "I'm sure it wasn't Whitehead, either, but we'll have to do a proper comparison to be sure. Give me your opinion."

"Whitehead was at home, in Oxford. His wife was out; he wanted a break from his work. He logged on to Sophie's website. He saw the murder and he panicked. Maybe he drove up to London to find out if what he'd seen had really happened. Maybe he just ran straight for Brighton. But he didn't come forward, and he tried to get rid of the evidence by reformatting his hard drive. He tried to hide what he saw, like the others."

McArdle thought about this, fingering one and then another of the folds of his face. "We could do him for obstruction and withholding, but it wouldn't advance the case. Still, I don't like being lied to. How are you set for overtime at T12?"

"I'm working off the books."

"Good man. I think we should have another word with Mr Whitehead as soon as possible."

15

James Whitehead was brought in an hour later. He stood when we came into the interview-room, and McArdle said, "Please sit down, sir. No need for formality."

As Whitehead resumed his seat, his solicitor patted his hand reassuringly. I started the video and the tape recorder. McArdle recited date and time and the names of those present, and told Whitehead, "Thank you for coming in so promptly, Mr Whitehead. I'm sure you know what this is about."

Whitehead's solicitor said, "My client wants to make it known that he is here of his own free will, to volunteer information that might be pertinent to your investigation."

He was a fat young man, with skin as white and smooth as wax, in a chalk-stripe Jermyn Street suit and polished brown Lobb Brothers shoes that probably cost more than I got for six months' work.

McArdle lit a cigarette and locked his gaze on Whitehead's and said, "We need to talk about what we found on your computer."

The solicitor said smoothly, "Again, my client has allowed you to examine his portable computer of his own free will."

McArdle ignored him. "You know what we found," he said to Whitehead. "The question is, do you want to talk about it?"

"Of course I want to talk," Whitehead said. "I'm here, aren't I?" He was a professionally arrested adolescent with an unlined, artificially tanned face and a facile, ingratiating manner. His black hair was shaved around the sides of his head and grown long on top, so that it looked like a small animal had fallen asleep on his skull. He said, "It was just a silly mistake, that's all."

McArdle drew on his cigarette and said, "A mistake, sir?"

"Is it okay if I smoke too?" Whitehead didn't wait for permission, but pulled out a slim transparent packet of black cigarettes and lit one. "You should try these," he told us, with a smile intended to charm, and pulled a couple of sealed packets from inside his jacket and dropped them onto the desk. He wore loose trousers of some silvery, silky synthetic, a collarless jacket of the same material, and a white shirt, top button fastened, no tie. A cheap, clunky watch hung loose on his wrist, its dial stamped with the star-in-a-circle logo of an American company that traded in athletic gear. The same logo had somehow been burnt into the silvery material of his jacket and trousers, a densely repeated pattern visible only at certain angles.

McArdle said mildly, "You were going to tell me about this mistake, sir."

"Of course," Whitehead said. "Sorry. I just happen to be very enthusiastic about these cigarettes. Well, this is the thing. I said before that I didn't know anything about Sophie's website. I'm rather afraid that wasn't true."

"Did you ever watch it, sir?"

"Sure, but purely as a favour, yeah? Sophie said that she wanted feedback."

"You looked at her website because she wanted feedback."

"Yes."

"And what form did this feedback take? Did you send her any emails, for instance?"

"No, that wasn't the deal."

"Did you ever comment on her site at all?"

"Not by email. She made a bit of a fuss, because she wanted something she could incorporate into her work, but I told her that I didn't want to be part of that. That we had a private deal."

"A private deal."

"Well, we were neighbours. We talked. I gave her the benefit of my expertise. And that's all there was to it."

"Remind me again, sir. How well did you know Ms Booth?"

"I knew her as a neighbour. Apart from her website I suppose we were on nodding terms. I gave her a few samples every now and then, but that's part of my job."

"Samples?"

"Cigarettes. Free software. T-shirts. That kind of thing. I run teams of student brand-managers, yeah? They give out samples of the latest software, beers, cigarettes, chocolate bars. Shit like that. You know, to increase brand awareness. Sometimes I had stuff left over, and I would give it to Sophie. I suppose that I should have told you this before."

"That's all right, sir. So, you gave her these samples, and she told you about her website."

"She explained to me what it was, and I thought I would take a look. And, what I came here to tell you, is that I did take a look that night."

"The night she was murdered."

"Yes." Whitehead leaned towards McArdle, eager to deliver his story. "I received an email from her, telling me that she was going to give one of her performances, and I thought I'd take a look. It seemed a bit extreme, compared to her other stuff, but I didn't think it was for real. It was only when you caught up with me in Brighton that I realized what had happened. And then I'm afraid that I panicked."

"And you didn't tell us the truth in your previous interview because you were panicked by what you had seen."

Whitehead nodded vigorously. "That's right. I mean, I've never been involved with something like this before."

McArdle made a production of consulting the file he had brought in. He said, "You told us that you knew nothing about Sophie Booth's website."

Whitehead nodded again. "Yes I did, but I admit now that I was very foolish. What I saw—"

"We'll get to that in a minute," McArdle said. "You gave Ms. Booth freebies, and she allowed you to view her website. Would this have been on a regular basis?"

"I can't really say."

"Once a night? More than that?"

"Not as often as that, I think."

"Once or twice a week, perhaps."

"It wasn't really my thing," Whitehead said.

"You mean the arty-farty performance art kind of thing, or the young woman naked in her room kind of thing?"

"Well, both."

"But you were aware that Sophie Booth displayed herself in that way."

Whitehead coloured up under his fake tan. "Of course I was. She told me."

"I must object," the sleek young solicitor said. "I find this line of questioning aggressive and demeaning to my client, and an invasion of his privacy. He has come forward of his own free will and has admitted to viewing Ms Booth's website, and to being an inadvertent witness to her murder. He has admitted that he foolishly concealed those facts from you on the occasion of his first interview, but he now freely admits his mistake. Unless you have specific charges, I really think I must ask you to bring this interview to an end."

"Not yet, sir," McArdle said. "Perhaps I should remind you

that we asked Mr Whitehead to come here. He did not volunteer."

"Nevertheless," the solicitor said, "he has volunteered to tell the truth."

"Yes," McArdle said, "and I have to say there are a couple of points I don't quite understand. So let's try and clear them up, shall we?"

"Why not?" Whitehead said. He leaned back in his chair, trying to look nonchalant, but his hand was shaking when he fed his cigarette to his lips.

"You saw pictures of Ms Booth being killed, but you didn't alert the police."

"Because I thought it was a performance."

"And on the same night, you left your house in Oxford and travelled to Brighton."

"I had some work there. It's what we in the trade call a hot spot, yeah? Lots of students and young singles with good disposable incomes, lots of clubs. Tremendous demographics."

"But you didn't tell your wife where you had gone."

"To tell the truth, we had a bit of a row that evening. Technically, I suppose, you could say we're looking at a separation, but we still share the house."

McArdle stubbed out his cigarette. "You had a row. Your wife went to work. You took a look at Sophie Booth's website."

"I looked at my emails," Whitehead said impatiently. "One said that Sophie was giving a performance. So I took a look."

"And then you went to Brighton."

"That's right."

"You told us at your first interview, sir, that you were at home when your wife returned. Are you sure about that?"

"Well, perhaps we missed each other by a few minutes."

"You drove straight down to Brighton."

"Yes."

"What route did you take?"

"I don't know. The usual one, I suppose. M40, M25, M23."

"And you didn't see the news about Ms Booth's murder."

"No. I don't watch much TV."

"And you didn't answer your mobile. We got the number from your wife, Mr Whitehead, and called you several times."

"I leave the message service on because of my work," Whitehead said. "Work at night, sleep at day, yeah?"

"But you didn't call us back."

"I suppose that was a mistake."

"Despite the fact that you had seen something that resembled a murder."

Whitehead stubbed out his cigarette, avoiding McArdle's gaze. "Okay, it was a mistake. I fucked up. But that isn't a crime."

"You didn't call us, but you did try and erase the evidence of what you had seen." McArdle looked at me. "What was it he did?"

"He reformatted the hard drive," I said.

"But that didn't erase the picture files."

"We were able to recover them."

"Look," Whitehead said, "I told you. I panicked."

McArdle said, "So by then you were fairly sure, sir, that you had seen Sophie murdered. But you still didn't contact us."

The solicitor said, "I do hope this is leading somewhere, Chief Inspector."

"I'm trying to establish why Mr Whitehead tried to erase those files," McArdle said.

"You don't have to say any more, James," the solicitor said. "Not unless they charge you with something."

"No," Whitehead said. "I want to clear this up. What if I did think that I had seen Sophie Booth murdered? It wasn't as if I was actually there, was it? It was just pictures on my computer."

"Yes," McArdle said, "pictures of the pretty young girl next door who gave you the means to spy on her any time. I can understand it. You have problems with your marriage, you have those long evenings alone. Nothing wrong with a bit of voyeurism as long as the subject is willing. And it's art, too. Even better. Except the pictures you saw on Saturday June 5 were of a real murder, and by downloading them you became an accessory to that murder."

Whitehead shook his head. His solicitor said, "Am I to understand that you are going to charge my client?"

McArdle ignored him. "Did you have sexual relations with Sophie Booth, Mr Whitehead?"

"My client won't answer that," the solicitor said.

"No," Whitehead said, "I want to answer. And the answer is no."

"Because wanking isn't real sex, is it?" McArdle said. "Is that what you were doing last Saturday, when she was killed?"

"Now that really is enough," the solicitor said.

Whitehead said, "Look, can I have a private word with my solicitor?"

McArdle and I waited outside. A few minutes later, the solicitor came out, grim-faced. He said, "My client has made a foolish mistake, but he's willing to make a formal statement about it."

McArdle said, "He saw a murder and he didn't report it. He lied about his alibi, and he tried to hide the evidence, too."

"The alibi was a genuine mix-up," the solicitor said. "But he's willing to cooperate now."

McArdle said, "He could have driven up to London and done the deed."

The solicitor said, "Do you have evidence that he did?"

"We're still checking the traffic cameras," McArdle admitted.

"I see. Then unless you find positive evidence that my client wasn't where he says he was, I assume he is free to go."

McArdle said, "I did a background check on your client. He earned a couple of cautions as a student, one for public drunkenness, another for possession of marijuana. He also has a history of poor credit, and his cards are maxed out."

"Hardly the makings of a serious criminal," the solicitor said.

"Who knows what else we might find if we start some serious digging?"

"I hardly think that is called for," the solicitor said.

"I can't promise anything," McArdle said, "but Mr. Whitehead will probably be all right so long as he agrees to make a full statement. That includes everything about his relationship with Sophie Booth, nothing left out. He's admitted his marriage is over, so he hasn't got anything to worry about on that score, has he?"

The solicitor thought about this for thirty seconds, then nodded. He knew that McArdle could issue a blanket Information Disclosure Order, open up Whitehead's email and web browser cache, ransack his bank accounts, credit-card and phone records, and run the data through an expert program that would reconstruct his life and look for anything that suggested possible criminal activity. Under that kind of intense scrutiny, no one appears entirely innocent. Regular withdrawals of cash from the same machine suggest a drug habit; unexplained credit-card transactions correlated with visits to certain websites suggest addiction to pornography; purchase of books or spikes from foreign Web retailers suggests at the least evasion of VAT payment, at worst, importation of material contrary to the 2006 Internet Regulation and Content Control Act. The feather of your innocence can never counterbalance the mass of information your life accrues.

"I'll apprise my client of the seriousness of his position," the solicitor said. "He has come here to cooperate, and I'm sure that he will."

"He had better," McArdle said. "Otherwise I promise you that I will take a very long and very hard look at him."

"There's one other thing," the solicitor said. "My client would like to know when he can have his computer back. He says that he needs it for his work."

16

It was almost eleven when I got home. I cracked open a beer and nuked a frozen pizza and unboxed my new toy.

The manual had been written by a lying bastard with the technical competence of a four-year-old, and translated into English from the original Japanese by someone with no working knowledge of either language. At best, a pocket dictionary had been involved at some point. But after an hour or so, I had more or less worked out how to use the thing's basic functions.

It was a web-book the size and thickness of an old-fashioned mouse mat, a piece of illegally imported greyware whose use explicitly broke the 2006 Internet Regulation and Content Control Act. It had a built-in modem dedicated to the American freeserve ISP that licensed it, a pressure-sensitive mouse pad, a voice-recognition program, and a palm-sized screen made of a layer of silicon circuitry just fifty nanometres thick, deposited on a flexible polyester support. You could roll it up and use it to swat flies. Eventually, you could get the modem to dial up the ISP, and find the messenger menu within the dumb browser.

I dictated an email.

We can talk privately now. If you're as good as you say you are, you'll know why. No promises, no guarantees, but I'll listen to what you have to say.

It seemed like too much. It seemed like not enough. I sent it in reply to the message I'd received from the remailer in Cuba.

Five minutes later, my mobile rang. My heart turned over, but it was only Julie, who wanted to tell me about her evening out.

"I was taken to, you won't believe this, a puppet theatre."

"Puppets?"

"It's about two hundred years old. The guy who's acting as liaison between us and the office management insisted that we went along. The longer you stay in this country, the stranger it gets. Tell me about your day, Dixon. How goes it?"

I told her about my day. I said, "I wish it was going somewhere, but none of the leads seem to add up to anything. Of course, we could get lucky, and forensics will find a fibre that's only produced by goats on the south slope of a certain Peruvian mountain, which our suspect just happened to have visited only last month."

"You have a suspect?"

"There are about a hundred suspects from all over the world, and most of them are hiding behind anonymous freeserve accounts."

I was sitting on the flat's tiny balcony, stripped down to shorts. It was just gone midnight, but the old bricks of the wall still radiated heat and the air was hot and heavy. A thunderstorm rumbled far off to the north. Every time sheets of heat lightning flickered at the horizon, the phone connection popped and crackled. Archimedes the Wonder Owl sat on his perch, somehow managing to look wisely attentive. Lou Reed was singing a twenty-year-old song about the Last Great American Whale.

Julie told me about the badges she and Tim Leyland had given the office workers, each tagged with the wearer's job and top five work priorities, readable by tiny scanners spiked to the walls.

They were constructing a picture of the human traffic in the offices, webs of affinities, patterns of attraction and avoidance. From this data, they could begin to apply space syntax to the reorganization of desks and services and departments.

I got up and went inside to get another beer from the fridge, the mobile tucked between my shoulder and ear. Archimedes turned his head through 180 degrees as he tracked me.

"Aha!" Julie said. "Another beer." Then, "What's up, Dixon?"

I had stopped in front of the diagrams Julie had once given me. On a silly sentimental impulse, I'd stuck them to the kitchen's bulletin board. I could barely make them out in the gloom. A stadium, an advertising-agency office, a hospital, stripped down to corridors and voids overlain with lines shading from green through yellow and orange to red, thickening, thinning, spattered with clots where people gathered. Associative knots, solitary loops, dense channels of flow. Beneath them was a small photocopy of a diagram I had found in Greil Marcus's *Lipstick Traces*, recording the movements of a student in the sixteenth *arrondissement* of Paris over the course of a year. The black overlay on the map of Paris looked like an agitated mosquito blurred by long exposure.

Julie said, "Are the tales of my fabulous working life boring you? I tried to phone you earlier, when I got back from the puppet show, but your mobile was switched off."

"I was in the middle of an interview."

"Then I fell asleep while watching truly bad TV. Why is all TV in Europe so horrible?"

"They don't think that TV's really culture."

There was a faint metallic whisper as Archimedes shuffled on his perch by the window. Julie said, "What are you looking at, in the dark in London? I hope you aren't brooding about us. Either it'll work out or it won't."

Of course I had been brooding about us, but I couldn't admit that. I said, "I was wondering about Wreckless Eric."

"He must be a musician. No, wait, I know him. 'Reconnaiz Chéri.' "

"And 'Whole Wide World.' His two hits."

"I even remember a bit of that one," she said, and sang a line of the refrain.

"He was part of the pub rock scene, signed up with Stiff Records. There were a few singles, every one lower in the charts than the one before, a couple of tracks of *Live Stiffs Live*, several LPs that sold less and less well, a *Best of* I used to own. He had a brief moment in the light, and then he vanished without trace."

Julie laughed. "Is he a suspect?"

"I was revisiting my past. You take things you know for granted, and then suddenly you want corroboration."

"You could ask Nick. Or there'll be something about him on the Web. Everything is on the Web."

"I always think of that as cheating."

"It's where the information flows, Dixon. It's where you and I are right now, in the space between our phones."

"You think it's a real place. I know it isn't."

"There's no distance between us, that's how real it is. I could be right there in your ear, Dixon. I could be right there in your head."

"Like a mosquito."

"Buzz buzz buzz," Julie said softly, and rang off.

17

I had been sitting in the Transit van with four uniforms for more than twenty minutes when Alan Rudd, the Man With The Plan, finally climbed into the shotgun seat and told us that we were ready to go.

Even though the Transit was parked on the shady side of Vine Street station's yard, it was swelteringly hot inside, and smelled strongly of sweaty coppers and their breakfasts. It was ten past ten in the morning and already over eighty-three degrees. There was a 5 per cent possibility of rain. Ozone, nitrogen dioxide and carbon monoxide levels exceeded recommended guidelines; the elderly and those with heart complaints were advised to stay indoors. Alison Somers was slated to give evidence in the Martin trial this afternoon. I'd received no reply to my email.

Alan Rudd told the uniforms, "You'll wait outside until you get the word, lads. No nonsense, all right? Let any punters leave nice and orderly. We just want the naughty stuff today, not warm bodies."

The uniforms nodded. They were eager to get into action. As far as the good old British bobby's concerned, there's nothing like a bit of book-burning first thing in the morning to set you up for the rest of the day.

Alan Rudd had a warrant for a raid on a shop in the back end of King's Cross, following up the first real break on the case. He had set ADESS on Ben Perry's tail, and yesterday evening, not twelve hours after the interview in his headmaster's office, the system had followed the boy all the way from his home in West Hampstead, along the Northern Line to King's Cross, and a back-street shop well known to be fronting a porn outlet. Alan had shown me on his mobile the last scene of this jerky, two-frames-a-second movie, a dry cold narrative that was all action and no reaction, Ben Perry's small figure highlighted by a pale aura, an unwitting star seen almost entirely in long shot as ADESS switched from camera to camera, up the escalators of King's Cross and out onto the streets. Caught in this ruthless unsleeping gaze, we are all of us reduced to strutting meat puppets, the individual dramas of our lives exposed as nothing more than a string of banal contingencies.

"I'd say he was getting more stock," Alan said, when the boy, seen from across the street, vanished into the shop. "The little toerag wants to be back in business as soon as possible."

"Have you talked to him yet?"

"Oh, I think we'll pull him after we do the shop, don't you? After all, he's going to be safely in school all day."

It was a slim lead, but we didn't have anything better to do. No one had made any headway in finding out who was making the data spikes. Rumours of an illegal spike-burning operation in short-term-rent offices at the edge of the City had turned up nothing; Alan Rudd reckoned that someone had been having some fun at our expense.

We all piled out as soon as the Transit van pulled up on the double yellows outside the shop. Some comedian dragging a dog on a string with one hand and clutching a can of Special Brew in the other gave an ironic cheer. The uniforms took up their positions; Alan Rudd and I went through the plastic strips that curtained the doorway. The inside was not much bigger than a single-car garage. A long time ago, probably in the previous century, it had been painted white. One wall was lined with racks of face-out sheaths and jewel cases. A selection of Disney movies hung like shiny fruit from a metal tree topped by a cardboard outline of a cartoon crow wearing a homburg. A fan pushed stale warm air about.

Alan Rudd showed the warrant to the pimply boy behind the little counter, and started right in.

"I have a warrant to search these premises under the Protection of Children Act . . ."

The boy had been reading a thick textbook, *The Physiology of Insects*, laid open on the counter between the grubby cash register and the six-inch monitor for the CCTV camera mounted over the doorway. He closed it and said wearily, "Take anything you want, all right? I only work here."

Rudd said, "How old are you, lad?"

"Look, I was told all this was legal. Will this get back to my college?"

"Only if you want to tell them. When I've finished with you, you can give the owner a call. I expect he'll want to know what we're about. Meanwhile, you'll take a minute to listen to this," Alan Rudd said, and started to read out the warrant again.

I called in the uniforms and we all went into the back. The tiny stockroom smelt of mould and was lit by a feeble bulb hanging from a fraying electrical cord. There was a broken sink in one corner, a stack of empty cardboard boxes, four identical grey metal cabinets. I rattled the locked doors; one of the uniforms produced a huge pair of bolt cutters and snipped the cheap padlocks one by one by one, the noise hard and bright in the tiny space.

No spikes or DVDs, just slippery piles of magazines in plastic wrappers. Danish and German stuff with the usual subtle titles and covers. *Anal Rampage. Anal Lust. Schoolgirl Sluts.* That scholarly feminist tome, *Big Fuckin' Tits.* That affectionate examination of the love act's tenderest moment, *Cum All Over.*

I dropped a selection on the counter, and Alan Rudd said to the boy, "You've never sold any of this stuff?"

The boy looked at the slew of magazines and said, "Honestly, Officer, I've never seen these before."

"Come off it, lad," Alan Rudd said. "This is the kind of stuff you sell to those special customers, isn't it? The ones who know what to ask for."

"This is a video shop," the boy said, in case we hadn't noticed.

I said, "And I suppose you only sell kosher spikes."

The boy shrugged.

Alan Rudd sighed. "Hear no evil, see no evil, eh? I've got your name and address, lad, and you've made your phone call, so there's no point you hanging around any longer. I suggest you take your book and go and find more regular employment to pay off your student loan. Go on. Get out of here."

"I should wait for—"

"We'll have a word with your boss. I doubt very much that he'll be in the mood to give you your severance pay, so I suggest you piss off before I think of something to charge you with.

"Young idiot," he added under his breath, as the boy stuffed his book into a backpack and hurried out into the sunlight.

I stood outside with Alan Rudd while the uniforms fetched plastic evidence crates and started to load them.

"I have a feeling that the spikes will turn out to be kosher," I said. "Someone knew we were coming."

Alan Rudd plucked a spike from a crate carried out by one of the uniforms. *Snow White*, according to the card mount. "We're going to have to look at every one of these anyway," he said, "just in case they're not what they say they are."

"Dork, Sloppy, Groucho, Peepy, Retardo, and I forget the other one. Why is it you always forget the last dwarf?"

Rudd laughed. "You only managed five."

"I'm thinking of *Snow White and the Six Dorks*. Wallace Wood. A comic, not the movie, but you get the idea."

"Sleepy, Sneezy, Dopey. Doc. Grumpy, Happy . . . Shit."

"You see my point."

"I must have watched that fucking movie about a hundred times. My kids love crap like that. I always thought it would have made a better plot if one of the dwarfs had been a plant. Someone working undercover for the Wicked Stepmother."

"She had her own form of surveillance, as I remember."

"There would be a dramatic revelation when he was discovered tying shoes to his knees. The dwarfs would suddenly realize why he was called Lofty."

It was pleasant to stand in the sun and exchange a bit of banter while the uniforms loaded the shop's stock into the Transit. Most British police spend their spare moments pissing and moaning or talking about football. We're rank amateurs of the conversational interlude compared to our American colleagues, who, if you can believe the books and movies, philosophize in paragraphs so nicely rounded they could be seamlessly inserted into the opinion pages of the quality newspapers. I felt that Alan Rudd and I were doing our bit to redress that imbalance.

I said, "You don't know anything about a raid just this Sunday past, do you? A journalist out in Walthamstow."

"What were we after?"

"Horror flicks. One of my colleagues went along. He was wondering if the guy was going down for it."

"That kind of thing, usually it's the result of a silly little squabble between neighbours. Generally isn't worth a prosecution. One party informs on the other, and, next thing, we're knocking down the door, marching out with some poor bastard's movie collection, and notching another point on the crime stats.

Unless some kiddy porn turns up, there'll be a formal caution and destruction of any unlicensed material, and that'll be an end to it."

A silver Mercedes two-seater city car, the sort of runabout that looks like the front half of a bad chop job, pulled up sharply behind the Transit. Alan Rudd made a point of consulting his watch and said, "A better response time than we can manage with bells and sirens."

A heavyset middle-aged man with a hectic complexion and a shock of unnaturally black hair hauled himself out of the Merc. He wore a yellow mohair suit with a red handkerchief in the breast pocket, and polished black shoes with gold chains across their tongues: Mr Toad dressed by Alexander McQueen.

"I know this cunt of old," Alan Rudd told me. "Before they turned Soho into Disney World, he ran a licensed sex shop in Frith Street. Trading standards did him for passing off 1970s sex comedies as hard-core."

"My God," the man said, pointing to a uniform carrying an evidence crate full of magazines to the Transit. "My God, Mr Rudd, you don't have a right to do this to me."

Rudd handed him a copy of the warrant, showed him one of the magazines. "We found them in lockers on your property, Harry. Don't tell me: you were looking after them for a friend."

"I've never seen those before," the man said indignantly. "You planted those on me, Mr Rudd. I'm shocked."

"I also have reason to believe that a number of video spikes on sale at these premises have been illegally imported from the United States. I'm sure you know it's an offence to sell spikes which haven't been approved by the British Board of Film Certification, Harry, what with you being a film buff from way back."

Harry pulled the handkerchief from the top pocket of his jacket and mopped his florid face. His fingers were heavy with gold rings. "The magazines must belong to the previous tenant.

I've never opened those lockers, Mr Rudd. I don't even have keys for the padlocks."

Rudd took out his phone, tapped his pen on the blank screen, and said archly, "And who might the previous tenant be, Harry?"

"You would have to ask the letting agency, Mr Rudd. And while you're doing that, perhaps I'll be having a word with my lawyer. He will certainly want to examine this." Harry flapped the copy of the warrant.

"If I were you, Harry," Alan Rudd said, "I would definitely have a word with my lawyer."

"I'm a respectable businessman," Harry said, "as you know very well, Mr Rudd. I have nothing to fear from the likes of you."

The uniforms were carrying out the last of the haul. They had run out of plastic crates, and were using cardboard boxes. I said to Harry, "Perhaps you know the name of the seventh dwarf in *Snow White*."

"I sell them," he said, folding his handkerchief into his top pocket with great dignity, "but I don't have to watch them." He was already thinking of getting the place restocked and finding a replacement for the lad who'd sensibly legged it. He knew we hadn't found anything important.

18

I was helping Alan Rudd sort through the booty from the raid when Roger Court phoned. Tim Coveney had turned up at the workshop, taken his pieces, and left.

I said, "How did he seem?"

"What do you mean?"

"Did he seem nervous or excitable in any way?"

"I suppose he seemed a bit preoccupied."

"Did he say anything to you?"

"Not really. Nothing out of the ordinary."

"He didn't say where he was going."

"He just wrapped his pieces and left."

"And you didn't mention my visit yesterday."

"I was starting up the furnaces," Roger Court said, "and he was wrapping his pieces. We barely exchanged ten words."

I made my excuses to Alan Rudd, dialled the Bunker and entered the account number I just happened to have read off an invoice that had been lying on top of Tony McArdle's In tray last night. I had Tim Coveney's meagre file in my mobile's cache, including a copy of his driver's licence, and I squirted it down the line.

"About time," I said, when an ADESS operator finally called me back.

"We are processing your request as quickly as possible, sir," the ADESS operator said, "but we're currently working at 87 per cent capacity."

By now I was in my Mini, navigating the permanent traffic jam of Piccadilly Circus. I said, "What's your name?"

"Dana, sir."

"Listen up, Dana. The suspect is probably on foot, perhaps on a bus, most likely somewhere in the Kingsland/Dalston area. You have your microwave links and polygonal forcing routines. You have your eight crucial physiognomy points. Make all that stuff work for me."

"I'm doing my best with what I have, sir."

"What's the point of putting photos on driver's licences if you can't use them?"

"The licence is two years old, sir."

I cut in and out of the taxis and buses and delivery vans along Shaftesbury Avenue, gunned through an amber light at Cambridge Circus. A traffic camera flashed above me like an exploding star.

"Fuck."

"Sir?"

"The traffic is terrible, Dana. Help me out here."

"He's in the system, sir. It's searching now. Please be patient."

I saved some time cutting through the back streets of Bloomsbury, hot dirty air blowing through the open windows of the Mini. Cameras hung from walls at the corners of every street. An invisible electronic net spread across London, flexing in inquisitive knots. An intelligence vast and cold and unsympathetic at play in the world. I was in a queue at a set of traffic lights, waiting to turn onto Gray's Inn Road, when Dana said, "I may have him, sir."

"Where?"

"It's only an 81 per cent recognition factor, sir. The driver's licence—"

"Is he carrying anything?"

"He has a bag slung over his shoulder. He's just entering the Dalston/Kingsland station."

I did a quick triangulation in my head, cut out of the queue. Horns blared and another star exploded in my windscreen as I pulled hard left through the red lights and accelerated towards King's Cross.

"He's on the westbound platform of the North London line," Dana reported. "I have a squad car about ten minutes away, if you require backup."

"Leave him to me, Dana."

Traffic was solid in the one-way system that fed into Euston Road. I got out of the Mini and clambered onto the bonnet, saw that the four lines of traffic were being funnelled down to a two-lane roadblock.

Dana said, "A train has arrived. Subject has entered the train. I have him on the carriage camera."

"I didn't know you could do that," I said, and restarted the Mini and pulled into the empty bus lane (another star exploding overhead), drove all the way up to the concrete barrier, parked and flashed my warrant card at the peace warden swaggering towards me.

"Watch the car," I told him, and ran.

I flashed my card again at a startled ticket inspector when I barged through the barrier at King's Cross, nearly took a tumble as I flew down the stalled escalator. Luck was with me. A train was standing at the platform of the northbound Northern Line Tube when I arrived. I strap-hung two stops, my entire skin greasy with sweat, the headset of my mobile hooked around my ear. Dana told me that Tim Coveney was still on the train at Highbury & Islington, that he was still on the train at Caledonian Road.

Nearly everyone seemed to get off the tube at Camden. Holding my warrant card above my head and yelling *police business* didn't do much to make them step out of my way. Just as I went through the barrier at the top of the escalator, Dana said, "I see you, sir. Suspect leaving the train, at Camden Road."

I was already running past the glass-and-steel canopy of Nicholas Grimshaw's Sainsbury's, and got to the entrance of the station thirty seconds later, just as Tim Coveney came out.

B e careful," Tim Coveney said. "They're how I make my living."

We were sitting on a wooden bench in a little triangle of bushes and dry grass across the road from the station. I was looking through the shallow bowls nested in cocoons of Bubble Wrap inside his black rubber shoulder bag: white glass shot through with a swirl of lustrous bronze, thickly bubbled translucent green glass, clear glass with alternating layers of suspended flakes of gold and silver and aquamarine, clear glass that blushed a delicate violet beneath my touch . . .

I said, "How much do you get for these?"

"You're looking at fifty quid a go, more for the smart pieces."

Tim Coveney was a thin, tall lad with a sulky face, hair cut short and dyed black, a silver ring through one ear. His faded green T-shirt unironed and torn along the seam under one arm, the front specked with burn holes, baggy camo-pattern army-surplus trousers, dirty white Converse high-tops. He visibly relaxed when I closed up the flap of the shoulder bag and handed it to him.

"You've got more than enough in there to get a long way from

London," I said. When he didn't say anything, I added, "Roger Court told you about my visit, didn't he? He told you that the police were looking for you, and you decided to make some quick money so you could get out of town."

"It isn't like that."

"But you were on your way to Camden Market, weren't you? Which is where you sell your stuff."

"I told you. It's how I make my living."

"So you said. The trouble is, I don't believe you. You move out of your room, and now you're looking to make some quick money. Someone more suspicious than me might think that you have something to hide."

"I already talked to you lot. Why are you giving me a hard time?"

"I want to clear up a few things," I said. "We can sit here and get our breath back and talk, Tim, or we can make it formal. I could charge you with obstructing a police officer. An interview-room, a tape recorder and a video camera, or a nice little chat here in the sunshine. Your call."

"I don't need to talk to you, all right, because I haven't done anything."

"Calm down, Tim, calm down. Do you want one of these?"

"Jesus, don't you have proper fags?"

I lit up, blew smoke. "Are you always this nervous?"

Tim Coveney said, with a feeble flicker of bravado, "You lot make me nervous."

"What have you got against the police, Tim?"

"Look, I don't want to talk about it any more, all right? That's all it is. It does my head in." He looked at me and said, "Give me a fag, will you?"

I gave him the packet and my lighter. He lit up, trying to hide his trembling fingers.

"Where are you staying at present, Tim?" A pause. I said, "I think I told you that I know you moved out of your room."

"I'm staying with a mate, all right? You don't have to bring him into this."

"I'll need his address."

Tim Coveney blew out smoke, and gave it.

"Why did you move out of your room?"

"Because I felt my head was coming apart."

"But you were still able to do your work at the glassblower's."

"Roger isn't a glassblower, all right? And I wasn't hiding, otherwise I wouldn't have gone back there."

"Come off it. You went back to get this stuff because you needed to raise some quick cash. You're frightened of something. Why don't you tell me about it?" Silence. I said, "Let's talk about Sophie's work. You helped her with her performances. With the little bits of theatrics she put out on her website."

Tim Coveney shrugged, his eyes on the traffic moving along the road beyond the edge of the little park. The grass was dry and sun-bleached. The cracked earth under the bushes twinkled with crushed cans and shards of glass. He said, "I wasn't the only one helping her, and it was just messing about, that's all. Having a laugh. Look, I already talked about this."

"I just need to go over it with you again, to get it straight. You know how it is with police, Tim, they always like to get things straight. That's all this is. We're just having a quiet word. No corroboration, nothing on the record. I've already talked with Lucy Matthews, and she's told me the kind of things the three of you did together. Was anyone else involved?"

"I wouldn't know."

"And did you and Sophie do anything without Lucy?" He shrugged again, and I added, "Lucy said that you did. What kind of things did you get up to?"

"I told you, it was just messing about."

"Let me tell you about police work, Tim. Mostly it's trying to get at the truth, because for some reason people find it difficult to tell the truth to the police. Even honest people start leaving stuff out when they're talking to us—lies by omission. Or they play down their part in something, or say they didn't see anything when really they saw it plain as day, because they don't want to get involved. As is only natural, since police work deals with the messy side of human nature. But all this means the police get very good at telling when someone's being truthful, and when they're not. And I'm very much afraid that you're not being truthful with me, Tim. So let's try again, and let's make it straightforward, because I think that in your heart of hearts you want to tell the truth."

"I have been telling the truth. We were just messing about, right?"

"You don't think much of her art."

"What do you mean?"

"You said you were messing about, but it was her final-year project, wasn't it? It was as important to her as your bits of glass are important to you."

"No way. Performance art, conceptual art, all that stuff, it isn't the same at all."

"You don't like it."

"I think it's middle-class shite."

"But you helped out Sophie."

"Yeah, well. Anything for a pal, you know?"

"She was a friend, then."

"Of course she was!"

"And what did you two get up to, as friends?"

"It wasn't like that."

"Like what, Tim?"

"Like whatever you were trying to say."

"You're making something simple very hard, Tim." He didn't reply. I said, "How did you two get to be friends? You were doing different kinds of art, and you're from very different backgrounds."

"That's not supposed to matter," he said with some bitterness. "Not in college."

"But it does."

"Yeah. 'Course it does. It always does. That's why this country is so fucked up. People only see what they want. So someone like me, someone from Liverpool, from a working-class family, he just has to be a bit of a hooligan, doesn't he?"

"I take it you didn't make many friends in college."

"I have plenty of mates at home."

"You have a girlfriend at home, Tim, is that right?"

"This isn't anything to do with her," he said sharply. He was hunched at the edge of the bench, all elbows and knees and exposed nerves.

"And the other student who was helping Sophie. Lucy Matthews. How would you say that she was like you?"

"Lucy's a Goth. The only Goth in the whole college. She's so out-of-date it isn't even ironic."

"So you were both out of the mainstream."

"I suppose, yeah."

"And was Sophie out of the mainstream too?"

"She didn't give a shit about anyone. That's what I liked about her."

"Were you sweet on her, Tim? I know you might think it's private, but it would help me if I could understand your relationship with her."

A pause. "I liked her."

I said, "And she liked you."

"Yeah. Yeah, she did."

"Did she have a boyfriend?"

He shrugged.

"Lucy Matthews said she was a bit of a flirt, Tim. Did she flirt with you?"

"We were mates. It wasn't like that."

"Did you ever log on to her website?"

"Maybe. Once or twice. For a laugh, like."

"It wasn't just the performances, was it? She did other stuff as well. I've talked with her tutor about it."

"She left the cameras on, yeah. You know, put her life on the Web. Hardly a big deal. Millions of people do it."

"Not in this country. Or at least, not the kind of things she was doing. I've seen some of it, Tim. And I know she was running her site on an illegal server. How often did you watch her?"

"Just for a laugh sometimes."

"Did you see her wanking, Tim?"

"What? No, wait, that isn't—"

"Because I know she was into that kind of thing, Tim. One of her fans put the pictures up on his website. Come on, just between you and me. I need to know what else she did." Another silence. I said, "Do you want Sophie's killer caught?"

"Of course I do!"

"Then forget about any laws she broke. That doesn't matter now. Just answer my questions truthfully."

"I am. Christ. I already told you lot everything I know."

"I've read the transcript of that interview, Tim, and pretty thin reading it makes. There's Sophie's computer, for instance."

"What about it?"

"Not the one her uncle bought her a month ago. Not the G10, and not the old one she was using as a server, either. But the one you have. The laptop."

"You mean the one that was stolen? I don't know anything about it."

"Don't lie to me, Tim. I can smell the lies coming off you and I'm liking you less and less because of it."

"It was stolen," he said.

"If it was stolen, how was it you were using it to look at Sophie's website?"

"I wasn't. I didn't."

"But you said that you did look at her website."

"Maybe I used the college's computers."

"I know about your record in Liverpool, Tim. Breaking and entering, stolen cars. How did a little tearaway like you get into a nice place like St Martin's?"

"Because I've got talent. They know about my record. It was all juvenile stuff. I've not done anything since I came down here."

"I wonder," I said. "I wonder if there aren't a few b and e's that might have your fingerprints on them. Perhaps from last night, when you were so hard to find."

"I was in the pub last night."

"Can you prove that?"

"The Old Meeting House over in Kentish Town. I played some pool, had a few drinks. I'm known there."

"If that checks out I'll take a look at b and e's on some other night, then. Don't think I won't do it, Tim, when I find out you've been lying to me. And you know I will find out. I'll put you away somewhere quiet and get a warrant to search for that laptop in your bedsit and in your mate's place. I know you have it because I know you won't have thrown away an expensive bit of equipment like that. I even know what you and Sophie did, because I read up on your police record, and I read the report she gave to the police as part of her insurance claim. You slim-jimmed her car door, an old Peugot 205 as I remember. You left the slim-jim lying there for the police to find, and Sophie told her insurance company that the laptop had been taken. So you had the laptop, and she got the insurance money."

"Look, suppose I explain what I did. Will you give me a break?"

"Let's hear it first."

"All it was, me and Sophie were friends, right? Good mates, all that kind of thing. And it came off the insurance, so it wasn't like it cost anyone anything."

"Is that how you put it to Sophie?"

"It was her idea, all right? She wanted a bit of excitement, she said. She'd locked her keys in her car once, and I showed her then how I could get the door open. When it came to the other thing, with the laptop, I told her she'd be better off smashing a window because that's how it's done around here, no one bothers with a slim-jim or even a coat hanger, but she didn't want to pay to have it fixed. And she said . . ."

"What did she say, Tim?"

"That it was more elegant."

"She got off on it, associating with a bit of rough like you."

Tim took a last drag on his cigarette and screwed the stub into the ground. He said, "You don't know her at all."

"And you didn't think to mention it to us."

"I didn't think it had anything to do with anything."

"I'll need to look at the laptop, Tim. That's all right with you, isn't it?"

"There isn't anything on it. She got rid of all her stuff before she gave it to me. She took it into her uncle's offices, and someone wiped it clean for her."

"Really. Why would she do a thing like that?"

"I don't know. But that's what she did. So you won't find anything on it, all right?"

"Still, I'd like to take a look. Where is it? Come on Tim, we've got this far, let's not spoil it."

He was watching the traffic again. He sighed, surrendering, and said softly, "In my room."

"Okay. Now, did she give you anything else?"

"What do you mean?"

"I mean disks, spikes, anything like that."

"No." It came a little too quickly.

"Because that's what people do. They exchange backups with people they trust. Did she trust you, Tim?"

"I told you. We were mates."

"Good enough mates that she'd trust you with her backups?"

He didn't say anything. I told him, "I'll look for them, Tim, in your room. And if I don't find them there, I'll turn over your mate's place."

"You won't find anything."

"Where is it then?"

He didn't reply.

I said, "It may have information on it that can help us find the man who killed Sophie."

"There's just the one."

"A data spike? Where is it?"

"I posted it."

"Where to?"

"To myself. At college."

"Do you know what was on it?"

"I didn't look. She said that it was for her show."

"The graduation show."

"She said that if anything happened, I was to play it then."

"If anything happened? What kind of thing?"

"She didn't tell me everything, okay? But she was excited about it. She said everyone would see." He twiddled his fingers. "Let me have another of those piss-awful cigarettes."

I gave him a tab and lit it for him. He sucked in smoke, and said, "How much trouble am I in?"

"I don't know, Tim. Why do you think you're in trouble?"

"She got a lot of emails about her work. Stupid stuff, most of it. Kids asking her to show more. Someone even proposed marriage. But there was this one guy, his stuff was different. Nastier."

"Where did these emails come from?"

"From Cuba. That's why Sophie didn't take it seriously."

"From an anonymous remailer in Cuba? He could have sent those emails from anywhere in the world, Tim. From next door."

Tim Coveney shrugged. "I wouldn't know about that. He said he knew all about her. He said that only he understood her. He called himself the Avenger. Creepy stuff. She kept copies. You must have seen them."

"Her computers were stripped out."

"Fuck. Well, she set up this email account, all right? She copied everything to it. She had a master list of the email addresses of everyone who made comments about her shows, too."

"At Wizard Internet. I know. I found out about it, but it had been stripped out."

Tim drew deeply on his cigarette. "I knew it. He's clever. She tried to set up a filter to keep him out once, but he got around it. He was some kind of hacker, I suppose. I told her to be careful, but she laughed it off. She said she had him under control."

"Do you know what she meant by that?"

"She said she'd made a deal with him. She was acting like she had this big secret."

"When was this?"

"A few days ago. We had an argument about it. I told her he was crazy, that she shouldn't encourage him."

"It probably doesn't help, Tim, but you were right."

"There's one more thing. I took a look at her site that night. I did most nights, you know? Not just when, well, when she asked me to. Just to see what she was doing. There was something creepy about it, but there was something that made you want to watch, too."

He was talking to himself now. He was working it out, making it into a story. I let him. I thought I knew where it was going.

He said, "Anyway, that night she sent me an email, saying that I should take a look at something special. So I did, and I saw her. There was a man with her. I watched a couple of minutes and she was there, naked in the chair. I didn't know. I didn't know what it was. If I'd known what it was, I'd have done something. Called you lot. Something. But I didn't know."

He looked at me, angry and defiant and scared.

I said, "You just saw a glimpse, and you got angry."

"I thought she was fucking someone. I thought she was doing it to get back at me because of the argument. It sickened me. It really did. I switched it off."

"What did you do then, Tim? Come on, give it up. It'll make you feel better when it's out. You won't have to carry it around any more."

Tim wouldn't look at me. "If I'd known . . . But I didn't know, all right? So I went out and had a few drinks. And all the time . . ."

"I know what you saw," I said. "And I think it wasn't enough for you to realize what was really going on."

"I could have saved her," he said.

"I don't think so," I said. "You were on the other side of London. It would all have been over by the time you got there."

"It was quick, then?"

I lied. "Yes. Yes, it was. But don't think about that. Think about what you saw. Was there anything you recognized? Anything that can be of help to us?"

"I saw that she was sitting on a chair. She was naked, and this fella was standing behind her."

"A big man."

He looked at me. "You've seen the pictures too."

"I want to know what you saw, Tim."

"He was big, yeah. A big fella. Long hair."

"It's all right, Tim. This is for Sophie."

"Well, he was holding her breasts. Lifting them up and squeezing them together. That's why I thought . . ." He took a breath. He said flatly, "I thought it was sex."

"Did you recognize him?"

"No. He was wearing something, too. A mask."

"What kind of mask?"

"It was that mad old woman from the last century. Sophie

asked me to look and that's what I saw. He was wearing a mask, that's why I thought it was one of her stupid little performances." Tim was crying now, tears running into two pulsing streams on either side of his nose and dripping from his chin. He said, "She didn't want people close to her. I thought she was fucking him to get at me."

I got the rest of it out of him in bits and pieces. He hadn't saved the two pictures. He'd banged off the computer and gone out to his pub and got drunk. He'd been jealous. He'd been angry. He thought he'd seen something meant to taunt him. And when he realized what had happened, when he realized what he had really seen, he got scared. He said that he had moved out of his room because he knew that the email must have been from Sophie's killer, not from Sophie, that the killer must have known about Sophie's website, that he must have got hold of the master list she kept, the list of people who had sent her emails.

"She was going to use them in her work," he said. "As a soundtrack or something."

"So you think he emailed everyone on that list."

Tim nodded. "That's what Sophie did, before we started one of her performance things. That's why I have to get out of town. The man who killed her knew about me."

19

I went with Tim Coveney to his friend's flat for the laptop, then caught the Tube to Holborn, walked over to St Martin's main building at Southampton Row, and had one of the porters retrieve the envelope Tim had sent to himself. My Mini was where I had left it, in the bus lane by the roadblock. A traffic ticket was stuck under its windscreen wipers. The peace wardens affected nonchalance as they watched me rip up the ticket and drive away.

An hour later, at T12, I switched on my computer and inserted Sophie Booth's data spike.

The computer's screen blanked; for a moment I thought a virus had booted itself up, but then a full-screen picture of Sophie Booth slid down. She was sitting cross-legged on her bed in the room where she had been murdered, looking up at the webcam in the corner of the ceiling, dressed in jeans and an oversized white shirt, the sleeves rolled up on her pale arms. Swags of stars twinkled across the ceiling. Candles burned in the fireplace.

She smiled and said, "I'm sorry, Tim. I know you'll have

been frantic, wondering where I've gone. That's why you're looking at what you thought was my backup spike, isn't it? I can't tell you where I've gone—I can't tell you *anything*. That's harsh I know, but that's how it has to be. It'll all come out soon enough, and then you'll know how I did all those tricks. Remember what I said, about fortune favouring the brave? Well, I deserve this, Tim. I saw my chance, and went for it. And now I'm gone."

I stared at my grainy reflection in the suddenly blank screen. The drive clicked and whirred and wouldn't give up the spike. I managed to reboot the computer, but there was nothing at all on the spike now.

How was I supposed to know that the file Sophie Booth had left behind would eat itself?

I put the spike back in its sheath and went upstairs, where I discovered that Charlie Wills had finished with Sophie Booth's laptop.

"Someone did a good job on it," he told me. "It was reformatted about a month ago, a very clean job by someone who knew exactly what they were doing. Every sector was overwritten with zeros before the operating system and programs were reinstalled."

"What about the web browser cache?"

"It had been set to purge itself every day, but no problem. I managed to retrieve most of the files that accumulated after the reformat." Charlie Wills swung to and fro in his chair. His long hair was loose today, flowing down the back of his clean white lab coat. He handed me a spike and said, "I found some dirty movies, just as you expected."

I asked him to take a look at Sophie Booth's spike, and went back to my computer and checked the compilation he had made. The beginning of the murder sequence, cut off before the killer settled down to his work, confirming Tim Coveney's story. A dozen clips of Sophie's solo home-made porn. And three sessions in which she was only the co-star.

I watched one all the way through, skipped through the other two. Everyone lies to the police.

There was one other movie clip, made three days before her murder.

Night, a medium-angle shot of the narrow street outside the building where Sophie Booth had lived and died. She stood underneath a streetlight in a long white dress. In the lower left-hand corner was some kind of aerial number, a date stamp, and a digital clock patiently accumulating seconds and minutes.

Sophie stood quite still for more than two minutes by the clock. Then she slowly spread her arms—the sleeves hung down like angel wings—and vanished, and there was only the street-lamp and the dark street beyond, and the uninterrupted count of the clock.

I watched the sequence again, and then again, trying to understand what I was seeing. The angle suggested that it had been taken by the security camera over the office door, the one Anthony Booth had used to demo the ADESS prototype in his salad days. Sophie must have had access to its output, made a recording, done a simple splice to make it seem that she disappeared, and edited in the clock.

It had the profound simplicity of the best magic tricks, I thought, as I watched it for the fourth time, but it was also haunting. The dark street, the girl in a halo of neon who suddenly becomes an angel, and disappears . . .

The phone rang. It was Charlie Wills. It seemed that the data spike had been wiped clean, everything overwritten with zeros except for a file-eating virus in the boot sector.

"A nasty little thing," Charlie Wills said. "It looks like it was triggered after a specific file was opened."

"Really. You can't recover anything?"

"Not a chance. It overwrote everything but itself about a hundred times. There's not even a ghost left."

On the screen, Sophie Booth smiled and spread her arms. And vanished.

Neither Tim Coveney nor his friend answered the bell at the tall narrow house in Kentish Town where he'd taken refuge, but I thought that I knew where he might be.

The Old Meeting House is an old-fashioned drinking den with two high-ceilinged bars and a back room with a big plasma-screen TV and a couple of pool tables. It was given low-level cosmetic surgery about ten years ago, but remains defiantly unthemed, unless the theme is drinking and smoking and watching sports TV—a pub-theme theme-pub.

It was midweek, midevening. Half a dozen hardened drinkers clung to the bar like limpets at the edge of a tide pool; a TV hanging over the raked bottles was showing the highlights of a Slovenian tree-felling contest.

Tim Coveney was sitting on one of the benches in the back room, a pool cue crooked between his legs and a pint of Guinness in his hand, watching as a boy his age, in baggy shorts and a mesh T-shirt, made a stretch at the table and missed a corner shot. I sat on a stool at the bar and ordered a Kronenbourg and fired up a tab and waited for Tim Coveney to notice me. He wore the same army-surplus trousers as this afternoon, and a denim vest open over a bare chest. He had a ring through his right nipple. He and his pal played with deliberation and elaborate banter, pausing between each shot like chess players so as to stretch the two pounds it cost for each game.

A pine tree fell in slow motion on the TV. An old bloke curled up on one of the bench seats in the corner woke briefly, fumbled out a flat bottle of Scotch and took a nip and went back to sleep.

After ten minutes or so, Tim finished his Guinness and came over for another, stopping halfway when he saw me.

"I don't believe this," he said.

"I've already ordered your drink," I said.

I had, too, and another Kronenbourg for me.

"I'm playing pool, all right? I'm in the middle of a game."

I went over to the table, winked at the boy in the mesh T-shirt, rolled the black ball into one of the corner pockets, and told him to get lost when he started to protest.

"I want a word," I told Tim. "The same deal as before. You can do it here, or in a cosy interview-room."

We sat at a table in the corner. I stretched my left leg straight out. It was aching badly, a sharp pulse deep inside the thighbone. I really had to start running again. Tim hunched over, drawing loops in the condensation on the outside of his pint glass of velvety black porter. He said, "When do I get that laptop back?"

I laughed at his cheek. "Apart from the fact it's evidence in a murder investigation, I think the insurance company might have something to say about that."

"Well it's mine, isn't it? You said you wouldn't tip them off. Look, what's this all about?"

"We're having a quiet word, Tim. Just you and me. No corroboration, nothing on the record. No fair, no foul. Do you understand that?"

"Make it quick."

"All right. I'll ask you straight. It's about what you got up to with Sophie."

"I told you about that."

"You did, up to a point. But now I need to get a few details straight."

"Will it help catch the fucker who did it?"

"I hope so." I stared into his face. "I want you to be honest with me, Tim. Nothing can hurt Sophie now, and if you're holding

something back because you think it will, you're not doing anyone a favour. Least of all yourself."

He looked down. "All right."

"You said that you did stuff with Sophie for her project. Sometimes it was you and Sophie and Lucy Matthews, but sometimes
just you and Sophie. I want to know the truth about the kind of
things you two got up to."

His eyes evaded my gaze. "I have been telling the truth."

"Most people think they know something about computers,
Tim. And some of them really do. Sophie did, for instance. But
most don't. The place I work at, T12, is very good at retrieving
computer files people think they've erased. Like those dirty little
movies you and Sophie made."

He jumped up and ran, knocking over a stool as he twisted
away from my lunge. I chased after him, through the doors and
across the pavement and into the road. Horns and brake squeals,
angry shouts. I slammed against the side of a rusty Vectra that
slewed across my path, the driver's face a white blur yelling
something I didn't hear. Ahead of me, Tim vaulted the square
bonnet of a parked Volvo and landed awkwardly on the pavement
on the other side, and I was on him before he could get up. He
tried to stand, but I had a good grip on his wrists and we both
staggered a couple of paces and fell over. A taxi's wheels
crunched past a foot from our heads. Someone was dodging
through the traffic towards us. It was Sandra Sands.

I yelled at Tim, my face a scant centimetre from his, "Tell
me, Tim! Tell me that you fucked her!"

He dropped his head and spewed a taupe stew. Not all of it
got on my shoes. He spat and coughed and then looked at me
and said, "I killed her, didn't I?"

Sandra Sands told me that Tony McArdle had learned about
the ADESS surveillance I'd placed on Tim Coveney when

the paperwork had arrived at the Murder Room for his signature. She had been sent to have a word with Tim; ADESS had tracked him to the Old Meeting House.

"I called this in, sir. I've been ordered to bring him back."

She looked very determined, her face pale in the orange glow of the streetlights, one hand gripping Tim Coveney's arm just above the elbow.

I said, "I'm already up to my neck in it, so another ten minutes won't make much difference."

"DCI McArdle is very pissed off, sir."

"You can wait in your car, DC Sands, or you can give me a hand."

"Is that a direct order, sir?"

"Absolutely."

We got Tim Coveney back to the pub and made him sit in a corner. I ordered a Coke and two double Jack Daniel's. The manager, a young man in a cheap suit and slicked-back hair, was reluctant to serve me, grumbling even after I had showed him my warrant card. "I nearly called the peacers," he said. "And I don't care if you *are* police, you're not local."

"Just give us the drinks," I said, "and I promise we'll keep it quiet."

"You should clean your shoes," he said, as he set the glasses on the counter. "I can smell them from here."

When I put the glass in front of him, Tim said, "I hate whisky," and drank half of it off and wiped his mouth with the back of his hand and gave me a truculent stare.

I lit a tab and took a sip of Jack Daniel's. My hands weren't shaking too badly.

"What now?" Tim said.

I took another sip. "I have to get this straight, Tim."

Sandra Sands said, "Do you want to talk about it here, Tim? Or would you rather talk to us somewhere quieter?"

"I want to talk," Tim said.

"That's good," I said. "You'll feel better for it, Tim, really you will. The two of you, it was her idea?"

He nodded.

"I don't need the details, but when did it happen?"

"She wanted more people to look at what she was doing, so she came up with this idea. She'd already done that other stuff by herself . . ."

"It's all right. I know. She can't be hurt now, Tim."

"Well, hers wasn't the only site on the Web with cameras in a room, all right? There are thousands and thousands. And a lot of them show people having sex. Sophie thought she'd get a bigger audience if she did the same thing. Especially as it was against the law. I agreed to mess around with her, you know, not go the whole way, but . . ."

I stubbed out my half-smoked cigarette. "One thing led to another."

Tim nodded. He looked very young and very wretched. I thought of the two of them in the crossfire gaze of the webcams, daring each other on like naughty children.

I said, "And afterwards, you downloaded the movie clips from her website. When did this happen, Tim?"

"It started about a month ago."

"Just before she got the new computer for her birthday."

"The last time was three days before she was killed. You see? You understand? He saw us, the dirty rotten fucker, and he was jealous."

Sandra Sands said, "You'll have to give a full statement, Tim. We'll try and keep it low profile."

Tim Coveney drank the rest of his Jack Daniel's. He looked up at the ceiling and said, "I thought it would just be me and her. I mean, I knew the webcams were there, but I thought it wouldn't matter, that I'd forget about them. But the thing was, I didn't forget about them and it didn't matter." He looked at me. "It made it exciting. It was the best fucking sex I'd ever had."

W hile Sandra Sands and DS Vine nursed Tim through a statement, I was reamed out by Tony McArdle. He wasn't much mollified when I gave him the spike of movie files Charlie Wills had retrieved from Sophie Booth's laptop, and told him about the messages she had received from the anonymous remailer in Cuba.

I said, "According to Tim Coveney, this so-called Avenger kept at her. At some point she tried to block access, but he got around it and taunted her about that. I think she tried to show him that he had no control over her by making love to Tim Coveney, and that's when he flipped. That's why he killed her. Or rather, had her killed. It has Barry Deane's prints all over it, sir."

McArdle tapped the data spike against his chin. He said, "I've come around to the opinion that someone had her killed, all right, but I don't think that it was Barry Deane. He has a solid alibi and nothing to connect him to the scene. Forget him."

"Sophie thought she could control him. She copied all his emails to the account at Wizard Internet as a precaution. But he attached a mail spider to one or more of his emails, and that erased everything. And when she tried to show him she could do what she wanted, when she fucked Tim Coveney in front of the webcams, he set up an alibi for himself and had her killed on camera."

"That's just cheap psychology," McArdle said. "We don't have anything to connect Deane with Sophie Booth. And worse than that, it sounds like you think she was asking for it."

"No, sir. I don't."

"There's been talk like that in the squad. I won't have it."

"She didn't see it coming, sir. She didn't know what he was."

"I should write you up for what you did. You could have fucked up an important witness."

"I had to know, sir. I thought——"

"It doesn't matter. We have a serious suspect, and when I've finished with you, I'm going to have a talk with him."

"A suspect, sir?"

McArdle leaned back in his chair and laced his hands together on top of his head and said, "We have a match with the sperm on the sheets. It's Anthony Booth's."

I had the peculiar sensation of riding an express lift while remaining perfectly still.

I said, "It doesn't mean that Booth killed Sophie."

"No, but it certainly gives him a motive, doesn't it? An uncle who's sleeping with his niece, especially an uncle who's in the public eye, if he thought it might come out in the press, he very well might resort to murder to keep it quiet. And if Sophie happened to have recorded one of those encounters with her webcams, it would explain why the hard drives were ripped out of her computers. You don't look very happy, John."

"Perhaps I'm stunned, sir."

"We're waiting for Anthony Booth to come in. With his solicitor, of course. We'll talk to him all night if we have to. Not a word of this to anyone outside the team, I hope that goes without saying."

"Can I ask, sir, if NCIS have become involved?"

"They are already involved. I asked them to try and track the origin of the fax sent through the remailer."

"If they told you that they could help you with that, sir, they're wrong. Cuba won't give up anything."

"NCIS have a different opinion."

"But——"

"End of discussion," McArdle said. "You've done enough here, John. Do you remember what I said about team players?"

"If this is about the ADESS thing, sir, I needed to find Tim Coveney urgently. It seemed the best way——"

"It was a stupid stunt that could have compromised an important witness. Count yourself lucky that I don't put you on report. Fuck off home, John. If I need you again, I'll give you a call."

David Varnom was waiting outside McArdle's office. From the way he smiled into my face as I went past, I knew he'd heard everything, knew exactly how badly I'd fucked up.

PART TWO

Wreckless

20

I went home. I changed into shorts and a T shirt, nuked a
couple of frozen burritos and sat on the balcony and ate
them. I drank a bottle of beer and talked to Julie for a few
minutes about nothing in particular. Afterwards, I cracked open
another beer and flipped through the copy of Barry Deane's file
I had downloaded onto my mobile. It was very hot. The sky was
bruising over to the east; there might be a thunderstorm later. A
helicopter was up, its searchlight restlessly probing a cluster of
high-rise towers. Sirens twisted in the evening air from two different directions. Someone was playing music very loudly in the
block of flats beyond the canal and its line of trees, and somewhere else a baby was crying.

I thought about Sophie Booth.

I thought about McArdle's warning, and David Varnom's
smirk.

I knew I couldn't let it go.

I opened another bottle of beer. I played the first four songs
of *London Calling*. I played *The Boatman's Call*. Nick Cave's

piano and dark brown preacher's voice, stark songs heavy with loss and the ache for redemption.

I filled two sheets of paper with names and arrows and tore them up, and started over.

Deane had a habit of stalking, although there was no particular pattern. One of his victims had been a single mother of twenty-two, a dishwater blonde with wary eyes and sharp features worn to the bone by poverty and hard luck; the other a divorced businesswoman of forty, a Mediterranean Earth Mother with an abundance of dark, curly hair and eyes as black as olives. The single mother had been living in a warren of council flats off Essex Road, where Deane had been renting a room after he had been fired from his first and only job; the other woman owned a drinking-club where well-known villains mingled with TV actors, crime writers and journalists of the old school. Perhaps Deane had fixed on them for no better reason than the simple fact that they were there, that he saw them every day.

I remembered the photograph of Sophie on the whiteboard in the Murder Room: laughing, her face flushed with health, so young.

I wondered how Barry Deane had found her, why he'd picked her website. There were so many sites. That he had to pick someone didn't seem good enough.

I didn't doubt then that he was the self-styled Avenger.

I wondered if Damien Nazzaro, who had travelled with Deane to Cuba and back, was an accomplice or a stooge.

I wondered about the deal Sophie had tried to make. She had dared Tim Coveney to fake the theft of the laptop from her car. She had made a dare with the whole world. She had hated her parents' stifling good works, the voluntary poverty, the extended family of sponsored children. She had loved exposure, the excitement of being on the edge.

I wondered about Anthony Booth, who liked pornography and made no secret of it, who allowed his niece to use his old flat, who bought her computers and rented a fat line so that she could run her website. I wondered if he had watched her silly, uncomplicated sex games. I wondered if he had done more than watch. I wondered about that sperm stain. I wondered about the web-cams, and simple blackmail.

By now, I was on my fourth or fifth beer, and was flipping a cloth mouse across the room for Archimedes' amusement. The robot owl seemed happy to swoop after the fake mouse any number of times. He would pick it up in his beak, waddle across to me and drop it at my feet, flutter up to his perch and watch me expectantly, waiting for me to do it again. Something was beeping, and after about a minute I realized that it wasn't coming from Archimedes, but from the web-book.

There was a message:

I see you. Getting fat on beer when you should be working.

I switched off the lights and went to the uncurtained window and looked out. No one on the towpath. In the kids' playground in front of the block of flats, perhaps, or on one of its walkways. I said to the web-book, "Are you using a mobile?"

Don't try and find me. I chose to talk with you. I can choose not to. Put the lights on so I can see you.

I didn't put the lights on. I went out of the flat, pressed the lift button. I said, "What do you want to talk about?"

The web-book didn't work in the lift, but it beeped as I walked out of the underground garage into the warm, close night.

You know what I did.

I was walking quickly down the road towards the bridge over the canal. I said, "If you know something, you should come forward."

No reply.

"You want to tell me something. You wouldn't have gone to all this trouble if you didn't. If you don't want to meet me directly, then we can arrange something else."

You know what I did. You know, and you can't do anything about it.

Crossing the canal. The gate to the steps down to the towpath was shut and locked. I walked quickly along the tall chain-link fence at the side of the playground towards the block of flats.

"We could meet any time you wanted. Face-to-face."

It must be frustrating, knowing what I did and not being able to touch me for it.

"You want to tell me," I said. "If you want me to know, you have to tell me everything."

Try 4th.

I broke into a run, up the first flight of steps, ducking around to check the lighted walkway—nothing—ducking back and starting up the next flight. I found it on the fourth floor, fresh red spray paint over older tags.

Avenger.

The paint smeared under my fingertips. A car started up on the main road. I ran to the far end of the walkway, and saw a silver car pull away.

21

Soho. 10 P.M. Tourists and clubbers queuing at the Old Compton Street security gate, watched by a posse of peace wardens. The narrow streets as crowded as a Mardi Gras party. Swarms of buffed gays (the area around Old Compton Street was still notionally theirs, despite the efforts of the Decency League to close down their pubs and clubs), tourists, media brats, and third-generation yuppies outside every pub and café. Resting actors in the motley costumes of Merrie Olde London: pie sellers, fruit sellers, tumblers, fire-eaters, coquettes, a town crier in red frock coat and tricorn hat ringing a handbell. Some kind of cartoon fox mobbed by kids outside the Nintendo store. A trad-jazz band in striped waistcoats and bowler hats playing "When the Saints." A TV comedian squiring two young women into the Soho House. Rickshaws nosing through streams of ambling pedestrians. At the corner of Wardour Street and Brewer Street, men and women in silver shorts and halter tops, their synthetic tans dusted with sequins, were handing out free beakers of green-gold syrup with glittering flakes suspended in it.

Everything watched by cameras slung under streetlights, fixed to brackets on the walls of street-corner buildings. Ever since the beginning of this case, I'd become hyperaware of their avid gaze, and the inscrutable intelligence that lived behind it.

Twentieth Century Eros was a licensed theatre club in a basement on Brewer Street. The woman who sat in the ticket booth, beneath a board that in fluorescent green letters on shocking pink advertised *Live! Girls! Live!*, knew that I was police before I opened my mouth, and told me that she didn't know of any Damien Nazzaro when I asked her where he was.

"You don't know your own boss?"

"I generally don't know much, and that's the way I like it," she said.

A fortysomething bottle blonde, hair brittle as old wire, crows'-feet around her seen-it-all eyes. Orange lipstick and brilliant blue eye shadow, traditional as a clown's mask. She sat on a tall stool, idly waving under her chin a plastic fan in the shape of a lotus leaf that advertised the club's website. Her short red vinyl skirt was hitched up, giving me a good look at her white thighs and red silk knickers. She saw me looking and winked.

"All part of the show, dear. It's in the licence."

"I need to talk to the man in charge," I said. "Whoever he is."

"Just wait there," she said, and pressed the button next to the credit-card swipe. A bell rang somewhere, and on its echo a heavy-set young man came bulling up the steep stairs. He had a shaven head, gold chains around his thick neck, gold rings in his ears and on his fingers. There were traces of steroid-abuse acne along the sides of his jaw. Scaly, plastic-capped spurs grafted to his wrists poked out of the cuffs of his *faux*-Armani suit jacket.

He glared down at me and said, "On your way, fella. This a legitimate club."

"*Klaatu barada nikto,*" I said, but it went straight past him. Before I could say anything else, he pulled me as close as a dancing partner, lifted me without effort, took two steps, and dumped me on my back in the gutter. A pedicab swerved, its bell ringing, as I picked myself up. A family group of tourists had stopped to watch, no doubt thinking that this was part of the zone's street entertainment.

"He's police," the woman in the booth said loudly. "He wants to see the manager."

"For true? Shit man, sorry 'bout that." The bouncer pulled me up, nearly wrenching off my arm. I straightened my jacket, and discovered that one of the pockets had been torn.

"You lucky me 'ad me caps on," the bouncer said, and pulled one of the clear plastic caps from one of his spurs to show me the black, razor-sharp tip beneath. "Brand-new thing, man. They take your cells and fuck up the DNA, grow these ickle buds they stick under your skin, and those buds, they grow into this. Severe shit, real wicked in a fight."

"When would you get in a fight in a tourist trap like this?"

"You be surprised," he said, as he recapped the spur. "I have these horns put in next. Make me like a bull, man."

"Or a goat. Take me to your leader, son. As long as you can do it without dropping me down the stairs."

How to describe the club? It was a gussied-up toilet with flashing lights and loud music, a naive Merseybeat confection that thumped and banged off the low ceiling. It was hot and humid and stank of sweat and disinfectant. The brick walls were painted with a crude moonscape of craters and jagged mountains under a starry sky. A rack of TVs played grainy black-and-white clips of *Ready Steady Go*, *Dr Who*, and *Steptoe and Son* above the tiny bar, where a waitress in silver shorts and a silver halter, two glittery stars on springs sticking up from her headband, was talking with the cold-eyed barman. A scattering of punters in the semicircle of booths watched a girl in a white vinyl bikini, fake tan and Dusty Spring-field wig shimmy listlessly on the stage.

I followed the bouncer through a beaded curtain into a narrow corridor made narrower by kegs of beer and lit by a buzzing fluorescent light, to a tiny office where a balding gnome of a man bent over a desk overflowing with paper.

When I shoved my warrant card under his nose, he barely spared it a glance. "If you're here to look at the license, it's up-to-date. Everything's up-to-date, and our girls' costumes are fully compliant."

"Are you Damien Nazzaro?"

The man sat back. "No, son, I'm Tam Burrows. Why would you want to be talking with Damien?"

"I take it you do know him."

Burrows's faded blue eyes, magnified by the lenses of his spectacles, were wary. He was in his late sixties, with a creased face and a bad comb-over, shirtsleeves rolled up to his elbows to show the riot of tattoos on his forearms. He told the bouncer, "You run along, Troy," and told me, "Have a seat, son. Tell me what this is about."

I sat down on the kitchen chair wedged between the desk and the door. A fan whirred above Burrows's head, but all it did was move the stale hot air around. "You'll have a drink with me I hope," he said, pulling a bottle of Bell's from a drawer in the desk.

"As long as it's not the watered stuff you sell to the punters."

"As if."

He slopped whisky into two dirty glasses. We drank, and I lit a cigarette.

"I see you're trying to give it up," Burrows said. "Or are those your girlfriend's?"

"What's it like, working for the Vitellis?"

"You know, I used to work the doors of places like this when I first came down to the Big Smoke. Full circle, eh? But like to say, it's only temporary. The last fellow left a bit sudden, and I'm just filling in. There's talk of another crackdown on the clubs, and no one is making any long-term plans. In a couple of years, this place will no doubt be another Disney shop, or a juice bar."

My mobile rang. I took it out and switched it off and said, "I understand that Damien Nazzaro manages this place."

"I know him, of course," Burrows said. "Just over from Malta, the oldest son of Andreas's wife's sister, doesn't know much but thinks he does. He's on the papers as manager, but that's because old Andreas likes to keep a member of the family in every bit of the business. He comes in once a week, takes maybe an hour to check the books. He has a couple of other jobs—looking after the slot-machine business, and one of the games arcades."

"Is he a smart lad?"

"He doesn't know much but he's not stupid. Clean record, nice motor, flash suits. Likes the ladies. Shaves his head to look harder. What kind of trouble is he in?"

"None at all."

"Is that so?"

"Really. I just want to check that he was in Cuba recently, and who he was with."

"Oh, he went there all right. That's where most of the Vitellis' business is these days. It's all fucking computers and the World Wide Web."

"Where can I find him?"

"This time of day? He's either getting ready for one of the clubs, or he'll be at the games arcade just round the corner."

"The one on Wardour Street?"

"That's the one. He likes the combat games."

I finished the Scotch and stood. "I might be back. I hope you'll have sharpened up the manners of your staff by then."

"Troy isnae mine," Burrows said. "He's from this security firm we use. I'll put in a word, but you can't blame him for the misunderstanding. No offence, but you have to be the least-likely-looking copper he'll have ever come across."

Damien Nazzaro was easy to spot. He was lit by a thready cone of laser light in the middle of the arcade, weaving and ducking as he ran in place on a kind of trampoline. The gun in his hand was linked by a cable to the big wraparound TV screen. Laser threads made a complex mesh over his body and flickered over his close-shaven scalp. He wore a tight white T-shirt that showed off his tan and his gymnasium muscles, tight grey pants with a gold-link belt, a stainless-steel Rolex. An avatar mimicked his movements on the big screen in front of him, dodging this way and that between piles of rubble and burned-out cars in some post-apocalypse version of New York, blowing away tattered zombies that lurched out of doorways or reached through the broken windscreens of wrecked cars. Gunshots and the ripe splatter of rotten flesh punctuated a pounding heavy-metal soundtrack. A few pallid kids stood around, cheering him on when he made a fancy move.

Emboldened by the shot of Bell's, I reached into the cone of laser light and waved my hand in front of Nazzaro's face, which did peculiar things to the shape of the avatar's head. Nazzaro missed a shot at a zombie, squared up and blew its chest open, then threw down the gun and saw the warrant card I was holding up like a shield.

The kids who had been watching suddenly got interested in machines on the far side of the room. Nazzaro shrugged and stepped down from the trampoline. Overhead, the cone of laser threads winked out.

I said, "Do you have an office?"

"This is it. You can talk to me here, like everyone else. That's a fucking silly name for a policeman, by the way. What are you, first cousin to that old TV detective? You should be dyeing your hair blond, mate, and wearing a cardigan and flares."

"You're thinking of the actor who played him."

"Oh yeah? Anyway, you look more like that other one, Columbo. Except you don't have a dirty raincoat."

"Or a glass eye. I understand you're the manager here."

His shrug was both haughty and casual. "It's one of my places, yeah. I like the games. I know all about them."

"Fronting for your uncle, Andreas Vitelli."

He was suddenly wary. His uncle was a touchy subject. "What's this about?"

"Just a couple of routine questions."

Nazzaro's eyebrows were a straight black bar over the bridge of the narrow blade of his nose. Now a dent appeared in the middle. He said, "This place is legitimate. The licence is by the front door, and we get inspected twice a week. Look all you want, there isn't a thing out of place."

"I'm not interested in your premises. I'd just like to ask you about your recent trip to Cuba."

"You've already talked to me about that."

"Not me."

"Some other police, then."

"You went to Cuba with Barry Deane."

"Not my choice."

"You were escorting him?"

"My uncle said, 'Go with the little fuck, he'll get into trouble if you don't.' So I took care of him, there and back. I flew club, he flew coach. We stayed at the American Hotel, the best in Havana. Had myself a fine time while he was working. Havana, man. Fuck, I'm going back there soon, and this time I'm taking my girlfriend."

"Mr Deane was working there."

"Fixing up some computer stuff. We have a lot of fucking computers in Havana."

"Does one of them host an anonymous server?"

"I wouldn't know about that."

"That's strange, because computer pornography is where most of your uncle's money comes from these days."

Nazzaro's smile showed more teeth than seemed humanly possible. One of his incisors, top left, was sheathed in black ceramic, with an inset diamond. "I like my women live and direct. The other stuff, that's for really sad people."

"And is Barry Deane working here, too?"

"I guess."

"He lives in Cuba, and he came here a couple of weeks ago. I don't suppose he's on holiday, so he must be working."

"Whatever you say."

"You're not looking after him here?"

"I might drop by now and then."

"But you don't know what he's doing. I find that hard to believe."

Nazzaro passed a hand over his shaven scalp. "It's computer stuff. You ask him, man."

"It must have been a tough job, baby-sitting him."

"He likes to think he's hard, but he isn't, not really. Nah, it was a piece of piss. Why are you asking all these questions?"

"We're very interested in Barry Deane. We have him under surveillance twenty-four seven."

"Is that so?"

"We're watching him, and we're watching his flat."

Nazzaro showed all his teeth again. "I wish you good luck, man. Are we done?"

"You've been very helpful, sir. I'll let you get back to your work."

Barry Deane had the top flat in a four-storey building a few doors down from the John Snow pub, just outside the protected zone. I told the squawking speaker who I was, very much aware that I was in line of sight of the CCTV camera angled high on the corner of the pub.

"I don't need to talk to you."

I risked a lie. "I can come back mob-handed, or you can talk to me now, alone and off the record. Your call."

Barry Deane buzzed me in. He was waiting at the top of the stairs, neat as a choirboy in a white shirt and pressed blue jeans and box-fresh Timberlands, the same smirk on his face that I'd seen in the interview-room.

"Anyone would think I'd done something," he said, "the way you keep hassling me."

I nerved myself to brush past him and walk into the flat. It had the empty feeling of a short-term-rental place. Good quality carpet and clean light blue paintwork, a flatscreen Sony hung on one wall, opposite a primrose-yellow Heals sofa and a smoked-glass coffee table. A laptop was open on the coffee table, cabled to a mobile phone. Half a dozen posters of naked, glossy-skinned girls were tacked to the walls, the interactive kind that blew you a kiss or lifted their breasts for inspection if you drifted too close. An expensive hi-fi was playing the sort of free-form jazz that sounds like bad plumbing.

"Very nice," I said, denting the slats of blinds and looking out at the night-time rooftops. "Nice view, too. Where's your telescope?"

"What do you mean?"

"I thought you liked to watch."

"You must think you're one of those clever cops." From the way he said it, I knew that his smirk was back in place.

"Yes," I said, "and I'm here to find out what you're about."

"I'm the wave of the future," he said.

I turned to face him. It wasn't as hard as I thought it would be, but my palms were suddenly pricking with sweat. I said, "I wouldn't be so sure of that, Barry."

"Look, just tell me why you're here. I want to get back to work."

"Sending emails or building porno websites? I do hope you're not messing around with porn here, by the way. It's against the law."

"You don't have anything against me. That's why you had to let me go."

"But you won't let it go, will you, Barry? That's why I'm here, and you know it."

"I paid for the old, and no one has ever fitted me up for anything since. Nor will you."

"Yes, but you know how it is, Barry. Once you get a reputation with the police, we like to pay you a visit now and then to see what you're up to. Maybe I should have a proper look around, what do you think? I might turn up a couple of stolen hard drives at the very least."

"You won't find me doing anything wrong," he said, and sat on the soft yellow sofa. Something relaxed or unclenched inside me. He'd just had his hair cut, short on the sides and fluffed up on top. It made him look younger than ever, a child with the lines of premature experience carved deep in its skin. He smirked at me and said, "I'm an upright citizen. I have a regular job. I make a lot of money. I've even been known to pay taxes."

"And what work is that, Barry?"

"Right now I'm working on a link that responds in unpredictable ways to a mouse click. It's a random cascade, really, so you never get the same sequence twice. Two or three young girls taking each other's clothes off and showing everything they have, shot from lots of different angles. Want to see? It's sexy."

His tongue touched the middle of his upper lip, retreated. He was trying to look casual, but there was tension in every line of his skinny body and he sat right on the edge of the sofa, as if ready to spring up.

I said, "I'm from T12, Barry. I've seen all sorts and I doubt that your stuff is any different. And you should know better than to be showing pink sites to a policeman, not in this country."

"I know about T12. Word is, it's going to be closed down, what a shame. Someone from a crufty old place like that, I don't think you can appreciate what I can do. Maybe you should just go."

"In a bit. We're just having a nice quiet chat here, that's all. After all, you've got yourself an alibi. You've nothing to worry about."

"If you checked it out, you know it's solid."

"You made sure it was, smiling right at the camera like that. You shouldn't have done that, Barry. You might have thought it was a clever touch, but it's the kind of clever touch that can cause all sorts of trouble. That, and sending the fax."

"I don't know what you mean," he said.

"Yes you do. It was sent to Scotland Yard, saying that a woman named Sophie Booth had been murdered, and it was routed through an anonymous remailer based in Cuba, which is where you were at the time of the murder."

"Anyone could have sent it," he said. "That's the point of an anonymous remailer."

"The fact is, you took far too much trouble to establish your alibi, and just because you happened to be in Cuba when Sophie Booth was killed doesn't mean you're not involved. You saw the murder, and you sent the fax. You think you can't be touched, you think you can do what you like. But I don't agree."

"If you ask me, the silly girl who got herself murdered was begging for it."

"So you think she deserved to be taught a lesson."

Barry Deane said, smiling up at me, "Well, that's what she got, didn't she? She got it hard, the silly little cunt."

"Why don't you at least admit that you watched the murder, Barry? I know you did, and you know I know. There are just the two of us here, so let's get it out in the open. Admit it. You saw it and it turned you on hard, especially as you think you can't be touched for it. Why, you even sent me a picture of it."

"Fuck you," he said. "You don't know what I can do."

"Sending nasty pictures, that's about your level. That, and spying on young girls over the Web."

"You don't know what I'm capable of," Barry Deane said. "You watch out. I might show you."

His eyes were glittering and flat, like bits of glass stuck in a flesh-coloured mask. Suddenly, it was very hard to stay in the room with him, but I knew that if I showed any weakness he would be on me in a moment.

I said, "We're just talking, Barry. No more than that. We don't want to get into anything serious, do we? Tell me about your work, Barry. I know you enjoy it."

"The thing about sex is that everyone wants it. Everyone thinks about it. Most of the top sites on the Web are about sex, and a lot of the top sites are mine. I'm the best. I earn a lot of money. More than you. A lot more."

"It's a pity that with your record you can only work for villains like the Vitellis, isn't it?"

"It's a respectable business. I'm well looked after. I have no complaints, and they don't have any complaints about me."

"Yes, but I expect they'd be unhappy to hear about the extra-curricular side of your life."

He said nothing.

"How were they about you being taken in the other day?"

"They know how it is with me and the police. If I'd have wanted that lawyer I could have had him. But I didn't need him, did I?"

"Have you been out and about, Barry?"

"I go where I want, do what I want, and leave no trace. I'm the invisible man."

"Perhaps someone took you for a drive. Damien Nazzaro, perhaps. I wonder what kind of car he has."

"I wouldn't know."

"It's silver, isn't it?"

Deane shrugged.

"Tell me about you and Sophie, Barry."

"I told you, I was in Havana. And even if I did see something, there's no harm watching, and there was no law broken. Otherwise you would have arrested everyone who saw it."

"None of the others were involved with her," I said. "But you were, and that's why I'm here. I know she had something she wanted to sell. She thought you could help her, didn't she? But all along you planned to kill her."

"You're mad if you think I'd tell you about that," he said. He was putting a lot of effort into his smile, as if he didn't really know how to do it, but was trying to get it just right.

"You make good money peddling pornography, don't you, Barry?"

"More than you ever will."

"How much did it cost, I wonder, to have her killed? But to someone like you, earning so much money, perhaps cost isn't the point."

"I don't know what you mean," he said, but he was giving me a wary look now.

"You paid for it, Barry. You paid for someone to do it while you were in Cuba. You paid for it and you watched it."

"I don't want to talk to you any more," he said.

"Who was it, Barry? If it was a professional, we'll find him quickly enough. There aren't that many of them. Or was it someone you know? Someone you met in prison?"

That went home. "I think you'd better fuck off," he said, and jumped to his feet, his hands curled into fists. "I don't know what I might do if you don't."

"That's fine, Barry, because I'm done with you for now. But don't go too far away, I'll back again soon enough."

He followed me out of the flat. It was very hard not to turn around, but I managed it.

"You don't know anything," he shouted, as I went down the stairs. "You don't know anything about what I can do."

———

I paid the ransom for my Mini at the NCP multistorey in Chinatown, and almost immediately got stuck in a traffic jam outside Leicester Square Tube station. And saw, on the stall outside the entrance that sold early editions of the next day's papers, tiled over and over and over, hundreds of copies of Sophie Booth's face.

I jumped out of the Mini, bought the *Sun*, the *Mirror*, the *Mail*, the *Guardian*, ripped through them one-handed as I drove home through stop-go traffic.

It was all there: everything McArdle had wanted kept from the press. Lurid details of Sophie's murder, her website, photographs of the "cyberdeath room" (the *Sun*), of "Sophie's sexgame partners" (the *Mirror*), the "tragic student pranksters" (the *Mail*). The *Guardian* had a second leader on cyberstalking. The *Mail* asked why pornography was encouraged by Britain's leading art college. And the *Mirror* had an exclusive: selected pictures from the murder sequence, Sophie Booth's breasts and thighs overlaid with black bars in a hideous parody of discretion, blurred close-ups of the killer in the Thatcher mask. No mention yet of Anthony Booth, but that was only a matter of time.

When I got back to my flat, it was nearly midnight.

A dozen boxes of bananas were stacked outside the door.

22

Alan Rudd phoned me at half past six the next morning. "Christ," I said, "I thought the point about Vice was that you left dawn raids to Customs and Excise."

"I need the overtime to pay off my unreasonably high mortgage. You didn't get my messages."

"Obviously."

"I left a message on your mobile. I left a message at T12, too, but never mind that. Remember there were so many magazines we ran out of evidence crates?"

"Vaguely," I said, and yawned.

Sunlight burned through the weave of the tall yellow curtains, dropped a starry pattern across the rumpled sheets of my bed. The bedroom door was open, and I could see, on the far side of the long living-room, Archimedes the robot owl sitting on his perch, a compact shadow against the sunlight burnishing the sliding glass doors. The red light at the perch's base indicated that he was recharging. When you were as short of sleep as I was, it seemed like a useful ability.

Late last night it had taken me an hour, listening to more

versions of "Greensleeves" than I cared to think about, interspersed with random fragments from all four of Vivaldi's seasons and a lifetime's supply of classic Rolling Stones tracks scored for soupy strings, to find someone in the online supermarket's chain of command who could make the decision to take back the bananas. The order had been genuine, made against my credit card, but I finally had a talk with a supervisor who, although he adamantly refused to believe that a hacker could have penetrated his company's firewalls, did finally concede that perhaps it had been caused by a typing error, and promised that the bananas would be taken back, no charge.

While I was working my way through the phone tree to the supervisor, I dictated a message to the web-book, sent it via the Cuban remailer:

Are you trying to make a monkey out of me?

A reply arrived ten minutes after I had finished with the line manager.

You're no better than the other police. None of you can touch me.

"Let's talk," I told the web-book, certain that I was talking to Barry Deane. "Because you do want to talk. If it's easier to talk this way than face to face, I'm happy to go along with it. Tell me what you want. Tell me what I can do for you."

There was a pause long enough for me to make a cup of tea. I didn't know if the delay was caused by routing of the message or because my correspondent was thinking hard. Perhaps he had logged off. My right elbow was stiffening; I had banged it badly when I had tackled Tim Coveney. "Talk to me," I whispered, watching the words walk across the web-book's screen. "I used to talk to people for a living. I used to be halfway good at it. If you won't give it up face to face, give it up here. Boast about it, you little fucker. Let something slip."

The web-book beeped. I started, spilled tea on my bare feet.

I'm going to get away with it. And there's nothing you can do.

I cleared the web-book's screen and said, "Let's talk about Sophie Booth. Tell me how you found her. Tell me what you wanted from her."

The rest of the police don't care. Only you. What are you going to do about it?

"Why did you have her killed?"

You can't do anything about it. You won't do anything. Because you're a coward. Spitalfields proved that.

"I know that she thought she was making a deal with you. Tell me about it."

There was no reply.

I had a bad night. While Archimedes waddled about the bedroom, his claws scritch-scratching the wooden floor, his wings rustling as he pounced on electronic ghosts, my thoughts circled restlessly around the idea that the man in the mask was not a professional but someone Barry Deane know. And how had Anthony Booth's sperm got on his niece's sheets? Was there some kind of connection between Booth and Deane? And even if Anthony Booth had been fucking his niece, perhaps it had nothing to do with her murder . . . Around and around and around, and when at last I fell asleep, there were dreams I'd rather not go into.

So I was still only half-awake as Alan Rudd said in my ear, "We took some of the cardboard boxes that happened to be lying around in the back of the shop. They contained blank spikes, once upon a time."

I found the remote and switched on the TV. On the twenty-four-hour news channel, Sophie Booth's face dissolved into a three-quarters shot of a reporter talking outside the building where she had been murdered. A uniform was standing in the left-hand doorway, in line of sight of the CCTV camera over the right-hand door.

I said into the phone, "That doesn't mean anything."

"There was a FedEx receipt stapled to one of the boxes."

"And the address on the receipt wasn't the address of the shop."

Now Tony McArdle was stonewalling at a press conference.

"One of these days you're going to make a fine detective, my boy," Alan Rudd said. "I had a warrant sworn last evening. I'm going to make a little unannounced visit."

He gave me the address, in a little cul-de-sac just west of Wardour Street and the barriers and gates of Soho's protected zone. He added, "It's owned by the Vitellis."

"Really?" That was interesting. "Do you think the Vitellis might keep a spike burner on one of their properties?"

A brief shot of Sophie's mother collapsing into the arms of her husband at that first press conference.

"I don't expect that kind of luck," Alan Rudd said. "But I do think it might be a convenient place for storage."

"This is small stuff for the Vitellis."

"Perhaps one of their many offspring has a sideline. Perhaps it's part of something else. I can't help wondering," Alan Rudd said, "if that little piece of shit we pulled a couple of weeks ago might not have something to do with this after all."

One newsreader was watching the other tell me about three black youths found shot dead execution-style in an abandoned office block in Hammersmith.

I said, "Barry Deane?"

"The very one. I just might have another word with him. Anyway, if you want to be in on this little jaunt, be there in an hour."

A woman walking her dog on Clapham Common had been badly wounded in a drive-by shooting.

Alan Rudd said, "You're up for it?"

A woman's body had been found in the River Lea, tied to the bodies of two dogs.

I switched off the TV with an impatient flick. "I'll be there. I'll even buy you breakfast afterwards."

"I should warn you now," he said, "that I'm not a cheap date."

The computer came sailing out of the window in two parts. First the screen, which imploded crunchily when it hit the pavement, then the box, trailing cables and smashing apart in the road a few feet from the police van.

One of the constables had clearly been working hard on his bored, seen-it-all-before attitude. He said, "I'd give it a 6.3 for style. He would have got the full ten if he'd actually hit the Transit."

Alan Rudd had been ringing the doorbell of the office of *Protempo Productions*, one of the Vitellis' front companies, when the computer crash-landed. "Fuck this," he said, and squared up to the door and kicked it in.

I was hard on his heels as he barged into a dingy hallway. There was a padlocked door to the left, but we galloped straight up the narrow stairs. The door on the first-floor landing was unlocked, opening onto a hot and fetid room with a desk in one corner and a fold-down bed with a sleeping bag on it in the other. A half-eaten pizza had congealed in its box and there was a clutter of empty beer bottles by the bed. Plain cardboard boxes were stacked along one wall. A scrawny middle-aged man in a string vest and stained Y-fronts was hopping about in the middle of all this, trying to pull on his trousers.

"Take your time," Rudd said. "I'll read the warrant to you. You two," he told the uniforms crowding in with us, "check out upstairs."

"That's a private flat," the man said, and was too slow in putting his hand to his face when I pointed my mobile at him.

"We saw the sign at the door," Rudd said. "What does she model, exactly?"

"I wouldn't know nothing about that. I'm just the caretaker." The man was trying to fasten his belt, but his hands were trembling. His comb-over had flopped to one side, a greasy curtain hanging down by his raddled unshaven cheek. Grey hair curled through the mesh of his string vest.

My mobile beeped; half a dozen lines scrolled up on its little screen. "Pat Cloudsey," I told Alan Rudd. "Sent down eight years ago, out just last month."

"Eight years?" Alan Rudd said. "We have a dangerous man on our hands."

"Burglary with aggravated assault. He raped an eighty-three-year-old woman after he'd broken into her house."

"I hate the modern world," Pat Cloudsey said.

Alan Rudd said, "Are you working for the Vitellis now, Pat? They must be desperate, taking trash like you."

"I'm just the caretaker," Cloudsey said. "None of this is to do with me."

"I wonder if your parole officer knows about your little job," I said.

Cloudsey's face crumpled. "Don't come the acid. I'm chipped, mate, can't even take a piss without them knowing. I never looked in any of these boxes, all right? As far as I know this is a legit place. I just look after it at night."

Rudd said, "And I'm your fairy godmother, and the woolly suits I brought with me are really white mice."

Muffled voices raised a racket overhead. A woman's indignant screech, the sound of footsteps coming back down the stairs.

"She don't like her beauty sleep disturbed," Cloudsey said.

Alan Rudd was inspecting the stacks of cardboard boxes. He said, "Does she throw you any freebies?"

Cloudsey grinned, showing a mouthful of brown stumps. "I wish."

"Really? I'd have thought she'd be a bit young for you." Rudd unzipped the tape of one of the boxes with a penknife and pulled open the flaps and lifted out a handful of spike sheaths shrink-wrapped to bits of card. "What would the Decency League think," he said, showing them to me.

Colossal Blowjobs. Girls Who Drink Cum. Blondes Who Blow.
"I don't know what's in any of those," Cloudsey said.

Alan Rudd opened another box. This time the spike sheaths were unmounted and unlabelled. "Finish getting dressed," he told Cloudsey. "We'll take all this away and you'll come along with us and sign the receipt when we've made an inventory."

"I can't sign anything. I'm just—"

"You'll do," Rudd said. "You can sign here or at Vine Street. Your choice."

"You're never taking me in. Jesus, have a heart."

"We could do you for suppression of evidence," Rudd said. "You shouldn't have thrown the computer out of the window."

I told Cloudsey, "Obviously no one told you how hard hard drives are."

"I must have had a nightmare," Cloudsey said, and tried out an ingratiating smile. "That's why I did it. Panic attack, innit?"

Rudd said, "Did they tell you to chuck the computer if the place was raided?"

"I wouldn't know what you mean," Cloudsey said. "I must have sort of banged into it and it went flying out the window."

Rudd had one of the uniforms take Cloudsey down. "That's your evidence fucked," he told me.

"Not hardly. He might have wrecked the computer, but you could bounce a hard drive from the top of Canary Wharf and we'd still get something out of it."

At T12, I settled at my desk and used the web-book to check for emails, the third time that morning. Nothing. I read through Barry Deane's file and made a phone call to Wandsworth. I pulled a couple of files from HOLMES. I made a phone call to the parole service. I sat back and thought about what I had found. It seemed too easy. McArdle's team should have found it as quickly as I had. But they hadn't taken Barry Deane seriously.

I went upstairs. The hard drive and spikes from the raid were in the system, waiting their turn, but the laptop confiscated from Nick's journalist friend had at last been processed and returned to the exhibits room. I signed it out and called Nick and told him the good news. I killed time before my lunchtime appointment by initialling the circulars that had accumulated on my desk and sending them forward without bothering to read them, on the principle that if they contained anything important I'd soon hear about it. I sorted and filed papers on a case that had been passed on to NCIS, but which was going to peter out before it reached court because the principal suspect had died of a coronary.

There had been a time when paperwork had meant everything to me. When a properly cross-referenced database could make my heart sing; when reducing the chaos of a case to four or five document boxes of sorted and indexed evidence dockets, interview sheets, scene notes, FSS forms and time sheets was to create a thing of beauty. Now, I was consumed by Sophie Booth's murder. A reckless wind blew through me. I worked through a pot of coffee. Every thirty minutes I stood outside the fire door and smoked a Tropica down to the filter, pretending that I could actually taste it. I ran the little movie in which Sophie vanished, ran it over and over. I diagrammed and rediagrammed possible relationships and motives in the margins of memos. When it all got too complicated, overloaded with speculation and wild guesses, I reduced it to the bare facts. To the one thing I needed to know.

Eventually, I took my life in my hands and tried to make contact with the man who could have told me exactly what it was Sophie Booth had taken. But I didn't have Anthony Booth's personal phone number, and I couldn't get any further than an emollient secretary somewhere in his company whose promise that my message would be passed on was about as believable as anything Barry Deane had told me. Perhaps it was just as well, I thought, when I put down the phone. If I spooked Anthony Booth, he had enough weight to squash me flat.

Around eleven o'clock, Rachel Sweeney came into my office and sat on the edge of my desk. There had been a spare chair once upon a time, but someone had borrowed it and I hadn't bothered to get it back. That left my swivel chair, with tufts of yellowish foam rubber working through its frayed cushion, three newish battleship-grey filing cabinets, and a metal desk dominated by the flatscreen monitor of my computer. A travel poster of a Swiss village had been taped to one wall by the previous occupant; I knew it so well that I could have drawn from memory accurate copies of every pitched-roofed stone-and-timber chalet, right down to the pots of red geraniums on the balconies and the boulders on the roofs.

"I hear you did some overtime yesterday," Rachel Sweeney said.

"I won't put in for it. I know how tight the budget is. Anyway, here's the news, I'm off the case."

"I know. Tony McArdle called, gave me a not very convincing excuse about NCIS."

"Well, they have become involved, Boss."

"Of course they have." Rachel Sweeney was wearing plum-coloured lipstick, a dark brown skirt and matching jacket. She brushed at stray hairs that had escaped her French braid and added, "I shouldn't wonder that NCIS leaked that stuff about the murder to the newspapers."

"I have my own idea about that," I said. "How's the Martin case?"

"The summing-up is today, which is why I can't spare the time to give you a bollocking about dropping the ball."

"Consider me chastened."

Rachel Sweeney gave me a long, considered look. A look of

weary forbearance and measured pity. A look she often practised on the recidivists and screw-ups and green recruits she had to work with. She said, "How long have you been here, John?"

"A year, more or less."

"I remember this office when you first moved in. Still the same. What does that tell me?"

I waited.

Rachel Sweeney said, "It tells me you don't see yourself as part of my team. It tells me that you think this post is just a way of waiting out your service until you get your pension. Well, this might be a backwater, but it is not a rest home. You will work here as part of the team. My team. You will acknowledge my authority. Am I or am I not your boss?"

"If you were a man, I'd say that you were the Man."

"I *am* the Man. And I say that you will do better next time. What's the progress on those bootleg porn spikes?"

I told her about that morning's raid, although I neglected to tell her about the connection with the Vitellis, who just happened to employ Barry Deane.

She said, "Press on with it. Take an active role. It will do you good. All this paperwork is making you pallid."

"I like paperwork. I like filing. I like writing reports. I'm good at it, always have been. It appeals to a puritanical part of my soul."

"Nevertheless. And you should brighten up your office, John. Look at it."

"I like the poster. I want to live there. I want to wander through the flowery Swiss meadows, leading a string of children while singing a merry song."

"A picture of something you like on the walls, some plants, a photo of your girlfriend on the desk."

" 'Edelweiss.' Or the one about doe, a deer."

Rachel Sweeney gave me a long hard appraising look. "You

keep looking at your watch, John. Am I keeping you from something?"

"I have a bit of business in town."

"If NCIS are on the murder case now, that means we'll be kept out. End of story. Stick with the bootleg spikes. It might be small beer, but we need the points."

The *we* was a nice touch, I thought, as I drove into town for my lunchtime appointment, with the floating feeling I used to get when I cut school. On the way, I called the parole office again, and was again told that I'd be called back as soon as the man I wanted to talk to had returned to the office.

Laura Sills was wearing a purple T-shirt with a scooped neck that showed the tops of her breasts, loose khaki shorts, and the same transparent sandals as before. This time her fingernails and toenails were painted orange, but not the same shade of orange as her hair. Her office was hazed with cigarette smoke, and she got through two more cigarettes as she listened to me explain a little of what I thought I knew.

"I think Sophie took something from her uncle," I said. "I don't know exactly what it was, except that it was something she thought was worth a lot of money, so most likely it was something to do with the RedLine chip and ADESS. For whatever reason her uncle was very indulgent towards her. He bought her a new computer every birthday, although he insisted that she wipe the old one clean before she got rid of it, which leads me to suspect that there was something to do with RedLine on its hard drive. That she learned something about RedLine or he told her, and she persuaded him to let her have access to whatever it was. I saw a sequence she did which seemed to be taken off the CCTV camera at the place where she was living, the one her uncle once used to demo ADESS—"

"Slow down," Laura Sills said. "This is a lot to take in."

I took a deep drag on my tab, drew smoke all the way to the

bottom of my lungs before blowing it out. I said, "I'm sorry. It's only just now coming together."

Laura Sills stubbed her cigarette into an ashtray and lit another and said, "I get the feeling that you are going to tell me that you think Sophie was murdered because of what she did."

"In a way," I said. "But the more I find out about her, the more complicated it seems. The more sides she seems to have."

"Men always have a problem with women's sexuality," Laura Sills said. "I don't suppose the police are different. You might try hard not to think it, but always at the back of your mind is the idea that when a woman is attacked, she was asking for it. That she was where she shouldn't have been, that she was wearing the wrong kind of clothes, that she said the wrong thing to the wrong person. That it was somehow her fault. Shifting the blame like that is a matter of control, of defining the kind of sexuality woman are allowed to display. Because it isn't what women do that's the problem, it's what men do."

"Are the newspapers still bothering you?"

"Not so much since I changed my telephone number."

"I'm sorry."

Laura lit another cigarette, tossed the matchbook onto the clutter on her desk. She was full of a restless energy. Her orange hair was brushed up in little spiky tufts. She rocked back and forth in her chair and said, "Sex and murder, it's the perfect combination in this country. The public can have their cheap thrill and moralize at the same time. She was murdered, John, and she's being condemned because she dared express her sexuality."

"I don't think it was anything to do with sex. I found Sophie's old laptop. One of her student friends had it. Its hard drive had been professionally erased and reformatted, but her friend had been using it to look at Sophie's website, and I saw one sequence that appeared to have been recorded by the CCTV camera outside the building where she lived. She was dressed like an angel, and raised her wings and disappeared. At first I thought she'd just hacked into that one camera—it used to belong to her uncle, and he used it to demo the first version of the RedLine chip and ADESS. But I also found out that she was trying to sell something when she was killed, and I'm beginning to think she had some kind of access to ADESS. She thought she'd found someone who could help her sell it, but he killed her."

"How did she find him? Who is he?"

"He found her, through her website. She thought she could use him, but he used her. He's a bad man, Laura. Someone who has served time for stalking, someone driven by a fixed, psychopathological obsession. Some stalkers continue to send harassing mail to their victims after they've been convicted and jailed. They are relentless. They constantly shift their mode of attack, exploit every weakness. They even track their victims from country to country. Once a stalker has become attached to someone, he won't stop stalking them until he becomes attached to someone else."

"Or until he kills her," Laura said.

"Not all stalkings end in murder, or even escalate into violence, but in this case, yes, I think he had Sophie killed. He had her killed so that he could take what she was trying to sell. He set it up so he could watch it over the Web while he was out of the country. So he got his disgusting thrill, but also had a perfect alibi."

Laura thought about this. Her hands, wrists crossed, lightly clasping her knees. Her lower lip girlishly caught between her teeth. She smiled when she saw how closely I was watching her, and said, "He had to rely on someone else."

"His accomplice can't give him up without giving himself up too. But the thing is, the man who had Sophie killed wants to give it up; he's dying to share it. That's how people like him are—they can't bear to be thought ordinary. That's why I wanted to talk with you about Sophie again. I thought there might be some clue in her performance pieces about what she took from her uncle."

"How official is this, exactly?"

"I'm just looking for a way to break him open," I said. "You showed me one of her pieces . . ."

Laura nodded. "There are two more."

The first was what Lucy Matthews had called a candle rite. Faint white shapes that might be faces floating around each other in darkness above flickered smudges of pixellation that might be candle flames, a sibilant multivoiced whisper.

The second was something else.

Laura Sills said, "Are you all right?"

"I know that place," I said. "It's where I run."

It was where I'd seen a fox caught in the implacable gaze of ADESS.

Shoreditch Park. Night. A figure in a floating white dress dancing through overlapping ovals of light that with a machined grace swooped and glided after her. But unlike the fox she could dance away into the night. The lights would switch off one by one, and then, after an interval of darkness, would suddenly come on again all at once, centered on her floating shape.

It lasted five minutes, and at the end the camera panned around to show the Gainsborough Studios apartment block at the northern end of the park, zooming in on a figure that stood at a lighted window.

"She didn't give you even one clue about how she did it," I said, a little while later.

"Not one," Laura said. "I remember she was very mysterioso about it."

We were sitting at a rickety corner table in the pub next door to St Martin's, leaning towards each other so we could talk. It was very hot and noisy, crowded with tourists and tourist-haters. Laura had a bottle of Korean lager. I was drinking Jack Daniel's and Coke, a double.

"Lucy Matthews didn't know either. She thought it was a situationist thing."

Laura leaned even further forward, her knees almost touching mine. I was aware of the scant inch between us, the cleft between her small but not insubstantial breasts. She said, "That trick is what got her killed, isn't it? It wasn't anything to do with stalking."

The smallest of movements, and we could have kissed. I said, "It might have been to begin with, but greed won out."

"There's something about our culture that makes us want to share in other people's lives. It goes beyond voyeurism—we want to share other lives because their very ordinariness validates our own. Sophie was playing with that idea, and using it to validate herself. I think she needed the same kind of attention a movie star craves. She wanted to be wanted. She told me a little bit about her parents and their extended family. She once said that she felt like a ghost in her own house."

I thought about Barry Deane. For him it was desperation— he desperately wanted what he did not have and could not understand. An ordinary life, ordinary feelings.

I started to say something about this, but Laura said, "Don't," and touched a finger to my lips for a moment. "Let me tell you about Sophie."

"All right," I said. The place where she had touched me tingled.

"The Web lets people open up their lives to everyone. That's the real fascination of webcams. Sex is a draw, but it isn't why most people stay interested in a particular site. They are intrigued because they're given the ability to participate vicariously in a life not their own. It could end up as a billion sites showing a billion boring lives—but there's the promise that we'll really be able to look into other lives, to see how different we all are. Sophie stumbled onto this. She wasn't particularly analytical about what she was doing, she was feeling her way into it, but I could see how it gave her confidence. She was beginning to understand her own self, and that's the first prerequisite for an artist. Or rather, the search for understanding is. She saw a way to assert herself, her identity. And then she was killed, but no matter what she did, she didn't ask for it. She didn't deserve it."

"I'm going to get the man who did it," I said.

"Even if it means breaking the law?"

My phone rang. It was the parole officer I'd been trying to contact. He gave me an address, and I wrote it down. "I'm sorry," I said.

"You have to be somewhere," Laura said, but she was smiling.

"I have a couple of things to do."

Laura took out a pen and wrote something on a corner of a beer mat, tore it off. "I don't usually do this," she said. "This is my mobile telephone number. Any time you want to talk to me, give me a ring."

"I will," I said.

23

We can track anyone, anytime, anywhere. We're the business. We work fucking magic in here, John."

I was somewhere deep under Whitehall, in one of the Cold War spam-in-a-can bomb shelters that had been designed to protect ministers and senior civil servants from the consequences of nuclear war. It was one of the Met's surveillance centres now, a hangar-sized room that had been made over by an architect who must have been a big fan of 1960s sci-fi movies. Operators in swivel chairs hunched before racks of TV screens, catwalks, low-level blood-tinted lighting, the smell of warm plastic, the crackle of static. A hushed calm broken only by the clatter of keyboards, the hum of air-conditioning and whir of computer fans, men and women muttering into the mikes of their headsets as they guided distant cameras.

I was sitting at one of the racks of TVs, a big master screen set over four smaller monitors in a two-by-two grid. The master screen displayed a view of the Marble Arch end of Oxford Street, looking down on two streams of pedestrians moving past each other in opposite directions. Don "Donald the Duck" Fowler worked a joystick, zooming in on a wedge of kids in T-shirts and baggy overalls and straw hats muscling their way through the crowd, isolating one cropheaded boy with the red deer logo of an ancient American brand of gasoline printed across his chest. Fowler thumbed the button on top of the joystick, and the picture on one of the monitors centred on the boy and began to track him as he moved along with his mates.

"Look at these silly fuckers," Fowler said. He was a heavy man whose neatly pressed short-sleeved shirt was a size too small, so that intervals of flesh pressed between the straining buttons. He had the grainy, translucent skin of a cave-dwelling animal, a fat lower lip he kept perpetually moist. Light slid over the slab-like lenses of his glasses as he looked from screen to screen. "Look at them," he said. "They're so busy pretending to be hard boys they've forgotten all about the cameras. I just know that sooner or later they're going to try it on with some stupid low-level crime. I have an eye for it. The system's good, it's smart, it's learning all the time. But it isn't as good as me, not by a long way."

The view on the monitor switched to another, more distant camera, which zoomed in on the boy as it took over the task of tracking him. I thought of the fox, running back and forth, trying to outpace the overlapping circles of light. I thought of Sophie Booth blithely dancing away from the cameras' attention.

Fowler said, "The cameras are above the normal line-of-sight of pedestrians. Hardly anyone notices them. Most people forget about them. Frankly, I think they should all be painted fluorescent orange and fitted out with big flashing lights and signs saying 'surveillance camera.' *That* just might reduce crime. As it is, it's like shooting fish in a barrel. Of course, you know what happens if you don't shoot fish in a barrel." He waited a beat. "You get a barrel-full of fish. We can feed into cameras on buses, the Tube, most of the big stores. We have over half a million cameras in central London alone. And if a subject leaves London, it doesn't matter for how long, ADESS will pick him up when he returns. It will lock on to his car on the M25, or find him when he steps down from a train. It never sleeps. It never grows tired. It's fucking magic." He pushed back in his chair and folded his arms and looked at me. "Now, who was it you want surveilled?"

Don Fowler and I went back to the beginning of my career as a negotiator. He'd been a spycam operator, piloting a camera platform about the size and shape of a Frisbee, with three fat gyroscopes, a whisper-quiet fan motor, 360-degree vision, and microphones that could pick up a rat's fart at five hundred metres. Now he was a shift boss in the Bunker, always happy to show off his toys. He was also the world's worst parker, a serial abuser of loading zones, double yellow lines and red routes, a cardiac infarct in the traffic's clogged arteries. His proudest achievement was the time he backed up the A10 for two miles when he double-parked so he could pick up his dry-cleaning.

"You're already watching him," I said, and gave him Barry Deane's name and address.

Don Fowler turned to his computer and pulled up a database. "We *were* watching him," he said. "Surveillance ended yesterday afternoon, seventeen hundred hours. I can start it up again and run it off the books for two days max, but it'll have to be worth my while."

"How many this time?"

Fowler smiled. "Eight."

"I could make five vanish." I had received four tickets of my own yesterday, for driving through red lights, for using a bus lane, for parking in a restricted zone.

"It has to be all eight. The fuckers are threatening to take away my licence."

"Eight if you watch my man twenty-four seven for as long as it takes."

Don Fowler leaned back in his pneumatic chair. TV light slid over his slab glasses. "That's the beauty of the system. Once it latches on to someone, it never lets go until you ask it nicely, or until the money runs out."

A n hour later, I was in the wastelands of Essex beyond Walthamstow, a long hot crawl along the A10, the A503 and the A406. Half the lanes of the A503 had been torn up for resurfacing. Big pots of tar simmered under clouds of acrid fumes. Yellow bulldozers belched black smoke as they gouged tarmac. As I inched over the bridge at Ferry Lane, both windows wound down, New Order's funereal disco thumping from the tape deck, I had a good view of a crime-scene tent pitched by the concrete channel of the River Lea, blue-and-white tape fluttering gaily in the hot dirty breeze.

The offices of FourSquare Security Ltd were at the edge of a blasted-looking industrial estate. A sprawling, flat-roofed, one-storey building that looked like a good wind could take it away, with cars and white Packer vans with the FourSquare logo on their sides parked in front, and flat sere wasteground stretching away towards the embankment of the M11 at the back. The receptionist was unimpressed by my warrant card and told me to take a seat and wait.

I sat and smoked three cigarettes, stubbing them out on the scarred linoleum floor, watching men in cheap brown trousers and white shirts with clip-on brown ties drift in and out. The air was hot and sticky and stank of industrial disinfectant—the same stink as in Twentieth Century Eros's dingy basement. At last, an overweight man in a striped shirt and red braces bustled over and said that he could look after me.

"Malcolm Robinson," he said, and held out a pale, waterlogged hand. When I didn't take it, he said, "You wanted to take a look at our time sheets. Well, I'm the dispatch supervisor, so it's my area of expertise. What is your query pertaining to, exactly?"

"It pertains to a murder enquiry."

"Oh dear. Well, come this way and I'll sort you out. I've pulled some files, and I'll walk you through them. We're always glad to help the police, of course, since we're in what you might call the same business."

He kept up the chat as he led me through to a room at the back, where file boxes had been stacked on a battered table. The metal-framed windows were wide open, but the air that drifted through them was hot and stank of dogshit. Beyond a wide, weedy patch of concrete, Alsatians ran about in wire pens or lay in the shade of corrugated iron shelters, their tongues lolling. One or two were trying to bark, but no noise came out; their vocal cords had been cut.

I said, "How can you stand the stink?"

"The dogs? Oh, you get used to it, they're our bread and butter after all. Much cheaper and far more reliable than human guards. Do sit down, Inspector. What's this all about?"

Malcolm Robinson really was eager to please—too eager, I thought, and nervous with it. There were half-moons of sweat under his arms, and his forehead shone greasily. He pulled the knot of his tie away from the top button of his shirt and tried out a smile.

I laid a piece of paper on the table and told him, "For a start, sir, I want to know the names of everyone who was on duty at this address last week."

"That won't take long," Robinson said, and started leafing through spreadsheet printouts.

I said, "What's your computer security like?"

"Very clean and very secure. Password-protected, swept for viruses once a day, the backups lodged in a safety-deposit box."

"And who has access to it?"

"Just myself and the managing director. We're the only people who can access the records once they've been typed in. We're very strong on security, Detective Inspector, as you might imagine. Don't worry, these time sheets are an accurate representation of our employees' movements. They'll stand up in any court."

"I hope so," I said, "but the problem is that not all the names on them are real."

Robinson coloured up, an unhealthy flush that mottled his fat face. "I don't know what you're talking about," he said.

"Now that's not true, is it? For instance, I think one of those names you're about to give me is Craig Stevens. He works as a security officer, but according to his parole officer he's on your payroll as a janitor."

"It's true that some of our staff sometimes have to be seconded to other duties. We lose many of our trained staff to the peace wardens, so we require our workforce to be flexible."

"I'm sure. Let's talk about what kind of job Craig Stevens was doing on the evening of June 5."

Robinson shuffled through spreadsheets, ran a finger down a column. "As it happens, he was on the patrol rota. Purely in a temporary capacity, I expect, but in any case, he wasn't responsible for the address you asked about."

I lit up a tab and said, "I still find him interesting."

"I wish you wouldn't smoke," Robinson said. "I have asthma."

"Then sit by the window and breathe the country aroma of dogshit, sir, and tell me why you're employing a known criminal as a security guard, one recently out of Wandsworth after serving a long stretch if I'm not mistaken."

I felt confident that I could get what I wanted out of this nervous fat man. I was charged up by secret information.

"That would be a matter for Personnel," Robinson said.

"And can they tell me where Mr Stevens is right now, or will you do that?"

"Look, I'm perfectly willing to cooperate on this matter, but don't start throwing accusations around. We're a respectable firm. I believe we have several contracts with the Met."

"Yes, the accountants contracted this firm because you're rock-bottom cheap, and you're cheap because you use recently released villains with fake certification who can't find any other kind of regular employment."

Robinson started to stand, spluttering that he wasn't going to take this.

"Do behave," I said. A little part of me noted that I was enjoying this far too much, but I didn't care. "Sit down. Of course you're going to take this. You've been told to cooperate with me because your bosses want to know who I'm after, they always do when the shit starts flying. When I'm done I'm sure you'll run off and tell them like the good boy you are, but meanwhile you can tell me whether your Mr Craig Stevens also worked security at the doors of this tourist trap in Soho." I flattened a second sheet of paper on the table, turned it around so Malcolm Robinson could read it. "Owned by the Vitellis, who also, I'm not surprised to have found out from a phone call to Company House, have a stake in this firm. I'll want copies of Craig Stevens's worksheets, all the places he worked at, and the times he worked."

Robinson blotted sweat from his jowls with his shirtsleeve, pulled out more copies of spreadsheets and said, "You can't have the originals."

"That's fair enough. While you're at it, perhaps you can tell me where I can find him."

"He's off today. Our men work five-day shifts, one day off. This is Stevens's day off."

"Where does he live, then?"

"I'll have to ask Personnel."

"You do that, sir, and make a copy of his file for me too, while I admire the view and take in the air."

Robinson went out and I lit another cigarette, watched the dogs in their pens in the hard, hot sunlight outside. I was certain that my guess was right, that Barry Deane had wanted Sophie Booth killed, but couldn't or wouldn't do it himself. So he had arranged for her to be killed while he had been in Havana, and he'd used someone he knew—someone who had been in prison with him. And that same person had taken the hard drives of her computers, because they contained some kind of program that gave access to the RedLine chip and ADESS. I was also certain that Barry Deane had used it to watch the police coming and going at the murder scene. He'd quoted my own T-shirt at me.

When Robinson came back, I took the papers and said, "I appreciate your cooperation, sir. There's just one more thing. I need to see your office."

"My office?"

"Lead on. It won't take more than a minute."

There was a flatscreen and keyboard on his desk, flanked by framed photographs of three young girls. When I pulled out the drawers and ran my fingers around their undersides, Robinson said, "You won't find it there, Inspector."

"What would that be, sir?"

"The password. I'm not so foolish as to leave it lying around." He prodded his forehead. "It's in here. Easy enough to remember, because it's based on the birthdays of my daughters."

"I see, sir. Let's hope hackers don't think to try that idea. Now you can phone your bosses, and don't forget to tell them that it's the Sophie Booth murder I'm especially interested in."

I read Craig Stevens's file as I drove back into the city, stop-and-go through the roadworks. FourSquare was a shady firm working on the edge of the law, but it was thorough. I had copies of Stevens's time sheets for his every working day; I had copies of his parole reports; I even had a blurred photocopy of his FourSquare ID card.

Stevens was in his fifties, a career criminal. I'd learned from his HOLMES file that he had just finished a ten-year stretch for manslaughter. He had badly beaten a man after a Spurs-Arsenal match and his victim had died a week later. He also had a record for burglary and aggravated assault—he'd break into a house, tie up the owners, and beat them until they told him where any valuables were hidden—and he'd served four years for using a craft knife to carve up a jeweller reluctant to give the combination to his safe. He had been on the same cell wing as Barry Deane while Deane had been serving time for harassment. Two like-minded men with plenty of time to develop their fantasies together. Stevens knew Deane, he'd been out for a month, he was a knife artist, and he was working for the security firm that regularly checked the empty office of Mobo Technology, the office owned by Anthony Booth, who had rented the flat above it to his niece. Stevens might not have been on the rota that night, but he had access to the keys for the building's front and back doors—a stop-off at a locksmith's at any time in the past month would have given him a set of duplicates in a couple of minutes.

Stevens's address was in Tooting, the top flat in a subdivided redbrick two-up-two-down Victorian terrace house on a quiet, ordinary South London street. I parked and watched the flat, drinking a can of Coke and making a late lunch of a dubious meat pie and a couple of packets of cheese-and-onion crisps I'd bought from the shop on the corner. The curtains of Stevens's flat were drawn. The street simmered quietly in the heat. Even with the windows all the way down, the inside of the Mini was sweltering.

I phoned Nick, told him that I probably wouldn't be able to meet him that evening. "I have the laptop, there's no problem there. I just . . . Something came up."

"Are you okay, John? You sound, I don't know, a little excited."

"I'm in the middle of something, Nick. I'll see you later."

I phoned Sandra Sands, and she told me again that she really shouldn't be talking to me.

"This is just a friendly social call, to see how all my old friends in the Murder Room are getting along without me."

"I'm really sorry they took you off the case, sir, but that's—"

"John. It's John now that I'm no longer on the case. I was wondering if I could see you again. We could meet for a drink. How would six o'clock suit?"

"You're putting me in a difficult position, sir."

"I don't mean to. Just a quick half, what do you say?"

"I get off-shift at eight. I can meet you at half past. Just for ten minutes, on my way home."

Sandra Sands gave me the name of a pub. I wrote it on the back of my hand. I watched and waited until schoolkids started coming home, walking in twos and threes along the shimmering street in the summer afternoon light, voices high as birds. I got out of the Mini and stretched and went across the street. There were separate doors for the two flats; I leaned on the bell for Stevens'. No answer. I phoned his number and stood outside the door while the phone rang inside the flat, looked through the letterbox and saw half a dozen flyers and menus from restaurants on the mat. No key on a string inside, no key under the plastic flowerpot with the dead geranium by the door.

A woman was standing behind the window of the house across the street, Decency League and Neighbourhood Watch stickers on the glass in front of her face. I walked across the street and showed her my warrant card, and after a minute she opened her front door as wide as its chain would allow. A plump, black woman in her early sixties, with a frilly apron over her loose, flower-print dress. She didn't know much about Craig Stevens, only that he had moved in three weeks ago, and that he worked for FourSquare—he was dropped off by one of their vans at odd times in the day or night. She had been at the wedding of her goddaughter on Saturday, and didn't know where he had been that day.

"Have you seen him today?"

"He's done something bad," she said, eyes widening as she placed a hand flat beneath her throat. "I know it."

"This is just a routine enquiry, ma'am. Nothing to worry about."

"Don't talk nonsense. I saw your warrant card. You're from one of those special units, not the local police."

"It's routine, but I'd appreciate it if you didn't repeat our conversation. Have you seen Mr Stevens today?"

"I have a job at the supermarket, the big Sainsbury's down the road? I was there from seven until one o'clock." She added, "I could tell he was no good from the way he smoked his cigarettes. Hiding them in his hand? I said to myself, I don't care if he works for a security firm, he's just out of prison, that man."

I gave her Barry Deane's description, and she apologized at length for not having seen him.

"Perhaps you can do me a favour now," I said. "I have to go into Mr Stevens's flat. As you're a member of the local Neighbourhood Watch—"

"Street coordinator," she said proudly. "People blame that computer war for the way things are now. I say they have only themselves to blame because they do not do anything about it. My husband, he is a peace warden, and I am street coordinator for five years now. There will be security cameras in this street next year because we organized a petition. We are glad to do our duty."

"Coordinator. That's even better." I wrote the number of my mobile in my notebook, tore out the page and gave it to her. "I'd like you to keep a lookout for Mr Stevens. If you see him coming, and I'm still inside the flat, call that number and let me know."

"I don't know," the woman said. "It doesn't seem right."

"I'm working for T12, the special computer unit. I'm acting under an emergency IDO, an Information Disclosure Order. I need to enter Mr Stevens's premises to discover some information."

"It doesn't seem right," she said again. "You wait outside most of the day and now you go in alone."

"I can see why they made you coordinator. Did you notice me on the phone just now?" When she nodded, I said, "I was checking with my superior for my orders."

The cheap Yale-type lock on the door to Stevens's flat yielded easily to my credit card. I went up the dark, narrow stairs softly, holding my breath, my heart pumping hard, half-expecting to see Barry Deane materialize in the gloom at the top, where a stained-glass window laid a jigsaw of red and green light on the worn carpet, and wishing that just this once I was carrying a gun.

There were only three rooms: a tiny bathroom at the top of the stairs; a bedroom at the back; a living-room with a galley kitchen crammed in one corner. The bedroom was mostly filled with a stained double mattress, a sleeping bag that smelt strongly of Stevens's sweat crumpled on top like a shed cocoon. A suit on a hanger swayed like a ghost behind the door; a plastic bag stuffed full of clothes stood in a corner. The windows were uncurtained, overlooking a tiny garden full of weeds.

I pulled on a pair of vinyl gloves and went through the bag of clothes, laying them out on the mattress one by one, failing to find any bloodstains. In the living-room, a sofa with a faded red velvet nap faced a TV perched on a coffee table. There was a video camera on top of the TV. It was plugged in, but there was no spike in its slot.

I stood in the middle of the room and scoped out everything slowly, looking for anomalies, finding nothing. No loose floorboards, nothing behind the curtains. There was nothing between

the pages of the dog-eared copy of the South London Yellow
Pages for 2006 by the telephone, only a can of lager and a carton
of date-expired milk in the tiny fridge by the sink, a box of tea
bags and a couple of tins of tomato soup in the cupboard above
it. The bathroom was stark and very clean, half-empty bottles of
bleach and lemon-scented cleanser on top of the toilet's cistern.
Bath and toilet gleamed. I tested the worn cork floor tiles one
by one, looked inside the cistern, stood back and let my gaze
fall where it would.

One of the panels at the side of the bath was very slightly
crooked. I undid the screws with the point of my penknife. The
panel came free, and a buff padded A4 envelope fell on the cork
tiles. Inside was a data spike.

I drew the curtains and switched on the TV and plugged the
spike into the camera. I sat back on my haunches and watched.

Snow, then a brief blackness, a slow wipe and something else
coming up, a view of a wrecked office from a low-slung and shaky
camera, shadows moving as it panned so at first it was difficult
to see what it was circling:

A naked girl in a chair, blonde hair falling down her white
back, her arms twisted against each other and fastened by tightly
looped wire. A fat white blur moved close to the lens, fingers
adjusting something. The contrast flared for a moment, and there
was a jump cut. The camera's gaze was steady now, looking
straight at the naked girl and the man bent over her. He wore
black jeans and a black sweatshirt and Margaret Thatcher's face.

I started to sweat all over my body. I wanted to look away but
I couldn't. I wanted to reach in there and save her even though
I knew that she was dead. I watched as he made the first cuts,
her screams coming out muffled, then got to the bathroom just
in time and threw up into the pristine toilet. I drank from the
sink tap, went back into the living-room. I punched the TV off,
pulled the spike from the camera.

I had what I wanted, but I didn't know exactly how I could

use it. The murder I'd just watched had enough similarity to Sophie Booth's death to tie Stevens straight to it. But who was the girl? Was she something to do with Barry Deane and the deal with Sophie Booth, or was she someone Stevens had killed for his own reasons?

After some thought, I wiped the spike with my handkerchief and put it back in the envelope, tucked the envelope behind the bath and screwed the panel shut. I tipped bleach into the toilet, flushed it, went out into the late-afternoon sunlight.

The woman was still at her station in the window. I gave her what I hoped was a convincingly cheery wave as I climbed into the Mini, but it was a good ten minutes before I could stop shaking and drive off.

The pub where I had arranged to meet Sandra Sands was a few doors down from the Petty France passport office, opposite the Wellington Barracks. Tourists of half a dozen nations had colonized pavement tables; inside, it was mostly men and women in suits, conference name tags pinned to their lapels, briefcases and laptops between their feet.

I was working on my second Jack Daniel's when Sandra Sands arrived. I bought her a dry white wine while she explained that she couldn't stay long.

"I didn't want to talk on the PoliceNet," I said, "because every call is logged and monitored. But I think we're safe enough here."

Sandra Sands sipped her wine, looking at me over the rim of the glass. "You make it sound like an affair," she said.

"I appreciate that you came."

"You're still chasing Barry Deane," she said.

"Am I being watched, DC Sands, or is that a wild guess?"

"Dave Varnom says that you have it hard for Deane, that that's why McArdle let you go."

We were in a corner of the bar, talking in low voices.

"I was let go because NCIS was brought in. Was it Dave Varnom who leaked the details of the case to the newspapers, by the way?"

"Actually, sir, it was someone in San Francisco, by the name of Glenn Bower. He logged into Sophie Booth's website, saw the murder, but didn't realize that it was for real until we contacted him. He retrieved the movie from his browser's cache and sold it to a news agency, and the agency sold the movie to two dozen newspapers, websites and TV stations around the world, including the *Mirror*. The *Mirror* told us what they had, and we couldn't block publication because by then they'd already published stills from the movie, and pirate copies were all over the Web. We had to have a press conference."

"What's the state of play? Is Anthony Booth going to be charged?"

"The things a girl gets asked," Sandra Sands said, "on her first date."

We had established a comfortable level of banter. We were keeping it light because we both knew how serious it was.

I said, "He hasn't been charged yet, has he? The papers would have picked that up right away."

"He's very much in the frame."

"Is that so?"

She gave me one of her clear-eyed looks and said, "Very much so, sir. I'm sorry."

"Don't you think that there was something odd about the way Anthony Booth's sperm just happened to be on the sheets in his niece's flat? I was there when Varnom first interviewed him, and he's a clever man. Too clever to overlook something like that."

Sandra Sands didn't dismiss this straight away, and I liked her for that courtesy. She thought about it. She said, "You think it was planted there."

"Or perhaps he *was* sleeping with Sophie, but that was nothing to do with her murder. After Sophie was killed, the place was fluff-bombed with rogue DNA to confuse the forensics. If Booth killed her, why would he leave sheets stained with his own sperm? No, it isn't credible. What's wrong?"

Sandra Sands was smiling. "I can't help noticing, sir, that the way you talk depends on who you're talking to."

"I'm very labile, DC Sands. I'm strongly affected by other people's speech patterns. It was considered an asset when I was in the Hostage and Extortion squad. When you're trying to talk someone out, it helps if you can talk like them, if you can get inside their skin."

"Is that what you're doing here, sir? Getting inside my skin?"

"I wouldn't dare try. We were talking about Anthony Booth."

"DCI McArdle got a warrant for Booth's laptop, and it went off to NCIS. And I don't think that I should tell you any more than that."

"Anthony Booth knows his way around computers. If there were any files on his laptop's hard drive that he didn't want found, he would have deleted them and overwritten them with zeros until there was no residual signature left. That's what he had done to Sophie's laptop after all, when she told him she was going to sell it to Tim Coveney. I really should have another word with Tim."

"He was released, sir. He's gone back home to Liverpool."

"Shit."

"We could hardly arrest him, sir."

"He colluded with Sophie Booth to defraud her insurance company. He didn't fully cooperate with you during his first interview, and I doubt that he told you the whole truth when you talked to him again."

"We took his statement and we're chasing every lead. Anthony Booth's been interviewed again, and we're looking at his movements in Scotland at the time of the murder."

"Checking traffic cameras, I expect. Varnom likes to think that they can track people around the country."

"And checking on Booth's business associates and his girlfriends, sir."

"His girlfriends?"

"We interviewed three today. He likes them tall and blonde and willowy, but what man doesn't? And they're all well-off, too, but then again, so is he. Are you all right, sir?"

"I'm fine."

"They were also working girls," Sandra Sands said.

"Really."

"Apparently Mr Booth was quite upfront about it. He said it was easier to pay for what you wanted than go to the trouble looking for the right girl and wooing her."

"He actually said that? Wooing?"

"They have websites, take credit cards. It's all very twenty-first century."

"They were very alike?"

"Not only physically; they were all stamped from the same mould. Pretty, well-educated, living in expensive flats in trendy areas." She wrinkled her nose. "I hated them all."

"You've been very frank with me, DC Sands. I appreciate it. Let me repay the compliment." I gave her the address of Craig Stevens's flat. I said, "Don't go there alone. And take a very careful look at the bathroom. You'll find something of interest there. I can't tell you any more than that. After all, I wasn't there."

"But you have a good idea of what I might find, don't you?"

"The tradition is, I have the idea and later on I explain everything to you. But I will tell you this much: Craig Stevens works for FourSquare Security, which looked after the empty office below Sophie Booth's flat. He had access to keys for the front and back doors. And if you check his prison record, you'll find he was banged up with Barry Deane. He was doing time for man-slaughter, and he's been known to use a knife. Don't tell anyone else about this, DC Sands. Work on your own. And when you've put it together, take it straight to Tony McArdle. He's a fair man. He'll give you your fair share of glory."

"He'll guess you're behind it, sir."

I drained my Jack Daniel's and banged the glass on the table. "Deny everything."

"Where are you going, sir?"

"I think I'm about to go and do something very stupid, DC Sands, but what the hell, I'm feeling reckless."

24

I t's me," I said, an hour or so later.

Barry Deane buzzed me in. He stood at the top of the stairs, arms folded across his chest, looking down at me as I climbed towards him, the usual smirk stuck on his face. He said, "Lucky for you I'm in a good mood, or I'd tell you straight away to fuck off. As it is you'll have to be quick. I'm just about to go out."

"It doesn't matter what kind of mood you're in," I said, "or where you're going."

I was braced by secret knowledge and by Jack Daniel's, the two I'd had in the pub while waiting for DC Sands, and two more I'd had in the John Snow while nerving myself up to do the deed. I pushed past him and went into the flat. The laptop was on the coffee table as before. I pointed at it as Deane drifted in, and said, "Have we been working hard, Barry?"

"You'll know all about it soon enough."

"I already know most of it," I said. "I wonder if there's something interesting on your computer, for instance. Something to do with RedLine chips and ADESS."

"Even if I did have something like that, do you really think I'd keep it here?"

"Not if you're as clever as you think you are. But you couldn't resist playing with what you stole from Sophie Booth, could you, Barry? You hacked into the camera outside the place where you had Sophie Booth killed. Information wants to be free? It really wasn't very clever of you to mention that."

He didn't say anything.

"I know you and Sophie had a deal, Barry. Or at least, Sophie thought she had a deal. But in the end you just went and killed her instead."

"I was in Cuba at the time," he said, "and now I'm going back there."

"Not without your passport."

"I got it back. You didn't have anything on me when you took it, and you still don't. I don't know why you're here, stinking of booze and looking so fucked up, and I don't care. I'm out of here, and there's nothing you can do about it."

"Have you been out at all today, Barry?"

"Sometimes I don't go out for days," he said. "I don't need to. I live in my head most of the time. I'm very self-sufficient that way."

"Is that how you got through jail, Barry?"

"I didn't let it touch me. I read a lot. Thrillers, philosophy. Anything, really."

"I would have thought that a pervert like you would have had a hard time of it in jail. It's funny, almost touching, don't you think, the way the hardest men in jail really don't like perverts. It's like a twisted kind of chivalry."

"I generally don't think about it," Barry Deane said. "It's behind me."

"You're wrong there, Barry. From where I'm standing, it's very much in front of you, and for the rest of your life too if I'm not mistaken. No, you'll soon be back inside, eating UFO stew and surprise pie, and this time you won't have anyone to watch out for you. That's what Craig Stevens did, didn't he? Or was it something more tender than simple protection? Were you sweethearts, perhaps? Did he pitch and you catch?"

At the mention of Stevens's name, a sudden change came over Barry Deane. It was like watching a cloud shadow run across a meadow.

I said, "Let's save a lot of time, Barry. Let's cut to the chase. You tell me that you know Craig Stevens from the time you served together, all cosy and lovey dovey in a cell in Wandsworth. Tell me that you met up with him when he was let out just this last month, when you came back here from Cuba for the first time in a year. Tell me about the little deal you and he cooked up together. I already know something about it, Barry, and when I've put everything together you'll go down hard. Unless, that is, you decide to help me."

He took two steps towards me then, banging into the side of the couch and not noticing, his face working around his anger as if he was chewing a bitter cud.

I was seized with a powerful urge to run. I said, very loudly, as if speaking to a sleepwalker, "Stop there, Barry."

He blinked and ran his tongue over his thin lips. He said, "I could kill you, right here, and no one would know."

"Don't be a fool. There's not a copper in the land would rest until you were caught. ADESS has you under surveillance, Barry, twenty-four seven, and it will have seen me coming in."

"I'm the invisible man. No one can catch me."

"No one can hide any more, Barry, not even you. Not even using what you stole. You see, I do know about that. And I know about the girl too. The girl with the blonde hair that Craig Stevens killed, just like he killed Sophie Booth. Yes, I've seen the little movie Stevens made. Were you there, Barry? Or did you just wank off to it, here on your yellow sofa? I think the last is more your style."

Deane's laugh was forced, harsh as a seal's bark. One of his hands, his left, went into the pocket of his neatly pressed blue slacks and came out with a butterfly knife. He held it in front of his face, flicked it open with a quick supple movement of his wrist, flicked it closed. He said, as if to himself, "They always make a noise when they see the knife. That's when it starts. I have to make them shut up."

"Come off it," I said. The fear was creeping up on me. It was right at my back. I more than half-believed that this wasn't one of his silly boasts, that he was nerving himself to do something. It was as if a dangerous dog had suddenly come into the room, the kind that goes quiet and still before it leaps at you. I said, "I know how you are, Barry. A bit of a romantic who can some-times let a harmless impulse get too serious. You can't let go, you can't take rejection. The anger builds until you have to let it out. Was that how it was with Sophie and the other girl? Who was she, by the way? How did you come to know her?"

"They don't understand me," he said, "that's true enough. They don't realize what I can do."

He was still flipping the knife open, flipping it closed. He seemed to have forgotten that he was doing it.

"I'm not sure that you really did it to anyone, Barry. A nice university-educated boy like you. You come on hard, but that's just show."

"Oh, don't you worry about what I can do," he said, and added, with chilling pride, "The wave of the future, that's me."

"We've already talked about your future," I said, "and it's a lot closer than you think if you don't put that knife away."

"I could make you go," he said, and stepped forward and started sweeping the knife back and forth, grinning at me all the while, his eyes glassy now and the tip of his tongue caught at the corner of his mouth.

I stepped inside one of his swings and caught his arm, but he was stronger than I thought, and I'd drunk too much before I'd come up to see him. He wriggled halfway out of my grip and whipped the knife back and forth when I tried to catch hold of it. There was a sharp slicing pain in the heel of my left hand and a jet of bright red blood jumped out. I managed to catch his wrist with my right hand, though, and I bore down, bending his whole body with the weight of mine until he let go of the knife. I kicked it across the room and pushed him away and grabbed hold of my left hand with my right.

Barry Deane giggled. "I cut you," he said.

"It's nothing. Don't you worry about it."

But it was a deep slice down my wrist into the meat of the palm of my left hand and it was bleeding quite badly, in little gasping spurts.

"I don't want you messing up my carpet," he said. "I think you should go."

"I think you should go in the bathroom and get me a bandage. Go on." I was leaning against the window so that my trembling wouldn't show. I knew then just what a fool I had been, going in single-handed, thinking I could pull off the kind of confrontation that works only in fiction.

He went out sulkily, slamming the door behind him. I crossed the room and picked up the knife, feeling dizzy when I bent. I closed it and put it in my pocket and wondered what else he might have. Another knife perhaps, or a gun. Ten minutes in the right pub, you could buy an automatic or a revolver for the price of a good meal in a decent restaurant. For the second time that day, I wished that I was carrying, like a real policeman.

When Barry Deane came back, his hand was behind his back and he was smiling. I closed my left hand over the knife in my jacket pocket. He saw that, and his smile broadened and he tossed a rolled bandage at me. I wrapped it around my hand, and the web of white cotton over the wound immediately reddened all the way through.

"That's a bad cut," he said happily. "Really, I think you should get it seen to."

"You don't get rid of me that easily," I said. "It would take a lot more than that. Look, Barry, I know why you're frightened. It's all right."

"I'm not frightened. Not me."

"I think you are. I think you're frightened I'll catch up with your friend Craig Stevens, who shared a cell with you in Wandsworth and who now works for FourSquare, the security firm that takes care of the office in the building where Sophie Booth lived, where she was murdered. Stevens was handy with a knife, and I shouldn't wonder he's where you got your talk from. Yes, he looks very good for the murder of Sophie Booth, and he's square in the frame for the other girl, the blonde. I wonder what he'll say to keep himself from going away for the rest of his natural. He might just drop your name, what do you think?"

Barry Deane managed a smile. He said, "I think you're full of shit."

"When the Vitellis find out that I'm looking for Craig Stevens, when they find out why I'm looking for him, I don't think you'll be making use of their lawyer. I don't think you'll have a job with them any more, or use of this nice flat, either. It might be better, Barry, if you gave some serious thought about helping me, because pretty soon you're going to need my help."

The tension in the air was deafening. The pain in my hand beat like a pulse.

Barry Deane smiled. He said, "I don't need anything here any more. I'm going. I'm gone. Soon enough you'll see. You'll see how clever I am."

"I don't think you're clever at all, Barry, which is why the next time I see you I'll have it all worked out."

I had to turn my back on him when I went out. I had the knife, but it was still hard.

A car was parked on the double yellows outside, a silver Saab with smoked-glass windows. As soon as I came out onto the street, the Saab's passenger door opened and DI David Varnom got out. He was smiling so hard it seemed that he had no lips at all, a shark's smile stretched from one angle of his jaw to the other.

"Get in," he said, and gripped my arm just above the elbow. "Get in now."

I climbed into the back. The driver turned to look at me. It was DI Anne-Marie Davies of NCIS.

"I do hope I'm not interrupting a tryst," I said.

"I think you'd better tell us why you paid a visit to Barry Deane," Varnom said.

I knew then what was going on. What these two sweethearts had cooked up together. Who my mystery correspondent had been. With a feeling of falling through space, I said, "I take it you're not here because you like Barry Deane for Sophie Booth's murder."

I was holding my left hand with my right. Blood was leaking from the sodden bandage; I could feel a warm wet worm running down inside my jacket sleeve. The wound was starting to hurt badly now, with a deep sharp ache.

Varnom said, "I'm here because you're a rotten excuse for a policeman."

DI Davies was watching us in the rear-view mirror. I said to her, "Dave Varnom doesn't like me because of Spitalfields. What's your excuse? Do you sing in the same church choir?" Then I knew. I should have known. A simple check with the personnel records would have told me. I said, "Both of you were at Hendon with Toby Patterson."

"I'm here to help out a colleague," she said coolly.

"She's our liaison with NCIS," Varnom said. "You, though, are off the case. You must know that, because Tony McArdle made it quite clear. And yet here you are, stinking of drink, coming out of the home of someone who may be implicated in a suspicious death. I suppose you drove here in that wreck you call a car. I should add a DUI to the rest."

"You set me up, didn't you? You made sure I'd go after Deane."

"I wouldn't know what you mean," Varnom said.

"You knew about the anonymous remailer in Cuba because that's where the fax about Sophie Booth's murder came from. I told you all about it, and you had DI Davies route emails through it. You pretended to be Barry Deane and taunted me about Sophie Booth's murder. You lured me out of my flat to a wall tagged with the handle Deane used to sign off emails he sent to Sophie Booth."

"I'd like to see you prove any of that," Varnom said.

"You overheard me tell McArdle about the emails Sophie Booth was getting. I bet there's a spray can of red paint in the boot of this car. And I reckon that if I took a look at your phone records, I'd find you'd been sending emails to a certain webbook."

"You're not going to get the chance," Varnom said. "It's all over for you, cop-killer."

I went for him then, but I was weak with blood loss and shock and he pushed me away easily. All I managed to do was get blood on his shirtfront.

"Christ," he said in disgust, and started dabbing at his shirt with a handkerchief, "you really are a mess."

"It's in the nature of an industrial accident."

DI Davies turned in her seat and shone a torch on me. She said, "He's been cut, Dave."

"He probably did it himself," Varnom said, still fussing with his handkerchief and his shirt. "Christ, he's bleeding like a stuck pig."

"It's nothing," I said, although I knew that it wasn't. I felt very tired, and the pain in my hand was making it hard to put words together.

"I'm taking him to a hospital," DI Davies said.

"After we get his statement," Varnom said.

"I know arterial blood when I see it," DI Davies said, and started the motor. "I don't want him dying on us."

Varnom said to me, "Hospital or not, you're still going to have to explain why you were interfering with a suspect in a suspicious death."

"Save your puff," I said. "I was just having a private talk with Mr Deane, who according to you isn't a suspect." I was holding my right hand tightly with my left, but I couldn't seem to stop the bleeding. My sleeve was sodden from cuff to elbow. I added, "Perhaps you should put on a bit of speed, DI Davies. I think you were right about the arterial blood."

"Look at you," Varnom said. "Drunk and generally messed up, thinking you can front a psychopath on your own."

"You might hate my guts," I said, "but I think that we both care about getting justice. Barry Deane is right in the middle of this case, alibi or not. He's close to telling me everything, and I don't know if he'd open up for anyone else."

"Bollocks," Varnom said. "We don't have a thing on him. He was in Cuba when Sophie Booth was killed, and that's all there is to it. You might have been able to look after a bunch of filing clerks once upon a time, but I doubt that you could even manage that now. And despite the fact that four fine policemen were killed because of your incompetence, you have the persistent and completely wrong-headed delusion that you can do real police work. You have to be stopped. For your own good, and for the good of the force."

"What about you, DI Davies?" I said. "I know you must have helped this man bounce those emails through the anonymous server in Cuba, because, frankly, I don't think he even knows how to type. I know you did it because you were a friend of Toby Patterson's. But do you really want to let Deane go free? Because that's what will happen if I can't get him to talk."

"You're in a lot of trouble," DI Davies said, "and making wild accusations won't help you. But if you tell us everything, John, I promise you that we'll have Deane put away for assaulting a police officer."

"That wasn't his fault," I said.

She looked at me in the rear-view mirror. A very cool, calculating look that was more unsettling than Varnom's angry disgust. She said, "I can understand why you don't like Deane. But he has a solid alibi for Sophie's murder, and you know that the DNA evidence points towards Anthony Booth."

"That's good, using her first name," I said, "but it won't get you any closer to me."

"I want to help you do the right thing, John," DI Davies said. "If you swear out a complaint against Deane, if you explain exactly what you were doing there, we could put him away for hurting you."

"He owes a lot more than that," I said, "and I'm not about to incriminate myself by swearing out a complaint. Do your own dirty work, I'm not that kind of police."

"No," Varnom said, as we drew up in front of the entrance to Westminster Hospital's Accident and Emergency Centre, "you're a fucking fool."

Varnom followed me inside, although I kept telling him to fuck off. He followed me all the way to the reception desk, where a nurse told me to quieten down and mind my language.

"Police," I said, and fumbled out my warrant card one-handed and flipped it open on the tall counter. The lights seemed very bright in there, piercing all the way to the centre of my head, and gravity seemed to have increased somehow; I found that I had to brace myself against the counter. I was getting blood all over it, too.

The nurse glanced at my WC and said, "I don't care about that. Everyone gets the same treatment here."

"I'm sure we're all impressed," Varnom said nastily. "We'll certainly keep it in mind next time someone starts cutting up rough in here and you call for some bodies to deal with it. Now light a fire under you, missy, and get a doctor for this man."

"Do fuck off," I told him. "You're about as good as me when it comes to playing the hard case."

I wanted to sit down, and because the rows of orange plastic chairs, with their scattered contingent of the battered and damaged and deranged, were too far away across a field of linoleum that gleamed like ice, I sat down on the floor under the counter, seeming to fall further than was necessary while someone somewhere shouted for a doctor.

They bundled me onto a trolley and wheeled me into a cubicle, where a haggard young man in a white coat did various painful things to my hand while I watched, happy to be lying down and shot of Varnom. I desperately wanted a cigarette, but knew better than to ask.

"I just need a few stitches," I said.

"I think you need a bit more than that," the doctor said. "Your radial artery has been nicked—that's where all the blood is coming from. You're lucky the nerve wasn't severed. It was a knife, yes?"

"It's in my pocket," I said.

"Christ," the doctor said, "how I hate knives. We get at least two dozen bad stabbings every Saturday night. They can be worse than any gunshot wound. There was a perforated bowel in here last week—a fifty-centimetre gash that almost cut down to the spinal column, done with a Japanese sword. You wouldn't believe the stink." He pulled on vinyl gloves and set acrylic goggles over his steel-rimmed glasses, took off the compress and probed the wound with a blunt steel needle, rotated each finger. "You need a suture in your artery," he told me, "and then I'll stitch the wound."

"But Doctor, will I ever be able to wank again?"

"That's the spirit," he said absently, as the nurse started to set out steel instruments on the green paper that covered the top of a trolley.

I said, "Do me a favour. Tell my colleague out in the waiting room that I'll be kept in overnight. We're working an important case, and I don't want him hanging about unnecessarily."

"I'll see to it," the nurse said. "I don't much care for his attitude."

"Neither do I," I said.

I didn't feel the deft suture in the nicked artery, but I felt every one of the fifteen stitches that closed the wound. The doctor wrote out a prescription for painkillers. After I'd had it filled at the hospital's dispensary, I went out through the main entrance of the hospital, past the shuttered flower shop and a row of vending machines. It wasn't even midnight. I called a number on my mobile, then fell into a taxi and let it take me away.

25

My mobile rang a few hours later. I rose naked from the bed, managed to find my jacket on the unfamiliar floor, and answered.

It was Sandra Sands. She was calling from a phone box. She said, "There's been another murder," and gave me an address. "Wait an hour, they're just clearing the scene," she added, and rang off.

I used ring-back, but no one answered.

Laura Sills switched on a bedside light and sat up, the sheet falling from her small pale breasts. She watched me pick up my boxer shorts and pull them on. She said, "I've had longer dates."

"I'll make it up to you."

"My mother warned me about policemen."

At least she was amused. I said, "Your mother was right."

"It's not because of . . ."

"I was tired. I was drunk. I was in a strange state."

"You had lost a lot of blood."

"That too," I said, grateful for any excuse. At its worst, before we decided to give up and try to sleep, it had been like trying to thread a dead caterpillar through the eye of a needle. I added, "I think I said too much, too."

"I think you've been wanting to tell someone that story a long time, but not necessarily to me."

"You're a good person."

"I'm a fucking walkover," Laura Sills said.

But she was still smiling.

She added, "Your hand is bleeding again, by the way," and took me into her scarily bright bathroom and rebandaged my hand. Her naked, me in my boxer shorts, in a dazzle of chrome and white tile and white porcelain.

"I think I've got your attention now," she said, when she was done, and gave me a tweak that was still tingling when I got into my Mini ten minutes later, after whispered regrets and half-meant promises and quick shy kisses.

Just after midnight, the traffic sparse under orange streetlights. I triggered two speed cameras on the way to the murder scene, but frankly I was beyond giving a shit.

I knew the address Sandra Sands had given me. It was a wrecked office block just beyond the silver griffins that, on pedestals either side of the A10, guarded the boundary of the City. Every sheet of glass in the windows of the first two storeys had been smashed, and the boards that had been bolted to their steel frames were thick with the leavings of aerosol bandits and felt-tip merchants, anticapitalist and situationist slogans (*Year Zero! We live like Insects. King Mob. Find the Beach!*) overlaid with gang tags (*Yvonne a bullet in mi art. Fuck you white hand. Enkow = positive*). Beyond the wrecked building, level ruins stretched away towards the luminous green and yellow tents a Korean company had built over the remains of Broadgate and New Broadgate, a froth of gigantic soap bubbles lapping at the abandoned towers of what had once been the self-proclaimed financial centre of Europe.

Sandra Sands was waiting for me by the steel security gates that, covered with torn and graffitied FourSquare stickers, closed off the building's entrance. "I shouldn't really be doing this," she said, as one of the two uniforms on guard duty undid the padlocks.

"Did you get the warrant for Stevens's place?"

"We found what you wanted us to find, if that's what you mean. And we have an ID for the woman. She was one of Anthony Booth's girlfriends."

"I bet that gave Dave Varnom a hard-on. How did you find out that she was killed here? Is her body still inside?"

"It was dumped in the Lea."

I remembered the white tent pitched in glaring sunlight by the river's concrete channel.

I said, "The woman tied to two dead dogs."

"Yes, sir. Two Alsatians."

"Would those be Alsatians which had their vocal cords surgically removed?"

"I don't know, sir."

"How were they killed?"

"They were fed raw hamburgers laced with warfarin."

"That would do it. Cheap security firms like FourSquare keep their dogs hungry at night so they stay alert. Is this where the woman was murdered? You still haven't told me how you found the place. And you said that there had been another murder."

"Yes, sir. Craig Stevens was found here. I'll have to talk you through it. The crime-scene technicians didn't leave much to see."

Sandra Sands used her torch to find a bank of switches. Half a dozen fluorescent lights came on. The limestone floor of the atrium had been swept clean of debris, but it was still marked with the blackened circles of half a dozen fires. The marble cladding of the reception desk had been attacked with sledgehammers, leaving white stars centred on radiating fractures; its computer terminal was a candled slump of blackened plastic. The waist-high bars of the security turnstiles had been bent and twisted by sustained hammer-blows. The leather-and-steel seats beyond had been set alight, leaving rows of char and twisted metal.

Sandra Sands said, "Are you all right, sir?"

The last time I had seen this place, the fires had still been smouldering. The Transit van had driven past it at speed, swerving around overturned burnt-out cars, in hot pursuit of the two bandits on a scooter. When they'd made a sharp turn, heading towards Spitalfields, their scooter had gone into a skid and come to grief. The Transit slewed to a halt; in the back, I lost my grip on the strap and was thrown from the bench onto the ribbed metal floor, so I didn't see the bandits take off in different directions. When I picked myself up and scrambled through the Transit's back door, I saw only the girl, and the four police chasing her down.

The third day of the InfoWar: after a protest march on the G7 conference had turned into a riot and the riot had spread; after hackers and microwave bombs had brought down the country's telephone, Web and broadcast networks, wiped bank and credit-card data, and wrecked the National Communication Data Storage Service supercomputer; after car bombs had shattered key buildings in the City of London and flash rioters had done their best to wreck the rest. The riots had been organized by a spontaneous alliance of libertarian anarchists, anticapitalists, radical greens and neoLuddites, and Irish loyalist groups had taken advantage of the confusion to plant the car bombs, but it was never clear who had paid the hackers and planted the microwave bombs. The government blamed an unholy alliance of Cuba, Libya and the enemy within, but there was no proof, only conflicting facts and claims. It was a very modern war.

I had told my own war story to Laura Sills only a few hours ago, dizzy and weepy and only half-coherent, sledgehammered by the evil mix of painkillers and Jack Daniel's. It was only my version of the truth, of course, and truth was the biggest casualty of the InfoWar. After the InfoWar, nothing was certain. Facts were no longer absolute but slippery and provisional; memory could not be trusted.

I'd been supervising the evacuation of records from the offices of an insurance company which had lost all its windows to a nearby bomb blast, and had hitched a ride with Toby Patterson's squad. We'd driven through the wreckage of the City. It was close to midnight and every streetlight was out, but the sky was clear and bone-white moonlight shone on the facades of the tall office buildings. Every window shattered, the streets full of paper and broken glass. A big crater where a microwave bomb had gone off inside a van, one of three whose intense pulses of electro-magnetic radiation had wiped every hard drive in the Square Mile. Liverpool Street station and Broadgate were still burning in places, and it was by the fitful light of those bale fires that Toby Patterson, riding shotgun, had spotted the scooter.

The girl hadn't been able to run far; she'd hurt her leg when the scooter had spun out in a long skid. Toby Patterson and his men were on her almost at once. And then the screams began, high thin screams that were utterly inhuman in their intensity. When I caught up, Toby Patterson was watching as the other three police thrashed at the girl's prone figure with their batons. Bulky as medieval knights in visored crash helmets and body armour, their batons rising and falling like the pistons of some horrible engine. Christ, how they beat her! Expending three days of frustration and humiliation and rage. By now, she was curled in a foetal huddle, and the only sounds she made were guttural grunts each time a blow to her ribcage drove out her breath.

I shouted at Toby Patterson, and he put his face in mine and told me to take my turn and tried to push his baton into my hand. "Them or us," he said. "Make the choice."

Two of his men had stopped and were watching us; the third was still whaling away, aiming licks at the girl's elbows and knees.

I shoved Toby Patterson's baton away. I told him that I was going to call for backup. My thoughts were blundering through a claustrophobic roaring in my head, but I had a heightened but detached awareness of everything around me. I saw clearly as in one slow sick second Toby Patterson reared back and snapped his arm forward. His baton, a rubber pipe loaded with lead shot, swept towards me with the lazy inevitability of a train wreck; then everything speeded up as in a blur it smashed into the side of my face. Split my lips and broke my cheekbone. Shattered four teeth and knocked me down.

"Don't let her go," someone said, and someone else said, "Let me! Let me!"

I was on my knees, cupping my ruptured cheek and spitting blood and bloody gravel. I remember very clearly seeing my blood spot and spatter the thin uneven drift of broken glass that covered the cobblestones.

The girl writhed, her arms gripped by two men as Toby Patterson tried to strip off her jeans. The other man reached into his fly and hooked out his cock and started pissing on her; one of the men holding her stepped back when the steaming stream splashed his boots, and she almost kicked free as her bunched jeans tugged free of her ankles. But then the man who'd pissed on her planted his boot on her neck. Her face, white and desperate in the light of the Transit's high beams, was only a few feet from mine, pressed sideways against broken glass.

I don't know if I went for them again. I do remember running towards the Transit. My face was loose and hot and numb, but I had the clear thought that although PoliceNet and every mobile phone network in the country was down, the Transit had a bulky army field radio with a whiplash aerial on its front seat. I had almost reached the Transit when someone ran past me, running fast, head down, arms pumping. I only got a glimpse, and my right eye was already swollen shut, but I'm sure it was the driver of the scooter, coming back to save his comrade. He shouted something. I like to believe that he shouted her name, but I don't remember. And then he triggered the bomb he was carrying. I didn't hear the explosion. I remember flying for one clear, calm painless moment, and then I slammed into the side of the Transit in a hail of hot metal.

I think I could have stopped him. He brushed right past me. I could have laid a hand on him, that at least. Perhaps I could have stopped him and swung him around in a drunken clinch. I think he would have triggered the bomb then: he was ready to do it. Toby Patterson and the other three police would not have died. Perhaps the girl would have lived, too. They had badly beaten her but I do not think they would have killed her.

I've spent over a year riddling this simple algebra and have never yet exhausted it. The other police I cannot care about, but I could have saved the girl. I was exonerated because I survived, but Andrew Fuller's death-bed statement that I had panicked and run when the squad confronted two terrorists was not completely suppressed, and everyone who heard about it condemned me. In my worst moments I believed it too: guilt exaggerates our fears and poisons our trust in memory. The reason why I had never told Julie my story was not because I was afraid that she would not believe me, but because I was afraid that I would not be able to believe myself.

So I was brimful with poisonous apprehension as I followed Sandra Sands up two sets of stalled escalators to the second floor and the wreckage of an open-plan office, where the half-burnt hulks of desks were piled along one wall like an overturned barricade, bundles of wiring hung down from holes smashed in the low ceiling, the wrinkled carpet was marked with white tide-marks of a flood, and piles of dogshit lay everywhere.

I paced the perimeter of this filthy space. The hot, close air still faintly stank of rot and char. It was a horrible place to breathe your last. The crime-scene people had been thorough, but they had left behind the chair where the blonde woman had died, and the steel-topped table, its green paint chipped and scored, where her killer had from time to time placed his instruments; there were drops and smears of blood everywhere on the green paint. There was a great deal of blood under the chair, and a smaller spray pattern a few feet away.

Sandra Sands told me that the murdered woman's name was Veronica Brooks. Or rather, that was the name she used in her work. Her real name was Jackie Grant. She was twenty-five years old, a high-class escort who worked out of a flat in Swiss Cottage. She was listed with an American website, Worldwide Exotics, shared a black server with a dozen other working girls. She had more than thirty regular clients, mostly businessmen. She charged two thousand pounds a day with a two-day minimum, her clothes and car service on top. She had a degree in Modern Languages from Cambridge, and more than twenty thousand pounds in savings accounts and bonds. Anthony Booth had been one of her clients, a fact that had pushed Dave Varnom's buttons hard. And she had a boyfriend: Damien Nazzaro, the junior member of the Vitelli family who had accompanied Barry Deane to Cuba. She had died here early yesterday morning, and Craig Stevens had been killed on almost the same spot some eighteen hours later, at around the time I had gone to Barry Deane's flat.

Had Veronica Brooks any hope at all when she'd been brought to that dreadful place? Perhaps she had seen the dead dogs in the atrium and had tried to run, but Stevens had made her climb the dead escalators, had made her strip. He'd forced her to sit in the chair, had lashed her tight. Light shining hard and bright in her eyes, the video camera's greedy black eye behind it as he bent to his work. Her screams would have echoed off the low ceiling, but the windows were boarded up and there was no one around to hear but the man who was killing her.

I said, "Is there a working phone line in the building?"

"Not as far as I know, sir."

"It doesn't matter. He could have used a mobile. Or perhaps he simply videoed it."

"Who, sir?"

"Craig Stevens. He got the keys to the building from the FourSquare offices. He killed Veronica Brooks here and killed the guard dogs too. He videoed the murder, dumped her body with the dead dogs, returned the keys to FourSquare, cleaned up at his flat, and made a copy of the video he'd made, no doubt for his own personal use. And then he went off to show Barry Deane what he'd done."

"I saw the video, sir."

"So did I. How was he killed?"

"He was shot in the head. Right by the chair where she was killed. The spray pattern suggests that he was kneeling at the time."

"Execution-style. No one deserved it more."

"If you know anything more about this, sir, I think you should tell me. Or better still come with me and make a statement to DCI McArdle." Her look was unforgiving. "You do know something, don't you?"

"What happened to our banter, the cheerful to-and-fro, the rueful acknowledgement of my superior deductive technique?"

"I think it only fair that you reveal pertinent information, sir."

"Why am I suddenly reminded of Tony McArdle?"

"He thought it might be easier for you if you talked with me," Sands admitted.

"And he was right. Well, then. Stevens killed Veronica Brooks, I think that much is obvious. I don't know why, but I think Barry Deane wanted it done. Then Damien Nazzaro found out. Perhaps Deane showed him the video of the murder. Or more likely,

Deane emailed a copy of the video to him. So Nazzaro went after Stevens. He lured him here or brought him here at gunpoint, and he shot him. I think you need to find Damien Nazzaro, DC Sands."

"Don't worry, sir. DCI McArdle came to the same conclusion, and sent out an APB."

"He thinks it's what? A lovers' tiff? Jealousy? Some kind of deal between Nazzaro and Anthony Booth?"

"I have to tell you, sir, that DCI McArdle will take it very badly if you do anything else."

"Like visit Barry Deane again?" I held up my bandaged hand. "I've already learnt my lesson."

Another lie. By now there were so many, one more didn't seem to matter.

26

A high-class call girl with links to Anthony Booth and a junior member of the Vitelli family. A call girl who had her own website. And Barry Deane, who designed websites for the Vitellis.

A bad man, a *femme fatale*, a patsy.

I drove fast down City Road, down Pentonville Road, overtaking whenever I could, earning an interesting assortment of angry gestures. The Clash on the tape deck, distortion loud. Oncoming headlights battering the windscreen, warm air rushing at my elbow.

It was all coming together. I thought I knew most of it.

Armagideon Time.

Tony McArdle's Scorpio and two patrol cars were double-parked outside the building where Barry Deane had his flat. I carded myself past the uniform at the door and was confronted by Dave Varnom at the top of the stairs, just where Barry Deane had been waiting for me a few hours earlier.

"We must stop meeting like this," I said.

Varnom was wearing white plastic coveralls, the hood cinched tight around his face, vinyl gloves and white boots. I could see the shape his shoulder holster made under his left armpit. He said, "I thought I made it clear you're not on the investigation. Clear off."

"I feel responsible. So should you, seeing as two people were murdered because you used Barry Deane as bait in your silly little scheme."

Varnom came down two steps, close enough to touch. My face was level with his belt. "Fuck off, you silly little man. There'll be plenty of time for you to try and explain the mess you caused. In front of a disciplinary board, just to start with."

"I know what this is all about now," I said, "and I very much doubt that you do."

"You don't know anything. Go home under your own steam, or I'll have someone take you."

I went back down the stairs and phoned Tony McArdle. He came out of the building five minutes later, pushing back the hood of his white coveralls, stripping off his gloves as he looked around. When he saw me leaning against a patrol car he threw the gloves into the gutter and stalked over, his face congested.

"I don't want to cause trouble," I said, "but I know why Deane was killed."

"Sandra Sands told me that you were at Craig Stevens's flat yesterday," he said.

"She told you that?"

"Of course she did. Besides, a neighbour took down the number of your car and passed it on to the local plods. Then you came here, and got badly cut. Dave Varnom told me all about it, so don't even start with any excuses. You fucked up, and you're going down for it."

"I expect you've seen the video showing the murder of Veronica Brooks, a.k.a. Jackie Grant. Craig Stevens killed her because she was involved with a blackmail attempt on Anthony Booth. Sophie Booth took something from her uncle. Barry Deane had Craig Stevens kill her and steal the hard drives from her computers, and was blackmailing Anthony Booth over them. Damien Nazzaro found out about it or was told about it, and killed Stevens and Deane."

McArdle unzipped his coveralls, pulled out his cigarettes and lit one without making the ritual offer. "Nazzaro came here all right—we have video footage of him smashing in the door. But Barry Deane had already gone. As far as we know, he's on his way back to Cuba. We're turning over the place and getting a DNA profile as a matter of course, but I don't expect to find anything significant." He sucked on his cigarette and added, "What the fuck did you think you were doing, spooking an important witness?"

"This isn't an excuse," I said, "but as far as you were concerned, he wasn't anything to do with the case. And he was already right on the edge when I saw him, and no wonder. He must have just told Nazzaro about Veronica Brooks, and he wanted to be on his way to the airport while Nazzaro was chasing down Craig Stevens. I know I fucked up, but I was right all along. He had Sophie Booth killed."

"Go home, John," McArdle said. "Go home, or go back to T12, I don't really give a flying fuck. You're out of your depth here, and it's my fault, I should never have let you in."

"Deane took something from Sophie Booth. He realized what she had when he saw one of her performance pieces. It's almost certainly on his laptop."

"If Deane has a laptop, it's not up there," McArdle said, and dropped his cigarette and screwed it under his shoe. "Go home. Get some sleep, then write everything up. You're going to have to explain why you broke into Craig Stevens's flat, and why you visited Barry Deane."

"I knew that Deane was involved in another case, concerning

dodgy data spikes being sold in schools. I think Deane and Nazzaro were in that together, which is how Deane met Veronica
Brooks."

"Write it all up," McArdle said, and turned his back on me
and went inside again.

I drove home.
As soon as I opened the door to the flat, Archimedes
swooped at me out of the darkness, spurred feet aimed at my
face. I ducked, grabbed at him with my one good hand, missed,
and fell flat on my behind. Archimedes smashed into the brick
wall and dropped to the floor. His wings scrabbled madly on
polished beech until his claws found purchase; he sprang upright
and darted off with surprising speed, banging into the side of
the sofa and spinning around, his wings whirring madly, slightly
out of synch. He was about to charge the sliding glass doors to
the balcony when I caught him.

He threshed in my hands, head wagging and wings flailing, a
light, vibrant shell full of crazed electricity. Each time I put him
down he tried to fly off: to fly at a wall. He must have been doing
that for some time. The glass visor of his face was starred and
cracked; his body was scored and dented under the tight weave
of nylon feathers. There were marks in the bare brick walls
where he had flown into them at speed. At last, I managed to
prise open the flap in his white-feathered belly and switch him
off.

I showered, my bandaged hand wrapped in a plastic bag. I
lay down on the bed for just a minute and woke seven hours
later. I drank enough coffee to do serious damage to my stomach
lining. There were eight messages on the flat's answering machine. I deleted them all. I phoned Julie, and told her about
Archimedes.

"I'm in a spot of bother," I said.

"I'm not sure if I want to hear about it."

I told her anyway. I told her that I had been shut out of the case. I told her that I had followed up on a couple of leads anyway. I told her that there had been two more murders.

I said, "It's possible that I'll have to face a disciplinary board."

"Which you've done before."

"That was a whitewash. This will be different. I didn't follow established procedures."

"Did you do what you thought was right?"

"I may have been mistaken."

"If you fucked up, at least you fucked up on your own terms."

"Is that supposed to be consoling?"

"You didn't have to do what you did. But you did it anyway. Hopefully because it was the right thing to do."

"My one last shot at glory, according to some of my fellow officers."

"Then they can't think much of you."

"If I caught a Eurostar . . ."

"No, John."

"I could be in Brussels in five or six hours."

"That is absolutely not a good idea."

"I have something to tell you. A confession. Or not a confession, not exactly. A half-assed attempt to explain why I'm so fucked up. Something I should have told you from the beginning. I want to tell you now, Julie, but not over the phone."

"Something that's too important to tell me over the phone, but not so important that it can't have waited a year."

"I don't blame you for being bitter. I could catch a Eurostar. I'd be there in time for breakfast."

"You fucked us up, Dixon."

"I know. I was an idiot. I was afraid."

And I was afraid. My hand was sweating on the mobile's plastic shell. My throat hurt, the way it does after you've been crying.

Julie said, "You didn't trust me."

"I didn't trust myself." Silence. I said, "I was thinking of a quiet café, or that park you told me about. The one in front of the palace."

"You've waited this long time to tell me. A little longer won't hurt."

"And meanwhile we're, what? Just Good Friends? Telephone buddies?"

A silence. A small sigh. "You'll have to trust me when I say that I'm not fucking you over on that. When will it happen, this disciplinary board? If it does happen."

"I haven't been told officially. But I have that feeling you get when you're in a Tube station and a train is about to arrive. When the air it's pushing ahead of itself stirs up a wind."

"But you can't see the lights coming down the tunnel. You can't hear the rumble."

"Not yet."

"Meanwhile, can you manage to stay out of trouble?"

"This thing isn't exactly over. Two of the men behind all this are still at large. And I don't know what Anthony Booth—"

"I think you should sit down and sort out your life, Dixon. Think about what you really want to do. I'll be back in two weeks. I know it's a strain, being sundered from my fabulous existence for so long, but bear up. Be a man. And then I promise, I'll listen to everything and anything you want to tell me."

She means it," Nick said. "Why would she still be talking with you if she didn't mean it?"

"I don't know," I said. "Pity. A misplaced sense of charity. Guilt."

We were sitting at one of the rickety wooden picnic tables on the terrace of the Head. The place was slowly filling up with lunchtime drinkers. Trains of small, fast-moving clouds filled the sky from edge to edge. The light was bruised bronze. The air was packed with wet heat; the overlapping shade of the terrace's big umbrellas provided no relief. Most of the blanket traders along the edge of the pavement beyond the terrace were wrapping their goods in newspaper and nesting the parcels in plastic milk crates or frayed cardboard boxes.

"You have a fucked-up sense of self-worth," Nick said. "You should wake up every day proud to have a girlfriend like Julie. Instead, you spend your time wondering how on earth it could have happened to you, and worrying about when she's going to come to her senses and leave."

"Well, she did leave."

Nick rapped the weathered grey planking of the tabletop. His fingers were knuckly with rings, the nails bitten raw. "Wake up, man! She went to Brussels on a job. She'll be back."

"We split up a month ago," I said. "Because she wanted to work out if she wanted to stay with me."

"And if she'd didn't want to stay, would she still be talking to you? I don't think so."

"I'm going to tell her. About Spitalfields."

"Good. You should have told her a long time ago. Instead, you've let yourself feel more and more guilty about not telling her, to the point where you wanted her to go because it was easier than facing up to what you had to do."

"Maybe."

"Absolutely," Nick said, and sucked a couple of inches of beer from his uptilted bottle of Sol and wiped foam from his lips, as if he'd made the point that had clinched the discussion. With his stubbly scalp and heavy dark glasses, leather waistcoat and black leather jeans, he looked like Roy Orbison posing as an East End heavy.

"Anyway," I said, lifting up the laptop from where it had been resting between my shins, and laying it flat on the table, "this is why we're here, and here it is."

"It's okay?"

"There isn't going to be a prosecution, so it isn't needed as evidence."

"I mean, his stuff is all there?"

"Of course it is. It hasn't even been switched on. What they do is plug a Bates Box into the back. It bypasses the operating system and takes a forensically pure snapshot of the hard drive without adding or removing anything. All your friend's files are still there. The copy of the hard drive taken by the Bates Box will be filed away. I doubt that anyone will even look at it. End of story."

"Not exactly," Nick said. "Jeff is thinking of going back to the States. The local Decency Leaguers heard about the raid and picketed his house. Someone threw a brick through the window last night; his wife and kid have moved out. I tell you, John, this kind of shit has made me think that if I do go on this trip to Mississippi, I might take the whole family, and not come back. When the Regulation of Investigatory Powers Act was passed, I thought, fuck it, it's a stupid law that can't possibly be enforced. We don't make stuff in this country any more, we're an information economy, and you can no more stop the free flow of information than you can stop the tide coming in. But they put in the black boxes and the RIP cutters, and then they passed the Internet Regulation and Content Control Act and they passed the Protection of Children Act, and I thought, it's like Prohibition. Keep your head down and it'll go away. But then the InfoWar made things worse because it gave the Decency Leaguers and the Little Englanders a real enemy, an excuse to pitch the whole country back to 1950. Single-sex schools, chastity pledges . . . I have a niece, man, who just turned sixteen. *She* took the chastity pledge last month. And then she went through my brother's record collection and burned everything on this list her local chapter of the Decency League had given her. She told him it was for his own good, he was lucky she hadn't taken them to the police. So fuck it, I'm seriously thinking about splitting before they start rounding us up."

"I might come with you," I said. "To Mississippi, I mean. It looks like I might have some time on my hands."

I drove to T12. The offices were crowded with technicians and secretaries and police drinking white wine from plastic cups or lager from cans. Pete Reid pushed a cold can into my hand and said, "It went down!"

I had forgotten about the Martin case. I saw Alison Somers talking animatedly at the centre of a knot of her colleagues. She'd reached escape velocity, and I felt so heavy that I might have been marooned on Jupiter.

"Three hundred years for Martin," Pete Reid said, "and a ton each for Locksley and Kernan. A solid result, my son."

Rachel Sweeney was making her way across the room towards me. You didn't have to be a detective to see that the news she was bringing was not good.

PART THREE

Spook Speak

27

Two days later, exactly a week after Sophie Booth's body had been found, I was on a KLM Airbus 340 out of Schiphol, bound for Cuba. I had been suspended with full pay pending a disciplinary hearing, something that wasn't even a sidebar in the news stories about the deaths of Sophie Booth, Veronica Brooks, and Craig Stevens—murderees and murderer, people I had never met but who had played crucial roles in my little drama. Ghosts who were never so alive as when they were dead.

McArdle was playing it as a blackmail attempt masterminded by Barry Deane. According to his version of events, Stevens had killed Sophie Booth and with the help of Damien Nazzaro had planted DNA evidence to implicate Anthony Booth in the murder of his niece. Then Veronica Brooks, the woman who had supplied the sample of Booth's sperm, had threatened to go to the police. After Deane and Stevens killed her, Nazzaro shot Stevens in revenge, but failed to find Deane, who had already fled the country. Nazzaro had escaped too. He'd caught a shuttle to Paris an hour after he'd broken into Barry Deane's empty flat, and by the time the warrant for his arrest had been lodged with Interpol, he was on a Cubana de Aviación flight to Havana.

Anthony Booth was going along with this story, which although essentially true made no mention of black websites, missing hard drives, a back-door into ADESS, Sophie Booth's complicity, or the faked email on her Wizard Internet account that had fingered Barry Deane. But it was in Anthony Booth's interest to keep quiet. He knew what Deane had taken from Sophie. He knew why she had been killed. He really had been blackmailed, but not over anything he had or had not done with his niece.

I might have left it there, if certain pieces of information had not come my way.

After Rachel Sweeney gave me the news about the disciplinary board, Charlie Wills came over and said that he had something interesting to show me.

"It's a small world," I said, five minutes later.

On the screen of Charlie's computer, the index page of the spike came up again. All black at first, and then a little flower of flame dancing in the middle. A naked figure appeared within the flames and walked forward and flicked open a fan whose folds were clickable entry points to the spike's contents.

One of the technicians had found this while doing a routine inventory of the unlabelled spikes I had brought in from Alan Rudd's dawn raid.

"It's nice work," Charlie Wills said. "High resolution, good refresh rate, all from a nicely compressed kernel."

The woman had Sophie Booth's face, but the heavy-breasted voluptuous body had been borrowed from someone else.

"There's a sound file," Charlie said, and clicked his mouse.

"Come on in," a breathy woman's voice said over the computer's speakers, as the figure in the flames wafted her fan over her naked breasts. "My sluts are wet and waiting."

"The very first thing you were supposed to see," Charlie said. "He's very cheeky."

"You know who did this?"

"I have a good idea, but not one that will stand in court. What else did you find?"

"More than ten thousand picture files and movie clips in different combinations. We've sorted them by size and the last twenty lines of code, and more than half of them were also found on the other spikes you brought in. It's possible that two different sets of people were pulling material from the same sites, but the burn codes show that these spikes were produced on the same machines as the others."

"Could he have taken her face from one of the news sites on the Web?"

"No way. Most picture files on commercial sites are compressed jpegs, but this is a tif, rich in detail. You can see the pores in the poor girl's skin if you blow it up. There's other stuff you should see, too."

Charlie clicked through the menu. There were pictures of Sophie I had seen before, the pictures duplicated on Mr Iggy Stix's website, and pictures of Sophie having sex with a variety of men and women.

"He patched her head onto other bodies," Charlie said. "Here and here, see? I think the shoulders might be hers in this one, but the right arm doesn't match the left. It's a lot cruder than the index page. Anyone with a halfway-decent graphics program could have done it."

I wondered if Barry Deane had emailed these pictures to Sophie. No, I was sure that he had.

I said, "Do you have all the specs? I have to write this up."

"I'll send them to your machine."

I wrote out a report. I sent a copy to Alan Rudd, and phoned Sandra Sands.

"I really can't talk with you, sir."

"I thought you might like to know what one of T12's technicians found." I told her about the spike's index, and the associated pictures. "Now we know what Barry Deane was doing here. Probably with Damien Nazzaro, since these spikes were found on property belonging to the Vitellis. How does McArdle feel about losing his two murder suspects?"

"He's sanguine, sir."

"Your vocabulary is improving, DC Sands. I'll send the report over, no charge."

I wrote up the report and sent it, and belatedly remembered to check my email. Amongst the usual newsgroup extracts and circulars and memos was an email with a bulky attachment, from the anonymous remailer in Cuba.

My blood stopped moving. I subjected the email and its attachment to my antivirus software and opened it:

Received: from post.mail.police.net ([128.345.0.104]) by pcnetmail1.police.net (HyperMail v3.2) with message handle 182390_367526_0_pcnmail1_smtp; Fri, 11 Jun 2010 12:28:32 for js134@js134.police.net.uk
Received: from anon02830@aglet.cu ([158.152.221.123]) id 1025602; 11 Jun 10 12:14 GMT
Mime-Version: 4.2
Content-Type: text/plain; charset="us-ascii"
To: js134@js134.police.net.uk
From: anon02830@aglet.cu
Subject:
Message-ID: <109277872.2099928.0@aglet.cu>
Don't try and find me. I'm everywhere.

It was unsigned, but I knew who it was from.

The attachment was a picture of Julie, taken across a busy street as she left her hotel, her pale, red-lipped face and slim body in sharp focus beyond a blurred foreground of little cars and scooters.

I phoned her at once, warned her that someone was following

her, that she was to tell the local police and arrange for them to escort her to her hotel. I told her, "I'll catch the first Eurostar. I'll be there in five or six hours."

"I can look after myself," she said.

"This is a bad man. Three people have been killed because of him. Please, Julie, do what I say."

"I'm not about to become one of your causes," she said.

"It's not about that."

"It is exactly about that. I left you because you make everything revolve around yourself, Dixon. Everything has to become part of your story, your little pit of misery. I can look after myself, thank you very much."

She rang off and didn't return any of my calls, but a couple of hours later she phoned me back. I had bought a ticket online by then, and was in a taxi on the way to the Eurostar terminal at Waterloo Station.

"It's sorted," she said. She was trying to sound matter-of-fact, but there was a wicked glee bubbling beneath her words.

"It isn't the kind of thing that gets sorted."

"You're absolutely wrong. I went for a walk. Tim hung back, saw the man who was following me and phoned me and told me what he looked like. I went into a café, and when the man came in I went right up to him and asked him what he thought he was doing."

"You went right up to him. Jesus."

"Are you cross because you think I was being stupid, or because you didn't get a chance to be stupid on my behalf?"

"There are ways of dealing with these people. Going right up to them isn't—"

Julie said, "Tim was with me. We all sat down. We had coffee together. We talked. It was all very civilized. He's a private detective from an agency in Holland. He was told that I was having an affair—he actually thought he was working for my husband. He was sort of relieved when I told him the truth."

The taxi was stuck in a jam in one of the back streets near Waterloo. Ordinary houses, ordinary lives.

I said, "What's his name?"

"I checked him out, Dixon, all on my own. I took his card and I phoned the number. It was genuine."

"Give me his name, Julie. The number might have been a blind."

"Harry Boomsma. He's a nice man, Dixon. An ordinary man who happens to be a private detective. He showed me pictures of his wife, his children. He has three. He lives in a place called Groningen. We talked, and then Tim and I saw Mr Boomsma on to a train back to Holland."

"You and Tim."

"Do I sense a teensy bit of hostility?"

"Point one. 'Harry Boomsma' might have lied to you. He might not be a private detective at all—the ID and the family photos he showed you could all have been faked. Point two. He could have got off the train at the next stop and got right back on your trail, or he could have passed the job to an associate. Point three—"

"We're not stupid," Julie said. "We went straight to the police after we saw Mr Boomsma on to the train. We made statements. *Don't worry*. It really is sorted out."

The taxi, finally released from the jam, accelerated and made a sharp right turn. I said, "Even if he is what he claimed to be, didn't you stop to wonder why a Dutch private detective was following you?"

"I don't know. Perhaps they don't have private eyes in Belgium."

"The people involved in this were also involved in pornography, and before Cuba and the other data havens opened up, Holland was a major clearing house for porn. Your nice family man, Harry Boomsma, is probably connected to all kinds of shady characters."

"Well, he said his job was finished."

"Of course it was. They'll have someone else watching you now. I'll be there in four hours, Julie."

"There's no *need*. I took care of it."

"You and Tim," I said again.

"I don't want to see you here, John. Okay? I'm no damsel in distress."

"And I'm no knight in shining armour?"

Silence, except for the subtle hiss of the connection. At last, Julie said, "I have a job to do. I'm working in one of the most secure buildings in Europe. The local police have agreed to drive me to work, and to drive me back to the hotel at the end of the day. Don't come here, Dixon. I mean it. Don't think that if you come here I'll swoon gratefully into your arms."

"I just want to be sure that you're safe."

"You have your life to sort out, Dixon. I'll be back in a few days. We'll talk then."

I could have gone anyway. I could have skulked around the hotel bar behind dark glasses and a newspaper, under a hat and a wig. And if Julie saw me . . . that would be the end of it. We wouldn't even be Just Good Friends.

The taxi drew up at the side of the great glass swoosh of the International Terminal. I rapped on the partition, told the driver to take me home.

When Julie had delivered Archimedes into my tender care, she had given me the address of someone who could fix him if anything went wrong. I drove over there that evening, with the Wonder Owl and his perch. It was a studio flat in a Victorian housing association block on Rosebery Avenue, with floor-to-ceiling shelves crammed with electronic gear and obsolete computers and printers, a workbench under the window, a rumpled bed walled off by boxes of parts. I sat on a listing kitchen chair and smoked two tabs while Gabriel Day, an unreconstructed six-tysomething hippie with long, grey hair brushed back from his bald patch, bent over Archimedes' stripped chassis. He rummaged in the piles of junk on his workbench, sucking on his coffee-coloured tombstone teeth, and found a hydra-headed lead. He plugged one end into Archimedes and the other into a battered laptop, and with his nose a scant inch from the screen peered at the lines of close-packed gibberish that scrolled up.

At last, he put on glasses with heavy black plastic frames and smeared lenses, and told me, "What it is, your owl's been hacked."

"Hacked?"

"Sure. See, he's been modified so that you can patch into his sensorium remotely."

"I know."

"Well, I put the chip in myself, and it's working fine, but someone hacked it. Pretty crude—like sticking a spoon in your brain and sort of stirring around."

"Someone got into my flat to do that?"

"No need. The chip links your owl's CPU via an infrared modem to a backup memory in his perch. It's a common mod on these older models. You can use it to access him remotely, and if something goes wrong with his built-in memory you just reset everything from the backup and carry on from there. What happened is that someone dialled up his modem and fucked around with his software. I can reboot and rebuild him from the last memory dump, but it'll take a little while."

"What about the dents and the rest of the damage? I want him as good as new for when my girlfriend comes back."

"No problem. I'll have to order a new visor, though. That'll take a week. It has to come from Japan."

I knew who had done it, and wondered when he had hacked into Archimedes. *I'm everywhere.* The thought that Barry Deane had been watching me in my own flat was not a nice one.

Gabriel Day pointed to a line of numbers on the screen. "If it's any help, this is the phone number of the computer your hacker used. Maybe he didn't know that your owl's modem does a hard handshake, grabs the number of anyone who dials into it. Or maybe he does, in which case this is probably a spook number, a random string set up in a use-and-lose shell."

I wrote it down, left Gabriel Day with Archimedes and a wad of cash, and drove over to T12, where I spent an hour checking out Harry Boomsma's credentials. I had a very short telephone conversation with Tony McArdle, who promised to follow it up. I phoned Anthony Booth, and then fired up my browser and sent a message to Barry Deane.

See you soon.

28

I spent most of the next day worrying about Julie. Even though Tony McArdle called to tell me that the Dutch PI was genuine and had been given a severe bollocking by the local police, it was clear that Barry Deane could reach out across the world to play his nasty little fuck-with-your-head games. He was like a malignant cell cruising your blood system, looking for weak spots.

I phoned Julie four or five times, but she wasn't picking up. I left messages—anxious, plaintive, angry, apologetic—and she finally called back at lunchtime. "I'm *fine*," she said, when I had finished expressing my concern. "Really I am. Tim has promised to look after me, which is sweet of him, but I can look after myself."

I told her that I thought she was taking this too lightly. I said, "I still have that ticket."

"Save it, Dixon," she said, and told me she had to go, she had a meeting in ten minutes.

"On Saturday?"

"I'm a popular girl. I can't talk now, Tim's waiting for me."

"In your room?" I said, and wanted to take it back at once.

"Downstairs in the lobby," Julie said, exasperation sharpening her voice. "With the nice policewoman who's going to drive us to our meeting."

"I didn't mean—"

"I really have to go," Julie said, and rang off.

Well, I had meetings of my own.

Late in the afternoon, I had an uncomfortable rendezvous with Sophie Booth's mother. We met in the terrace café of Somerset House. "One of the last places in London where you can sip a decent glass of wine and smoke at the same time," Angela Booth told me when I found her, full of apologies for my lateness. Although she clearly hadn't slept much since her daughter had been murdered, and despite the bitterness that hardened her eyes and drew down her mouth, she was a handsome woman, elegant in a white T-shirt and blue jeans and spike-heeled snakeskin boots, her long hennaed hair caught at her shoulder with a wood-and-leather clip, her lipstick a defiant red slash. She smoked steadily, reaching for the next tab even as she stabbed the butt of the last into the ashtray, and was halfway down her bottle of Pinot Blanc.

"I'm splitting up with my husband," she said.

"I'm sorry to hear it."

Angela Booth waved that away. "It was going to happen anyway."

"Still, it seems—"

"You think I should wait. That we should get through this thing together. See if it makes us stronger."

"I don't—"

"That's what my sister-in-law said. That's what my friends say—the ones who still dare to talk to me. There's nothing like having a child murdered," Angela Booth said, "to bugger up your social calendar. Anyway, Simon and I agreed to split up last Christmas. We planned to stay together until Sophie had finished her degree, but that doesn't matter now, does it? End of story, as they say. Move on. Start over. Although of course I won't get over it."

She screwed a half-smoked cigarette into the ashtray, pulled out another. I lit it for her, and lit one of my Tropicas.

She said, "The man who was killed. Is it true he was involved in what happened to Sophie?"

"Yes."

"And the other two, the ones who ran off to Cuba. They were involved too."

"Absolutely."

"And they can't be brought back."

"No. I'm sorry."

"Simon and I supported the old Cuban government. In fact, we went there for a holiday long before it was fashionable. No beaches or bars then—it was tours of factories and hospitals and model farms, and lectures every evening. Ten years ago, while the trade embargo was still in place, we were involved in a scheme for getting proscribed medicines into the country. Thank you," she told the waitress who set down my bottle of Tiger beer and refilled her glass.

"We don't have an extradition agreement with its government," I said. "Because of the InfoWar."

"Even though no one can prove that Cuba was involved in the bloody war. That was the one thing that Sophie and I could agree on at the end, you know. That the war would eventually bring an end to this government's ridiculous policies, that eventually everyone would see their pursuit of 'the enemy within' for the sham it was: an excuse to prosecute and lock up anyone who dared disagree with them. I'm sorry. You must think that I'm a flint-hearted lefty bitch, giving you the party line less than a week after my daughter was murdered. You must be wondering why you agreed to meet me."

"I'd like to know about her," I said.

"Then you're not like the rest of the police. They're interested in Sophie only as a victim. Not as a person."

"This isn't exactly police-work. I suppose I'm working in a private capacity."

"Twenty-five dollars a day and expenses? I loved those old black-and-white films." Angela Booth took a sip from her glass of wine. "Well. What can I tell you? I didn't know Sophie very well in the last few years. Oh, she was still my daughter, but we had grown apart. I suppose you might have noticed that I have strong opinions. So did Sophie. Poor Simon rather suffered, always trying to be the peacemaker."

"She disagreed with your politics."

"She resented our good works, our extended family, and all the rest. And she always did like attention; in that respect she was just like her mother. And I'm sure she began to encourage Anthony's attentions for just those reasons. Lord knows she didn't really like him, and she certainly didn't like his support for the government. She was a libertarian if she was anything, and not just because it's fashionable and 'shocking' "—Angela Booth drew ironic quote marks in the air—"to run black servers and play with porn."

"You knew about that."

"Simon and I brought our daughter up to speak her mind. She told us what she was doing. She *was* trying to be shocking, of course, but I think she was serious about it, too. It was as much a political statement as anything else."

"Information wants to be free."

"And all that. Yes. Of course, she made the mistake of equating money with freedom. She didn't see that it was a trap. Fuck it," she said, and dabbed at her eyes with the back of her hand.

"I'm sorry," I said again. I couldn't apologize enough.

"Fuck it," Angela Booth said again. "All I ask is that you do what you can."

"I'll do my best."

But I knew that wouldn't be enough either.

I was shown to the terrace of Anthony Booth's fuck-off flat by Bob, the silent, Armani-clad butler. A sweltering wind blew upriver, thick with the smell of decay. It ruffled Anthony Booth's fine blond hair and sustained the wings of his silk gown as he faced into it, standing at the prow of his silvered-wood terrace like an intrepid explorer scrying new horizons.

It was eight o'clock in the evening. Ninety-two degrees. The humidity over 80 per cent. A 50 per cent chance of rain in the next twenty-four hours.

As I walked out on to the stage of the spotlit terrace, Anthony Booth said, without turning around, "You're an interesting man, Detective Inspector. Too interesting for the police, I'm given to understand."

I said, "A little local difficulty. I think your own problems may be more global." I had so many questions to ask him. About Sophie. About the ADESS back door. About what I had learned from Don Fowler—about invisibility. I was pretty sure that I wouldn't get satisfactory answers to any of them, but I was determined to do my best. I held out the buff A4 envelope I'd brought, and said, "I've been doing some research."

Anthony Booth still did not turn around. A brilliantly lit pleasure cruiser was making its way downriver, music thumping out across the river's black flood, but I did not think he was watching it. He said at last, "All programmers leave themselves a way in to the heart of what they make. A trap door, a back door, a twist, a cheat, a hack. You do it for yourself. You do it because you can. You do it because, when you make something and let it out into the world, you want to retain control of what you made—it proves you know more about it than anyone else in the world.

You're the maker, and the little secret you hide in your creation makes it yours for ever.

"The vanity of a creator is one weakness I will admit to, Inspector, but not stupidity. Never that."

"I brought some photographs you might be interested in," I said.

Two were stills taken from the caches of the security cameras in front of this very building; the other three were outtakes of one of Sophie Booth's performance pieces. A long shot of Sophie posed under the streetlight, arms raised in her angel-winged white dress. A grainy close-up of her hand as she pointed towards the CCTV camera, pointing something like a TV zapper. And the very next frame in the sequence, time-stamped a tenth of a second later, after she had disappeared.

The invisible girl. Don Fowler had told me that her image had been overwritten by a pixellation process that patched in approximations of the background. Magnifying that single frame had revealed a kind of Sophie-shaped fringe or halo of displaced and compressed pixels where she was standing, a barely visible shimmer containing all the information needed to make a picture of her.

When it was clear that Anthony Booth wasn't even going to look at me, let alone the photographs, I said, "Sophie was killed because of your vanity, sir. And Barry Deane was blackmailing you over it."

"I was called as soon as Sophie was dead," Anthony Booth said. He might have been talking about a business deal. "I was sent pictures. And I was told what had been taken from her flat, and what it would cost for its return."

"But you didn't go to the police."

"The RedLine system is my child, Inspector. It has been adopted as the standard surveillance system in this country and by fifteen major cities in the US. My company is currently negotiating its sale to more than a dozen governments. It is a dispassionate witness, an unsleeping policeman. It learns and grows. It is self-motivated and infinitely flexible. It will transform the world."

"A just machine to make big decisions," I said, but clearly Anthony Booth wasn't a Donald Fagen fan.

"Surrendering a little autonomy is a very small price to pay for safe streets, for orderly cities. Since ADESS was set up in London, there has been an 18 per cent drop in street crime and a 35 per cent increase in arrests. Machines are fairer than people, more accurate, more efficient, more dispassionate. We trust them with so much else, why not maintenance of law and order?"

"Perhaps we trust them too much," I said. "When you put in the back door, was that just vanity? Or was it because you were afraid of your creation?"

"I have more than half a dozen interviews lined up tomorrow, Inspector I'm more than ready to give a full and frank explanation of my position."

Yes, I thought, the questions vetted, the time and place—even lighting and camera angles—specified, approval on the final cut contractually guaranteed. Booth's kind make the rules, and make sure that the rules don't apply to them. They pretend to act out of benevolence, but really it is out of fear. And I knew that Anthony Booth was afraid: his butler was carrying a pistol in a shoulder holster, and had searched me thoroughly before I had been allowed into his master's presence.

I said, "How much of the truth will you tell?"

"As much as I can. I have to be circumspect about certain things. As do you."

"I wasn't thinking of going to the newspapers with what I know, sir."

"It doesn't matter where you go. A public interest immunity certificate has been issued to all newspapers and TV and Web channels. It prevents any mention of RedLine in relation to Sophie's murder. And of course, as a policeman you are subject to the Official Secrets Act. If you go to the press, nothing you say will be reported, and you'll be buried five fathoms deep by your own people. You can try and hurt me, Inspector, but you'll only hurt yourself."

I believed him. After Don Fowler had helped me unpick Sophie's trick, I had told him that it was a feature of the RedLine chip sanctioned by MI5, that it was covered by the Official Secrets Act, that if he breathed *so much as a word* he would be disappeared to a UN listening station on the border between Zimbabwe and South Africa. And it had worked: it had scared the shit out of him. But Don Fowler cared about what might happen to him, and I no longer cared about what might happen to me.

"I'm sure all that's true, sir," I said. "But the thing is, I have nothing to lose, as you pointed out yourself."

"You'll ruin yourself. And for what?"

"It may sound silly to you, sir, but I think that the truth should be known. For Sophie's sake."

"I gave Sophie everything she asked for, and more. I helped her get away from her parents. She desperately wanted to escape. I gave her the flat, the computers, everything."

Yes, I thought, but not out of love. Or not the right kind of love, not out of the unqualified love that does not seek to possess, to suborn.

"You did take a close interest in her," I said.

"Be careful, Inspector. This conversation is being recorded. Don't be tempted to take a cheap shot."

"Let's make things clear, then, for the record," I said. "Even if it's only for your record. For whatever reason, you gave your niece a copy of a back-door program that allowed her high-level access to ADESS. That allowed her to control any CCTV camera linked to the system."

"For her performance pieces, yes. She wanted to use security cameras—I didn't see the harm in that. I suppose I was flattered that she took an interest in my work—that she wanted to make use of it. I didn't know what her real agenda was."

I saw that he was planning to justify himself by pretending that his generosity had been rewarded by deceit and betrayal. That made him easier to hate.

I said, "But there's more, isn't there? I know that you also gave Sophie a device that turned on some kind of stealth function. It made her invisible to the cameras. She was literally written out of the picture."

"Ah. You know about that."

"I saw her performance pieces, sir. At first, I thought it was just a matter of switching cameras on and off, or clever editing of recordings. But then I realized that it was more subtle than that, and I had a technical friend of mine take a very close look at the recordings."

"I had it especially made for her, Inspector. It's one of a kind."

"Barry Deane saw Sophie's performance pieces and worked out that Sophie must have had access to ADESS. He told her what he knew, and she thought that she could use him to hurt you. Because I don't think that she liked you, sir. I don't think that she liked you at all. But Barry Deane went back on the deal he'd made with her. He arranged to have her murdered, and took her computer's hard drive so he could get the back-door program and blackmail you over it. And he took something else, too: the gizmo, the zapper, call it what you will."

"Sophie was so very persuasive, and I, well, I'll admit a weakness for her. We shall," Anthony Booth said, with unexpected dignity, "call it a fond uncle's indulgence. I was fond, and I was foolish."

Yes, I thought. You gave Sophie the ability to disappear: and she disappeared.

I said, "You must have been very fond of her, sir, to give her something so powerful."

"We grew very close in the last two years, Inspector. She was much more like me than Simon and Angela. She said so herself."

I saw then how Sophie had manipulated him. How she had used his pride and his vanity to get what she wanted. At bottom, he was still the younger brother, still eager to please, still seeking approval.

I said, "Barry Deane learnt about it, and had Sophie murdered to get it. And the man he paid to kill Sophie also planted sperm taken from a condom you used when you fucked a prostitute called Veronica Brooks."

I stepped hard on *fucked*.

"I make no secret of my sex life, Inspector."

"Trying to implicate you in Sophie's murder seems to me to have been an unnecessary touch. Deane must really hate you."

"It's easily explained. I once employed Barry Deane as an outworker. I used a lot of freelance programmers when I was developing the code for ADESS and the RedLine chip. Deane was one of them."

"When was this, sir?"

"Two years ago, just after he was released from prison. Someone started sending my female workers the worst kind of pornography, I traced it back to Deane, and he was sacked."

"I've seen his file, sir. There's no mention of that."

"I didn't report it because it was an internal matter, Inspector. I discovered what he was doing and I got rid of him. It didn't seem necessary to involve the police."

"I suppose it would have been embarrassing for a firm involved in security to have to admit to having unwittingly employed someone with a criminal record." When Anthony Booth didn't say anything, I added, "What I don't understand is why you didn't tell the police everything after Sophie was murdered."

"I didn't know then that Barry Deane was behind the theft of the back-door program and what you call the gizmo."

"And Sophie's murder."

"And that too, of course."

"Come off it," I said. "You wanted to handle it yourself. You wanted to pay up and keep quiet. You wouldn't have told the police even if you did know who was blackmailing you, and I do think you knew that it was Barry Deane. Because he would have wanted you to know that it was him. That's his style."

"I admit no more than I want to admit, Inspector."

"Yes, that's always the way with people like you. You like to think you're in control."

"I did what I could, given the circumstances."

"Like faking an email from Barry Deane, and sending it to Sophie's email address at Wizard Internet? Hoping that the police would take the hint? Hoping that they'd follow it up and pin the murder on Barry Deane, but wouldn't find out what he'd taken?"

"If I had done something like that, Inspector, I would have to express my disappointment that the police failed to follow through."

But I had followed through. In my eagerness to become what I was not, I'd allowed myself to be comprehensively used—not only by Anthony Booth, but also by David Varnom. Don Fowler had also analysed the picture of Sophie Booth's body sent to me via the Cuban remailer. I had thought Barry Deane had sent it, mocking me with a picture of Sophie Booth a few moments after she had been murdered. But it was a fake. It had been doctored. It was one of the pictures taken by the crime-scene photographer, the telltale lividity—her socks of congealed blood—erased by a image-processing program. It had been bait, dangled by DI David Varnom and DI Anne-Marie Davies. And I had swallowed it.

I told Anthony Booth, "You must be so disappointed in the police, sir. The problem is that we don't play games. We live in the real world, the world of cause and effect, where you can't reset, you can't go back, if you do something wrong. There was a dead girl, horribly murdered, and there were traces of her uncle's sperm on the sheets. What else were the police going to think? You should have told them about the blackmail attempt. You should have told the whole truth."

"What else could I do, as a private citizen? Have him killed?"

"I bet you thought about it. Perhaps you even made enquiries. I hope you did, in fact, because we'll find out about them. But Barry Deane was owned by the Vitellis, and no hit man in his right mind would take the job."

"It isn't against the law to make enquiries, Inspector."

"As a matter of fact, sir, it is. An admission of conspiracy to murder would get you at least five years, although unfortunately a man with your connections would probably serve minimum time in one of the open prisons."

"Then I admit nothing. However, I will say that I am as disappointed as you in the way things have turned out."

"I wouldn't describe the way I feel as disappointment."

Anthony Booth shrugged. In all this time he had not turned around. I was trying to imagine that it was out of shame, not arrogance. He said, "There are loose ends. The official story is very neat, but we know that two of the principal players have got away."

"Are you concerned about justice for your niece, or for the things Barry Deane took with him?"

"He has contacted me, Inspector. He says that if I do not buy the back-door program from him, he will publish it on the Web."

"I'm sure that someone as smart as you could rewrite the program and close the door."

"In theory, yes. But the program is hardwired into the RedLine chip that forms the basis of ADESS. Every RedLine chip in every security camera would have to be replaced, and the present configuration of ADESS would be destroyed. ADESS isn't just a computer program; it's a complex phenomenon arising from the interaction of tens of thousands of simple elements. Autonomous and distributed. It has been growing and learning for more than two years. It's as much an individual as you or me. Think of it as a child, Inspector. My child. As far as I'm concerned, if the RedLine chips were pulled, it would be very like murder."

"That depends on your point of view, doesn't it?"

"I would have thought every policeman would approve of something as useful to them as ADESS, Inspector."

"I have no objection to ADESS itself, sir, or any properly managed surveillance system." If the CCTV cameras had been working that night in Spitalfields, if their cables hadn't been cut, their lenses spray-painted, their chips blown by microwave pulses, if their control centres hadn't been crippled by power cuts and computer viruses, there would have been no question about what had happened. I said, "I've even made use of ADESS in this investigation. The problem is that if even one person has privileged access to it, its veracity is completely undermined. You said that it is a dispassionate witness, but that isn't true, is it, as long as some people are able to evade its gaze."

"I can give you money, Inspector. Let's say it's for the pictures."

"I'm not surprised you've resorted to desperate measures, Mr Booth. I expect the government and those fifteen major US cities that bought ADESS weren't very happy when they learnt about your back-door hack, and I'm sure they'll be even unhappier when they learn that there's another special feature you didn't tell them about."

"A lot of money, Inspector. It would give you the freedom to pursue Barry Deane. To avenge Sophie's death."

"You don't know much about people, do you?"

"ADESS is as dear to me as any child to its parent. I'm prepared to pay very well to make sure that it comes to no harm."

"I don't think so. Apart from everything else, I think you already have someone working on that."

On the way out, I dropped the envelope containing the five photographs on the silvery wood of the decking. They were only copies, after all.

29

The whole wide world is no longer big enough to hide in. Everywhere is connected to everywhere else. Everywhere—the air of the most desolate desert, the wind above the waves of the most remote part of the oceans: *everywhere*—is laced with electronic chatter. We once believed that the world was packed, wingtip to wingtip, with invisible and omnipresent angels whispering the word of God to His entire creation, leaning through our skulls to speak to our souls. Now, our flesh is continually swept by an invisible and omnipresent rain of information, quantum packets, strings of zeros and ones, on its way from somewhere to somewhere else. How different are our dreams?

I knew one of the passengers on the plane. It wasn't a coincidence. You can't fly directly from England to Cuba, but KLM provides a convenient connection between Heathrow and its twice daily Schiphol–Havana route. Using PoliceNet, it had taken me only a few minutes to obtain the passenger lists.

Once the seat belt lights had gone out, I levered myself out of my narrow seat and picked my way down the shuddering aisle, brushed through the token flap of curtain that separated Economy from Business Class. I felt airily disconnected, like an angel cut off from God's sight. Horizontal light poured in through the windows: up here, above the clouds, the sun always shone, and the only information my watch would divulge was the time.

DI Anne-Marie Davies lay back in her aisle seat, eyes masked with goggles, ears plugged, and her fingers fluttering in the air, each finger wearing a ring, and each ring connected by infrared light to the little computer that rested in her lap. It looked like a sleek oyster which had benefited from an extra billion years of evolution, with a fluted shell that appeared to be made from real pearl, and tiny gold switches and red blinking lights peeking shyly along its curved and recurved edge.

I pulled the goggles forward—complex light shone in DI Davies's eyes as they turned towards me—and let them fall back with a sharp slap. The businesswoman seated next to her looked up, and when I gave her a fuck-off stare pretended to be tremendously interested in her epaper.

"DI Davies, what a nice surprise," I said.

DI Davies pulled the goggles down around her neck and pressed a button on the side of her seat, which caused it to surge upright. Its squarely padded expanse was about twice as wide as my seat in Economy. She said, "You shouldn't be here."

"We're both going to Cuba, it seems. Are you all alone this time, or is Dave Varnom hiding somewhere?"

"I really don't want to talk with you," she said. "You shouldn't be here."

"Not even when we happen to be on the same plane, going to the same place to see the same person? I assume you're acting on my report."

DI Davies gave me a cold look and pressed another button. A light flashed overhead: she had summoned one of the cabin staff. She said, "I mean you shouldn't be here. This is Business.

You're in Economy, with the rest of the cattle. I don't know what you're going to do in Cuba, I hope I don't have to care, and I certainly don't want to talk about it, so just fuck off back to where you belong."

The businesswoman hunched as far away from DI Davies as she could, flattening her epaper, with its scampering words and crawling images, against the oval eye of the window.

I said, "It doesn't matter where I'm sitting. I'm on the same plane as you, travelling at exactly the same speed towards the same place. I expect to be seeing a lot of you in Cuba, given our mutual interest."

"I don't want to see anything of you," DI Davies said. Her pale face was hard to read, a stern, bony face like a Presbyterian preacher, resolute, scrubbed clean. The black bowl of her hair, I realized now, was like Joan of Arc's, or an untonsured monk's. A soldier-saint of the InfoWar. She moved her jaw from side to side, as if she had discovered a bad taste in her mouth, and added, "If you have any sense, you'll stay away from me. You'll have a nice holiday and go back fit and rested for your disciplinary hearing."

"Are you working for NCIS, or for your friend Dave Varnom? I hope it's NCIS, although I still don't see what you can do in a country we're technically at war with. If you're not careful, you could be heading for your own disciplinary hearing."

A stewardess had disengaged herself from the task of slotting pallets of ready-cooked meals into the maw of her trolley, and was coming towards us—coming towards DI Davies, to find out what she wanted. DI Davies hooked her goggles over her eyes, plugged the foam speakers into her ears and leaned back in her chair, becoming as remote as a statue of herself on a tilted catafalque.

I didn't argue with the stewardess. I went back to my battered sling in Economy. I desperately wanted a tab, but I couldn't smoke on the plane. I couldn't even smoke Tropica Ultras, which as everyone kept telling me weren't real cigarettes. The brick of tabs I had bought in Heathrow's duty-free shop was in the sealed carrier bag under my seat, and I couldn't break into them until I left the plane. And I hadn't bought any nicotine patches because they were too much like real cigarettes. This, I thought, is going to be more difficult than I expected.

30

Despite its new status as a data haven and free information zone, Cuba is still a revolutionary socialist country. It still proudly cleaves to principles of the February 24 constitution and the Fidelista ideology. It has outlasted the Special Period of the American economic blockade. It has outlasted the fall of the Soviet Empire, the declaration of the Chinese Second Way, and the reunification of Korea. Even so, travellers arriving in Cuba still deplane from the front to the back; DI Davies was off the plane, through the airport, and on her way into Havana while I was still stuck with the rest of the Economy passengers in the towelly heat of a long concrete corridor (the single floor-mounted fan was surely a malign joke) that led to the undermanned wooden cubicles of Immigration and Customs. After only an hour of slowly shuffling past no smoking signs and faded notices in five languages apologizing for the temporary inconvenience caused by the second phase of the expansion of the José Marti International Airport, I was finally released onto the main concourse, the glass wing of its roof floating with no visible means of support high above a vast marble floor crowded with people of every colour and every age, in shorts and brightly coloured shirts, wrap dresses, leotards and T-shirts. They hauled wheeled luggage or slouched along beneath enormous duffel bags and rucksacks. Women balanced crates of fruit or live chickens on their heads. A line of people in motorized wheelchairs glided past, following a guide who held a furled umbrella like a battlestaff. As I drew on my first cigarette, I spotted a tall, thin young man standing still amidst the streams of people, holding up a torn strip of cardboard on which my name had been laboriously misspelled in green felt-tip pen.

My contact was just twenty years old, a friendly, enthusiastic computer geek by the name of Marcos Panama, the sole human employee of a data vault owned by a cabal of British netheads, T12's Charlie Wills amongst them. It was through Charlie that I'd made contact with Marcos Panama; the first thing I did after shaking hands was give him the envelope with half his fee in US dollars.

"The rest when it's done," I said.

"No problem," Marcos Panama said, folding the envelope into one of the pouches on his belt. "I have already been earning my wage. For instance, I know where Señor Nazzaro is staying."

"The Hotel Sevilla. He stayed there last time, and I made a long-distance call to check. Not a family man, our Mr Nazzaro. And what about Barry Deane?"

"I am desolate that I do not know where Señor Deane is. He has a bungalow in Miramar, but it has been empty for more than four weeks. That is your luggage?"

An overnight bag was slung over my left shoulder, and I had the brick of duty-free Tropicas in my right hand.

I said, "It's all I need."

Marcos Panama grinned. "Then we get going. Trust me, man, this is going to be fun."

He really was very young, a slightly built boy with smooth

olive skin, his black curly hair cut short except for a skinny plait that hung to the small of his back. He wore an oversized Japanese T-shirt, baggy yellow shorts and a broad, many-pocketed belt, cheap sandals. He was a university dropout—he could make more money from the information economy than he ever could in the profession (dentistry) his parents had chosen for him.

I learned this and much more as we drove into town in a tiny electric bubblecar painted the vivid green of a hummingbird. The paint was a spray-on coating of tiny solar cells that topped up the bubblecar's battery; the shell was made from recycled coconut husks bonded with resin. It was so cramped I had to sit with my overnight bag on my knees and the plastic bag on my feet because there was no other place to put them. I didn't mind. I was too busy smoking to mind.

Marcos Panama told me that Barry Deane was using a broker to front for him. "A man by the name of Ibrahim Iznaga. He came back to Cuba after the end of the Special Period, and has run various small import-export businesses with little success. Currently, he owns several small pornographic websites, and an anonymous remailer."

"Aglet dot cu?"

"You know of him."

"An interesting coincidence. Perhaps you can find out about this anonymous remailer. I'd be interested in discovering where its server is located. And I think I should have a long talk with Mr Iznaga."

Marcos Panama pushed his mirrorshades up his nose and said seriously, "If you want to talk with him, you will have to bring something to the table."

"I'm not interested in what Deane has to sell, only in finding him. Iznaga must know where Deane is staying," I said, and lit the fourth tab in an unbroken chain.

"Now you're in Cuba, man. I get you a real smoke. Cohibas, Coronas, Romeo y Julietas, Trinidads. You name it. All at the best price."

"I'm trying to give it up."

"Smoking those? Believe me, it has happened. Smoking those, you are not a smoker."

We had managed to drive through the traffic jam in the airport, and were now driving through the traffic jam on the road to Havana. It was being torn up so that a new expressway could be built, and for most of the time the road was down to a single lane. Although Marcos Panama steered his nimble little bubble-car in and out of the queue of larger vehicles—huge trucks converted into buses, tractors, tourist coaches, taxis, cars, all sputtering thick diesel fumes into the stiflingly hot air—a horde of other bubblecars were trying the same trick, along with motorcycles, scooters, mopeds converted into rickshaws, and motorized tricycles hauling trailers stacked high with TVs or computers or air-conditioning units, and sometimes drivers on the other side of the road got bored with their jam and cut through ours instead. People seemed to prefer to use their horns rather than their brakes, although the blares and beeps were not like the little stabs of anger sounded by London motorists, but more of a musical dialogue. The stripped wrecks of cars dotted the shoulder of the road, turned to impromptu shrines by faded flowers and photographs of the dead fastened to buckled doors and smashed windscreens.

"Now we all have cars," Marcos Panama said, "we are learning to express ourselves with them."

We passed a convoy of ambulances I thought must be going to or returning from a particularly bad wreck, but Marcos told me that they were medical tourists come to Cuba to take advantage of treatments which in the rest of the world were either banned or too expensive.

"Many come now to get their cellular clocks rewound," he

said. "Telomere extension, it is the latest thing in longevity treatments, and our clinics are the best."

There were tall, drooping palms topped with improbably small
clusters of fronds raised against a blue sky so bright it hurt to
look at, huge colourful billboards that mostly advertised Com-
munism (I remembered Julie's description of the bleak little
Communist shop in Brussels, with its forlorn mementos). There
was a hillside crowded with shacks made from packing cases
and flattened cans—the homes of palestinos, Marcos said, mi-
grants from the countryside. There were factories behind chain-
link fences, strings of scabby apartment buildings, microbrigade
housing built of unpainted cement blocks by untrained volun-
teers during the Special Period.

We were in a different traffic jam now, beeping and weaving
down a commercial street crammed with electronics bazaars.
There was a raw trench down the middle of the road where glittering skeins of fibreoptic cable were being spun into colour-
coded pipes. Children on street corners were selling single
cigarettes and plastic lighters. The sweet corrupt smell of sewage
cut through the diesel fumes.

Havana.

My hotel was a five-storey concrete cube on a nondescript
busy highway with terraced apartment blocks stretching away on
either side, and my small, hot room had all the charm of a condemned council flat. The carpet, laid directly on the concrete
floor, was grey by default rather than choice, and stained and
wrinkled under the window, where rain had leaked through the
corroding aluminium frame. The ceiling fan didn't work, and the
lights above the bed's rickety headboard buzzed ominously.

Marcos Panama surveyed this with eloquent sorrow and told
me that I had been swindled, that he could get a better deal
renting the apartment of a good friend of his.

"I don't plan to spend much time here," I said.

I took a shower and changed into a clean white shirt and

chinos, and went out with Marcos and bought a mobile phone at one of the bazaars. I used it to call the Hotel Sevilla. Nazzaro wasn't in his room, but Marcos said that it would be easy enough to find him.

"Like you, he must use a native phone, and all phones sold to visitors are registered."

"If he used his real name."

"Did you use a fake name? No. Because you had to show your passport when you bought the phone."

"If he used his own passport." I was amused by Marcos's earnestness. He was deeply into his role of the sidekick, the magic kid in possession of esoteric but crucially useful knowledge.

Marcos said, "His room is registered under his own name, is it not? No worries, as your people say."

"I think you're confusing me with some kind of Australian."

"I know many Australians," Marcos said. He had unclipped his phone and was using its Web function, frowning heavily as he scrolled through screen after screen.

"You can access police records?"

"All phone numbers are public knowledge. Why should they be private? Here," Marcos said, and handed me his phone as the phone at the other end began to ring.

Nazzaro answered, and told me to fuck off as soon as he realized who I was.

"We should talk about our common interest," I said, but I was talking to a dead line.

Marcos Panama took back the phone, and after a few bleeps and chirps its screen displayed a street map centred on a red dot.

"It is easy, as you see," he said. "Information is useful only if you can use it, and that is what our system does. It is the Cuban way."

"And does Barry Deane have a phone?"

"I have looked, of course. If he does, it is a ghost. Not registered. Perhaps he has one such from his broker. You would like to see Señor Nazzaro?"

"Absolutely. I want to make him an offer, and perhaps he knows where Barry Deane is. But wouldn't that be too easy?"

"Well, he is not far from here. Two minutes, maybe three."

It took fifteen, because we got tangled in one of the Santería processions that were staged twice a day for the benefit of tourists: women in white blouses and layered red or white skirts sewn with coloured tags whirled in mock ecstasy to the beat of dozens of drummers led by a figure in top hat and tails and a skull mask. This was in the old part of Havana, where the Spanish-style houses, with their balconies and wrought-iron, arched windows and wooden shutters, their tiled roofs and plastered walls painted in fresh pastels, looked too real to be real, looked like immaculate reproductions of themselves.

I took pictures using the phone's camera function, and emailed them to Julie. It had grown hotter. The air was heavy with unshed moisture. The sky was the colour of new copper and huge purple ranges of clouds were massing to the south, looming over the rooftops. My watch told me it was just past two in the afternoon; my body thought it was early evening.

There was a small park of trees and threadbare grass, and a bar in the basement of one of the pastel-coloured apartment buildings facing it, a crescent of tables in front of the broad steps down to the bar and more tables in the small, wedge-shaped park across the road. Nazzaro was sitting at a wooden table under a pepper tree with two young men and an even younger woman, whom he tipped from his knee as I approached. She wore a yellow Lycra swimsuit and tight white shorts, and gave me a look of bored appraisal from beneath a cascade of black ringlets as she sashayed away.

I said, "Can't shake the old habits, Damien? You pretend to be a ladies' man, but really you just like whores."

For a moment, there was a glint of anger in Nazzaro's dark eyes. Then he smiled. "I saw how you looked at her. I know you think she's beautiful. Young and beautiful and willing."

"That is Havana," one of the young men said. He had a straw hat with a red crown, and a slight squint. His unshaven companion showed several gold teeth when he smiled at me, and casually rested his hand inside a canary-yellow ruffle-fronted shirt split to the waist.

I told Nazzaro, "A whore is still a whore, even if she charges two thousand pounds a day. Is that what Veronica Brooks charged you, Damien?"

"With me she did it for love," he said, his face suddenly wary. He wore white toreador pants and a black mesh T-shirt, and he was fingering the edges of a big strip of adhesive bandage on the ball of his right shoulder. His upper arms were tapestried with tattoos, the plain old-fashioned kind—a dagger dripping blood, a fan of playing cards, a skeleton with a scythe—and three animations: a skull with flickering flames in its eye sockets; two naked girls writhing over each other like snakes; a cobra with smoking venom endlessly dripping from its fangs. He said, "You like these? I can get you fixed up."

"Tell your friends here to fuck off, and then we can have a quiet chat."

"I have these done the last time I was here," Nazzaro said, fingering the cartoon-bright pair of girls writhing above his left elbow. "They're the best in the world at this animated shit."

"That is Havana," the man in the straw hat said again.

I pulled up a chair and sat down and said, "I'm serious about that talk, Damien."

Nazzaro's smile disappeared. The boy in the hat gave me a sullen eye-fuck; the one in the yellow shirt said something in Spanish to Nazzaro, who shook his head and said to me, "I don't remember inviting you, but okay, what the fuck. Speak your piece."

"First tell your friends to fuck off."

Nazzaro's smile returned. "No, I don't think so. You tell me why you are here."

"You know why I'm here."

"Look, I didn't have nothing to do with Sophie Booth, okay?"

"Why bring that up, Damien? Is it on your conscience?"

"Why should it be?" he said, but he wouldn't meet my eyes.

A waiter in a long white apron came over. I told him that I was just here to talk with my friend; Nazzaro ordered a daiquiri, and told me, "You should try one. You should take it easy. Relax. This is Havana, not London. Is that your helper over there?" Pointing at Marcos Panama, who was leaning against his illegally parked bubblecar. "You'll need more than some kid."

"I can fuck him up," the boy in the hat said.

I ignored him and said, "Why are you working for Anthony Booth, Damien?"

"Who says I am?"

I unfolded an envelope and took out two photographs and laid them on the table, next to Nazzaro's ice-filled glass. Both had been downloaded from the caches of the security cameras at the front of the building where Anthony Booth had his flat. They had been taken two days after Nazzaro had returned to London, and showed him strutting up the steps towards the lobby, one a full-face portrait, the other a rear view clearly showing the building's brass nameplate beside the revolving door.

Nazzaro glanced at both of them, shrugged. "So what?"

"I think you were planning to frame Barry Deane. I don't blame you, because I know how he suckered you. It was supposed to be a simple blackmail scam, and it ended up with two women dead, and you, Damien, on the run, wanted for murder."

"You don't know anything about it."

"I know that Deane told you about this girl he had been

watching. She had something that messed up security cameras and she was willing to make a deal. The plan was to fake the theft of her computer and blackmail Booth for its return. Not only that, but your girlfriend saved a condom with Anthony Booth's sperm in it—Booth was a regular customer of hers—and it was planted in Sophie's flat, to stop him going to the police. A nice touch that. Whose idea was it? Sophie's, or Barry Deane's?"

Nazzaro shrugged.

"Anyway, you were to be the go-between. All nice and easy, except that Barry Deane had Sophie killed, and Anthony Booth refused to pay up."

"Deane's a sick fuck," Nazzaro said. "He's not right in the head."

"Absolutely. He sent Anthony Booth a video of Sophie's murder, didn't he? And he let Anthony Booth know that he was behind the murder, because he had a solid alibi and he wanted so badly to gloat over what he'd done. But Anthony Booth wouldn't pay up. Not only that, he started asking around, looking for someone who would kill Deane. That's when it occurred to you to play it another way, to contact Anthony Booth directly. Don't deny it, Damien, here are the pictures of you paying a call on his flat. Were you working for him when you shot Craig Stevens? I saw the way you enjoyed that shoot-'em-up arcade game. Was the real thing even better?"

Nazzaro told the boy in the hat, "You believe this shit? He accuses me of murder."

"Does your family know about all this?"

"They aren't bothered about my private deals."

"I suppose the bootleg porn you and Barry Deane were involved with was also one of your private deals? Penny-ante stuff for a man who likes to think he lives as large as you, Damien. No wonder you went for the chance of big money when Barry Deane told you about the RedLine back door."

"You don't have any proof I had anything to do with that," Nazzaro said, with great dignity, "and these pictures don't prove anything either. You still haven't told me why you are here. Not on business. London police have no business here."

"Not in Havana," the boy in the hat said.

The waiter came just then, with Nazzaro's daiquiri. There was a little ritual as Nazzaro offered a credit card and the waiter ran it through his machine and showed the screen to Nazzaro, who laboriously signed it, tongue caught between his lips. The air was growing closer and the light was changing: becoming harder, more metallic.

I said, "You must be the only villain who doesn't pay cash."

"Nah, I never liked it."

"Most of you like to carry a big roll, like a secondary prick."

"I don't have no need of artificial aids in that department," Nazzaro said, and rubbed his buttoned crotch and smiled at me and his two boys. "Anyway, the exchange rate is better on credit, and even the girls take cards."

"Anthony Booth wouldn't give you cash up front, would he? You didn't have time to get hold of enough cash when you went on the run, and you can't ask your family for help because you didn't tell them about your little deals. That's why you're staying in the Hotel Sevilla instead of your uncle's *estancia*. That's why you have to fix things up by yourself."

Nazzaro said, "Maybe I'm here to negotiate for the return of Mr. Booth's property. He's willing to pay a fair price, I'm here to see that he gets it. But that has nothing to do with you."

The first few fat drops of rain had begun to fall, spotting the cobbles and the grey wood of the tabletop.

"How are you going to get close to Barry, Damien? He'll do a runner if he so much as glimpses you, because he knows you want to hurt him. He had your high-class whore girlfriend killed and you have to make him answer for that. It's rule one in the thieves' code of ethics."

"You don't know anything about it," Nazzaro said, smiling at his two boys. "What movies you been watching? Not ones about the real world."

The boy in the hat laughed, and a moment later the one in the yellow shirt laughed too, although it was plain he wasn't able to follow the conversation.

I said, "You killed Stevens because Barry Deane sent you a video clip showing Stevens killing your girl. You would have killed Deane that night, too, but he'd already taken off. So now you've had to leave the job you were given by your family and you have a murder hanging over your head, all because of Barry Deane. He got you in a lot of trouble, it's natural enough to want revenge, I have no problem with that. That's why I'm here. I want to help you."

"No. No, you don't. What you're doing is fucking with me."

"I'm serious, Damien. Never more so. I don't care that you killed Craig Stevens. I saw what he did to your girlfriend, and I saw what he did to Sophie Booth. I can help you, Damien."

"Put your hand on the table," Nazzaro said. "Go on, you lying fuck. Do it."

When I didn't move, Nazzaro spoke a single sentence in Spanish, and the boy in the yellow shirt took his hand out and flicked it so the thin blade of his gravity knife clicked down.

It was beginning to rain hard now, striking through the leaves of the pepper tree with a noise like sizzling fat, drops bouncing off the table, off the cobbles. Around us, people were gathering up their drinks and heading towards the bar. The waiter followed them, walking with slow, straight-backed dignity and holding his tray over his head.

I said, "We can talk inside. We both want the same thing, Damien. We can sort everything out."

"No," Nazzaro said, "I like it out here in the rain. I like this little scene. It is like a movie. You're the detective and I'm the villain, and this is near the end of the story. You find me and tell me what you think happened, yes? You tell me you want to help me, but you're police, I know you try to set me up. So what a shame, there's no happy ending for you because I don't let anyone fuck with me. Now put your fucking hand on the table. The left one."

The boy in the yellow shirt feinted with his knife, a happy smile on his face.

I put my left hand on the table.

"Hold him," Nazzaro said.

The boy in the hat leaned forward, the brim of his hat shedding water, and grabbed my wrist tightly.

"Don't be stupid," I said.

Nazzaro leaned in and smiled and said, "I bet it hurt, when Barry cut you. He was laughing about it, the crazy little fuck, when he called to boast about how he'd fucked me."

"What are you going to do, Damien, dress up one of your baby thugs here in a suit and send him to talk with Deane's broker? You can do better than that."

The rain really was pounding down now. My shirt stuck to my back, and I was sitting in a puddle which had gathered on the seat of the metal chair. The boy in the hat had a strong grip; I could feel the bones in my wrist grind together.

"Flatten out your hand," Nazzaro said.

"I can help you," I said again. "You want Deane because of Veronica Brooks. I want him because of Sophie Booth."

"I don't think so," Nazzaro said, and nodded to the boy in the yellow shirt.

I didn't see the knife come down, but I felt the hammer of the impact and the sharp tearing pain as its blade went through the meat of my palm and into the tabletop.

Both boys pushed away from me as Nazzaro stood up. "Enjoy Havana, Mr Police," Nazzaro said. "Just stay the fuck away from me."

When they were gone, I got a good grip on the knife's plastic handle and pulled it out in one swift motion. Red-black pain, blood reddening the sodden bandages, washing to pink, dripping down onto bloodstained wood. I bent over and was comprehensively sick on the cobbles.

31

Marcos Panama wanted to take me to a hospital; I opted for self-medication. The slim blade didn't seem to have done any serious damage; it was clear that my days as a touch-typist were over, but I could still flex my fingers. I bought a half pint of vodka at the bar, and in the tiny, white-tiled toilet poured it over the wounds in my palm and the back of my left hand. I let Marcos retie the bandage, then dried myself as best I could with paper towels, poured water from my shoes and threw away my sodden socks, and sat in the little basement bar and drank several glasses of dark, oily rum until my blood began to move around my body again and I could think about what to do next.

Marcos ordered food, but the pain in my hand and my displaced internal clock left me with little appetite, and he ate most of the coleslaw and fried fish and black beans while I made do with half a bowl of fish soup and dry bread and a couple more glasses of rum. We had a brief technical discussion. Marcos made several calls on his phone. By the time little cups of coffee had been served, Damien Nazzaro had been sorted out, and I had the name of the hotel where DI Anne-Marie Davies was staying.

It was still raining when we took to the streets, although a single shaft of sunlight pierced the clouds like God's own searchlight. We parked outside the Hotel Sevilla, and after a little while Damien Nazzaro came through the sliding glass doors, arguing with two police and followed by a bellboy pushing a luggage cart stacked with suitcases. Nazzaro ran through an alphabet of arm semaphores and hand gestures, then struggled furiously and shouted loudly when the police moved in and wrestled his arms behind his back and cuffed him.

It had been alarmingly easy to set up. I had dictated a fax, warning the local police that Nazzaro was a known forger using counterfeit cards, and for a ridiculously small fee one of Marcos's friends had contrived to make it seem to come from Scotland Yard's Fraud Squad. It wouldn't keep Nazzaro out of the way permanently, but it would seriously inconvenience him.

He was still shouting at the police as they started to force him into the back of their car. It was almost worth the pain in my hand.

D I Davies had booked into a brand-new hotel on the seafront. It was as efficiently impersonal as a shopping mall. A marble floor as big as a soccer pitch, fountains and plantings of tall palm trees, a Gap, a McDonald's, a Starbucks, a Republica cigar shop, and an anonymous newsstand. A vertical banner hung from the middle of the high glass roof mysteriously proclaimed that *Havana welcomes Elvis Presley!*

"This is very lovely," I told DI Davies, half an hour after I had called her room. "I do hope the British taxpayer is footing the bill. Otherwise I'd have to suspect that you were somehow on the take."

"I said that I'd give you five minutes," DI Davies said, with her usual icy hauteur. "I'll give you none at all if you're going to indulge in cheap insults."

We were sitting in the bar on the top floor of the hotel, with a tremendous view over the sea and the long curve of the seafront promenade of Havana, the Malecón. The sun was sinking beyond crowded rooftops and office blocks. A very old man with a cap of white woolly hair was playing soft, slow jazz on a shiny black grand piano. DI Davies had not yet touched her mineral water, but I was halfway down my frozen daiquiri. I had to admit that Damien Nazzaro had been right about them. I was wearing an oversized jacket made of violently red cloth the texture of a horse blanket the maître d' had insisted I put on, and I rested the palpitating ache of my left hand in the jacket's capacious pocket as I told DI Davies about Damien Nazzaro.

DI Davies had had her suit pressed since getting off the plane. Her cap of black hair looked polished and her face was as cleanly scrubbed as a nun's. She said, "All you're doing is making things worse for yourself, and I hope you'll have the sense to stop before you do any more harm."

"And what are you doing here, DI Davies? Making bids on behalf of the government for the stuff Barry Deane stole? He's involved in at least three murders. How do you feel about helping someone like that make a profit from his crimes?"

"My personal opinion has nothing to do with it. I'm here to do a job, to the best of my ability."

"Where do you live, DI Davies?"

"What do you mean?"

"Where do you make your home? Where do you park yourself of an evening? Where's your own little private space?"

"Shepherd's Bush, if you must know. I don't—"

"We have something in common. You know, that's my old manor. Where I was brought up by my grandmother. Grandma C., for Cecily. I can't see you in one of the Victorian brick terraces, or in one of those cozy cottages the BBC executives love so much, and I definitely can't see you in a council block, so that leaves somewhere modern. A block of flats carved out of one of those lovely old Victorian pubs, or a purpose-built development. I'd guess the latter, because when I first met you, out in Docklands, you seemed right at home."

"David Varnom was right about you," DI Davies said.

"Really?"

"He said you were a touchy little fucker with a bad attitude," DI Davies said primly.

"I can understand Dave Varnom. He's motivated by hatred, which is a very human emotion. But what about you, DI Davies? Help me out here. I'm trying to find some spark of humanity, some point of contact. What's your flat like? I can't picture it. Is it kitted out by Ikea, all clean lines and clever storage spaces, dried flowers in vases, a few cuddly toys on the bedspread? Or is it something starker, a Retro Moderne stainless-steel kitchen, a floor of that clear neoprene with dead leaves suspended in it? Because, quite frankly, all I'm seeing is an empty shell just as the builders left it. You come home of an evening, and two steps inside the door you set an internal alarm clock and switch off until morning."

"If you're trying to insult me, you aren't getting anywhere."

"I'm trying to find the human being inside the impersonal functionary, DI Davies. Because we are human beings as well as police. We can make compromises. We don't run on inflexible rules. We aren't limited by the parameters built into our software."

"I have a job to do," DI Davies said dryly. "My personal likes and dislikes don't come into it, so don't think you can prick my conscience and make me change my mind. You might have been with the Hostage and Extortion squad once upon a time, but if you don't mind me saying so, you're clearly out of practice."

"Well, you can't say I didn't try," I said. I was sweating inside the heavy jacket, and its wiry material was rubbing welts at my wrists and the back of my neck. "All right, we'll stick to plain facts about your job. Which is, as I understand it, to pay Barry Deane for what was stolen when Sophie Booth was murdered."

DI Davies sipped her mineral water. "For the hard drives and the remote control, yes."

"And you don't have any qualms about helping a murderer profit from his crime."

"The point is to retrieve items that endanger national security."

"Anthony Booth isn't cooperating, is he? He won't give you a copy of the program because closing the back door will mean killing his cybernetic child."

DI Davies rubbed her thumb over the rim of her glass, erasing a smear of lipstick she had left there. "What Mr Booth wants is irrelevant. He's out of the loop."

"Oh, I don't know. The police won't be able to hold Nazzaro for long. Can I ask you, DI Davies, if you have already made a deal with Barry Deane?"

"That's none of your business."

"Someone must be helping you find your way around, because you don't have any more power here than I do."

"That's none of your business either."

"I don't know much about politics, but I do know that Britain has no official diplomatic links with Cuba because of the information war. So either you're fronting for some MI6 spook, or another government is helping ours. I couldn't help noticing, for instance, that this hotel is very close to the American embassy."

"I do wish you'd come to the point, because your time is nearly up," DI Davies said, although she hadn't looked at her watch.

"I'm not interested in the stuff stolen from Anthony Booth. I'm not interested in the scandal which might result if it was learned that there was a back door into the RedLine system. Like Damien Nazzaro, I'm interested in Barry Deane. Only I don't want to kill him, just bring him back to Britain to stand trial for the murder of Sophie Booth. You do remember Sophie Booth. She was Anthony Booth's niece. Barry Deane had her killed. I think he ought to answer for that."

"There is far more at stake than a murder investigation, but I wouldn't expect you to understand that."

"Look, I don't care about the politics surrounding ADESS. All I want is to make sure that Barry Deane answers for what he did rather than profits from it. At some point you're going to want to verify that what Barry Deane wants to sell you is the genuine article. He's going to have to demo it. All I ask is that you let me know when and where. I'll come in after the handover, strictly on your say-so. If that sounds unreasonable to you, then I don't think we have anything more to talk about."

DI Davies stood. "For once," she said, "we're in complete agreement. I want you to stay away from me, and stay away from Señor Iznaga, too. You really have no idea about what's at stake here."

I went back down to the lobby. I sat on a marble bench and watched the lifts through a stand of tropical greenery. I bought a bottle of aspirin, and after some trouble with the child-proof lid downed half a dozen dry. The pain in my hand didn't lessen, but it slowly receded, as if it had stepped into another room. I ate a Snickers bar and smoked four tabs, screwing each spent butt into a pot of grey sand. The air-conditioning made the huge, well-lit lobby as cold as a tomb or a cathedral; I shivered in my grubby, rain-wrinkled short-sleeved shirt, my damp shoes. I was half-drunk, dead tired, and mantled in dried sweat—flop sweat, fear sweat. Bellboys in purple uniforms and pillbox hats pushed rattling trains of luggage carts across the marble floor. A party of forty or fifty grey- and white-haired tourists wearing pastel leisure clothes and stick-on badges made a noisy rendezvous and wheeled away like a flock of birds. Elvises in blue jeans and check shirts, in sharp houndstooth suits and silk shirts, in army fatigues, in Las Vegas rhinestone and white satin jumpsuits and aviator shades, wandered past in groups of two or three.

My mobile rang. It was Julie. Seven in the evening in Cuba; midnight in Brussels.

"Now you've gone and done it, Dixon."

So she'd seen the photos I'd emailed.

"I'm on holiday."

"What a fabulous lie."

"A policeman's holiday."

"You're chasing ghosts, Dixon. I don't know whether to laugh or cry, really I don't."

"Oh, he's real, all right. A very real and very bad man."

"I meant your own ghosts, Dixon, but I suppose you want to tell me about this bad man. Who is he? Is he the one who set the nice Dutch detective on my lovely tail?"

"Have you had any more trouble in that direction?"

"I've been managing to have my usual wonderful time."

DI Davies came out of one of the lifts and trotted on a purposeful diagonal across the lobby towards the revolving doors.

I said, "Julie, I have to go."

"I hope this isn't an elaborate ploy to get my sympathy."

"I really am here to do something important. My last piece of police work. And I really do have to go now."

"You stay in touch," she said, and rang off.

I rang Marcos while I loitered on the other side of the revolving doors and watched DI Davies consult her watch under the raked steel and glass awning. A black limo swung into the short arc of the drive and pulled up. A bellboy opened the door; DI Davies didn't tip him before she climbed inside. As the limo whispered away, I pushed through the doors, sprinted across the drive, dodging a yellow taxi, ran down a sloping stretch of springy grass, leaped over a low hedge of some kind of flowering evergreen, and almost fell on my face on the pavement as Marcos's bubblecar drew up. He opened the passenger door and I tumbled inside.

"Follow that car," I said.

I'd always wanted to say that.

The limo drove into the old town. Marcos kept three or four cars behind, switching lanes every two or three minutes. He was a natural at the tailing game, and I told him so.

"I learned it from American movies," he said. "Where do you think she goes?"

"I don't think she's going to hit the nightclubs."

Marcos drove past the limo as it pulled up at the steps of a wedding cake of an old hotel, turned at the corner and parked. I walked back past the limo and climbed the steps. As I entered the huge, marble-floored lobby, I saw DI Davies and a tall man with a bristly crew cut and a grey silk suit walk through a tall walnut doorway flanked by potted palms.

It was a ballroom, half its floor crowded with tables and tourists, the other half full of couples dancing to a twelve-piece band punching out a brassy *danzón*. Chandeliers blazed like inverted Christmas trees beneath the gold ceiling. Mirrors on the walls doubled and redoubled the lights and the dancers and the noisy crowd. I sat at the end of the long bar, near a pack of braying American businessmen and- women celebrating with champagne and oysters the conclusion of a deal, and watched as Crew-cut Man introduced DI Davies to a heavy, slab-faced man at a table behind the rail of the raised section at the far side of the room.

Slab-face picked up the receiver of an old-fashioned telephone and talked into it, watched by DI Davies and Crew-cut. He talked to the telephone for ten minutes, then talked with Davies and her friend for twenty. A thin, straight-backed old man in a red shirt and a black slouch hat joined the band and sang three numbers in Spanish strongly and clearly and with great emotion, the band playing as tightly as any I'd ever heard. I drank two very cold beers and fended off the advances of one of the American businesswomen.

Finally, DI Davies and Crew-cut shook hands with Slab-face and left. I drained my beer and walked through the crowded tables, climbed the wide, shallow steps, and said, "Señor Iznaga, I presume."

"I usually expect my clients to make an appointment," Ibrahim Iznaga said, "but out of respect for the British police I'll make an exception."

Iznaga was a charmless, insincere man in his early sixties, a chancer, a would-be operator whose greed had blinded him to the plain fact that he was a long way out of his depth. He affected an old-fashioned dandyism: white French cuffs on his pink shirt, a handkerchief meticulously folded in the breast pocket of his linen jacket. Thinning black hair that was surely dyed was slicked back over his scalp and curled at his collar. If he had been a character in a movie, he would have been played by Sydney Greenstreet. A web-book lay in front of him on the crisp white linen tablecloth, flanked by an incongruous brace of old-fashioned telephones with rotary dials and braided cords. His bodyguard, a very large and very polite gentleman with matt black skin and waved, oily hair, had frisked me thoroughly in the toilets, escorted me back to his boss and poured me a tiny cup of coffee from a silver pot, and now sat at another table, in the shadow of a pillar.

I told Iznaga, "I'm not exactly a client."

"And despite your impressive credentials, I do not believe that you are here as a policeman." I had shown Iznaga my warrant card and he had studied it carefully before handing it back, telling me that this was the second one he had seen in an hour.

Now he folded his hands on his belly and smiled at me and said, "So, what do you want? Tell me that it doesn't complicate my business, and I might listen."

I laid a photograph on white linen and said, "I'm here to find the man responsible for two murders. This man. The man you are representing."

Iznaga turned away from me and interested himself in the singer and the band at the far end of the long, crowded room. He said, "I know nothing of that business. It was in another country."

"If you give me an hour, I can give you the full story."

"Too bad, I don't have an hour to give you."

"Because you don't want to believe it? That would be a serious mistake."

"Because I don't give a shit about what happened in some rainy little island on the other side of the pond, if you want the harsh truth."

"Frankly, I'm not interested in the stuff Barry Deane wants to sell. As far as I'm concerned you can do what you like with it, and good luck to you, you'll need it. But I do want to bring Barry Deane back with me."

"Really? How are you going to do that?"

"I'll have a word with him, and make him see reason. Meanwhile, I'd appreciate it if you didn't close any deals, Mr Iznaga. I don't want Barry Deane suddenly coming into funds. It would make him even harder to find."

The song finished. Iznaga lifted his hands and clapped softly, adding to the loud applause that rose from the crowded tables under the chandeliers and the gold ceiling. The old man bowed from the waist and swung his arm vigorously, counting the band into the next number.

Iznaga said approvingly, "He is very good. One of the last of the old school. Did you understand his song?"

"My Spanish isn't very good."

"Of course. You are a stranger in this country."

"And you've been here, what? Five years?"

"He was singing of his lost love. *Perdito tu amor, no podré ser feliz jamás.* Now your love is gone, I will never feel happiness."

"You were just talking with a colleague of mine, DI Davies. I know that she wants to make a deal with you. And I know that Anthony Booth is prepared to pay a high price for the return of his property. Perhaps you are playing one off against the other. Unfortunately, Booth may have a little difficulty in closing the deal; his man here has been temporarily inconvenienced. He is currently discussing a problem with his credit rating with the police."

Iznaga studied me briefly. He said, "Señor Booth and your colleague may not be the only ones interested in this property."

"These would be real people, or stand-ins to boost the asking price? That's a dangerous game, if you don't mind me saying so."

"Now I do believe that you really are a policeman," Iznaga said. His smile made him look like a frog about to swallow a fly.

"You're not dealing in porn with small-time chancers, Mr. Iznaga. I would be very careful, if I were you."

"Please don't threaten me. I take threats very badly."

"I'm trying to be helpful," I said. "I want to talk with Barry Deane."

"Unfortunately, I do not know where you would find him."

"You do not know where your client is?"

"What can I tell you? I'm just the middleman here. He keeps in contact by email. Those interested in what he has to sell come to me, and then I tell him what they offer. He will meet them soon, to demonstrate what he has and then to hand it over."

"So you've made a deal."

Iznaga took out a cigar from the breast pocket of his linen jacket, drew it under his large-pored nose and sniffed it appreciatively. He said, "Here's some free advice. Be a tourist. Enjoy Havana. It's a great little town. But don't try and find Barry Deane."

"You're right. I'll sit at the bar and listen to this fantastic old-style singer while you tell Deane that I'm here, and that I'm looking for him."

Iznaga turned to his bodyguard and said something in Spanish. The big man stood up, showing me a small nickel-plated revolver. It looked like a toy in his big hand. Iznaga said, "Leon will show you out by the back way, and explain to you why that's such a bad idea."

As the bodyguard guided me down the steps, one hand clamped on my shoulder and the gun in the small of my back, I said, "Do you speak English, Leon? ¿Habla inglés?"

"Sure I do, but it won't do you no good to argue. This is just my job, man. Let me get it done and I won't fuck you over too bad, okay?"

The singer bowed to applause, his black slouch hat clasped to his chest, the band swung into a punchy mambo, and Leon bore down hard on my shoulder because I had tried to turn around; the white-jacketed waiter who'd just gone past us was Nazzaro's squint-eyed sidekick.

"Don't get me mad," Leon said. "You don't want to be doing that," and shoved me forward. We were almost at the doors when the first shot cut through the music. Leon pushed me aside and started to bull his way through dancers towards the raised section at the back of the room, where Ibrahim Iznaga was trying to stand up, his cigar still stuck in his mouth, as the squint-eyed boy shot him in the face and shot him again as he went down. Leon was almost at the foot of the steps when the boy coolly shot him twice and walked away, his gun held loosely by his side, blood all over his white jacket.

The music had came to a ragged stop. A woman screamed. Everyone in the big bright room rushed the doors. I went with them.

32

"It's plain Iznaga was murdered to force Deane into the open," I told Marcos Panama. "Nazzaro doesn't want to make a deal. He wants Deane, and not in a good way."

We were leaning against a wall scabbed with posters across the street from the hotel, sipping from little paper cups of strong sugary coffee bought from a street vendor's cart. Police cars and ambulances, light bars flashing, were double-parked under the leaning palm trees in front of the white icing of the hotel's spotlit façade. Traffic had been pinched down to one lane by hissing orange flares laid in the road; drivers were expressing their indignation with an off-key symphony of horns. Doormen waded amongst the slow-moving cars, searching out empty cabs for tourists fleeing the scene. I was feeling cold and jumpy, half-expecting the squint-eyed boy to amble out of the crowd that had gathered to watch the show.

I told Marcos, "We need to flush Deane out of his hiding place before Nazzaro finds him. What about this remailer, Marcos?"

"There is good news and bad. I have found the server that hosts Señor Deane's anonymous remailer, the one known as aglet.

It was not difficult. Unfortunately, the server that hosts it is impossible to reach."

"But you do know where it is."

"Certainly. It is in the Cube."

"The Cube?"

"It is where much of the hardware of the Internet servers is located. Señor Deane's remailer is embedded in a server owned by Andreas Vitelli."

"I wonder if Mr Vitelli knows about that."

"The Cube is very well protected, both electronically and physically. Not even the police can enter. Not even the government. Only licensed technicians."

"I find that hard to believe."

"It's true. It is why Cuba is a successful data haven."

"According to our mutual friend Charlie Wills, you don't need to physically access the server in order to close it down," I said, and I explained what Charlie had given me, and what I wanted to do.

"I think it possible," Marcos said. "It would depend on the quality of the server's firewalls, of course."

"It's my last chance, Marcos. That, or trail after DI Davies."

"Everything is simple if you know the right people," Marcos said. He looked very young and very determined, a geek ninja in baggy shorts and an oversized T-shirt printed with a picture of some Japanese cartoon hero with big eyes and a flamethrower. He smiled and added, "And you are lucky, because I know many people."

"That's good," I said, and asked him for another favour.

"Surely a gun would be better."

"I don't want to kill anyone, Marcos. I just need something that will stop them having a go at me."

"I think I can get something suitable."

"Good. Let's go and see your friends. The clock is ticking."

Marcos's apartment building was a crumbling brutalist block that had been built by the Soviet government forty years ago to house "special advisors" to the Cuban revolutionary government. By a psychogeographic irony, some of those "special advisors" had been the technicians who had constructed the big Russian interception station at Lourdes, just outside Havana, that had surveilled data from telephone calls and satellite links across the US, for now the building was home to an international community of netheads and white hat hackers and netrepreneurs—not only Cubans, but Chinese, Indians, Russians, Australians, and even a few Americans. Script kiddies, stringers, programmers, coders, Web designers, video editors, multimedia editors, streaming media jockeys, database analysts, channel editors, on-line researchers and graphic designers, a loosely affiliated tribe of technocrats careless of national boundaries. They were the wave of the future, as much a part of it as the offices and data warehouses going up all over Havana. They had turned the building's warren of cockroach-infested apartments into a cross between a student dorm and a backpackers' hotel. The breeze-block corridors, lit by buzzing naked fluorescent tubes, were ropy with graffiti and resonant with music mingling from dozens of sound systems; power lines from rooftop solar cells and swags and loops of fibreoptic cables were stapled to the ceiling.

Marcos had set up the meeting by phone as we drove across Havana. When we arrived, twenty kids were already crammed into his small, spartan apartment, sprawled on the mattress or sitting on rough-hewn chunks of foam rubber or on folding chairs they had brought themselves. Gawky boys and girls in nolabel baggies and T-shirts and sneakers, crew cuts and ponytails and dreadlocks, tattoos and multiple piercings. Some with palmtops or web-books like rolls of cloth or slabs of slate, others wearing chunky data spex. One girl wore a lumpy silver belt which, she claimed, contained more computing power than the Pentagon.

After I had given them a rundown of the circumstances of Sophie Booth's murder and described what Deane had stolen, they quickly agreed that it would be easy enough to do what I wanted, but the earnest discussion of the ethics of the plan, and whether they should risk their good names by hacking what might be an innocent site, took far longer. I went up to the roof and looked out at the lights of Havana and wondered where Barry Deane was, wondered if even now he was reaching out to DI Davies, arranging the deal, getting ready to vanish. I went back to the room. The kids were still talking. I nodded off, was woken by Marcos. My watch told me it was ten minutes to midnight; my body suggested it was some time in the next century.

Marcos was grinning. "We'll do it," he said.

They did it on the roof.

Twenty kids sprawled on old loungers and chairs scrounged from hotels and set up on a stretch of Astroturf beside a garden of satellite dishes and racks of black solar panels, typing furiously at laptops connected to mobile phones or flexing ringed fingers as if conjuring spells from thin air. There was a party atmosphere—candles flickering in coloured glass holders, red paper lanterns strung on a line, music from a boom box, Chinese food and beer, buzz colas and coffee coolers and Guatemalan weed. Marcos had ordered everything, and I'd paid for it.

The favour I'd asked Marcos to supply came half an hour later. A tiny glass ampoule of clear, oily liquid, and a plastic syrette with a single shot of antidote. It cost more than everything else, almost cleaning out my stash of paper dollars.

After Marcos had explained how it worked, I said, "Laughing gas isn't exactly what I'd asked for."

"It is not laughing gas," Marcos said. "It is a very specific releaser, made by bacteria genetically engineered here in Cuba. We have the best genetic engineers in the world. This stuff will disable someone as quickly as capsicum spray, and it is pain-free."

"People have been known to die laughing," I said, and added, when Marcos looked blank, "An English saying. How much longer do your friends need?"

"Half an hour. Perhaps a little more, perhaps a little less."

"Take me to the Cube, Marcos. When that server starts to drown in spook speak, I want to be ready and waiting."

33

Spook speak:

Rewson, SAFE, Waihopai, INFOSEC, ASPIC, MI6, Information Security, SAI, Information Warfare, IW, IS, Privacy, Information Terrorism, Terrorism, Defensive Information, Defense Information Warfare, Offensive Information, Offensive Information Warfare, The Artful Dodger, NAIA, SAPM, ASU, ASTS, National Information Infrastructure, InfoSec, SAO, Reno, Compsec, JICS, Computer Terrorism, Firewalls, Secure Internet Connections, RSP, ISS, JDF, Ermes, Passwords, NAAP, DefCon V, RSO, Hackers, Encryption, ASWS, CUN, CISU, CUSI, M.A.R.E., MARE, UFO, IFO, Pacini, Angela, Espionage, USDOJ, NSA, CIA, S/Key, SSL, FBI, Secret Service, USSS, Defcon, Military, White House, Undercover, NCCS, Mayfly, PGP, SALDV, PEM, resta, RSA, Perl-RSA, MSNBC, bet, AOL, AOL TOS, CIS, CBOT, AIMSX, STARLAN, 3B2, BITNET, SAMU, COSMOS, DATTA, Furbys, E911, FCIC, HTCIA, IACIS, UT/RUS, JANET, ram, JICC, ReMOB, LEETAC, UTU, VNET, BRLO, SADCC, NSLEP, SACLANTCEN, FALN, 877, NAVELEXSYSSECENGCEN, BZ,

CANSLO, CBNRC, CIDA, JAVA, rsta, Active X, Compsec 97, RE NS, LLC, DERA, JIC, rip, rb, Wu, RDI, Mavricks, BIOL, Meta-hackers, SADT, Tools, RECCEX, Telex, OTAN, monarchist, NMIC, NIOG, IDB, MID/KL, NADIS, NMI, SEIDM, BNC, CNCS, STEEPLEBUSH, RG, BSS, DDIS, mixmaster, BCCI, BRGE, Europol, SARL, Military Intelligence, JICA, Scully, recondo, Flame, InfoWar . . .

Spook speak. Keywords and alphabet soup acronyms that security service dictionary computers, ether peekers, packet sniffers and all the rest of the Web's electronic policemen and border guards sleeplessly search out in the endless flood of information, a list as long as the Bible.

Marcos's friends were dispatching thousands of clones of a freely available program to servers around the Web, cloaked in spoof addresses. Once launched, the clones would dial up Barry Deane's remailer, send a tiny program that would jam open any mail filter, and bombard the remailer with hundreds of thousands of copies of the spook-speak file Charlie Wills had given to me, a file constantly annotated and passed back and forth by hackers. Every electronic watchdog in the world, drawn by the spew of spook speak, would start dialling up the remailer too, until its server ran out of bandwidth. And if Barry Deane tried to use his laptop, the clones would dial up its modem, using the phone number left behind when he'd hacked Archimedes the Wonder Owl, and crash that.

We were going to shut him down. We were going to drown him in information.

It was highly illegal. It was mail bombing. It was denial of service. I had crossed to the other side. I didn't care.

34

Marcos Panama drove me across town to Havana's new commercial centre. We drove past the skeletons of half-built ten- and twenty- and forty-storey office buildings. We drove past completed but empty buildings surrounded by security fences and raw trenched earth and mounds of rubble, every window marked with an X as if by some demented lover. We drove past empty, wire-fenced parking lots punctuated by lush groves of palms and palmettos and banana plants, past a building clad in black mirror-glass, a building like a fantasy of a Moorish castle cast in concrete, with crenellated battlements and deeply recessed slit windows, a low rambling building whose every window at this late hour blazed with light.

And we drove past a modest three-storey, windowless matt black block with a forest of microwave antennae and satellite dishes and cooling units on its roof, surrounded by an artificial lake that was in turn ringed by security fences and cameras. This was the Cube, the physical location of much of Cuba's telecommunications industry, a data warehouse crammed with servers and memory chips, equipped with emergency generators and backup batteries and kilometres of optical cabling. Its cladding, like the skin of Marcos's bubblecar, was full of tiny solar cells; its moat was part of an elaborate heat-recycling system.

I watched it dwindle in the rear-view mirror as Marcos drove on. It looked exactly like the kind of facility that plucky hitech thieves, armed with laptops and laser deflectors, climbing equipment and ingenious little black boxes, were always trying to break into in blockbuster movies.

"It's time to phone your friends," I told Marcos. "It's time to send Barry Deane a message."

We parked at the edge of an empty lot behind hoardings painted with the faces of dead Communist heroes, across the road from a sprawling, spotlit steel-and-glass office building. Dead-looking shrubs and spindly trees stretched away into darkness; beetles and fat moths clumsily dive-bombed the bubblecar's headlights and clustered on its windscreen.

Marcos plugged into his laptop. It was a fat pod that looked like it had been picked from some exotic jungle tree, its reduced keyboard buried inside a slot, output sent directly to goggles, input through skinny gloves he pulled on with a snap.

"It is done," he announced, after a couple of minutes of air sculpture.

"It's done?"

"I mean that it has started."

"How long will it take?"

Marcos shrugged and waved his right hand through the air. His goggles filmed over and he said, "The clones must multiply and spread the good word. I will keep watch."

While Marcos sat cross-legged in goggles and gloves on the front seat of his little car, eating spoonfuls of a bacterial culture that looked like crude oil and smelt worse, I prowled around the car, strung-out and restless. When I got bored with kicking stones I walked a little way into the scrub and stood on the ridge of upturned earth by a rutted track and stared at the Cube, which squatted like some gigantic altar in the centre of its floodlit lake. Insect code buzzed all around me. I imagined that the black air above the Cube must be seething with information, as invisible but densely packed as a science fiction force field.

The bubblecar's horn sounded. I went back, and Marcos told me that the server had gone down, saturated with information spew. He said, "Do you think he will come?"

"I think he needs that server because he has to link to ADESS in Britain to demo what he stole. Now it's gone down, he'll have to come out here to reboot it."

"He has access to the Cube?"

"The Vitelli family own that server, and he's their computer expert. Of course he has access."

I wasn't as sure as I tried to sound, but it was the only plan I had.

"Then all we have to do is wait," Marcos said. He was still sitting cross-legged, the goggles pulled down around his neck, and now he stretched and yawned, cool as a cat.

I wondered if he truly believed that what we were doing was real, with real consequences. I said, "You can take off if you want, Marcos. Scoot. Go. Leave."

"I am fine. I finish this job. Maybe you give me a cut of what you get for these things your man tries to sell."

"I won't get anything," I said. "If I'm lucky, I get to hand Barry Deane to the police in England, and then I walk away, sadder and wiser, my honour intact and my faith in my fellow-man slightly diminished."

Marcos smiled and said, "You are I think a romantic."

"I'm a bloody fool. So are you, if you stay here."

Marcos reached for his goggles. "I shall keep watch on the server," he said. "In case your man finds a way around the information spew."

I found a good spot behind one of the billboards and smoked and watched the Cube. I watched a long time. A handful of cars went past, security guards or night-owl office workers. I smoked my way through a whole pack of Tropicas, parching my throat and making myself light-headed. At the foot of a billboard bearing a heroic picture of Che I pissed what seemed half a pint of salty whisky—too much beer, too many nerves. Che was staring into infinity with the bold resolve of a starfighter pilot. I was just shaking off the last drops when my new mobile rang.

I tucked myself away, zipped up. The mobile stopped ringing as soon as I took it out. Then it started again.

I remembered that you had to press the green button twice.

Barry Deane said in my ear, "You're a dead man."

"You seem agitated, Barry. I think that I should take you for a nice quiet drink, calm you down and sort everything out."

"I'll sort everything out all right," Deane said shrilly.

"A beer," I said, "or maybe something a little stronger. They do wonderful cocktails here, you really should try them. How about it? Havana's a late-night kind of town. I'm sure we can find a bar that's still open. A drink and a nice quiet civilized chat, just you and me." Deane didn't say anything, but I could hear him breathing. I said, "That's all I want, Barry. To talk."

"When I see you, it'll be for the last time."

"You're upset. I can understand why. It's all gone a bit pear-shaped, hasn't it? Your one-time partner Damien Nazzaro had your broker shot dead, and now your clandestine remailer has gone down. And I expect your laptop's fucked too. I got its modem number when you tried to fuck with me, Barry, and I've just now returned the favour. All of that must really be putting a crimp in the deal you thought you'd made, and I expect the Vitellis will be wondering why no one can access their lucrative porn sites."

Deane breathed noisily for half a minute. He said, "You think I care about the Vitellis?"

"But you do care about your remailer, Barry. It's your private access to the Web after all, and I can't help wondering what kind of files you have buried there. Pictures of all your women, copies of Anthony Booth's back-door program, all your little secrets. All gone. I really think you should talk to me, Barry. It's plain that Damien Nazzaro wants to hurt you, but I want to help you. I really do."

"Just stay there, and see what happens."

"I'll wait," I said, but he had rung off.

I went back to the car and told Marcos about the conversation while he fiddled with my mobile. I said, "Does your government use RedLine chips in their surveillance cameras?"

"Of course not." Marcos switched off the mobile and handed it back. "He uses an illegal clone, one I cannot trace."

"He knows we're here. If he isn't plugged into a camera network, he must be nearby." I looked at the dark windows of the office building. I thought of the cars that had passed by. I said, "He might call the police. He certainly won't come out while we're waiting for him."

"He will come," Marcos said, folding his arms and leaning against the door of his little car. "You said he needs the remailer, and if he is like me or any of my friends he will have an urgent need to fix it."

"Unless he's already made the deal," I said, and saw a car shark out of an intersection far down the road and put on speed, headlights on full beam.

Marcos Panama saw it too. He said, "Remind me of your plan."

"I don't have one, Marcos, but I do want you to go." I pointed. "There's some kind of track over there. Go now!"

The boy swung into the front seat of his car and grinned up at me and said, "I see you soon."

The car was only a couple of blocks away now. Marcos started up his bubblecar and slowly drove away through crackling scrub, picking up speed after he bumped over the ridge, vanishing into the night. I fumbled out the little syrette and flipped off the needle protector and pressed it against my thigh, noting with detached interest just how badly my hand was trembling. There was a brief sting, nothing more.

Then I walked out into the middle of the road and raised my hands.

The car braked in a swirl of dust that blew past it and blew over me. The tall, crew-cut man I'd seen with DI Davies at the hotel stepped out and came forward through the dazzle of headlights. The bib of a Kevlar vest was strapped under his grey silk jacket and he was pointing a stainless-steel automatic at me. Its bore looked as big as the Blackwall Tunnel.

I raised my hands higher.

"Stay the fuck where you are," he said.

DI Davies got out of the car. She was wearing a Kevlar vest too. I wished that I had one. I wished that I had a gun, a crack SO19 team, a get-out-of-jail-free card. Heat beat up from the concrete slabs of the road. The black air was so heavy that you could have cut wedges out of it with a knife. I could feel sweat all over my body. My arms were starting to ache, but I kept them high.

DI Davies looked at me in disgust and said, "That's him."

"Deane's out there, having a lovely time," I said, "watching you dance to his tune. He called you down on me, didn't he?"

"You're in the way," DI Davies said.

"You tried to fuck up the deal, guy," Crew-cut said, with a lazy drawl and a slow smile, "but now you're going to help us unfuck it."

"Right now Deane's waiting for you to take me away so he can get into the Cube."

Crew-cut shook his head. "No sir. What we're going to do is wrap up this whole thing right now."

"If you take me away from here, you'll lose your chance of finding Deane," I said.

"Oh, we know exactly where he is," DI Davies said.

"The deal is, we bring you to him," Crew-cut said. "You wanted to fuck up the deal, but now you're part of it. Walk over to the car, my friend, and assume the position."

I kept my hands on the hot metal of the car's roof as I was patted down. I imagined that I could feel the weight of the ampoule in my shirt pocket, that it must be outlined against the material. It seemed a very silly gadget now, no more than a joke-shop threat, but it was all I had. Crew-cut ran his hands under my arms, around my waist. He found the gravity knife in my trouser pocket, ran his hands inside and outside my thighs, around my ankles. He stepped back, said, "He's clean," and showed the knife to DI Davies, flicking it open, flicking it closed. He told me, "You couldn't have done much damage with this, my friend."

"I don't like guns."

DI Davies looked at her watch. "We're wasting time."

Crew-cut raised his automatic, pointed it at me, jerked it to one side. "In the car."

He put his hand on the top of my head as I ducked through the back door, then went around the back of the car and sat beside me as DI Davies started the motor.

I said, "Deane will want to kill me."

I said, "You must want what Deane has very badly."

I said, "It's like one of those moral problems we used to discuss at Hendon, isn't it, DI Davies? Whether or not you should risk one life in order to end a siege, for instance."

"There's no moral problem I can see," DI Davies said crisply. "You got yourself into this. You and your blundering arrogance. You shouldn't be here, but in a way I'm glad you are. I'm going to enjoy watching you work for us."

We drove past the Cube, razor wire and security cameras along the top of the high boundary wall, a rack of floodlights above the gate.

I said, "This won't do you any good. Deane will have made

copies of the back-door program. He may well have reverse-engineered the gizmo, the remote control. After all, he'll want to sell it to as many people as possible."

Crew-cut said, "I'm assured that only one copy of the back-door program is for sale, and that the remote control will be returned intact."

"And you believe that?"

"He doesn't need to know anything," DI Davies said. "Ignorance is his natural state. Ignorance and cowardice."

We drove past half-finished office blocks, their skeletons rising into the darkness that pressed above the streetlights. The car slowed and turned off the road and bumped down a track between piles of sand and gravel.

I said, "It's comforting to know I won't die in vain."

"No one's talking about dying," Crew-cut said.

"That's easy for you to say."

DI Davies said, "You're getting what you wanted. You're going to meet Barry Deane. And he's getting what he wants, too." I caught her gaze in the rear-view mirror. She wasn't looking at me in a good way. She said, "You can't run away this time. This isn't Spitalfields."

"I went to call for backup," I said. "While your pal Toby Patterson and the others were raping a civilian."

That cracked her shell. She leaned back and tried to punch me out one-handedly, and Crew-cut blocked her flailing blows as the car fishtailed to a halt.

"We're going to do just fine," Crew-cut said, "as long as we all stay calm. Tell me that you're calm, Anne-Marie."

"I'm fine," DI Davies said, and took a breath, and another. "It's old business. I'll tell you all about it when this is over."

Crew-cut said, "When this is over, fine. Set us up."

DI Davies opened a palmtop and plugged it into a mobile phone. The palmtop beeped. She said, "I have a line. We're in the system."

"Okay. Then let's get this thing done."

"We should mike him up. I'd like to hear him plead for his life. He likes to think he's good at that."

"We're going to do it just the way Deane wants." Crew-cut pointed to the shell of a half-finished three-storey office building shrouded in sheets of heavy, transparent plastic. "You're going to walk in there, my friend. Deane will give you a data spike and you will bring it out. The spike will contain a working copy of the back-door program. We're going to test it, and when it checks out you're going back inside with the cash for the hard drives and the remote. You understand all that?"

"I'm going inside. To meet Deane."

"You'll bring out the spike he'll give you. He's pissed off, he's nervous, and he almost certainly has a gun, so don't say anything to provoke him. It would be best if you don't say anything at all." Crew-cut jabbed me with the gun. "You hear what I'm saying, little fellow?"

"I feel sick," I said, and bent over, one hand on my belly, the other over my shirt pocket.

"Christ," DI Davies said, "not in the car."

The ampoule dropped on the floor. I ground it under my heel.

There was a faint smell of burnt garlic. Crew-cut got a lungful and started to laugh and kept on laughing, doubled over and breathless, tears leaking out of screwed-up eyes, his face congesting with blood as he howled and roared. He didn't try and stop me when I took his heavy stainless-steel automatic away but just pointed at me and laughed harder. Then DI Davies began to giggle, the pitch of her laughter quickly rising towards hysteria.

I got out of the car and pulled out my mobile and punched a number. The voice at the other end said, "What the fuck?" and I told it where I was and cut the connection and punched another number.

I told Marcos what I was going to do.

"You are crazy."

Crew-cut had started to snore. DI Davies was watching her hands flap feebly at the steering wheel. Her face was wet with tears and she was making helpless little hiccuping noises. The laughing policewoman.

I said to Marcos, "How long does this laughing gas last?"

"It isn't—"

"You know what I mean."

"That depends."

"They both got a good dose."

An irritating pause. I could imagine the serious expression on Marcos's face as he thought about it. He said, "Perhaps half an hour."

"Call the police in twenty minutes and tell them it's a murder," I said, and switched off the mobile and called out to Barry Deane.

There was no reply.

A steel-mesh gate was pulled across the entrance, but its padlocked chain had been cut. I pushed the gate open and went inside.

35

Heaps of construction sand and piles of cement bags on one side of what would soon be the lobby, a little dumper truck parked on the other, caught in the glare of the headlights of the car outside. A man in a brown rent-a-cop uniform lay face down in a puddle of blood and brains; I didn't need to look twice to know that he was dead. There was a lift cage beyond the body, and when I called out to Barry Deane a generator fired up with an unnerving splutter and the lift started down towards me.

It was no more than a steel platform caged with wire. A sheet of paper, **3** scrawled on it in black felt-tip pen, was pinned to the gate by a twist of wire. I pulled the gate open and stepped inside and pulled it shut, called out that I was coming up, and pressed the appropriate button on the dangling handset. I was afraid, but in a state where I didn't care that I was afraid. My left leg hurt like a bastard, and I was thinking of Sophie. The way she had died and how she had been found, naked and tied to a silver chair.

The lift rose past a dark empty floor and thumped to a stop.

I tucked the automatic into the waistband of my trousers at the small of my back and stepped out into an unpartitioned space punctuated by rows of concrete columns and full of huge shadows cast by the hissing hurricane lamp set on the floor in front of the lift. A warm wind scrabbled at long strips of plastic sheeting over window spaces. They lifted and fell, lifted and fell, lifted and fell like the valves of a heart. Through this unquiet curtain I could see a strip of black water I would later learn was Esenada de Atarés, and the heaped lights of the old part of Havana.

Barry Deane's voice came from somewhere in the shadows at the far end of the space. "Christ," he said, "it really is you." He laughed. "I nearly killed you."

"I've come for another of our talks," I said, and began to walk towards him, my shadow thrown across the dusty floor ahead of me.

Barry Deane was standing behind a carpenter's bench. A laptop lay on it, the plastic casing shattered. There was a gun in his hand and it was pointed at me.

"Stop there," he said, "or by Christ I will kill you where you stand."

"No, you won't," I said, and took two more steps. "You would have done it already if you wanted to."

He fired a shot at the ceiling, the noise shockingly loud. As a cloud of concrete dust fell around him, he said, quite calmly, "How's your hand?"

"It's fine." My voice sounded silly and flat through the ringing in my ears.

Deane said, "That's funny, because I thought I cut you up really badly. But being shot, I bet that'll hurt worse."

"I'll tell you what, Barry, I'll stay right here, seeing as how that makes you feel more comfortable." I was intensely aware of the cold weight of Crew-cut's automatic at the small of my back, but I knew that Deane would shoot me if I tried to take it out. He had shot the security guard in cold blood; he had a lot more reason to shoot me. I said, "How do we do this?"

"You do what I fucking say. That's how."

"You must have a hell of a hard-on, Barry, what with me being in your power, and the gun and all."

"I could shoot you right now, and still get the money."

"Where are you planning to go, Barry?"

"That would be telling," he said.

"Anywhere in the whole wide world."

"Well, it's true," he said. "I am a citizen of the world. Perhaps I'll pay a visit to one of my favourite girls. I've got plenty of them. We keep in touch over the Web, but sometimes it isn't enough." When I didn't say anything, he added, "You're going to take a data spike to the fuckers waiting downstairs, they'll check it out and transfer the money to my account. When they've done that, you'll come back here for the remote and the hard drives."

"And then what?"

"Maybe I let you take them down. Maybe I shoot you and leave you here for them to find. It all depends on my whim, doesn't it? Here," he said, and threw a data spike at me.

I let it drop to the floor. I said, "Tell me about Sophie, Barry. You and her."

"Pick it up, you fuck."

"I want to know about Sophie, really I do. I've talked to everyone who knew her, and no one seemed to really know her at all."

"You can't touch me for it. You can't even prove that I saw her being killed."

"I know you did, Barry, but I'll let that slide for the moment. Perhaps you didn't even want her killed. Perhaps Craig Stevens went too far and you weren't there to stop him. Was that it?"

If a suspect is desperate enough, they'll grab at any lame excuse or justification you offer them, because they think it's a way out. You tell them that you know all about it. That they didn't mean to do it. That it was in self-defence. That they didn't know it was loaded. And when they go for it, when they agree with you, that's when you've got them. Because that's when they put themselves at the scene, at the hot black instant when they crossed the line, and after that, everything else is dotting i's and crossing t's. But Deane didn't want a way out. He was happy to tell me what he'd done because he believed that I couldn't touch him for it. He didn't use what I gave him as an excuse or a justification, but as a prompt.

"I loved her," he said, "and I know she loved me. I thought she might be the one. I tried to tell her, but she was only interested in what I could do for her. She wouldn't listen, you see. She had to show herself off to everyone."

"Is that really true, Barry? Or had you always planned to take everything from her?"

"She didn't know what she had, the silly little cunt. Becoming invisible—there's nothing like it. To walk down any street and know nothing can see you? That's real freedom. The first day I used it, I walked into the Marks and Spencer on Poland Street. I took a pair of socks and put them in my pocket and walked out, right under the eye of the cameras. And they couldn't see me. I was invisible to them," he said, and smiled happily at the memory. "There's nothing like it."

"What a shame Sophie Booth had to die because of it. And Veronica Brooks, too."

"People can't be trusted, can they?" Deane said, as if he had just thought of it. "Nazzaro's tart was only killed because she was going to talk. There wasn't any pleasure in it."

"No, I don't suppose it was like Sophie, was it?"

"I loved her," he said. "I really did."

"So you say, but you know what? You really haven't told me anything about her at all, Barry, because you didn't really love her; you don't even know what love is. You think it's possession. You wanted what Sophie had. You wanted the thrill of watching her being killed because that's the only way you could ever have her, you poor sick fuck."

"You have to understand," Deane said, like a man trying to explain why he collects stamps, "that I can go anywhere in the world at the speed of thought. It's all mine. The killing was only a small part of it, and I can have it over and over again. It was the demonstration of my power that was important. That I can have everything, and go anywhere."

For a moment our gazes locked. I saw the thing inside him, looking out through his eyes, and I thought he was going to kill me because he knew I'd seen it. But then a noise outside broke that horribly intimate moment. Deane walked over to one of the windows, pushed aside the plastic strips that hung there, and looked out.

"There's another car," he said conversationally.

"Turn around, Barry."

He did, and saw that I was pointing Crew-cut's automatic at him.

"You fuck," he said.

"Put your gun down, Barry. Your friends down there are sleeping off a nasty attack of bad humour, and the other car is Damien Nazzaro's. And soon enough, the police will be here."

"You can't use that on me. You're here to talk to me."

"Perhaps I'm talked out."

My finger was on the trigger, and I'd pulled it back to the first notch. The effort of keeping it there, so that it only needed a fraction more pressure to go off, was already making my hand cramp up.

"You won't do it," Deane said, with a sly smile. "I know about you. I know about Spitalfields and how you fucked up. That nice DI Davies told me all about it."

"You come with me now, Barry. I'll look after you. I'll make sure that Damien Nazzaro can't get at you."

"I don't need your help!" he shouted, and said into the echo of his voice, talking quickly and intensely, "I don't need it, so just listen. First of all, information wants to be free. If I can't get money for that RedLine hack I'll let it go. I'd rather fuck up Booth than get money off him anyway. Second, I put a back door into the websites I set up. It lets me get in any time I want and do whatever I want. Those sites pull in thousands of dollars an hour, and I'll take all that money before anyone knows what's happening and I'll vanish."

"I shut those sites down, you sad man," I said.

"Not for ever," he said, and casually raised his gun and shot me.

A punch low in my side knocked the breath from me. The automatic went off even as I fell down, and I fired again through the noise. Deane's second shot kicked up concrete splinters that cut my face and I hitched myself behind a pillar, sharp pain slicing through the numbness of the blow to my side. My bowels were loose and watery. There was blood all down the front of my shirt and the waist of my trousers was soaking wet. I shouted into the echo of the shots, "Stay here, Barry!"

He didn't, of course.

He ran.

He shot at me as he ran, but the shots went wild. I didn't shoot back. The lift's gate rattled shut. The generator started up, ran on, stopped. I sat there, listening hard, straining to send my senses out into the world. The shots might have been cars backfiring. There were three of them. Then only the soft sound of the plastic sheets lifting and dropping in the warm tropical wind.

I managed to stand, and drag my numb leg to where the data spike lay. I put it in my pocket, and got to the bench and leaned against it, feeling things move around in my belly. Deane had shot his laptop at least once, but I supposed that all the information on its hard drive would still be there.

Outside, someone started laughing wildly. He must have

opened the car where DI Davies and Crew-cut lay asleep. A few minutes later, Damien Nazzaro's voice floated up the lift shaft. "I know you're there, Mr Police. I'm coming up."

"I wouldn't advise it," I said, and shot once into random darkness.

"Fuck you!"

I didn't say anything.

"I don't care! I've got his shit!"

"Then you'd better go," I said, "because the police will be here soon."

Two loud shots lit up the lift shaft, and then there was a long tense silence before I heard car doors slam, the whine of a motor pressed hard in reverse, a fading roar.

Some time passed. I sat on cold concrete in my own blood. At last blue light flashed at the shrouded windows. A little later, the lift started up. I pulled the magazine from the automatic and threw it in one direction, threw the automatic in another, and waited for the mercy of the police.

36

Barry Deane was dead, of course. He had been shot by Nazzaro, who was arrested a few hours later while trying to escape to Florida on a cigarette-smuggling boat. Nazzaro would stand trial in Havana for the murders of Deane and Iznaga. DI Davies had been deported in a minor diplomatic scandal; I hoped that she and David Varnom would be very happy together.

I learnt all this from Marcos Panama, the very next day. He had followed the ambulance to the hospital, and had managed to snatch a brief moment with me in the emergency room. I'd given him a phone number then, because I had been convinced that I was going to die, and he told me now, "I got through to that number."

"What did she say?"

"She wants to call you a fool to your face. How are you feeling?"

I had had my spleen and a shattered rib removed. My skin crawled with itches under the bandages they had lashed around my chest. "Never better," I said. "What about the other thing?"

"I am happy you gave it to me, rather than let the police take it."

"Information wants to be free."

"But of course," Marcos said seriously. He wore a neat olive suit and an open-necked white shirt, and looked ten years older. He said, "You are not much like the police I know."

"That's what everyone keeps telling me. I'm beginning to believe it might be true."

"Letting information go free, that was a brave thing. It's become very popular at once, playing with those cameras. Serious problems for your government."

"Until they fix the back door in ADESS."

"Yes, they say that soon they shut it down so they can change all the chips. Big trouble for the company that made them."

I had been following the news on the TV in the corner of my little room. It had several hundred channels, most either homegrown or from the US, but one of them was the news channel of the BBC World Service. Shares in Mobo Technology had crashed; there was talk of a takeover, a government enquiry. Anthony Booth would have let Sophie's killer go free to save his child, and in revenge I had put that cold and unsympathetic intelligence under sentence of death.

I told Marcos, "The man who owns that company deserves everything coming to him."

"And trouble for you too, I think," Marcos said. "But perhaps I can help you a little."

"I don't suppose you'll tell me who exactly you are working for."

He had the grace to blush.

"Fuck it, Marcos, you weren't even arrested. You have to be working for someone who has influence. And that bullshit about tracking Nazzaro through his mobile phone. He was being followed all along, wasn't he? In case he led you to Barry Deane."

"And so he did, in a way."

"What are you, Marcos? Some kind of police, or some kind of spook?"

"Merely a humble government employee. Every nethead in your country likes to boast of contacts with the wild and crazy hackers in Cuba. We store their information, give them access to remailers, to encryption, all the things your government so foolishly forbids."

"I suppose I should resent the way you used me."

Marcos smiled his placid, gentle smile. "You used me, I used you. We both got what we wanted."

"A nice arrangement. If only I'd known of it sooner." I didn't want to ask if he had been hoping that Barry Deane would kill me.

"Anyway, none of that matters now. The thing is done. We are all content. Here," Marcos Panama said, and lifted a plastic bag onto the bed. "I brought you some books."

Half a dozen ancient, broken-backed paperback mysteries that must have predated the revolution, full of those lovely romantic lies about neat endings and moral payoffs.

I laughed. It hurt. Then I had to explain to Marcos why I was laughing.

They had a police officer on duty outside the door of my private room, and a few hours after Marcos had gone I heard someone talking with him. The man he let in was young and tall and blond, with a raffish, breezy manner and a fringe that flopped over his blue eyes. His name was Hawthorne. He told me that he was attached to the EU trade office. He'd come for a little chat.

"Why not?" I said. "I don't have anything to hide."

Hawthorne sat beside my bed and looked at me and shook his head. "I suppose that you know you fucked up very badly," he said.

"That depends on your point of view. What's your opinion, Mr Hawthorne?"

"On a scale of one to ten, I'd say you scored an easy eleven. Sometime very soon my people will want a full statement from you, but if you can give me your side of things right now, I can make sure that it is represented in the final report."

"Which will portray me as what? Hero or villain?"

Hawthorne pushed back his floppy blond fringe. "Oh, I'd say half and half, all things considered."

I was certain that his careless manner was a finely played bit of misdirection. I said, "Are there going to be any charges?"

"You're still on suspension. And I'm afraid that you'll have to face a disciplinary hearing."

"Assuming I go back."

"I rather hope that you do. I'm sure that arrangements can be made, but frankly it isn't my department."

"What is your department?"

"I just want to hear what you have to say for yourself."

"You'll listen without prejudice?"

"I'll listen to you man to man," Hawthorne said. "That's all I can offer."

"Pour me a glass of water," I said.

I told him how Barry Deane had had Sophie Booth murdered by his prison mate, Craig Stevens, and what they had taken. How, in partnership with Damien Nazzaro, they had tried to blackmail Anthony Booth. How Stevens had killed Nazzaro's girlfriend, the deal Deane had tried to make through Ibrahim Iznaga.

"The problem I have," Hawthorne said, "is understanding how the information about the RedLine back door was leaked to the world. It's all over the Web. Every surveillance system that uses the RedLine chip is crashing because so many hackers and joyriders are trying to take control of the cameras. Red faces all around, rather."

"Especially Anthony Booth's."

"Yes, he will have to face some hard questions, by and by, and the publicity has done his company no good at all. Meanwhile, I understand that ADESS must be dismantled, every RedLine chip stripped from every CCTV camera . . . It's an awful mess."

"Perhaps you should leave it be," I said. "Let Anthony Booth's child live and grow. Let everyone watch everyone else."

"Yes, well, in an ideal world it might be an interesting experiment. I was wondering if perhaps you know how the information got onto the Web."

"It must have happened after the deal Barry Deane was trying to make fell through," I said.

"I see. Well, I mustn't tire you," Hawthorne said briskly, and dusted his knees and stood up. "We'll talk more about this later."

"I want to put this in the record," I said. "I got an admission off Deane before he was killed. He told me that he paid for Sophie Booth's murder. The whole thing was down to him."

"Not much use, though, is it," Hawthorne said, "since only you heard it."

"Whatever you say. But I'd like to put it on record anyway. Go away, Mr Hawthorne. I'm very tired."

I was, too. Later, I woke in unquiet half-darkness to find Sophie standing at the end of my bed. She wore her white long-sleeved dress, and smiled at me and raised her arms. I tried to say something, and the pain in my throat jerked me awake just as she vanished.

It was the same unquiet half-dark. I heard voices outside the door. Julie was talking to the young police officer, in Spanish. He told her in English that she should come back later, that I was asleep.

"No," I said. "It's all right. I want to see her."